Praise for
Her Lost Words

"A stunning homage to two legendary women writers. . . . Stephanie Marie Thornton's ability to bring historical women to life for the reader is unparalleled as she chronicles their passions, struggles, and legacy with impeccable research and emotional resonance. An extraordinary read!"

—Chanel Cleeton, *New York Times* bestselling author of *Our Last Days in Barcelona*

"Beautifully crafted, spellbinding, heartbreaking. . . . This novel is a masterpiece I won't forget, an ode to motherhood, to love, and to two brilliant women who changed the world with their words. One of the best historical fiction books of the year, and one that I'll be thinking about for a long time to come."

—Kristin Harmel, *New York Times* bestselling author of *The Forest of Vanishing Stars*

"Stephanie Thornton delivers a stunning historical fiction with lyrical prose and vivid description. . . . Set amid a cast of literary names we all recognize and love, *Her Lost Words* is sure to be a reader favorite."

—Madeline Martin, *New York Times* bestselling author of *The Librarian Spy*

"Thornton's prose sparkles with wit and wisdom about literature, romance, and family. The Marys are heroines for their time and ours, remarkable women with independent hearts and minds, true inspirations to anyone who dreams of making the world a better place."

—Kerri Maher, national bestselling author of *The Paris Bookseller*

"One would be hard-pressed to find two stronger or more significant female writers, and both are brought to life with elegant prose and wisdom."

—Renée Rosen, *USA Today* bestselling author of *The Social Graces*

"Immersive, elegant, engaging. . . . Readers will savor the details of this fascinating account of the making of two brave, brilliant women—mother and daughter—who defy the odds as authors and early feminists."

—Heather Webb, *USA Today* bestselling author of *Strangers in the Night*

"A vibrant, immersive portrait of two brilliant women! Both highlights as well as humanizes the Marys' extraordinary achievements. A timely inspiration."

—Evie Dunmore, *USA Today* bestselling author of *Portrait of a Scotsman*

"Thornton grips our hearts with prose on love and loss, grief and survival, and the power of art and expression to heal our very souls. An extremely moving and enlightening novel that is an absolute must-read!"

—Eliza Knight, *USA Today* bestselling author of *The Mayfair Bookshop*

"An extraordinary work of historical fiction, weaving together the journeys of two brilliant thinkers and writers who lived and wrote with a daring that was centuries ahead of their time."

—Christine Wells, author of *Sisters of the Resistance*

"Stephanie Marie Thornton has compellingly and sympathetically humanized an American icon. Well researched and beautifully written, *And They Called It Camelot* is compulsively readable historical fiction!"

—Laura Kamoie, *New York Times* bestselling coauthor of *My Dear Hamilton*

"Students of history will appreciate Thornton's exacting research and convincing portrayal of the First Lady and style icon, and Kennedy aficionados will feel as if they have an unparalleled access to Camelot. Thornton's magnificent portrayal of Onassis will delight fans of Kennedy-related fiction."

—*Publishers Weekly* (starred review)

"A sumptuous, propulsive, scandal-filled peek behind the curtain of American royalty. Thornton gives the reader a fascinating look at the masks worn by those who live in the public life."

—Erika Robuck, national bestselling author of *The Invisible Woman*

"As juicy and enlightening as a page in Meghan Markle's diary."

—*InStyle*

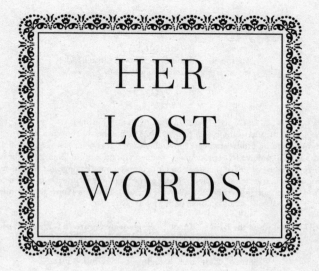

HER
LOST
WORDS

A Novel of
Mary Wollstonecraft and Mary Shelley

Stephanie Marie Thornton

BERKLEY

NEW YORK

BERKLEY

An imprint of Penguin Random House LLC

penguinrandomhouse.com

Library of Congress Cataloging-in-Publication Data

Names: Thornton, Stephanie, 1980– author.
Title: Her lost words: a novel of Mary Wollstonecraft and Mary Shelley /
Stephanie Marie Thornton.
Description: First edition. | New York: Berkley, 2023.
Identifiers: LCCN 2022034436 (print) | LCCN 2022034437 (ebook) |
ISBN 9780593198421 (trade paperback) | ISBN 9780593198438 (ebook)
Subjects: LCSH: Wollstonecraft, Mary, 1759-1797—Fiction. | Shelley, Mary
Wollstonecraft, 1797-1851—Fiction. | LCGFT: Biographical fiction. | Novels.
Classification: LCC PS3620.H7847 2023 (print) | LCC PS3620.H7847 (ebook) |
DDC 813/.6—dc23/eng/20220725
LC record available at https://lccn.loc.gov/2022034436
LC ebook record available at https://lccn.loc.gov/2022034437

First Edition: March 2023

Printed in the United States of America
1st Printing

Cover images: (flowers) Yagi Studio / Getty Images; (quill and inkwell)
Big Ryan / Getty Images; (letter) Roy Wylam / Alamy Stock Photo
Book design by Nancy Resnick

To my fearsome kraken of an agent,
Kevan Lyon
For her passionate and unwavering support of women writers

I do not wish [women] to have power over men, but over themselves.

Mary Wollstonecraft, *A Vindication of the Rights of Woman*

The memory of my mother has always been the pride and delight of my life.
Mary Shelley

London, December 11, 1800

My Dear Reader,

The past has not been kind to women. Those who strayed from the prescribed path and dared make a name for themselves were branded as witches or traitors, harlots or madwomen. And yet, despite all this, some women still dared. They dared to dream and hope and imagine and create.

We owe them a magnificent debt. Instead, we have been content to let these inconvenient women disappear.

History is shadowy even at recording broad strokes of important women's lives—the dates of their births, their schooling or lack thereof, the titles of their written works, their first loves, and the names of all their progeny. We know that Cleopatra fled at Actium and we can still read Queen Elizabeth's speech from Tilbury, but we may only guess at these women's deepest anxieties and wonder what monsters kept them awake at night. We possess the frailest skeleton of history but have lost the person.

Be warned that the pages herein lay bare woman's loathsome fears and scandalous dreams, searing romances and heartbreaking tragedies. At the time they occurred, these scandals threatened to drown those involved. Times will not have changed so much as to render these affairs mundane, but remember that some bold woman was the first to imagine that a girl might be educated in the same manner as her brother, that a wife and husband might be equals in their own home and before the law, or that the ideas conceived in the mind of a woman were as worthy as those dreamed by a man.

The pages that follow are filled with the hopes of a better world. To the benefit of all women.

With affection,
M. G.

PROLOGUE

February 1775

MARY WOLLSTONECRAFT

I yearned to disappear.

It had been two days since I'd last eaten and still longer since I'd bathed, but those were inconsequential trifles at this moment. Huddled in the corner of Hoxton's cold stone church, I grimaced at the poppy-blossom spatters of blood that now speckled the muddy hem of my threadbare muslin dress. I thought about my mother cowering on the scuffed wooden floorboards of our drafty front hall, her front tooth chipped and lower lip leaking blood. The weak winter sunlight had illuminated her like a fallen angel when she had turned toward me, her eyes pleading with me to *run*. Then my father had clutched her auburn hair with one fist, the other poised to land yet another blow.

"Stop!" I had yelled in a rush of breath. "Stop!"

"Shut your mouth," my father had growled, his breath reeking of gin as it had since he'd squandered the last shilling of his ten-thousand-pound inheritance. "Shut your mouth or I'll shut it for you."

But then I was on him, biting and hissing and clawing, *anything* to have dragged him away from my mother.

The mess of her blood and broken teeth had been the last thing I saw before he raised his fist again. Then my world exploded.

When I'd come to, everything had changed. With one eye swollen shut and my ears still ringing with my mother's urging to *go*, I'd run out of the house as fast as my feet would carry me, as if ravens had nipped at my heels and torn at the very threads of my soul. I ran as if I could escape this hell.

I told myself I was running toward a better life.

The howling winds brought me back to the present. The mild winter temperatures had plummeted and my fingers cracked and bled, the victims of my incessant picking at them as I worried over what to do next. It was a rare stroke of luck that Reverend Clare made a habit of leaving the Hoxton church door unlocked; otherwise I'd already be frozen stiff.

The recent horrors I'd experienced were still circling my ravaged mind when the reverend's wife found me curled in one of the front pews on that second morning.

"Jesus, Mary, and Joseph!" She clutched one hand over her heart as she peered down at me. The candle in her hand lit her up like a kindly seraphim, one with dimples and graying hair at her temples. "Who have we here?"

"No one so exalted, I'm afraid. Just plain Mary Wollstonecraft." My mouth felt as if it had been packed with wool as I rubbed my eyes, then winced at the throbbing pain rooted somewhere deep within my left eye socket.

"It *is* you, Mary." Mrs. Clare frowned as she touched her candle to those on the simple wooden altar. "What in heaven's name are you doing here at this hour?"

"Praying."

It wasn't truly a lie. Over the past two days I'd prayed for many things—a cure for my father, a new life for my mother, and a way to make everything better. Essentially, I'd prayed to rewrite the entire history of my fifteen-year-old life. Or to find a new one.

"Well, we could all use a little more prayer in our lives." Mrs. Clare held up the altar candelabra and offered her customary warm smile. Then she gasped.

It took a moment to remember that I must look an absolute fright. "I tripped," I mumbled, feeling my body cave in on itself: chin down, shoulders forward, arms clasped around my middle.

As if I might truly disappear.

Mrs. Clare hesitated, but I could tell her mind was churning from how her gleaming eyes darted to and from my face, like curious little minnows. We'd lived in Hoxton only a few months—this decaying village north of London claimed three crumbling insane asylums that rang at all hours with the screams of the unfortunate inmates locked within—but kindly Mrs. Clare slipped me a new book to read every Sunday: Voltaire, Diderot, Rousseau. I wanted her to like me, but today I desperately needed her not to send me back to my father's house. "A nasty fall, to be sure," she said, as if mulling over each word. "Does your mother know you're here?"

I shook my head, ever so slowly.

"Well, you'll catch your death of a cold," she announced. "Follow me."

I merely stared until she turned at the entrance, arms akimbo as she cleared her throat. "Do you usually dawdle?"

With downcast eyes, I hustled after Mrs. Clare, and breathed a sigh of relief when she opened the door to the rectory instead of leading me down the weed-choked lane to my father's house. "Miss Wollstonecraft is joining us for luncheon today," she announced matter-of-factly to Reverend Clare through the open door of his first-floor study. The reverend merely gave a distracted wave. He was a tougher needle to thread than his good-natured wife, given that I'd only ever heard him speak during his long-winded Sunday sermons. In fact, he so rarely left the rectory that I'd once heard him boast that he'd owned the one same pair of shoes for fourteen years. That might have been the case, but as I followed Mrs. Clare into a room down the hall, I discovered the one thing that the Clares did *not* scrimp on.

Books.

Beautiful, wonderful *books*.

The Clare library was merely a back room on the bottom floor, but it was crammed from floor to ceiling with all manner of volumes. Fat books, thin books, some freshly leather bound, and others so aged they looked ready to crumble at the slightest touch. I could feel a difference even in the air of that room, as if it were somehow heavier, weighed down by all that knowledge.

I thought of how glorious it would be to curl up here in the sunshine and spend an entire afternoon immersed in reading. Except this wasn't my house, and that sort of honeysuckle fantasy would never come true, certainly not for a girl like me, whose earliest memory was of my father hanging our family dog during a drunken rage. Not even my fist pressed against my lips could stifle the tears that stung my eyes then.

Mrs. Clare glanced my way, hesitating before thumbing through a shelf. "Sometimes, the Lord sends us challenges, to test our mettle and forge iron into our bones." Her delicate fingers flitted over several titles before finally pulling one from its shelf. "Reverend Clare and I hoped to be blessed by a passel of children, but our Heavenly Father had other plans for us. Thus, we transformed this room into a library." She handed the volume to me and closed my fingers over the embossed letters on the front. I expected the Bible, but it was Locke's *An Essay Concerning Human Understanding*. "Words have the power to transform us, Mary. They can lift us from our grief. The ideas they form can even offer humanity the hope for a better future."

My chin still wobbling, I recognized the rare door that Mrs. Clare had just cracked open before me. And, as she led me to a chair and offered me a luncheon tray of meat, cheese, and lemonade, I was suddenly famished, greedy for food but also for the escape of all those *words*.

So I opened Locke. And I began to read.

I stayed past luncheon. In fact, I'd been at the rectory the entire day when Reverend Clare finally called me into his study. Which meant I was going to be turned out.

I wasn't sure which was worse—being returned to my father or having to leave behind the Clares' marvelous library. Oh, I truly felt as if someone had given me a maharaja's sapphire and then commanded me not to look at it.

The reverend studied me through wire spectacles before folding his hands neatly upon his desk. "Mrs. Clare informs me you've been reading Locke."

I had *An Essay Concerning Human Understanding* with me, had sat unmoving the entire day until I'd nearly finished the first of its four books, which I now clutched tight to my chest, even as I wished to disappear and just stay here, unnoticed as I wandered within the wonderful worlds contained inside all those magical pages.

I swallowed, hard. "Indeed, sir."

"And?"

"And what?"

"What do you think of Locke's statements? Do you agree that there are no innate principles?"

Never before had I been asked my opinion on anything, certainly not about my beliefs regarding the stances of a famous philosopher. Finally, I gathered my wits long enough to speak.

"I'm intrigued by Locke's premise that observation and human experience shape a person's idea of what is true. It does seem accurate that infants come into this world without preconceptions." I swallowed. "Only . . ."

"Yes?"

I placed the book on the edge of the desk. It wasn't as if I were debating Locke himself, only his *ideas*. "Well, can't one also learn from someone else's experiences?"

"Explain."

I thought of my mother's life, of her dogged insistence that a woman's place was always with her husband and of the bottles of laudanum that were her constant companions. Already I knew her life wasn't for me. Except I couldn't very well speak of that with Reverend Clare. "Well, for example, I have experienced neither Judaism nor Islam, but I believe I can understand their basic tenets after reading Voltaire's *Dictionnaire Philosophique*." It was the first book Mrs. Clare had lent me, several weeks ago. "And I would wish everyone the opportunity to learn, even if they're not able to observe or experience something firsthand. Locke doesn't seem to account for that. At least not in this volume."

Reverend Clare rubbed his chin. The pause was so long I struggled not to fidget. "You read and speak French, correct? And are proficient in geography and the use of globes?"

I didn't understand the sudden change in subject, but then, Reverend Clare was known for his idiosyncrasies. "Yes. I am competent in both areas."

"Excellent. You have a sound mind, Miss Wollstonecraft, one that I fear will languish here in Hoxton. Mrs. Clare directed me to speak to your father this morning—we believe you would be ideally suited as a governess. Or perhaps as a paid companion. Unless you prefer to return home? Or are ready for a husband? I understand Farmer Jameson is looking for a new wife since being widowed last autumn."

I recoiled. Farmer Jameson was nearly twice my age and already missing half his teeth. No, marriage would not be the grand feature of my life.

"I'd happily be a governess or companion," I responded, "but my parents would never agree. And I lack the necessary experience or letters of reference."

"Your father has already agreed, so long as you send back half your wages to him here at Hoxton. And your mother was very enthusiastic about the idea." Which meant my mother knew this was my only chance to escape, and had given her blessing. I felt a pang of guilt, knowing she was trapped, for society would always condemn a woman without a husband. "Mrs. Clare and I will be your reference. In fact, I already know of one possible position—a former congregation member of mine, now Lady Kingsborough of Bristol—has two young daughters she would like educated. Does that sound like something you could manage?"

My head might well have popped off my neck from how fast I nodded. I'd only ever dreamed of leaving Hoxton, but that had been as likely as sprouting wings and learning to fly. Except I'd just been handed wings.

I rocked on my heels. "That would be ideal."

The reverend retrieved a fresh piece of vellum from his desk and tapped a quill into his inkpot. "Then it's settled." He stopped and shook the pen at me, so I feared I'd suddenly angered him. "But you must promise me one thing."

I would have promised to memorize every word of Locke's four volumes in that moment. And to recite them all backward. "Anything."

Reverend Clare gestured to the many books that lined the shelves of his study. "Knowledge is the fairest fruit and the food of joy. You must never forget that. And you must swear a solemn oath that you will never stop reading, or learning, or sharing that knowledge, like the philosophers of old."

"I won't," I said, then stuck out my hand. "You have my word."

A touch of amusement bloomed at the corner of Reverend Clare's mouth. His handshake was firm but not overly strong. "Excellent. Oh, and Miss Wollstonecraft?"

"Yes?"

The reverend's watery eyes twinkled from behind his spectacles as he nudged *An Essay Concerning Human Understanding* toward me. "You may keep this volume of Locke. And the other three, too—can't have a mismatched set, now, can we?"

I felt the rusted twin shackles of past and present fall loose in that moment, the sudden buoyancy of their loss making me nearly giddy. I no longer needed to disappear—surely that was the inevitable fate of most girls and women throughout all of history—not when I was about to do the impossible.

I, Mary Wollstonecraft of Hoxton, would use wings stitched from words and knowledge and kindness to soar my way to freedom.

And I hoped never to look back.

CHAPTER 1

❧

March 1814

MARY GODWIN

Mary tugged closer the tartan shawl that still smelled of Dundee's wild heaths, wondering if she was ready to shed the final lonely moments of her journey home from Scotland—that eyry of freedom where her father had sent her to be educated by an old radical friend so she might be brought up a philosopher like her mother.

At nearly seventeen years old, Mary understood her education was now considered complete even as she tucked into her reticule the well-loved volume of her mother's most celebrated—and vilified—book, *A Vindication of the Rights of Woman.* Mary had read every book written by or about her mother, save the one that her father had strictly forbidden her, but this was her most beloved, and she'd been rereading its fabric-soft pages since the *Osnaburgh* had begun its traverse of the murky Thames.

Live each day as if it were your last.

For a woman with no intention of living beyond the age of thirty-eight—the age her mother died—Mary reasoned, at best, she had only twenty-two years left to live. Truly *live.*

Ahead of her, London bustled beneath soot-filled skies, and

with the motion of the city came a return to her old life. Whether she wished it or not.

Standing on the deck, Mary rocked on her heels—London's frenetic energy was catching even from this distance—until she spotted her father's ramrod posture among the crowd milling about the wharf, a standout in his eccentric emerald waistcoat. Decorum forgotten, Mary waved wildly to catch his attention while burly sailors sprang to action to secure the *Osnaburgh*. Oh, how she had missed her father!

He had been her sole family for so many years. And it had been enough, at least for her. Her father had obviously needed something more.

Scotland's heather-speckled hills and the white-capped waves of the North Sea—the same that had caused Mary a week of seasickness and now made her striped cambric carriage dress hang looser on her bones—may never have existed as the weary *Osnaburgh* passengers jostled her forward onto the pier. Mary's sudden joy evaporated the moment she spied the gray-garbed wardress of a woman standing next to William Godwin. Mary wanted her father to be happy—truly, she did—but it was near impossible to find solace in her father's remarriage, to dour Jane Clairmont.

The noise and sun-rotten stench of the docks closed around her like a fist as her father and termagant of a stepmother approached.

"*Grata domum*, Mary." William Godwin kept both hands on his mahogany walking stick like a philosopher of old. The image was marred only by that eye-numbing emerald waistcoat.

"*Gratias tibi*," she responded in flawless Latin, preening at the pride reflected in her father's warm gray eyes. It was an old game of theirs, conversing in Latin. Once she'd mastered the ancient language of the classics, they'd moved to French until Mary could converse just as easily in both languages. She'd learned early how to capture her father's praise—through the accumulation of knowledge.

Jane—who also understood Latin—merely ignored their exchange. Mary recalled her stepmother responding once in the dead language during a dinnertime conversation. It was shortly after she'd joined the Godwin household, but Mary's father had ignored her, and Jane never again partook of their forays into Latin.

William Godwin rubbed the bend in his nose and appraised Mary with an approving nod—her stoic father abhorred tender embraces, especially in public, but his eyes had taken on an extra mistiness that made Mary hope he might embrace her, just this once. Instead, he gruffly cleared his throat before directing arrangements for the delivery of her portmanteau.

"You should have arrived an hour ago," Jane tutted under her breath, replacing the polished timepiece in her pocket. "Supper will be late and there's nothing to be done about it."

"My apologies. I learned much in Scotland, but not how to control the winds." Baiting her stepmother had been a favorite pastime before Scotland—like a tattered bear in a ring, Jane usually responded with growls and much gnashing of her pointed little teeth. Now that Mary was older, she had promised herself to try harder with Jane upon her return. In less than a minute, she was back to old habits.

Be kind, Mary, her father had implored when he'd first informed her of his upcoming marriage. *For me*.

More than ten years later and she was still trying.

"Please forgive me." Mary wished her father had come alone to meet her. "It's been a difficult journey and I'm out of sorts."

Jane scowled but didn't scold further, which Mary took as a small measure of progress.

"The porter assures me your trunk will arrive this afternoon."

Her father gestured with his walking stick away from the *Os-naburgh*. "Shall we?"

"Indeed. If we hurry, I might still salvage the chestnut soup." Jane was already marching through the crowd in the direction of Skinner Street, leaving Mary and her father to trail behind like unruly attendants.

"It *is* good to see you, *corculum*." At that moment, with the salt of the North Sea in her hair and the ground still pitching beneath her feet like the decks of the *Osnaburgh*, her father's words were a safe harbor. "I hope you don't mind the walk. I thought to hire a coach, but my wife reminded me that we must economize. And so . . . we walk."

Mary strolled alongside her father, hearing the hum under his breath and knowing it was because she was back home. However, she wasn't quite as content. London's cramped streets were a far cry from Dundee's wild heaths, and the city closed in on her, the ramshackle buildings blocking out the spring sunshine, the refuse and turgid brown waters gurgling down the uneven gutters. Even the poisonous black snake of the river Fleet was so different from the sparkling creeks she'd left behind in Scotland. London's grit settled on her like the finest ash as they passed first Newgate Prison, with its wagon of pallid inmates bound for the gallows at Tyburn Square, and then Newgate Market, where a forest of waxy hog carcasses with unseeing eyes hung on racks outside the butcher shops.

Mary heaved a sigh of relief when they finally arrived at 41 Skinner Street, the ground-level bookshop that had also been the Godwin family home in recent years. Her father opened the door to the accompaniment of the shrill yapping of Jane's three russet turnspit hounds. Mary ignored them because by then her eyes had landed on the best treasure of all.

Books.

The tiny shop and even tinier press of M. J. Godwin & Co. sold stationery, maps, and games. An avid reader, Mary's stepmother had named the entire enterprise after herself, although no one called her M. J. or Mary Jane any longer. The shop was a way to make ends meet, but the real prizes inside these four brick walls were the scores of glorious books stacked on every space that would hold them. Much of the shop was dedicated to the lucrative new business of selling children's books, but familiar names beckoned: Descartes, Locke, and Voltaire, along with the works of Erasmus Darwin, Thomas Paine, and so many others Mary's father had placed in her hands from the moment she could read.

It was Mary's first memory, her father teaching her to read amid the musty scent of spindle mushrooms and autumn's final decay at the St. Pancras cemetery. Seated on her father's lap atop her mother's grave, she'd shivered against the damp while a crow rooted among piles of decomposing oak leaves and William Godwin guided her tiny finger over the chiseled letters of the tombstone.

"M-A-R-Y." William Godwin's voice had caught on each letter. "Your mother's name was the same as yours, *corculum*."

"What does that mean," she'd asked with a wrinkle of her nose. "Cor-, cor-cul . . ."

"*Corculum*," he'd repeated. "It means *little heart*. For you're an offshoot of your mother, and I loved her very dearly."

She remembered watching her father remove an embroidered handkerchief from his hellfire-red waistcoat and blow his nose, this staid man who was greater and wiser to her than any other being on earth. Given his tender feelings for her mother, Mary still didn't understand how her father had developed any affection for Jane Clairmont, since her stepmother was the least sentimental—or kind—person she knew.

"Mary! You're back!" Ignoring the yapping dogs, Mary's stepsister Claire bounded down the stairs in a riot of shiny chocolate-hued ringlets and pink muslin ruffles. Less than a year her junior, Claire moved about the world like a shimmering hummingbird. A nearsighted, very *loud* hummingbird, who was still somehow endearing to everyone she met. "You'll never guess tonight's dinner guest!" She turned to her mother—Claire ignored William Godwin as much as Mary ignored Jane—and wrinkled her nose. "You didn't tell her, did you?"

Alas, the books—and any semblance of quiet—would have to be postponed.

"Where is Fanny?" Mary cared little for dinner guests but deeply for her half sister, who was conveniently missing from the melee.

"Mother had to pack her off to the country to visit our aunts." Claire's voice dropped. "One of Fanny's moods, you know."

A heaviness settled upon Mary's shoulders, for Fanny was prone to sweeping depressions and terrible crying jags. Suddenly Mary missed her eldest sister's tallow-scented embraces and thought of the solemn manner in which Fanny showed off her collection of pinned butterflies and other insects. That was Fanny's way—always quiet and deferential. Whereas Claire . . .

"Guess who is coming to dinner tonight, Mary?" Claire insisted. Her enthusiasm was catching. "*Guess!*"

"Hmm . . ." Smiling, Mary tapped a finger to her chin before removing her gloves. She couldn't help herself; her attempt not to needle her stepmother didn't extend to Claire. "Is it Mr. Burr again? I *did* enjoy performing speeches last time he came to visit."

Claire narrowed her gimlet eyes. Mary had won that particular speech competition with Aaron Burr and outshone her stepsister's efforts to impress the former American vice president with an ill-rehearsed song. "Don't be an addle-plot." Claire poked Mary in the ribs with a roll of her doll-like eyes. "Not Mr. Burr."

Mary removed her bedraggled travel bonnet and barely suppressed a fresh smile as her father switched into his sharp-toed crimson Moroccan slippers. Some things never changed. "Then who?"

"Percy Bysshe Shelley," Claire exclaimed, but only sighed at Mary's blank stare. "The poet?"

"You girls will be your most charming tonight"—Jane shook a stern finger—"no talk of politics or philosophy, only the weather and the state of the roads." Her long nose verily twitched with disdain as she placed a stern matron's mobcap—no frills, only one row of sensible English bobbin lace—atop her head. Mary's stepmother need never worry about being driven from the throne of beauty, given that she'd never had a place there to begin with. With one barked command, Jane shooed her precious dogs upstairs. "Percy Shelley is currently your father's best hope for solvency."

Mary turned to her father in alarm and watched in dismay as his ears turned the same color as his outlandish slippers. Money had always been in short supply in the Godwin household, especially since her father had taken on Jane and Claire, but things had improved somewhat after her stepmother had wrangled him into opening the bookshop instead of relying solely on his pen. (It seemed more prescient to sell other authors' works, considering that few cared to purchase William Godwin's writings in the salacious aftermath of Mary Wollstonecraft's death.) But what Jane was insinuating . . .

"Surely things aren't so dire that you're planning to marry off one of us to salvage your accounts?" The idea was anathema to Mary—her father's perpetual lack of funds had always meant there would be no dowry for the girls, and thus marriage was unlikely. The very thought of trying to pair one of them into a match somehow advantageous to the family finances would have been entirely out of character for a man who claimed to want nothing more for his daughters than education and independence.

Although, given the narrow scope of suitable positions for young women—most notably those of wife and mother—Mary had often pondered what options her future held. A paid companion or governess? Spinster caretaker of her father and stepmother into their dotage?

Fortunately, her stepmother was quick to assuage the first of Mary's fears, only to replace it with another. "Percy Shelley is already married with an infant daughter and a second babe on the way. However, if your father *did* arrange a marriage for you, you'd say your vows and be a dutiful wife. Jaws will flap if you're still unwed by your twentieth year. Four years may seem ages away, but they'll pass sooner than you think."

Mary ground her teeth so hard they nearly fractured. "I care little about the opinions of small-minded people, and furthermore, I plan to make my own choice when it comes to marriage, *if* I ever marry. Anything less is oppression."

"Of course you'll choose your husband, if and when you decide to marry." Ever the peacekeeper, Godwin cleared his throat even as Jane threw her hands in the air. "Addressing the problem at hand, Percy Bysshe Shelley is an ardent admirer of my early work and is in a financial position to help moth-eaten radicals such as myself."

"He's a baronet's son," Claire gushed as she sashayed up the stairs. "Just wait until you see him, Mary. He's so terribly noble."

"He may be nobility," Jane groused, "but his boots are filthy. He tracked a mess into the dining room both times he's come to call."

"Mud on the carpets is a worthy price to pay if Shelley will lower the ebb waters of my accounts." Mary was struck by the deep furrows between her father's brows. His expression softened once Claire had disappeared upstairs and Jane marched toward the kitchen, nattering under her breath about wayward daughters and chestnut soup. "Be forewarned," he said to Mary, "your sisters are both quite taken with Percy Shelley. Claire turns quite addlepated when he's in the same room, and Fanny falls ever more silent, if you can imagine such a thing."

The floorboards creaked overhead, and Claire started singing "Sweet William's Farewell to Black-Eyed Susan" upstairs. The songbird sound of the broadside ballad made Mary smile, albeit briefly.

"How bad is it?" Mary asked quietly while her father unlocked the glass case that held the shop's most priceless volumes alongside her mother's first edition works. There were so many of them—it boggled the mind to think that one person could write so many important works over the course of so short a life. "The accounts, I mean. Surely you have something set aside?"

Her father's sigh was fraught as he thumbed through the cloth-bound treasures, absentmindedly pulling them out and replacing them one by one. "Not this time, I'm afraid. If Shelley doesn't build me a raft with his funds at dinner tonight, you'll soon have to visit me in debtor's prison."

The announcement was as unexpected and painful as running into a brick wall in the dead of night. Imagining her father as some sort of heathen philosopher trapped within one of the infamous workhouses while overrun with vermin and deathly fevers made bile skitter beetle-like up Mary's throat. If her father went to such a place, he'd likely never come out.

There was already a gaping hole in her life left by her mother's absence; Mary couldn't fathom a life without her father.

Dust motes danced around William Godwin as he sighed and ran his hands over his bald pate—the last remnants of his hair had retreated while she was in Scotland. He picked up a rare blue cloth volume—*Memoirs of the Author of A Vindication of the Rights of Woman*, by William Godwin—and turned it over in his hands. Her mother had been so famous at the moment of its publication that he hadn't even needed to identify her in the title. Everyone knew who *the Author* was, although how humble Mary Wollstonecraft of Hoxton had become such a renowned—and vilified—writer was still a mystery to Mary so many years later. "This has been the way of things since I published this damnable book about your mother. I wish I'd never written the cursed thing."

And of course, its reception upon publication had created such a violent backlash that the publisher had refused another printing outside the tiny first run. So the book had condemned Mary's mother without even paying the bills.

"Why did you write it?" The question was tentative. Several years ago, her father had forbidden Mary to read it: *I'm afraid you'll get the wrong idea about your mother. You're still too young to understand who she truly was*, he'd said. *Few adults could comprehend her genius.*

William Godwin weighed his words so long she feared he wouldn't answer. "To beat out the dissenters who sought to discredit her radical ideas," he finally said. "And the opportunists who aimed to popularize on their fragile acquaintances with her. Your mother was famous, or infamous, depending on whom you talked to. I thought people would appreciate her if they understood what she'd overcome. Instead, I made things worse."

Mary *did* know, she'd learned from Claire—who had heard it from her mother—that Mary Wollstonecraft's life had scandalized society to the point where the entry for *prostitution* in the conservative publication *The Anti-Jacobin Review* read "*see*: Mary Wollstonecraft." As a child, Mary herself had suffered the aftereffects when parents refused to let their daughters play scotch hopper with her, one mother even going so far as to lecture young Mary, insisting that she had Mary Wollstonecraft's foul blood running in her veins. Surely this would incline the neighborhood's children toward licentiousness, just if they played with her.

And yet, Mary had never read her father's memoir. Godwin had kept this lone copy locked away, and Mary never had the pocket money to procure her own. She couldn't have found a copy anyway, given that it had been published so sparingly following the public outcry upon its release. That, and although she'd learned to talk politics from her father—a subject typically forbidden to women—he generally refused to speak of her mother.

However, she was a young woman of the world, no longer a child. Surely he would allow her to read it now.

Mary would have broached the subject then, except Godwin replaced the rare volume in the case and glanced with shining eyes about their cramped little bookshop. "God, but your mother would have loved this place," he murmured under his breath. "Did you know that we used to walk to the village of Sadler's Wells to visit the bookshop there before you were born? I always suspected you soaked up your love of books while still in the womb." He rubbed the purple crescents beneath his eyes, seeming far older than his fifty-eight years. "I always feel closest to her when I'm knee-deep in books."

Mary held her breath, hoping that he'd dole out more of these precious diamonds of memory. Her father so rarely talked about her mother and never in Jane's presence. Instead, Godwin only glanced around the shop and gave a groan worthy of the condemned. "And now I'm about to lose even this place."

Mary rested her hand on his forearm. Her heart contorted into painful knots seeing him so despondent. "You believe this Shelley fellow is the answer to all of your problems?"

Godwin straightened and the moment of vulnerability evaporated. "Percy Shelley is a spoiled charmer. However, there's more than cotton between his ears—he read my book *Political Justice* and called on me before traveling to Ireland. He wrote to me about the protests he organized against British rule there."

Mary leaned against the shop's battered wooden stool. "Well, Father, you *are* a bit of a luminary."

"Only among foolish young men who seek to emulate bent-backed revolutionary philosophers." Still, Mary could tell her praise lightened his mood, if only slightly. "Shelley promised to help my finances if I gave him advice, which I did. He even bottled my words as incendiary messages and cast them into the sea in Ireland to further fan the flames of actual rebellion."

So Percy Shelley was a rebel. And a dreamer, if messages in bottles were any indication.

Just like her father. Except dreamers needed to be tethered to this earth.

Mary brushed the shoulders of her father's jewel-toned jacket with two authoritative swipes, then straightened the lapels of the waistcoat. "Then it's his turn to hold up your gentleman's agreement."

Godwin turned a critical eye on her. "Indeed. I believe Shelley will enjoy conversing with the daughter of Mary Wollstonecraft. He mentioned during our last visit that he read my thoughts on marriage in *Political Justice* and your mother's condemnation of the institution in *A Vindication of the Rights of Woman*. Our views apparently informed his stance against marriage."

Mary arched an eyebrow. "But isn't he married?"

Godwin shrugged. "He seems to have been swept away by his bride, Harriet. Love can do that, you know, catch the most skeptical of us unawares."

Her father's faraway look made Mary suspect his mind had unspooled an even greater distance. "Never fear, Father. We'll make sure this Shelley fellow can't squirm out of his promise to you. You won't lose the bookshop," she promised.

Or be taken to a workhouse.

Godwin gave her shoulder a distracted pat before his hand fell. That thimbleful of affection would have to be enough. "I can always count on you, *corculum.*"

Mary watched her father's red-slippered retreat, noting the new stiffness of his walk. It was good to be home again, if only to help her father, although it wouldn't be long before her feet itched to stroll the moors or whisk her away somewhere new. But as an unmarried young woman—a *poor* unmarried woman—that simply wasn't done. No, she'd have no escape.

Which made her ever more thankful for *books*.

Mary ran her fingers over them, wondering which she'd take to bed with her that night. She loved the comfortable scent of aged paper and the creak of old bindings, the heft of a beloved volume in one's lap while immersed in words richer than the finest velvet.

Even more tempting than that daydream was the sudden discovery that her father had forgotten to lock the glass cabinet behind the counter.

The forbidden memoir about Mary's mother beckoned even as her father's prohibition circled like a storm of crows. This was the first time the rare and scandalous volume had ever been within Mary's reach. Who knew when the opportunity would present itself again?

You must live for her now too.

Mary recalled her father's constant admonition at her mother's grave. But how could Mary live for her mother if she didn't *know* her?

Moments later, the glass case's other volumes had been pushed together and the incriminating dust marks indicating the now-missing book had been blown away. Her shoulders hunched over a tartan-wrapped package, Mary hurried upstairs with her treasure of ink and paper.

First, dinner, where she might save her father from ruin.

Then she would read about her mother. And learn who she really was.

CHAPTER 2

❧

August 1787

MARY WOLLSTONECRAFT

No matter the season or time of day, London was a city that thrummed with vibrant, vivacious, unapologetic *life*. Regardless of who lived at Buckingham Palace or which party held the majority in Parliament, and despite the roiling sea of unwashed bodies and eye-watering odors, this would always be the city of Chaucer and Shakespeare.

This marvelous, terrifying place was where I planned to do the impossible: to make a new name for myself.

Which was necessary because I had just been turned out as the governess to Lady Kingsborough's daughters.

After I made the sixteen-hour drive from Bristol in a public mail coach, the hackney I'd caught for the last leg of the journey finally rolled to a stop outside St. Paul's Square. My legs were so stiff I felt at least twice my age of eight-and-twenty. Whereas Bristol had been quiet and overcast when I'd departed as a freshly unemployed governess (who could have foretold that encouraging Lady Kingsborough's nearly grown daughters to argue with their mother for a continuing education over marriages would lead to my dismissal *and* refusal of references *and* cause the entire town to scorn me?), stepping from the coach into London's summer cacophony felt like emerging into a different world that no novel could have prepared me for.

"You're sure this is right, miss?" the hoary old driver asked as I tugged my valise out of the carriage. "You've not mixed up the address?"

"I'm absolutely sure." I smoothed the front of my black homespun dress and tilted my face to the sunshine, removing my unfashionable beaver hat to smooth my mussed hair. *Why* did women have to be stylish when fashion merely proved that the soul lacked a strong individual character? Most men felt no such compunction—they were not reduced to dolls. Of course, it would have been nonsensical to wish for buckled shoes and velvet capes when I scarcely had two farthings to rub together. "This is *definitely* the right place."

I spoke with a confidence I didn't feel, and fervently hoped I'd made the right decision in coming to the only place where a solitary woman might blend into the landscape while going about her business. The driver grumbled something from beneath his grimy hat, but I didn't respond as he shifted in his box seat and flicked the reins. Bone weary and still smelling of the road, I had to stretch my eyes wide to take in all of London: the brick buildings leaning together like gossipy old men, the sharp clatter of horse hooves and carriage wheels, even the stench of putrefaction wafting from tiny cesspools gathered between the ancient cobbles.

If my family knew where I was right now . . .

I took both that unruly thought and my one-handled valise in hand. A few years ago, after I'd briefly returned home to care for her, my mother had died from a variety of ailments. My father and I didn't speak after that, and he had recently passed from a spoiled liver—which meant I was now as unmoored as a bit of dandelion spindrift. I'd traveled featherlight to come to London—only two extra dresses, a set of paper and quill, and most importantly, my freshly finished manuscript. My prized possession. Not a soul knew I was here and I planned to keep it that way, at least until I'd proven I wasn't a failure.

London was where I might finally be heard. Here, in this great city bustling with new ideas, no one would spit at my feet when I passed.

Here, I could start a new life.

I gaped at St. Paul's Square standing in the shadow of the famous cathedral, its Roman-era cobbles seething with tides of harried paper sellers, auctioneers, and book buyers surging toward the offices of the forty-odd publishers crammed into the district. A hundred years ago, books were the purview of silk-draped aristocrats who could afford them; now the sturdy middle class clamored for knowledge that would improve their minds and lives.

St. Paul's was the beating heart of the book trade in London. I loved it already.

Sheer mathematics—and my dwindling finances—demanded that I impress just one publisher today. Only a single person needed to say that magical word: *yes*.

That's what I'd reminded myself when I'd been let go by Lady Kingsborough and first set pen to paper to begin the essay that had grown into the 160-page manuscript at the bottom of my valise: *Thoughts on the Education of Daughters*.

Back in Hoxton, I'd wished to disappear, but that had been a child's dream. Now I'd honor my promise to Reverend Clare to never stop reading, or learning, or sharing knowledge. And I planned to do it with this manuscript.

Mine was a book meant to start fiery debates, a combustible tract in the tradition of Locke and Voltaire, Descartes and

Diderot. Except I was no renowned philosophe whiling away my evenings debating the latest intellectual ideas in Parisian salons. No matter how much time had passed, I was still just Mary Wollstonecraft of Hoxton.

If I failed, I'd be right back where I started—a governess or a paid companion to some mealymouthed dowager taking the waters in Bath. Even worse, without a letter of recommendation from Lady Kingsborough, I might be forced to marry a widower who required someone to raise his children in return for putting a roof over my head.

Damn me.

I tugged at my sleeves and replaced my beaver hat before marching toward the nearest building, its wooden sign hanging outside proclaiming it a broadside publisher. A few minutes later, St. Paul's shine had worn off.

"What's it about?" that first publisher asked from behind a desk mounded with books and pamphlets.

"It's a conduct book arguing that girls ought to be educated with sound morals, their intellect bricked up with analytical thought, and their characters solidified through hard work and useful skills. I state in no uncertain terms that England's women are more than decorative ornaments made for man's pleasure and that traditional feminine social graces are superficial fripperies."

"Are you soft in the head?" The man laughed so hard that spittle flew from his lips. I resisted the urge to wipe my bodice. "A book by a woman about educating *women*? Who would read that?"

I told myself the sting of that first rejection was a badge of honor.

It was difficult to be as sanguine about my second rejection, since the publisher suggested that perhaps he could *educate* me if I joined him alone in his back room. I responded by asking pointedly if he made that request of every *male* author that walked through his door.

From the way he blustered and foamed at the mouth, I took that answer as a decided *no*. Then I thanked my quick reflexes when I ducked a book that vulgar fool threw at my head as I announced I'd rather eat worms than spend one more moment in his vile company.

After that, the third publisher informed me that publishing my radical critique of the British government's education system could land him in jail, and the fourth scarcely glanced up before spurning my work . . .

The fifth publisher wouldn't even see me.

And the sixth?

"I don't publish women's novels," the ink-stained man had stated while chewing the end of his churchwarden pipe. The cramped room was filled with an acrid fug of smoke that set my eyes to watering. "My readers aren't interested in drivel about frocks, bonnets, or romance."

"I didn't write a novel. It's a conduct book about—"

"Show yourself out."

Damn me.

It seemed no one in the whole of the blasted British Empire was interested in contemplating the education of women, despite the fact that such ideas involved half the population. Heartsore and temper flaring dangerously, I was plunged into a seething cauldron of doubt.

What am I doing? Why did I think anyone would care about equality or education?

Still, I doggedly pressed on, losing count after at least a dozen rejections. Finally, as St. Paul's Square emptied and the sun set, I was forced to concede defeat.

I'd thought life couldn't get any worse than that bleak night in Hoxton when my father had attacked my mother and me. That had been my lowest point, but as I tucked myself into a dank alcove of a haberdashery to sleep for the night and tried not to touch the stained walls while ignoring the stench of old urine, I wondered if perhaps everything I'd tried to accomplish since then was all in vain.

The next day, I woke with a stiff back and a crick in my neck. I'd spent half the night trying to contort myself into a seated position that allowed sleep, the other half trying to keep a grip on my valise so no nimble-fingered thief made off with all my worldly belongings. Exhausted and in desperate need of a wash-bowl, I was disheartened but still trudged back to the publishing district, my heart and mind and feet numb by the time I entered the sixteenth—or was it the seventeenth?—office.

The brass doorplate of No. 72 St. Paul's Churchyard proclaimed simply *Joseph Johnson, Publisher*, yet as I knocked, I recognized the name from travel and advice books, sermons, poetry, and even romances, many of which I'd read during late nights after discharging my duties as the Kingsborough governess. Inside, an older man's voice beckoned me to enter.

I introduced myself to the trim man behind a lone desk that was piled so high with globes, books, and even a telescope that I wouldn't have been surprised to find a Hamlet-esque human skull hidden among the knickknacks. I was aware of how each previous rejection had blunted my delivery. He used his finger to mark his place on the pages before him and said, very matter-of-factly, "Leave the manuscript. Check back in a week." He barely glanced up at me. "I can't promise to read it by then, but I'll do my best."

He was actually going to read it? I was surprised, elated

even, except . . . "I—I can't leave the manuscript with you. I only have the one copy."

"Leave it or not," he answered. "The choice is yours."

Fortune favors the bold.

I wasn't sure where I'd first read the aphorism, and I certainly couldn't claim fortune had ever favored me, but after I had seen more than a dozen publishers, this was the first time my beleaguered manuscript had been invited out of my battered leather valise. I hesitated at the overwhelming feeling that I was handing over some precious part of me, suddenly terrified I was making a horrific mistake. If the book were lost, I would lose years of work, not to mention my lone chance to avoid backsliding into a life I had no desire to live. Still, I took a deep breath and set the twine-bound stack of pages on his desk before backing out of the office of Joseph Johnson, publisher.

In the week that followed, I found a place to stay in a dingy lodging house in the unfashionable district of Camden Town. The cramped room smelled of boiled trout and cabbage, but the daily rent was cheap given that I offered to watch the owner's gap-toothed twins, one of whom had already ripped a handful of pages from my precious copy of Locke's *Essay Concerning Human Understanding* and proceeded to use them to make spitballs.

I'd barely stifled a scream as I'd pried the remaining rumpled pages from the little demon's sticky fingers. Was this going to become my life? Had I risked everything to come to London only to become a governess again, this time to children who could barely read?

I waited seven days before returning to St. Paul's, then eight, mostly because I was terrified of another rejection. It was one thing to be turned away by publishers who hadn't read my words, another entirely to be spurned because my work was inferior.

Finally—one morning after the twins had filled my boots with mud—I couldn't stand it anymore. During my tea break, I hurried to St. Paul's Square, valise in hand and my feet still squelching in the swampy remnants of the twins' prank.

"Please sit, Miss Wollstonecraft. You've caught me at a good time." After the customary bows and curtsies, Mr. Johnson surprised me by gesturing to the chair across from his desk. He was a trim pea-stick of a man who wore a simple powdered wig and reminded me of Reverend Clare, only a decade or so more youthful. Seated behind a desk still covered from edge to edge with trinkets, Johnson removed a silver timepiece from his fob pocket and used the tiny key on the watch chain to wind the clock. "I tried to send you a message earlier, but I'm afraid you didn't leave an address."

I cringed inwardly and then heaved a sigh of relief as he removed my manuscript—the beloved child of paper that I'd verily left in his arms—from the shelf behind him and set it on the desk. *At least he didn't burn it with the rest of the day's rubbish.* I wished I could freeze this moment like a mosquito in amber— that breath where there was still hope, before everything came crashing down.

The nearby oak pendulum clock ticked away the seconds, and I forced myself not to fidget in the high-backed wooden chair as I reached for the inevitable conclusion that Johnson, too, was about to reject me. Coming to London had been a mistake. Misguided. I should never have dared dream above my station. My fingers twitched with the urge to snatch the pages back and tuck them into the safety of my valise.

Immersed in the bramble of my thoughts, I jumped when Johnson cleared his throat. "Miss Wollstonecraft, your ideas on the first pages are progressive. Even radical."

I gripped the edges of my chair as I prepared for the familiar judgment. *Too* radical.

"I understand it's dangerous to publish something so revolutionary." It was a rejection I'd heard from one of the many editors of St. Paul's, alongside finger-pointing rejoinders that my inflammatory text could land a publisher in jail for the treason of criticizing the government (to which I had bit my tongue against retorting that I wasn't criticizing the government—no, I was criticizing *everyone*). Suddenly, some small part of me wished I'd written the same sort of pointless drivel that already lined every bookshop's shelves. A romance or two would pay for a roof over my head. And perhaps some new boots, given that mine would soon be growing toadstools.

Johnson interrupted me. "I've published far more incendiary tracts than this. Firebombs are my specialty." He thumbed through the pages and frowned when something caught his eye. "*In a comfortable situation, a cultivated mind is necessary to render a woman contented; and in a miserable one, it is her only consolation. A sensible, delicate woman, who by some strange accident, or mistake, is joined to a fool or a brute, must be wretched beyond all names of wretchedness, if her views are confined to the present scene.*" He cleared his throat. "Do you truly believe this?"

I hesitated, but there was no point in dissembling. "I do."

Johnson frowned again. "Your writing is direct and accessible. No fancy turns of phrase to trip the reader, nothing flowery or overwrought."

A kind word before the inevitable ax crashes down . . .

Johnson folded away his spectacles. "Miss Wollstonecraft, it's almost as if you don't believe the commonly accepted idea that deep thinking overtaxes the female brain."

My tone was frosty. "I most certainly do not."

The white flags of Johnson's hands went up. "Please don't be offended—it's obvious from your manuscript that your brain is adept at all manner of deep thinking." He rapped the stack of pages with his knuckle. "You have extraordinary talent, Miss Wollstonecraft. I'll give you ten pounds for the manuscript."

"Ten pounds?" The shock of those very words caused me to collapse into my chair. That was more money than I could expect to make over several months as a governess. *He wants to publish my book. And for ten pounds!*

"I see great promise in you, Miss Wollstonecraft," Johnson continued, "and I'd expect more writing from you. Of course, I also take care of my authors to ensure they continue to produce. In return for my investment, I'd like consideration for all your future works."

It sounded too good to be true. I hesitated, knowing from experience that life rarely gave anything without taking something else away. But maybe my luck was changing. Perhaps this time, it would be real. Finally, I thrust out my hand.

"You have a deal, Mr. Johnson."

Johnson was already tapping the edges of the manuscript against his desk to even them up before setting my pages atop another stack of papers. "Excellent. Where may I address the payment and all future correspondence?"

Now, *that* was a bit of a quandary.

"I don't have a permanent residence." I bit my lip, a habit that had earned me constant reprimands from my mother. Before her laudanum days, anyway. "I'm staying at a lodging house in Camden Town." I quashed the urge to squirm as Johnson eyed my unfashionable dress and battered valise; I could fairly see him imagining the squalor of Camden Town.

"No, that won't do at all," he said. "We'll have to rectify that situation tout de suite. Luckily, I have a solution." He reached for his polished walking stick and shrugged on a wool overcoat that was far too heavy for the pleasant temperatures outside. Johnson merely held the door when I didn't move. "There's no need to fear for your safety or virtue, Miss Wollstonecraft. You're nearly twenty years my junior and remind me of my daughter. Now, follow me."

I insisted on carrying my own valise as Johnson locked up his office—I didn't want to be left without all my worldly belongings if this turned out to be a mirage.

I had no idea where we were heading. For such a slim and unimposing man, Johnson cut through London's filth-laden streets like one of the majestic dhows of old slicing through the wine-dark sea on its way to the Indies. Deftly sidestepping a particularly offensive puddle, he paused at a corner and waited for me to catch up, allowing a family of four, laden with a tattered picnic basket, room to pass. The youngest perched on his father's shoulders, dirt-streaked fingers in his mouth, and his sister held her father's frayed sleeve. "Papa," I overheard the little girl ask, "will his neck break when they kick the stool from under him? Or will he twitch and squirm like the last one?" I cringed as she clapped her hands in anticipation.

"So long as his eyes don't bug out." The sour-looking mother scowled as they all trundled past. "I hate that."

Damn me. Where was Johnson taking me?

"On their way to Newgate Prison to watch the day's hangings," Johnson announced as he hurried me along, his Malacca cane beating out a steady rhythm. "Common entertainment for common people. If only the herd read more books, they wouldn't be titillated by such base entertainments."

Ten minutes later, Johnson had led me over the new stone Blackfriars toll bridge to George Street on the south side of the Thames. Grim-faced toshers in oversized coats prodded through the muck of low tide with their long poles in search of bits of copper and other discarded treasures at the water's edge. Farther on, the busy waterfront was crammed with merchant ships anchored stern to prow, their old-pine masts making up a dense forest that hailed from all corners of the globe. And across from that, tucked away from life's hustle and bustle, squatted a quaint clapboard yellow cottage folded between a honeycomb of three-story buildings made of crumbling bricks and knotty timber.

"What is this?" I asked.

"You need a place to live where you can create, and I've been keeping an eye out for possible renters. Plus, this will cost you far less than a lodging house. There are enough creative characters on the south side that a woman living alone won't attract much notice." Johnson pushed open the door. "Take a look inside."

I steeled myself for an uninhabitable hovel furnished with gleaming-eyed rats, a sagging roof ready to collapse, or a cellar cesspool overflowing with night soil, but while the interior of the cottage was modest—whitewashed walls, a bed with fresh ticking, a wooden table, and two chairs left behind by the prior inhabitants—it was perfectly neat, if not fine. From the upstairs loft I could make out London's peaked rooftops as they stretched toward the coal-streaked sky.

A room with a pleasing view. And it was mine for the taking.

Emerging back outside, I cleared my throat to catch Johnson's attention. He raised both eyebrows.

I wanted to crow with excitement, but . . . "This is too good to be true, both the employment and this place. There must be something you haven't told me."

I knew I sounded suspicious, but Johnson simply said, "You're absolutely right. I should warn you that the chimney smokes and sometimes when the wind blows just right—or wrong, really—you'll have to stop up the windows to avoid the Thames's trademark stench. However, this neighborhood is safe, which is important for a woman living on her own."

I tugged at my sleeves. "My ideas have made me a trifle conspicuous," I admitted. "I came from Bristol in the hopes that London might be friendlier."

"Indeed. I think you'll find old Londinium a bit more forgiving of certain, eh . . . anomalies. Certainly more so than, say, Bristol."

Touché. "Is that why you're helping me?"

"Actually, I have a hunch that you're going to become one of my most productive writers. My hunches tend to be correct, which means you need to focus on writing. I've learned over the years that writers grow best with a little solitude, time, and a place to spread out."

I couldn't help the smile that tugged my lips. "Like some sort of potted plant."

"Precisely. It's my job as your editor to ensure you have those conditions."

It was a rarity that I was at a loss for words, but never before had anyone encouraged me to do what I loved—to *write*. The idea of a house of my own—a space to create and grow and breathe—was beyond enticing.

It seemed so simple. Serendipitous, actually.

"I'll take it."

Johnson's broad smile at my announcement was at odds with his otherwise austere manner. "Excellent! I'll send a basket in the morning to get you settled in."

I opened my mouth to protest this added boon, but Johnson merely lifted his hat. "I host occasional dinners for my authors and London's other brightest lights. Seven o'clock sharp every Friday evening—the food is simple, the conversation anything but. Rest up tonight, Miss Wollstonecraft, but feel free to join us tomorrow. We're just a short walk across the river whenever you feel the need for company—my carriage will see you safely home."

After giving me the address, Johnson whistled his way down the street and back toward Blackfriars. As I shut the door and fastened the heavy latch, I had only one thought.

As of today, I am wholly and truly an independent woman.

I wasn't even sure what that looked like, but I was eager to find out.

I awoke the next morning to the delivery of Johnson's aforementioned basket, along with a letter from my new employer.

After moving a chair to the second floor to better enjoy the view while I wrote, I broke Johnson's tiny wax seal and unfolded the message, all the while marveling at the difference one day could make in a person's life.

> *Dear Miss Wollstonecraft,*
>
> *It occurs to me that, given your position as a former teacher and governess, you may be adept at languages outside our lingua franca. If I am correct and you are interested, I propose keeping you on retainer as I have continuous—and fairly lucrative—translation opportunities to send your way. One learns to forge by hammering, yes?*
>
> *Sincerely,*
> *Joseph Johnson*

Unsure why the stars were aligning in my favor after so many years of struggle—and not quite trusting my newfound good fortune—I set aside the letter, then smoothed a fresh piece of paper and set about sharpening a goose feather into a service-able quill.

The first page in any new writing project was both terrifying and full of promise, its blank face begging to have words set upon it. One succinct tap in the inkpot and I sat straight as a ramrod at my desk, willing the sentences to flow from my mind down my arm and out my pen. Only the doubts about whether I was good enough for this—writing at all, this recent good fortune—grew to a fevered pitch until I could scarcely think. "Enough," I muttered to myself. "Doubts will get you nowhere, old girl."

I didn't need to write a masterpiece today—just find *one* idea for *one* book. I grabbed the back of Johnson's letter and began scribbling, scratching each idea out in its turn.

Two hours later, Johnson's letter was a mess of ink, but my writing page was still untouched.

There were too many ideas jostling for my attention, with the end result that none of them were quite good enough. And I required better than *good*.

I needed something that would shake the very stars from their moorings. And I was petrified I'd never find it. Or be worthy to write it.

I meandered downstairs, pleased to discover all the trappings for tea along with a crusty loaf of bread and a jar of blackberry preserves in Johnson's basket. Once the kettle whistled and I set the tea to brew, I crammed a bit of bread slathered with blackberry into my mouth, enjoying the fresh burst of summer before washing it down with a swig of sugary tea.

I couldn't fail Mr. Johnson, or myself. I had to start writing. So I did.

What I started scribbling was one of several ideas I'd been turning over. Girls were rarely taught more than embroidery and the occasional bit of painting or French, and that only if they were lucky. This new project could be a compilation of the original educational stories that I'd woven for my charges during my tenure as their governess, tales the likes of which might have made it easier to endure my father's drunken rages, the days of forced silence as punishment, and our family's constant grinding poverty. Not frilly fairy tales or fables, but stories of the good habits of two young girls crafted to inform and to *educate* those female charges who otherwise were instructed only to be frivolous and marry well.

Some hours later, the tea at my elbow had gone cold, but I'd finished drafting the first story of a children's book—tentatively titled "The Ant and the Bee"—when I realized I couldn't tarry any longer. I cringed at the stubborn ink stains on my fingers. They'd be impossible to scrub off before dinner. *Ah well, Johnson knew what manner of woman I was when he invited me.* Without time to make myself fully presentable, I scrubbed vainly at the worst of the stains in the washbowl and shoved back the stray tendrils of hair that had escaped my lopsided chignon before tucking a plain white fichu into the bodice of my sensible black dress.

"Good enough," I announced to my cloudy reflection in the mirror. I'd always eschewed the whole tribe of beauty washes, cosmetics, and oriental herbs that bid defiance to time. Before striking out for Johnson's home across the river, I consoled myself with the reminder that distinguished women in history were neither the most beautiful nor the most gentle of their sex.

Black rooks swooped in the pink blush of twilight, and happy laughter spilled out of taverns as I passed across the river. It was enough to coax a rare smile to my face.

"Miss Wollstonecraft, I'm so pleased you could join us," Johnson announced, ushering me inside. "My guests eagerly anticipate making your acquaintance."

My reply died in my throat as I entered the low-ceilinged

dining room, the air thick with pipe smoke. I gaped at the grim painting hanging in the place of honor above the cheery fireplace, its florid depiction of a pale beauty with her head thrown back in abandon while a dark demon sat upon her loins.

Damn me. What den of iniquity have I stumbled into?

"Ah, yes. That's *The Nightmare*." Johnson drew deeply on his pipe as he took in my line of sight. I couldn't read his expression. "A gift from our resident Swiss German artist Henry Fuseli himself." He gestured for me to turn about. Behind me, a bow-legged gnome of a man bearing a prominent nose and a buoyant wave of auburn hair offered a truncated bow. More introductions followed: John Bonnycastle, who wrote books Johnson published that attempted to make math accessible to all readers, and then the poets William Cowper and Erasmus Darwin. "Erasmus has caused quite a stir in London with the recent publication of *The Loves of the Plants*," Johnson explained.

Erasmus Darwin gave me a jaunty wink as we all took our chairs and a servant brought in plates of boiled potatoes and baked trout. Johnson cut into the latter with an antique knife marked with musical notes on the blade. "A notation knife," Johnson said when he caught me studying the tool, and inclined his head to the ivory-handled knife at my place setting, which bore a similar design. "I'm a collector of rarities, not just in my stable of authors but also in artifacts from the past. Back in the days of Leonardo and Michelangelo, diners could use these knives to sing the benediction for their meal." He glanced at the disturbing demon painting. "We could give it a try, but I'm not sure God listens anymore."

"If he ever existed in the first place," Fuseli muttered.

Honestly, I was relieved to be seated with my back to the rather foul painting, even if it did mean my neck crawled with the feeling that the infernal thing was watching me instead of being skyed at the Academy of Arts where no one could see it. I reminded myself that for a woman to cling to innocence was to remain in a perpetual state of childhood. "It was deemed too explicit for married women," Darwin said, so at first I thought he spoke of the painting. "My volume of poems," he clarified. "Apparently, the way I described the flowers was too *sexualized*."

Every admonition I had ever heard about the proper company for young women squawked like blackbirds about my conscience. Propriety demanded that I should plead a sudden headache and never return.

Except I was a grown woman who, while flustered, felt like some green-eared sailor of old, contemplating a journey around the globe for the first time.

Hang propriety.

"Well then." I cleared my throat and offered Erasmus Darwin a sly smile as I poised my notation knife over the steaming trout. After all, I could always plead a headache if things got out of hand. "It's a good thing that I'm not a married woman, then, isn't it?"

"What about you, Miss Wollstonecraft?" asked ruddy-cheeked William Cowper, whom I already found myself liking, if only because he was a fellow writer. "Johnson tells us you're the only female author in his employ."

Johnson took a tidy bite of trout and chewed thoughtfully. "She's the only one I'm aware of in all of London that's on retainer, actually. Not even Anna Barbauld or Fanny Burney have managed such a feat." I blinked in astonishment at the mention of the famed poetess and playwright as Johnson dabbed the corners of his lips with the white tablecloth.

"I fear you exalt me on quicksand," I replied.

"Not at all. You're a rare breed, Miss Wollstonecraft. As

such, I plan to position your work to cause quite a stir in London."

"Wonderful," Erasmus Darwin exclaimed with a clap. "So, tell us, what do you write?"

"Let me guess." Fuseli interrupted with an exuberant slug of ale. "Novels and other bits of fluff."

The way he sneered the words made the very idea of a novel sound cheap, even dirty. I wasn't sure what I'd done to offend him—other than being a female with a working brain—but his tone reminded me of Lady Kingsborough when she'd dismissed me. I tightened my grip on my cup. And allowed myself the indulgence of envisioning hurling its contents into Fuseli's face.

Well. Now, that wasn't very ladylike at all.

Still, I'd backed down with Lady Kingsborough and been turned out into the rain; I wasn't willing to cry off now.

"I do have an idea for a novel, yes," I admitted. "One that will elucidate how small-minded men subjugate women and hold back all of society by doing so. But my first book seeks to initiate and expand the education of women. My second project—which I began today—will instruct young girls on the strength of their own minds so they may look men in the eye and know they are not lesser."

Fuseli merely offered a stale smile. "Is that so? That sounds akin to dry and dusty instruction manuals."

I bristled. "Perhaps the world—and men like you—are in need of instruction."

Darwin and Cowper gaped at the jab, but Fuseli sniffed. "We're accustomed to discussing a more advanced sort of art here at Johnson's dinners."

I waved at the scandalous painting behind me. It was a truly dark and crude display, especially the leering demon. "Is this what you mean by a *more advanced sort of art*? Please. I've seen the same subject revisited ad nauseam in alleyway graffiti."

Not exactly true, but there *had* been a similar scrawl on the haberdashery alcove where I'd slept just over a week ago.

"My works deal with sex and lust and the darker sides of emotion, not clouds of fancy on a page."

I shoved my plate aside, my ears burning more with anger than the scandalous turn of topic. That same voice that had urged me to flee now resumed its argument and begged me to ignore the gauntlet Fuseli had thrown at my feet. Except I'd never been one to duck a challenge. I didn't claim that to be a wise trait, merely that it was my character, for better or worse.

I refused to address the theme of *lust*, not in public and certainly not with this man, but: "To speak disrespectfully of love is, I know, high treason against sentiment and fine feelings, but my works address the head rather than the heart. Or any baser organs." I offered a smirk even as my stomach roiled with nerves. "While you've been mired down thinking about cruder instincts"—I couldn't bring myself to say the word *sex*—"some of us have struggled to be taken seriously. A pampered man such as yourself wouldn't recognize themes of education and independence, given that you've been spoon-fed those gifts all your life."

There was a moment of silence, followed by Johnson's long, low whistle. "She's pinned you there, Fuseli."

Fuseli merely stared at me, then raised his mug of ale in a mock salute. "I defer to your exhaustive experience, Miss Wollstonecraft."

Foul-faced little gnome. I recognized female placation when I saw it, and it rubbed me raw. But I was a guest in the home of my new and very benevolent employer, which forced me to concede.

"Hear, hear." Erasmus Darwin seconded the armistice with

a lift of his glass. "And to the addition of Miss Wollstonecraft as the first female member of our supper club. You've certainly proven you can hold your own."

Johnson touched his cup to mine. "To Miss Mary Wollstonecraft, first of a new genus: the woman writer."

Torn between my ire and an unfamiliar rush of pride, I took a long sip of my ale as the conversation turned to talk of America's new Constitution and political tremors across the Channel in France. Despite men like Fuseli, with Johnson's help, I had so far escaped the pitfalls of my past mistakes.

I only wondered how many Fuselis—or worse—I would have to battle to keep this up.

CHAPTER 3

❦

March 1814

MARY GODWIN

The forbidden biography of her mother's life waited beneath the down pillow of Mary's bed, its very title beckoning her like a siren's song.

Memoirs of the Author of A Vindication of the Rights of Woman.

She knew her mother had been wildly accomplished during her short life—a governess turned author turned mother and wife. What Mary still didn't understand was how those accomplishments had somehow gone sour to the point where she was now reviled.

Tonight, she would find out.

Mary now tapped her foot impatiently while waiting for the door of the downstairs drawing room to open. Given the state of her father's finances, this dinner with Percy Shelley was critically important, but Mary was already impatient for the pudding dishes to be cleared. She calculated she had barely enough tallow candles to read through the night. It was a boon that she was a fast reader; she dared not keep the book from its case longer than this single night.

"It's a stroke of ill luck that Percy Shelley already has a wife," Claire sighed beside her. While Mary's pale complexion and unruly auburn hair were scarcely on this side of fashion, Claire's heart-shaped face and lustrous mane of dark curls meant she could have passed for a Greek goddess come down from Mount Olympus, an image heightened whenever she opened her mouth to sing. That might have been enough to make Mary jealous, had she and Claire not become perfect confidantes in the early days of their parents' marriage. It certainly hadn't taken long to bond over their mutual confusion regarding their parents' match. Claire patted the plaits of cocoa-colored hair looped around her ears. "Please don't show off in front of Percy and make me look silly like you did with Mr. Burr," she pleaded. "You know I can't debate philosophy and politics, not the way you can."

Mary blinked, hardly hearing that last bit. *Percy?* "When did you find yourself on such familiar terms with the Honorable Mr. Shelley?"

"Percy and I are two souls ruled by emotion, not decorum. I could easily imagine marrying a man like him." Claire's pert nose twitched in annoyance. "*If* he weren't already married, that is."

"Mind you don't say such scandalous things in front of your mother. Or my father."

Claire scoffed. "Your father would just ignore me as he always does. We don't have a hope of marrying well, Mary, and I merely enjoy talking with Percy. And perhaps flirting." She bumped her hip against Mary's. "Please, let me have fun tonight."

And therein lay the most telling difference between them— Mary was always seen as the responsible one, no matter how she yearned to fly away from all the mundane matters of life and see the world. "My only concern is to persuade Mr. Shelley to rescue Father from the workhouse."

"Miss Godwin and Miss Clairmont," announced their elderly maid in a fortuitous—if somewhat ridiculous—show of some sort of middle-class decorum. Even Mary knew that a maid should never announce the daughters of the house, especially in a house that lacked a noble crest. *Jane's doing,* she thought to herself. *We're poorer than church mice, but she's still more pretentious than a peacock preening before a Mughal throne.*

Her first glance at Percy Bysshe Shelley took her aback.

She'd expected a stiff and serious lordling with a velvet bow drawing back his powdered wig, his posture nailed into stiffness by gleaming gold buttons on his silk waistcoat. Instead, Percy Shelley, son of a baronet, was perhaps five years her senior and wore a severe black tailcoat—although there *was* silk cut velvet on the lapels—over a crisp white shirt open at the neck. His face was pale, but not unhealthily so, more as if he sustained himself on honey and dew. And yes, Jane was surely dismayed to find that his boots were indeed muddy around the edges, as if he'd come straight from tromping through some obliging field. No wig, but Percy Shelley's dark hair was disheveled and wild, just like the storm-tossed eyes that Mary startled to discover were studying . . . *her.*

"You know Fanny, of course, but this is my second daughter, recently returned from her studies in Scotland." William Godwin flicked gray coattails out of the way as he assumed his seat at the head of the table. His waistcoat tonight was the color of a sapphire in sunlight—inconspicuously repaired by Jane's nimble hand along the hem. "Mary, meet Percy Shelley."

Mary gave a concise curtsy, and Shelley lingered in his bow, the dark recklessness of his gaze skipping like a lake stone over her again. "Miss Godwin, I feel as though we have long been destined to meet," he said once he'd straightened. "I could go on for days about all I admire from your mother's vast collection of work, but I daresay you've heard plenty of people wax poetic on the subject."

"You're very kind." Despite her mother's notoriety, Mary had been proud to be Mary Wollstonecraft's daughter from the first time she'd read *A Vindication of the Rights of Woman*, but now that she was older, she realized how large her mother's shadow truly loomed. And she also wondered whether she would always be known simply as Mary Wollstonecraft's daughter.

The table was small—Percy Shelley and Mary sat at Godwin's left with Jane at the foot of the table, Claire on the other side, next to an empty chair.

Percy noted the absence. "Where is the eldest Miss Godwin? It seems ages since I've had the pleasure of conversing with Mary Wollstonecraft's elder daughter."

Claire reached for the bread basket that had just been set down. Rye and pumpernickel, neither of which Mary enjoyed. "Fanny went to the country for the fresh air."

"Well, I do hope she wasn't sent away on my account," Percy jested. "She seemed rather discomfited at my appearance during my last visit."

"Not at all," Claire said, but Mary could tell she was lying from the way she bit the inside of her cheek. "Our sister's health is delicate, you know."

Fanny's health had been delicate when Fanny was a child, but Mary couldn't recall the last time her sister was ill. And Claire was forever trying to shield Fanny from the harsh glare of the wider world.

Was Percy the reason why Fanny was sent to our aunts? Mary recalled her father's warning that both Claire and Fanny were quite taken with Percy Shelley. *Oh, Fanny, falling for a married man.*

Claire cleared her throat, splitting a rye roll and smearing more butter than was needed into its center, steadfastly ignoring her mother's knife-sharp glare at the unnecessary extravagance. "That chair was actually reserved for Mrs. Harriet Shelley," Claire added. "Is she indisposed this evening?"

To which Percy responded with a nonchalant nod, although Mary noted the way he suddenly fiddled with his lapels. "My wife sends her apologies for not making merry with us tonight. Her condition makes her poorly."

Of course. Because Percy Shelley and his wife were expecting their second child. Which made Claire's and Fanny's infatuations all the more ridiculous.

After that, Jane's steaming chestnut soup was brought in—for all her faults, Mary's stepmother was an admirable house-keeper who also saved money by assisting with the cooking—and Claire quickly commandeered the conversation by interjecting between mouthfuls about her fervent hopes to take up portrait painting. "You must return for tea tomorrow," she exclaimed eagerly to Percy. "Then you might sit for my first endeavor into portraiture!"

Claire was a gifted singer, but Mary had seen Claire's attempts at painting—she'd never tell Claire, but Percy Shelley would be better painted by the family dogs—yet she was even more shocked at Claire's audacity. It was one thing to bat one's lashes at a married man, still another to invite him to tea. "I'm sure Mr. Shelley has other appointments planned for tomorrow," she said in an attempt to rescue him.

"I'm afraid I could never sit still long enough for a portrait," Percy said. Was it her imagination, or did he wink at her? Something in his eye, perhaps. "Although I do recall that you met your first wife during a tea, isn't that right, Mr. Godwin? And I've seen the final portrait that was painted of her—it was in your memoir, actually."

Mary's father finished his final bite of soup—William God-win was rail thin but never wasted a drop of food—and dabbed a corner of his mouth with a serviette. "We met at a dinner party, actually."

Jane suddenly rose from her chair, causing Godwin to frown. "I must go see how the pie is coming along in the kitchen," she said. "Excuse me."

"Was it love at first sight?" Percy prompted Godwin. A brilliant poet he might be, but the man seemed oblivious to her father's discomfiture or how inappropriate it was to bring up one wife in the presence of another. "Did you stay at the table until all hours, reciting each other's works and discussing philosophy?"

It took Godwin an extra few beats to answer; his gaze lingered in the direction of the kitchens. Finally, he cleared his throat. "Quite the opposite. I'd label it loathing at first sight."

Mary leaned in. Ordinarily, she'd have shielded her father from an uncomfortable topic, but she was eager to hear this unknown part of her parents' lives. Except Godwin only folded his hands over his sapphire waistcoat so the maid could clear his empty soup bowl. "That's a dull tale. Tell me, Mr. Shelley, what is the latest news from Ireland?"

This time Shelley seemed to take the hint. "The Irish won't stop agitating until they're free from the British boot at their neck. Unfortunately, given the current state of Parliament, I fear that will be a long time coming." Jane chose that moment to reappear in the dining room, followed by the kitchen maid bearing the platter of eel pie sprinkled with parsley.

"Miss Godwin, what are your ideas regarding liberty and oppression?" Shelley asked as the savory meat pie was served. "Can you think of anything more valuable than the former? Or more despicable than the latter?"

These were common topics Mary had conversed about while in Scotland—after all, the Scots weren't free, so it was a favorite, albeit very vehement, topic of discussion. Ignoring the minute shake of Claire's head, Mary used her fork to poke at the flaky piecrust before answering.

"Liberty is the sought-after apogee of every society, is it not?" she asked, frowning at the pie. Eel was also not her favorite. "It is the ideal that the Americans, Haitians, and French have so recently spilled blood to achieve. Yet, it is also what each individual strives for in virtually every decision he or she makes. In striving for happiness, we also seek the ability to make our own choices and be free of every restraint that seeks to hold us back. Anything less is oppression."

The oppression of a young woman being expected to comment on nothing more substantial than the state of the roads, not to mention society's expectations that women be wedded and bedded before their twentieth year . . .

The dinner table remained so silent Mary feared they could all hear her swallow as she took a sip of watered wine and stared into her stoneware cup.

Her attention was so firmly on the dregs there that she nearly dropped it at the cannon boom of applause from across the table. "Eloquently spoken, Miss Mary," Percy Shelley announced. "I'd have expected no less from a child of Mary Wollstonecraft."

Mary was glad the candlelight was dim, given that she could feel the very tips of her ears flush with pleasure, even as Percy scribbled something in the tiny notebook he kept in his waistcoat pocket and Claire frowned in her direction. Right, because she wasn't supposed to dominate the conversation tonight. Still, perhaps it wasn't *so* bad to be renowned as Mary Wollstonecraft's daughter.

"I, too, aim to deliver as many creatures from oppression as

I am able," Shelley continued as he tucked the notebook away. "Why, in my youth I even contemplated kidnapping my sisters before my father could marry them off."

"And didn't you marry Mrs. Shelley to rescue her from a stifling home and a terrible match?" Claire leaned down to slip remnants of bread to the dogs, which had the added boon of displaying her pale décolletage, although their dinner guest seemed not to notice. "It's such a romantic story."

"A rather dull tale, I fear. My childhood was far more interesting—I spent much of my youth experimenting with all manner of science and cooking up mischief. In fact, I accidentally set our butler on fire when I was still in short pants, and later, when tinkering with a bit of electricity, I set my parents' baronial estate aflame. Both recovered—I was thankful Mr. Niles was merely singed around his edges." Shelley gave a frown, but his eyes sparkled with mischief beneath all that messy hair. "Although I'm still a bit disappointed that drafty old manor didn't burn down."

Mary noted the speed with which Percy Shelley changed the subject when his wife was mentioned. "Perhaps we should move the candles to the fireplace, then," she said with a smile. "We share space with a rather combustible bookshop, after all."

"I shall endeavor not to set anything aflame." Shelley's smile crinkled the corners of his eyes. His lashes were lush and impossibly long. "For tonight, at least."

The rest of the meal passed uneventfully—Percy Shelley easily juggled Claire's attempts at flirting with more philosophical discussion about Napoleon's legacy, even occasionally pausing to write more notes in that slim notebook he kept in his pocket—until the final serving platters were cleared and Jane stood. "The girls and I will retire now." She inclined her head in a clear command to Claire and Mary while Godwin motioned Shelley to retire to his private study. The room was the sacred lair that even Mary wasn't allowed in, where an oil portrait of Mary Wollstonecraft held pride of place. Mary wondered whether her father still kept the locket of her mother's hair looped over its gilt frame or whether that tiny treasure was now hidden in his waistcoat.

Normally, Mary would have been put out that she couldn't join the men to speak of weighty matters rather than retreat to write letters or darn socks. But tonight she could feign a headache and sneak upstairs to read . . .

Her train of thought was interrupted when a tiny ball of wadded paper—no bigger than a thumbnail—landed in her lap. Mary glanced up to see Claire had already followed Jane out of the dining room and the men had almost been swallowed by her father's study.

Except Percy Shelley lingered at the door, tiny notebook in hand. He turned back to glance at her, and . . . *winked.*

There was no denying the motion this time, but the door closed behind him before she could react. Mary unfolded the tiny bit of crumpled paper enough to see something was written inside—possibly one of the notes Shelley had jotted down over dinner—but Jane's voice rang out, impatiently commanding her to come along. Mary crumpled the paper.

Likely a question about my mother. Possibly something he didn't wish to say in front of Jane and risk further bruising her feelings.

Mary stashed the paper into the wide saffron ribbon at her waist, then rose and hurried after her stepmother and stepsister. Jane was already seated at the tiny writing desk, so Mary made a show of warming her hands in front of the hearth before pausing to rub her temples in an exaggerated show. "I'm afraid my journey has finally caught up with me," she said to Jane before yawning. "If you don't mind, I'll withdraw now."

"I'll need your help with the shelving tomorrow," her step-mother said. "We've a new shipment of pamphlets arriving. And some of that Lord Byron's poetry too. They're scandalous, but *The Corsair* sells so quickly we can barely keep it on the shelves. Claire certainly can't stop talking about his stanzas."

Rather than race upstairs, Mary forced herself to pause at the doorway. "It's good to be home," she said.

Jane temporarily set down her quill and glanced up from her accounts. "It's good for your father to have you near."

She went back to her accounts, but Claire winced in com-miseration before holding up four fingers. *Or five?* she mouthed to Mary before adding the thumb, recalling an old game they had played as girls, counting in a day each time one parent slighted the other sister. But Mary didn't feel slighted, even if Jane hadn't said she was glad Mary was home. Jane's statement was still one of the kinder things Mary could recall her step-mother saying. Mary supposed that was a start, especially if they were to be living in the same house now.

The walls of that same house seemed to close in on her—soon she would have to seek out the quiet and solitude of her mother's grave at the St. Pancras cemetery. Some might find a graveyard too morbid a place to linger, but for Mary, taking her books to sit in the warm sunshine while visiting her mother had always imbued her with a sense of peace. Perhaps she'd find an excuse to visit Fanny in the country next week. She was halfway up the stairs when she heard a frantic whisper. "Mary!"

It was Claire, of course, her lips turned down in a frown. "I just wanted to say sorry, for my mother. And that I, for one, am truly glad you're home."

"I'm glad too," Mary murmured. "And I'm sorry I talked so much about politics over dinner."

Claire sniffed, just once. "It's fine. It's only that I hate feeling like the lone dull-witted member of our family. We can't all have Mary Wollstonecraft as our mother, you know."

"True. Instead, you have a living, breathing mother who loves you very much." The words hurt to speak aloud, but they were true.

Claire recognized the sadness in Mary's eyes and stood on tiptoe to kiss her cheek. "Sleep well, sister."

Only once Mary was wrapped in the soft woolen quiet of the room she usually shared with Fanny could she forget about Jane's animosity and even her father's money problems, at least until dawn. And she had two things to look forward to—her father's memoir of her mother and Percy Shelley's mysterious note. *Which to read first?*

Her choice was entirely practical—Shelley's note was far shorter. Nose already twitching, Mary lit a pungent tallow candle and pulled free the tiny ball of paper from the satin ribbon at her waist.

Her heart—usually so steady and dependable—whirled like a dervish in an Arabian sandstorm as she read the miniature words seemingly sketched by a fairy's pencil.

> *How beautiful and calm and free thou wert*
> *In thy young wisdom, when the mortal chain*
> *Of Custom thou didst burst and wend in twain.*

Poetry? Percy Shelley had written *poetry*? About *her*?

Surely not, but there it was on the page.

Had he truly called her beautiful and calm and free? And, more importantly, wise?

Mary shook her head to clear it—the note didn't mean anything, coming from a poet who likely scribbled all manner of nonsense over the course of each day. Still, Mary tucked the paper into the nearest book—her well-loved copy of *A Vindication of the Rights of Woman*—and climbed into bed with the candle flickering at her elbow and her ears alert for the slightest sound from the corridor. Despite the strange fluttering in her heart, she refused to allow Percy's poem to distract her from the night's all-important task: reading her father's book about her mother.

She would have to read all night, but that was a challenge she'd happily meet.

Deciphering Percy Shelley's note could wait until tomorrow. Or forever.

Opening her father's forbidden book, Mary was surprised when a delicate piece of folded paper slipped from the front cover. It was written in her father's familiar script.

> *Curse on the icy mechanical medium of pen and paper.*
> *Shall I write a love letter? May Lucifer fly away with me*
> *if I do! When I make love, it shall be in a storm, as Jupiter*
> *made love to Semele and turned her at once to a cinder.*

Feeling like the lowest sort of thief, Mary flushed at the private love note her eyes were surely *not* meant to read. She returned it to its place behind the cover before opening to that forbidden first page.

Then she began to read.

Mary persevered until she finally turned the last of her father's pages just as a sleepy dawn stretched its rosy arms into the dark sky. Some parts she had reveled in, especially:

> A Vindication of the Rights of Woman *is undoubtedly*
> *a very unequal performance. . . . But when we consider the*

importance of its doctrines, and the eminence of genius it displays, it seems not very improbable that it will be read as long as the English language endures.

Despite her father's critique of *Vindication*'s method and arrangement, Mary agreed that her mother had written a volume that would become a classic. But then her father exposed truly shocking—and terribly private—moments from her mother's life. Mary kept reading, newly appalled that her father had strayed into topics that were so *intimate*. Not even honest and forthright Mary Wollstonecraft could have wished to have her premarital bedroom secrets so exposed for all to experience:

> *Her confidence was entire; her love was unbounded. Now, for the first time in her life, she gave a loose to all the sensibilities of her nature.*
> *Soon after the time I am now speaking of, her attachment to her lover gained a new link, by finding reason to suppose herself with child.*

It was no wonder Joseph Johnson, her mother's publisher, had refused a further print run. Nor why Mary Wollstonecraft had been pilloried as a concubine in its reviews.

Mary knew that she should feel ashamed at the truth of her mother's life, but instead she felt only relief, both that she would never again have to wonder why her mother was so vilified and also that her mother had found happiness, however fleeting that happiness may have been. However, Mary wished that she could demand answers as to *why* her father had insisted on the publication of such salacious secrets, but she dared not reveal that she'd read it. Instead, she only closed the book, wishing her mother had possessed the years to write her own memoir so that Mary might have truly known her.

Just before dawn, Mary slipped downstairs on silent feet and replaced the hateful volume in its case.

No one would be the wiser.

When she came downstairs the second time, it was to find a surprise waiting for her.

Her sister Fanny had returned from the countryside.

"I came home early, as soon as Father sent word that you'd arrived from Scotland," Fanny said as they embraced. The sight of the angry puckers of scarred skin that lined her sister's delicate jawbone always brought a stab of regret to Mary's heart— Fanny would have been this side of beautiful had it not been for an infant bout of smallpox.

"I'm so glad you did," Mary said. She'd planned to visit her mother's grave at St. Pancras today, but Fanny didn't like to be reminded of their mother's death. And a day chatting and sipping tea with her sister was an unexpected gift.

In this inconstant world, it was Fanny and their father who peppered Mary's earliest memories, Fanny who had sat by Mary's own bed when she was feverish and wove her a daisy crown for every birthday she could remember.

"Are you well and truly recovered?" Mary asked that night when they were both beneath their coverlets, their beds pushed together like old times so they could whisper long into the night. Fanny had brought a new glass-framed box of butterflies from the country and already hung it to the wall with a jaunty yellow ribbon. Mary always found herself quietly wishing she could breathe life back into the beautiful, innocent creatures and set them free.

"I'm as well as I shall ever be." Fanny resettled her childhood rag doll on the bedside table. Stitched by their mother just before Mary's birth, it was one of Fanny's most treasured belongings. "The darkness always nips at my heels."

Which made it all the harder to see Fanny's obvious infatuation the moment Percy entered the shop the following day. With Harriet at his side.

That day had started off with their father drinking his morning tea in the empty bookshop and waving a freshly delivered letter, all the while railing against Percy Shelley.

"He enjoyed the meal the other night—at our expense, I might add—and claimed over brandy that he considers himself my standard-bearer." Her father's usually calm tone was fraught. "Yet now he refuses to commit any financial assistance to ease my debts, despite his prior promises. It seems I shall have to try harder to persuade him."

"He's an irresponsible young brat," Jane muttered under her breath. Mary and Fanny exchanged an amused glance before Jane peered up from the book she was editing—a soon-to-be published version of *The Family Robinson Crusoe* that was her own attempt to make M. J. Godwin & Co. solvent. "If only you would write something new."

"No one would buy it if I did," her father grumbled.

"Or I could find a way to make the shop more profitable." Jane frowned before shifting her attention back to her book. "Mary, Fanny—the shop needs dusting before the shelving today. I left out the rags for you—Claire already shelved the latest order of the Robert Southey poetry we just ordered."

Tying threadbare striped aprons over each other's white morning dresses, the sisters set to dusting. Mary had nearly finished the first set of shelves when the bell on the front door announced a customer.

Not a customer. Two.

Percy Shelley. And his wife.

It was raining when the two ducked into the bookshop, Percy's overcoat dappled with waterdrops as his dainty wife shook out her white oiled umbrella. Mary's heart shriveled in her chest at her first glimpse of Harriet Shelley: a pale and cultivated beauty of the first order, like some rare breed of hothouse rose. Her periwinkle day gown was cut in classic lines with swags of fabric along the hem and a high waist that somewhat masked her advancing pregnancy. "Just the bookseller I hoped to see," Percy said to her after tipping his gray satin top hat. There was a full sunrise in his smile, Mary was sure of it. Why, oh why, did she have to be wearing an apron right now? And why did that suddenly matter?

"Oh?" she asked. "And why is that?"

"I'm on the horns of a dilemma—I just finished a book this morning and cannot decide what next to read. So, I thought to myself, who else could spend an entire day recommending authors and scenes and passages and grand ideas?"

More than an entire day, Mary wanted to answer. "I'm sure Fanny and I can make some suitable recommendations."

"Dearest Miss Godwin!" Percy's enthusiastic exclamation shook the walls as he spied Mary's sister in the corner, where she'd been studiously dusting one of the shelves. The man truly didn't believe in hiding his emotions. "Skinner Street hasn't been the same without you!"

"You are too kind." Fanny's already mottled face flared a painful shade of crimson before she made her excuses and hurried upstairs, retreating to the safety of the family's rooms.

"She's a dear little mouse. It's really too bad about her face." Harriet's lips pursed into a perfect moue, although their color was far too vibrant to be natural. Mary didn't have a chance to remark, not when Harriet turned her flinty stare to Mary herself. "And you are William Godwin's youngest?"

To which Percy stepped in to finalize the introductions. "Indeed. Harriet, meet Miss Mary Godwin. Miss Mary, this is my wife, Harriet Shelley."

"Mrs. Shelley, how wonderful to meet you." Mary offered a perfunctory curtsy that Harriet didn't deign to return, resulting in a rare flurry of nerves as Mary cleared her throat and sought a lukewarm topic. "So, you're both looking for books?"

"Not me." Harriet only plucked the lace at her cuff. "I'm sure there's nothing wrong with whiling away hours reading novels. If one works in a bookshop, that is." Her nose tilted up as she glanced at Mary. "You know, I've never cared for the smell of books, especially old books. So musty—it makes my nose twitch. But I suppose that can't be helped, in a place like this anyway."

The way she said it made Mary feel like some sort of insect discovered beneath an unpleasant rock and pinned within one of Fanny's glass cases. How on earth had Percy—a bona fide poet and dreamer—managed to wed such a tedious woman?

"I'm here for a copy of Lord Byron's *The Corsair*," Shelley said.

"I'm afraid we're sold out." Mary was about to offer to order Percy a copy from the London publisher, but Harriet merely shook open her parasol, scattering raindrops over Jane's pristine floors.

"No matter," Harriet said. "Come along, Percy. My father is expecting us. At the coffeehouse." Harriet's pert little nose tilted ever higher as she addressed Mary. "My father *owns* the coffeehouse, of course." She gave Percy a look that was fraught with meaning before her gaze darted to Mary. "Unless you'd prefer to stay here?"

What on earth?

Percy merely nodded, his attention already drifting toward the section on political theory. "Enjoy the coffeehouse."

Mary watched Harriet parade out the door, waited for the door to shut. "Your wife is a force of nature," she finally managed.

"My apologies for her behavior." Percy winced. "Especially her comments about your sister."

Mary had heard far worse things said about Fanny—and so had poor, long-suffering Fanny—but Mary didn't say so. "Thank you." She sought to move the conversation to safer ground. Unfortunately, there were few topics that seemed calmer. *Books, Mary. You can always talk about books.* "Surely Mrs. Shelley jests about her loathing of books."

Shelley's smile dimmed, but only briefly. "Nay, I fear Harriet truly dislikes literature. She prefers the theater."

Mary frowned. How was it possible that a poet and philosopher such as Shelley had married a woman who didn't love to read? "I'm sure I could find a volume even the most reluctant reader would enjoy."

"I shall accept your gauntlet in Harriet's name. Thus, I will happily purchase two volumes today."

"Tell me which two and I'll wrap them."

"Whatever you recommend for Harriet." Mary was already running through a list of titles in her head—*Sense and Sensibility* or perhaps Jane Austen's newest, *Pride and Prejudice*, which had come out only a year ago—but stopped short at Shelley's next pronouncement. "And the last book you read."

"Why that?"

"So we'll have more to discuss over dinner, of course. Your father invited me again next week."

Mary didn't care to ponder why her cheeks flushed then. *He's a married man.* And her father had only invited him in the hopes of persuading him to fulfill his financial promise. She must have mused too long, for Percy cleared his throat to gain her attention. "Miss Mary, I await with bated breath the title of your most recent literary conquest."

Mary hesitated, suddenly wanting to tell him of her father's memoir. More than that, she wanted to discuss it with someone. No, not with *someone.* With this man who revered her mother and who was well positioned to help her make sense of the conflicting views her father had written of.

She glanced about in case Jane might overhear—her stepmother had better ears than a well-bred pointer—and suddenly wished she could duck out with Shelley, propriety be damned.

And why not? If her father's memoir were to be believed, her mother had done all manner of improper things. A walk on a public street was hardly a corroding mildew upon her own virtue.

"Jane," she called toward the back room, "we need more binding thread. I'll visit the milliner and return shortly."

Shrugging off the hideous striped apron without waiting for an answer, Mary tied on the bonnet she'd hung by the door yesterday and darted outside before she could change her mind. Fortunately, the rain had stopped and, to his credit, Shelley followed as if they'd plotted this escape together. She was unchaperoned, but certainly not alone, given the many Londoners swarming all around them. This city was truly a place to disappear. "I had no idea you were such a free spirit," Shelley said.

"I find London confining after the freedoms of Scotland," she admitted. "And if you must know, the last book I read was my father's *Memoirs of the Author of A Vindication of the Rights of Woman.*"

"Truly?" Shelley assumed the gentleman's position on the outside of the curb as they fell into step together. "I'd have thought you'd cut your teeth on that volume."

"My father forbade it." A barouche driving through a puddle of questionable nature caused Percy to step closer to avoid both of them being splashed. "I finally sneaked it the other night."

"Soaking in rebellion by midnight and candlelight?" His hand went to his heart. "Why, you truly are subversive, Miss Mary."

Mary cut her gaze toward him. Was he insulting her? Or worse, *flirting* with her?

Either way, this was a bad idea.

"*Damnare!*" Mary's curse lifted Shelley's eyebrows. "I forgot coin for the binding thread."

She moved to turn back, but Percy's hand at her elbow guided her forward. "Press on, Miss Godwin. It's unfortunate that the market is out of thread today, but alas, we won't make that discovery until we arrive. Tell me," he prompted, "what were your thoughts after reading about your mother?"

Mary bit the inside of her lip. "I wished that she could have written her own memoir. And that I could have met her. *Truly* met her," Mary finally admitted. "It's not fair that we had only a few days together. None of which I remember, of course."

"True, but life *is* fair, you know." Percy leaned in as if explaining to her the location of the philosopher's stone. "If only because it's unfair to everyone."

If she'd known him better, she might have elbowed him in the ribs. Instead, she merely chuckled as they approached Skinner Street's infamous butcher stalls. Shelley's hand found the small of her back to guide her around a pool of greasy blood that had gathered at the base of one of the skinned hogs hanging from a hook. Mary felt suddenly unsettled, but thankfully, Shelley's featherlight touch disappeared once the danger of ruining her hem had passed.

"Well," he said thoughtfully as they approached the end of the butcher stalls and neared the district of the milliners and mantua-makers, "given that you can't meet your mother, you'll have to do the next best thing."

"And what would that be?"

"Retrace her steps. Walk where she walked. Read what she read. Talk with the people who knew her best."

"Easier said than done. My mother spent many of her years in Paris." Given her father's finances, Mary couldn't expect to travel much more than the familiar path to the milliner's shop. France was out of the question. "The majority of her friends rejected their acquaintance with her after the publication of my father's memoir." And her father—the man who'd known Mary Wollstonecraft best—rarely spoke of her.

"That *is* tricky." Shelley paused outside the milliner's and retrieved a shilling from his coat pocket. "You need thread, yes?"

Mary frowned. "I thought we agreed the milliner was out of thread today."

"Whoever heard of a milliner being out of thread?" Percy's eyes gleamed. "That was an excuse so we could continue our excursion."

Normally, she'd never have allowed him to pay for the thread, but she reminded herself that Percy Bysshe Shelley *had* made her father certain financial promises.

Inside the cramped shop, Percy exchanged the coin for a bobbin wound with coarse thread and tossed it to Mary once they were back out in the din of London. She caught it with both hands. "You can't blame Mary Wollstonecraft's so-called friends," he said matter-of-factly. "Most people are small-minded—your father laid bare many truths about your mother. The world wasn't yet ready for the likes of Mary Wollstonecraft. Still isn't, actually."

Mary moved the wooden bobbin from palm to palm to give herself something to do. "Nor was the world ready for her ideas."

"Particularly that of free love. I fear your sister Fanny has borne the brunt of your mother's choices and your father's later exposé."

Mary gave him a sharp glance, sure she'd see the usual twisted lips or grimace most people wore when speaking about—or, worse, *to*—her sister. It wasn't Fanny's fault she'd been publicly exposed as illegitimate or that she was so terribly disfigured from her bout with smallpox, but Mary worried that society's censure had worsened Fanny's natural timidity. She sometimes wondered if that had intensified her sister's love of insects, given that none of her six-legged subjects could ever ridicule her. Except there was no disapproval on Shelley's fine features, only a thin veneer of unhappiness.

"My father said you were an acolyte of his and my mother's views." They were only a few minutes from M. J. Godwin & Co., and Mary wasn't sure when she'd be able to speak so frankly again. All the better to ask the important questions, yes? "I was surprised to hear that you yourself are married."

Shelley removed a silver timepiece from his pocket and fiddled with it before answering. "When I married Harriet, I was an idiot who fancied myself a dashing Napoleon riding across the Alps on a white horse to her rescue. And Harriet believed herself a damsel in need of rescuing, which, as you've seen, couldn't have been further from the truth. It wasn't quite as romantic as all that."

Mary waited for his elaboration; her need to fill the empty space between them expanded until she finally responded. "Napoleon's passage through the Alps wasn't so romantic either. He actually rode an unkempt little mule into Austria."

Shelley's bark of laughter made Mary's heart give an inexplicable stutter. Why did being around Percy make her feel so effervescent? "You are a treasure trove of surprises, Miss Godwin." They walked in companionable silence for a few beats before Shelley continued. "Harriet and I barely knew each other when we ran away—we believed our elopement and experiment with free love to be a grand adventure. My father threatened to disown me; he still feels that the daughter of a coffeehouse owner is beneath the esteemed Shelley peerage. Unfortunately, our great adventure ended when Harriet fell pregnant and I was plagued by a guilty sense of hypocrisy—that in our quest for freedom I was dooming Harriet to a life of censure. So, we married." He sighed. "And we have both been miserable ever since. We're fundamentally ill-suited—she makes it clear every day that she wishes we hadn't married. We've agreed our marriage is in name only now—we're both happiest when farthest away from each other."

Mary didn't know how to respond, so she said nothing until they approached M. J. Godwin & Co., its hanging board with book and inkpot faded and peeling, the rusting chains it hung from squeaking louder than an old man's joints. "Well, Mr. Shelley," she said as she moved the bobbin from one hand to the other, "I fear this will likely be the end of our acquaintance."

Shelley's face fell—he was quite plain with his feelings, although perhaps that was the way with poets? "I've scandalized you, haven't I?" he said. "I must apologize for speaking so freely—I felt as if you were a kindred soul, that you might understand. Instead, I said too much."

"Not at all." Mary felt out of sorts for causing him a moment's angst. "I merely meant that we've discussed books, my mother's death, and your marriage. I fear we shall have nothing left to mull over during future conversations."

The flecks of sapphire fairy dust in his eyes sparked even brighter. "Ah, Miss Godwin, there's where you are entirely wrong."

"Oh?"

"I doubt you and I could ever run out of topics of conversation." He tipped his hat to her. "I look forward to our tête-à-tête next week over dinner."

It wasn't until he had gone—swallowed by London's unceasing crowd—that Mary stopped smiling and she realized one thing with a pang of guilt.

She'd never chosen a book for Harriet.

Percy Shelley did come to dinner the following week—sans Harriet, although Mary made sure to send him with her dog-eared copy of *Pride and Prejudice* in order to assuage her guilt over so thoroughly neglecting his wife the week prior.

That did little to soften her remorse when Shelley pinged her with another crumpled bit of paper on his way out. Especially when Claire turned at just the wrong moment and witnessed the tiny missive hurtling through the air just as Shelley shut the door to Godwin's study.

"What is that?" Claire's eyebrows nearly hit her hairline as she deftly plucked away the paper Mary had just caught, and danced out of the way, dark-lashed eyes flicking fast over the words Mary had yet to read. Her jaw dropped. "Percy Shelley is writing you *poetry*?"

At least Claire had lowered her voice. Mary could only imagine what sort of histrionics Jane would erupt into if she discovered Shelley's clandestine notes.

"I don't know what he's writing." Mary tried—and failed—

to sound as if she had the moral high ground. "Given that you swiped it away before I could read."

To which Claire recited in a stage-worthy whisper:

> *They say that thou wert lovely from thy birth,*
> *Of glorious parents, thou aspiring Child.*
> *I wonder not—for One then left this earth,*
> *Whose life was like a setting planet mild,*
> *Which clothed thee in the radiance undefiled*
> *Of its departing glory; still her fame*
> *Shines on thee. . . .*

Claire had just finished reading when Jane reappeared, brows drawn into a frown. "Girls, what are you doing?"

Claire's eyes widened just before she pulled Mary into an embrace and shoved the paper into her palm. "I was just telling Mary I'm overjoyed she's home with us," Claire babbled. "Haven't the past few days been idylls of pleasure?"

To which Jane gave her trademark half frown. "If idylls of pleasure involved creditors breaking down our doors. Come along—your father insists that you both spend time improving your minds after supper."

"We'll be right there." Claire's singsong voice was honey-sweet. She barely waited for her mother to exit the room before whispering to Mary, "I'd never have thought you capable of something so scandalous."

"It's nothing," Mary ground out from between clenched teeth. Given Claire's own infatuation with Percy, her stepsister's reaction was a relief, if puzzling. "I swear."

But Claire only waggled her eyebrows and gave an excited yip of laughter before trailing after her mother.

It is *nothing*, Mary reminded herself over and over, even as she patted the bit of paper more safely into her bodice. There was no doubt she would reread it by tonight's candlelight, even though she knew she should probably burn it.

She squared her shoulders, determined to quash the fledgling emotion that struggled to life there. Except . . . why did she feel so comfortable with Percy—so at *home*—when she often felt so out of sorts everywhere else?

Mary avoided working at the bookshop as much as she could over the next few weeks—she pleaded headaches and female problems to avoid running into Shelley again—but finally, Jane refused to entertain her excuses.

"You'll be a woman for the rest of your life, so there's no use grousing about it." Jane talked around the pencil pinned between her teeth, using it on occasion to edit a volume called *Tales from Shakespeare* while also darning Mary's father's woolen socks. Mary wasn't convinced her stepmother ever slept. "It's no wonder you've got bleary eyes and a clanging head when you're up all hours reading by candlelight—something to remember next week when you meet the gentlemen I've invited to dinner."

"Gentlemen?"

"The apothecary and his two sons." Jane wiped her hands on her apron before shaking a finger at Mary. "Don't you go turning your nose up—it's high time you think about marriage and settling down. The apothecary's family is completely respectable, plus, his eldest will inherit." Mary couldn't mask her grimace and Jane only sighed. "The bindings downstairs require finishing on *The Family Robinson Crusoe* and the shelves need alphabetizing."

Mary didn't correct her stepmother, nor did she comment that she had no wish to meet the apothecary's sons. And she hadn't been reading last night, not books anyway. Once Fanny's breathing had evened out, Mary had removed Percy Shelley's poetry and sat poring over the well-read scraps of paper until she could have recited each word contained within.

It wasn't fair of him to toy with her this way, so Mary was determined to be cold and aloof the next time she saw Shelley. Except her father still held out hope that the Honorable Mr. Shelley would be the answer to their financial problems, which meant she couldn't risk alienating him.

What she needed was an afternoon alone in which to clear her head and work out a solution to this puzzle.

Today was Sunday, so the shop was closed to the public. Mary could complete Jane's chore list and then visit her mother's grave at the St. Pancras cemetery. Though it seemed morbid, she looked forward to this moment every week, escaping the constant cacophony of Skinner Street to spend an idle hour in her mother's presence.

Mary hurried to alphabetize the political shelves and had just wrapped her Dundee tartan shawl around her shoulders and stepped outside with a basket bearing her lunch—a humble repast of day-old bread and fresh cheese—when her name was called.

Percy Shelley ambled his way from the crowd, alone today. His cravat was loose as ever, and his fingertips were stained with ink as if he'd been up all night writing. Which he probably had.

"Ah, Miss Mary, my fairy muse." He produced with a flourish a nosegay of sumptuous purple pansies hidden behind his back. "Your sister informed me yesterday that you'd fallen grievously ill, so I procured these magical blossoms to speed your recovery." The assessing smile he offered was honest and the sound of his voice was more soothing than piano music by moonlight. "I'm pleased to see their curative powers are no longer necessary."

Everything in her turned over and sighed at the sight of him. Mary felt the stone walls of her resistance crumble as she took the proffered posies. "I'm feeling much better, thank you," she mumbled. Surely there was no harm in being friends with this poet who shared her reverence for her mother. Was there?

Mary suspected that Mary Wollstonecraft would never have shied away from conversing in the open with a man as brilliant and passionate as Percy Bysshe Shelley.

And Mary reminded herself that she was a grown woman. She would be safe so long as she restricted their conversation to philosophy and politics, history and her mother's works. She could walk this knife-edge.

"I was just leaving on my morning constitutional," she said. "Would you care to join me?"

"Nothing could make me happier," Percy responded. *Damnare*, but his smile could make her forget her own name. Mary set the pansies in her basket with a reminder to add water to them later. Perhaps she'd even press some of them.

She shook herself at the ridiculous thought. *Discuss Edmund Burke's conservatism and the Napoleonic Wars. Do not swoon over sickbed flowers.*

Only, she didn't trust herself to do that. Unless . . .

"Claire will be joining us." Once the words were out, Mary couldn't undo them. Especially as they were for her own protection.

She didn't wait for Percy's reaction before slipping back into the shop and bounding up the stairs.

Claire sat at her dressing table, clad in a cheery sprigged lavender afternoon gown while making over an old bonnet at her dressing table—an insipid pastime Mary refused to take up, given her mother's rant against such fripperies in *A Vindication of the Rights of Woman.* The detritus of her stepsister's fashion exertions already littered the floor, the corpses of discarded bonnets and their ribbony entrails flung everywhere. "Aren't you supposed to be working?" Claire asked idly as she stabbed a hatpin through a frothy concoction of ribbons and feathers that Mary recognized as a piecemeal mélange of two of Claire's old hats. "Please don't tell me you've come seeking help for the dusting. You know how it makes me sneeze."

"I need you to come with me to St. Pancras." Mary folded her hands in front of her. It felt so *wrong* to invite Claire to visit the cemetery, the one place she'd never shared with anyone except her father, who had ceased going years ago. "*Now.*"

"It's a graveyard, Mary, and one I have no intention of visiting, at least not until I require a plot myself. You go there every week—you certainly don't need me to help you sit among the dead."

"Please." Mary shut the door, mindful that Fanny or Jane could walk past at any moment. "I told Percy Shelley I'd walk with him, and I can't very well do so alone."

Claire pivoted, her eyes wide. "You *what*? And you want me to, what . . . act as your chaperone?"

The world had certainly turned topsy-turvy if Claire were undertaking such a role of responsibility. "Whatever you care to call it, yes. Just hurry." Mary retrieved the plainest bonnet from the floor and gestured for Claire to put it on. "And whatever you do," she whispered, "you *cannot* tell Fanny."

Claire knocked the unoffending bonnet to the floor, choosing instead a garish confection of straw and feathers. "I'd sooner kick a lost lamb than bruise poor Fanny's feelings, but I'm surprised you'd take that chance." She tied the bonnet's violet lappets under her chin before slanting her eyes at Mary. "A walk to the cemetery seems excessively grim, even for you." Claire frowned at Mary before plucking a lacy eyesore of a bonnet off her bed. One actually adorned with a *peacock feather*. "Here. At least put this on so Percy has something to look at other than moldering gravestones."

Then Claire swept out the door, leaving Mary to frown at the gaudy bonnet. With one deft tug, she freed it of its ridiculous lace and the peacock feather, leaving only a serviceable white bonnet with a blue ribbon. She sighed and donned the thing, sparing only a brief glance in Claire's mirror.

Pinching her cheeks, Mary hurried after Claire, who had surged ahead. To Mary's surprise, her stepsister breezed past Shelley with scarcely a word, and once they were out the door, Claire stayed a respectable distance ahead. Was her sister trying to give them privacy? Or did she have some ulterior motive?

Mary knew Claire's penchant for gossip, and she'd have bet her favorite locket timepiece—her only timepiece, actually— that her stepsister was somehow eavesdropping to tease Mary upon their return. She'd ponder that mischief later.

"So." Percy offered his arm, which Mary duly ignored. "Where is our destination on this mysterious excursion?"

"My mother's grave." Mary wondered anew that she could speak the words so matter-of-factly. Had her mother died within the realm of memory, Mary was sure she'd have felt a pickax of pain at the statement; instead she felt only the usual echoing void.

She waited for Percy to squirm at the mention of death or its attached grief. Instead, he gave a sage sort of nod. "As a boy, I once slipped into our family's church to spend the night in the burial vault." He let Mary lead the way as she turned them down a damp and mossy side street that meandered to the cemetery. "I was hunting ghosts, of course."

"Naturally." Mary barely stopped herself from smiling. "Did you have any luck?"

"None, unfortunately. But I did spend the evening pondering whether electrical fire could animate the inanimate."

"A curious idea indeed."

Both fell silent as they reached the cemetery's outer gates. Claire sat on a bench outside, legs stretched before her so her dainty ankles peeked from beneath lavender skirts. "I'll wait here." She shuddered. "I don't care for cities of the dead."

The St. Pancras churchyard crooned its usual lullaby of rustling leaves and cawing crows. Mary knew it marked her as odd, but a sense of calm always settled into her soul when she opened the rusty gate that led to the pretty Norman church with its bower of weeping willows. Without speaking, Mary traced the familiar path to her mother's grave, the austere stone monument that marked Mary Wollstonecraft as the authoress of *A Vindication of the Rights of Woman*.

"Remarkable." Percy traced the curve of the stone so that Mary imagined those same elegant fingers tracing the line of her jaw. She shook herself. "To think she's actually *here*."

"I learned to read in this very spot," Mary blurted before smoothing a stray tendril of hair from her temple. "My father taught me how to spell my name from hers."

Mary expected some witty retort from Percy, or perhaps some well-rehearsed platitude about her mother watching over her. Instead, Percy studied her only a moment before closing the distance between them and lifting her chin. Mary knew she should step back, but her feet were rooted deeply to the damp earth. "What are you doing?" she whispered.

Percy fanned an errant lock of her hair between his ink-stained fingers. "It really is a blaze of red, so fine I fear to disturb its beauty." He lifted his gaze to hers, his blue eyes ocean-deep. And she was drowning in them. "I can see your soul, Mary," he whispered, "glowing like a lamp of vestal fire. And I've always been drawn to the beauty of fire."

Mary exhaled, her heart beating a wild and primal tattoo in her chest. She never knew exactly what happened next—who leaned closer or whose fingers reached out first or how her hands found Percy's chest or his threaded their way into her thick hair.

All she knew was that, like a woman drowning for air, her lips were on Percy Shelley's.

Touching, kissing . . . and then *devouring*.

CHAPTER 4

❧

August 1789

MARY WOLLSTONECRAFT

The months following my move to London were a storm of words. The raindrops of ideas tapped the panes of my mind from the moment I opened my eyes each morning until my thoughts were so saturated I could no longer think. Once the weather grew cold, I remained nestled among the down of my bed, scratching out sentences and paragraphs despite the chilly air, while wearing thin gloves from which I'd snipped the fingertips away.

Days passed, chapters grew, and winter steadfastly turned to spring.

When *Thoughts on the Education of Daughters* appeared in London bookstalls, I stood there gaping, my heart racing at the reality of my precious ideas on the shelf for all to read, my name embossed on the cloth cover. This success was quickly followed by *Original Stories*. Then I submitted to Johnson my first novel.

It had taken nine months to write. I never anticipated having a child of my own—no man desired a woman who cultivated her mind more than his ego—but this book I had struggled to create was my legacy, and so I named it *Mary*.

"It's brilliant," Johnson announced from his throne of a desk as he passed me a bulky envelope of banknotes.

It still felt so strange to be paid for my writing, and I couldn't help the flush that heated my cheeks. After so many years of being scorned for my dreams, I would never grow accustomed to Johnson's effusive praise. "I'm terrified of what the critics will say."

"The ones with sense will say it's absolutely bloody brilliant. Readers may chicken-squawk over the lack of a happy ending for your poor heroine, but then, I do love making the hoi polloi squirm."

I was mulling over the topic for my next project when word came of calamitous bread prices in Paris and angry French citizens tearing apart the Bastille brick by brick, of riotous fishwives led by former courtesan Théroigne de Méricourt storming the palace at Versailles and dragging Marie Antoinette back to the capital amid bloody pikes bearing the heads of her slaughtered guards.

I drummed my fingers while reading the latest edition of *The New Annual Register*, my neglected cup of tea already cold— always cold—at my elbow as I devoured a column by the liberal philosopher William Godwin, who I'd been startled to learn was only a few years my senior. He seemed so wise and experienced from his writing that I'd envisioned a bent-backed philosopher with a wispy beard of white trailing from his chin.

"Advice is received from Paris of a great revolution in France," I read aloud from this Godwin fellow, followed by an account of King Louis XVI's pestiferous royal transgressions, most of which I was familiar with, given my recent translation for Johnson of the works of the king's finance minister Jacques Necker from French to English. I read with keen interest that regular women like myself were clamoring for legal rights alongside the poor and hungry.

Rights for women, after so many centuries in the dark.

I'd sought London's safe harbor for myself, but each article about the tumult in France made me yearn to witness the history being made there. In my experience, gentlewomen were too indolent to be actively virtuous, but there in Paris, change was being wrought by everyday citizens. Everyday *women*.

"This revolution is the dawning of a new day," I announced to the calico cat I'd found on my doorstep during a rainstorm, shaking the *Register* for emphasis. The cat—whom I'd named Bet after Queen Elizabeth—licked her paws. "To be in France right now, can you imagine? Where Freedom, like a lion roused from its lair, rises with dignity, and shakes herself?"

Bet merely looked at me and continued washing her face, decidedly *un*lionlike. I felt as if the sunbursts of my soul might shine through my skin from the excitement.

Mind awhirl, I swallowed down cold tea before turning my attention to the next item in my reading stack, the bestselling pamphlet titled *Reflections on the Revolution in France*. Famed Whig philosopher and respected MP Edmund Burke bemoaned the French failure to revere government and warned that liberty should be treated with caution. In his conservative tirade, he even went so far as to write that the poor must *respect that property of which they cannot partake* and *be taught their consolation in the final proportions of eternal justice*.

"Horse manure," I muttered. My fingers itched to write a response, so . . .

"Where's my quill and paper?" I asked Bet. She was sitting on the latter and watched through slanted and entirely unconcerned eyes as I sharpened a fresh quill.

I didn't come up for air until the sun had set and my stomach growled in ardent protest. Who cared for food when such feral ideas needed trapping? I was nowhere near done snarling at the cloven hoof of Burke's despotism, but two things occurred to me as I reread my pages. First, that Johnson would rush to publish this argument, and second, that I—Mary Wollstonecraft of Hoxton—was going toe-to-toe against the greatest Whig writer and orator to date.

Not even David would have been so presumptuous against Goliath, I was sure of it.

Panic stilled the angry scratch of my pen, and I crammed my diatribe into my bag and force-marched myself to Johnson's town house before depositing the weighty bundle of ink-smeared pages in front of him.

"Tell me I haven't gone mad."

Perhaps Johnson was accustomed to unhinged writers showing up at his home after dark. It wasn't a dinner party evening, but he didn't blink, merely ushered me into his study and beckoned for my pages with a flutter of his fingers. "Writers need a little bit of madness to give birth to new ideas."

Finally, after several interminable minutes, Johnson sighed and ran a hand over his forehead. "You really don't care which wasp hive you beat with a stick, do you?" His lips quirked into a smile before I could snatch the paper and fling it into the fire burning in the grate. "I especially appreciate your rejoinder to Burke that it is *possible to render the poor happier in this world without depriving them of the consolation which you gratuitously grant them in the next.*"

"Well, Burke asked for it. He's advocating on behalf of the baneful gangrene of covert corruption." I bit my lip. "He'll come after me for this, won't he?"

Johnson rubbed his chin. "Yes, the mighty Edmund Burke will blow an ulcer, especially when he discovers it is a woman who has dared challenge him."

"A pen name would be best," I said quickly. My prior writings had garnered me modest attention, but I had no desire to become notorious for challenging the foremost politician of the empire. It was one thing to critique all of society for their failures toward women, quite another to call out an incredibly powerful man by name.

Johnson frowned. "Perhaps your initials."

"I'm not sure . . ."

"I insist. You must cease hiding that mind of yours. However, if your feminine sensibilities don't feel up to finishing, I can drop these pages in the fire right now."

"If I don't feel up to finishing," I muttered under my breath. Johnson knew exactly what turn of phrase would goad me to complete the essay. "You truly are insufferable, do you know that?"

Johnson's kindly eyes crinkled at their edges. "Whatever it takes to keep the ink flowing from your pen, Miss Wollstonecraft."

Twenty-eight frenzied days and one hundred fifty pages later, *A Vindication of the Rights of Men* was complete. True to his word, Johnson immediately dashed it off his press so my refutation of Burke's staid conservatism was timely and fresh. If my pen wasn't darting rapidly over pages during those days, I was frantically devouring every paper that came my way. Against all odds, the famed Society of the Friends of Truth salon in Paris continued to speak out in favor of abolition and had claimed once and for all that women deserved equal rights to men. Even more shocking was that their most outspoken leader, Olympe de Gouges, and her followers were willing to join the revolutionaries of the estates general to demand those rights. I had once excited laughter by positing that women should have their own representatives instead of being arbitrarily governed without having any direct share in the deliberations of government.

Now it seemed that was exactly what was happening just across the Channel.

Which was what brought me to Johnson's door once again . . .

"Burke is nearly apoplectic with rage, but reviewers are singing your praises for *Rights of Men*. Bookstalls can't keep copies on their shelves," Johnson informed me when I arrived for supper. "I'm already planning a second edition, although there's one change it's imperative we make."

I felt a chill at Johnson's impending critique that had nothing to do with slipping out of my wool jacket. "Oh?" I tried to sound blithe. "What sort of change?"

"The second edition must be published under your full and real name," he announced. The first version had been penned merely by M. W. "London has been exposed to your brilliance thrice already—it's time to show everyone that genius knows no bounds."

I found myself wringing my hands and made myself stop. *Too soon*, a pensive voice nattered in my head—I worried it might be right, but Johnson didn't give me an opportunity to protest.

"Also," he added with a flourish, "Thomas Paine himself is here tonight and eager to meet you."

A stiff man dressed in a fusty old coat and powdered wig approached, his discomfort writ clear even in the candlelight by the rigid way he held himself. I'd envisioned someone more genteel and less death's-head-upon-a-mopstick as the great Thomas Paine, whose fiery pamphlet *Common Sense* had helped unleash the glorious American Revolution, but closer inspection revealed this man with a pronounced cleft in his chin was far too young to be the renowned Paine. "Johnson," the intruder said, "I believe you promised to introduce me to the author of *A Vindication of the Rights of Men*. Is the fellow here yet?"

Johnson's eyes gleamed with mischief as he caught the tight shake of my head. *Don't you dare.* But Johnson always dared—it was in his blood. "I'm afraid *he* isn't here yet, but *she* is. Mr. William Godwin, may I present to you Miss Mary Wollstone-craft, author of *A Vindication of the Rights of Men*."

There was an overly long silence—I would quickly discover this was one of Godwin's several and annoying habits. "*You* are the author of *Vindication*?" he finally managed. "The same writer who accused Burke of *turgid bombast* and feminine *flowers of rhetoric*?"

"Indeed." I crossed my arms, balanced on the precipice of boasting or arguing with this man who was also one of the renowned contributors to *The New Annual Register*. "Please tell me you're not one of the hapless majority who believe women to be inferior in all areas of human development."

I really *did* want him to tell me that, to find another ally who believed that women weren't naturally less than men. Even if his reaction to my identity made it unlikely.

Godwin's cough was polite, albeit amused. "Not quite, although I do believe that, due to the softness of their natures and the delicacy of their sentiments, women stand in need of male protection."

Damn me. I snorted—actually *snorted*. Let him find the delicacy in *that*.

"Your moss-covered opinions sell us ladies short, sir. Have you ever considered that perhaps all that male *protection* keeps females soft and delicate? That perhaps you men couldn't handle women who were allowed to grow and thrive on their own?" I didn't wait for a response before sweeping away in search of more interesting conversation partners. I might have discovered deeper intellectual stimulation in striking up a conversation with the wall or window than listening to another outdated utterance from the likes of William Godwin.

Fortunately, I did locate famed corset maker turned revolutionary Thomas Paine and was delighted to parley with him about *Vindication* and the glories of America. Unfortunately, Paine was no great talker, although the bewigged pamphleteer occasionally threw in some shrewd and striking remarks. "People in America breathe the very air of freedom," he informed me, so I could almost imagine it. The thought of such contagious liberty was enough to make me fancy packing my bags and moving to Ohio or Virginia myself. To my elation, when the dinner bell rang, I found myself seated with Paine at my left.

To my dismay, insufferable William Godwin was seated at my right.

And the medieval ogre was determined to make polite conversation while a Scottish Tattie Drottle thick with summer potatoes and leeks was served.

I *loathed* polite conversation.

"Johnson informed me that you once lived in Hoxton," Godwin said, his soupspoon paused in midair. I winced, wishing he'd lower his voice. "I believe he said it was several years ago?"

"Indeed." Those were years I had no desire to discuss, nor did I wish to remember my family or the deplorable village I'd escaped, with its crumbling almshouses and howling insane asylum. Godwin didn't notice my unease.

"Those are the same years I attended Hoxton Academy," he exclaimed. *Why doesn't the man choke on his words? Or better yet, his spoon?* "The village is so small we were probably only a few hundred yards apart—I wonder whether our paths ever crossed. Perhaps we would have conversed further if they had."

My mood darkened the more I thought about Hoxton and the noose it had nearly slipped around my neck, of those silk-robed Hoxton students—all male—whom I had sometimes seen gliding about their lives of ease. For all I knew, this Godwin fellow had been among them. I certainly didn't care for him to parse out my sordid family history. "I doubt that very much, sir, given your antiquated notions of womanhood."

My comment was snide, but I'd have overturned my wine-glass into his lap if it meant escaping talk of Hoxton or the *softness of my nature*. "Mr. Paine," I asked as I gave Godwin my shoulder, "do you believe the American experiment with democracy will spread to France?"

"The ideals of *liberté*, *égalité*, and *fraternité* have taken hold across the Channel," Paine answered as the soup bowls were cleared and the steaming venison pie that was the main course was brought out. I kept my back to Godwin. "Miss Wollstonecraft, I do hope your ideas from *Vindication* reach our brothers in France so they know they have allies in the cause of revolution here in England."

There seemed no better segue . . .

"Indeed." I turned so Johnson could hear me. "In France there is undoubtedly a more general diffusion of knowledge than in any part of the European world, and I attribute that, in great measure, to the social intercourse that has long subsisted between the sexes. I would like to see such an exchange here in England as well, which is why I aim to write a second book. It will be a companion volume to *Vindication*, except this one will be about the rights inherent to *women*, especially their natural entitlements to equality and education." Next to me, Godwin choked on his venison, but I thumped him heartily on the back, enjoying it more than I should as he sputtered into his napkin. "I aim to prove that women's minds are not in a healthy state, given that both our strength and usefulness are sacrificed to beauty. I attribute this barren blooming to a false system of education that considers females as women rather than human creatures and has been more eager to make them alluring mistresses."

"From your pen to our minds." Johnson's benediction to my plan came easily. "I eagerly anticipate this new manuscript."

I swallowed. *And now comes the tricky bit.* "Once it's complete, I hope to travel to France. To be your eyes in Paris, writing on events as they unfold."

It was difficult to keep my heart from palpitating at the thoughts of both my new writing project and my fledgling plan to live in Paris. If I could build with my words a platform for the women of France—the women of the world—to stand on, why, I could see no better or more useful purpose for my life. To argue for equal education for women and then witness a revolution for equality with my own eyes? Now, *that* was something I yearned to see and not read about secondhand.

Johnson rubbed his chin, but Godwin interjected. *Of course he did.* "An Englishwoman traveling to France right now is absurd."

To which I responded, my tone cutting, "Is it so difficult to image a woman bearing witness to such history and reporting on it, instead of a man?"

"I have no quarrel with your sex, Miss Wollstonecraft." Godwin tugged at his collar. Did the man never cease fidgeting? "Merely your safety. A journey to France right now is incredibly dangerous, for a man *or* a woman."

I waved a hand as if accepting his token, instead of making a mockery of his Gothic manners and misguided chivalry. "And yet men travel to France unimpeded. It will take a great man with sufficient strength of mind to puff away the fumes of superiority he holds over women."

My implication was clear: *You, sir, are* not *a great man.*

I continued: "If men stopped trying to yank the reins against my dreams—and those of all womankind—then we women might be able to achieve great and impossible things. Like writing our own histories."

It was impossible to ignore the crimson flush creeping over Godwin's collar. "That may be so, but you might not have read that twelve thousand political prisoners were just murdered in their cells and Marie Antoinette's friend the Princesse de Lamballe was stripped naked and dragged through the city streets before her breasts were cut off and she was beheaded." The apple of his throat bobbed. "Her head was mounted on a pike outside the queen's window."

I shuddered involuntarily; I hadn't heard that. Still, I remained undeterred.

Godwin must have noticed the resolute set of my shoulders. "For your own sake, Miss Wollstonecraft, think of the hazards such a journey would pose!"

He seemed earnestly concerned for my safety, but all my annoyance with William Godwin evaporated as Johnson began that slow nod of his that I loved so well. Until: "Godwin brings up excellent points."

I nearly gaped. Of all people, Johnson should be on my side.

I leaned forward, strumming my fingers against the table for emphasis. "I'd rather risk my own life than do nothing while women are fighting for freedom on the other side of the Channel."

"As I said, Godwin brings up excellent points. Fortunately for you," Johnson continued so I couldn't argue further, "I have contacts in Paris who could arrange your accommodations and maintain your safety. *After*, of course, you write your women's companion to *Vindication*." He raised his glass of wine in my direction, which started a wave of salutes. Godwin most notably did *not* follow suit. "To Miss Wollstonecraft and her brilliant new endeavor," my beloved editor toasted. "May the world keep changing and us with it!"

Red-hot blood thrummed in my ears even as I spared a haughty glance at Godwin. This would be the start of something new for me, no matter the Fuselis and Godwins who tried to keep me—and all women—boxed in their iron cages built of worn-down traditions and outdated expectations.

I would go alone, and neck or nothing was the word.

I could hardly wait.

When I had arrived penniless and alone in London, my prized possession had been my first manuscript. Now, barely two years later, my carriage rolled down Paris's Boulevard Saint-Martin at dawn with a purse flush with pounds and a trunk containing copies of my five published works.

Including *A Vindication of the Rights of Woman*.

It was a four-hundred-page treatise written over six weeks where every minute had been consumed with netting my thoughts and pinning them forever to paper.

> *Women are told from their infancy and taught by the example of their mothers that a little knowledge of human weakness, justly termed cunning, softness of temper, outward obedience, and a scrupulous attention to a puerile kind of propriety, will obtain for them the protection of man; and should they be beautiful, everything else is needless, for at least twenty years of their lives.*

> *. . . Strengthen the female mind by enlarging it, and there will be an end to blind obedience.*
>
> *. . . If we revert to history, we shall find that the women who distinguished themselves have neither been the most beautiful, nor the most gentle of their sex. . . .*

If I was ever to be remembered, I believed it would be for this book, which had set my brain on fire, in which I stood in defense of one half of the human species. More than any of my other works, *A Vindication of the Rights of Woman* was the stamen of my immortality.

From a battered Hoxton girl, I had remade myself into a renowned published author, one who gave lectures at Johnson's dinner parties and overheard her ideas being debated in bookshops. I might even call myself a philosopher, and if there was anywhere that my nascent ideas might give birth to a new reality, it would likely be here in France, where playwright Olympe de Gouges had just published *Déclaration des Droits de la Femme et de la Citoyenne*—demanding equal rights for women while wittily claiming that if a woman had a right to mount the scaffold, so, too, did she have a right to the speaker's platform.

Some write of what was, *others of what* is, *but I shall write of what* will be.

Now I was here to witness history in the making, especially as the revolution in Paris had volleyed forward with terrifying speed . . .

The capture of the king and queen at Varennes.

The storming of the Tuileries Palace.

A new constitution ratified and a new French republic proclaimed.

For the next six weeks—perhaps longer, although for safety's sake, that was all the time Johnson had agreed to—I would record every moment and send my impressions home to further enlighten England.

In doing so, I'd prove what women were capable of.

A December chill now seeped into my bones as the coach jarred its way from one pothole to the next down the cobbled street toward 22 Rue Meslée. Tricolor cockades flourished like tropical birds, and the revolutionary sansculottes stood out everywhere in their distinctive striped trousers. The house of Aline Filliettaz—Johnson's contact here in Paris—was six stories high with wrought iron balconies and tall windows that opened onto a quiet side street deep in the Marais.

Nearby was the Temple, that turreted medieval fortress where Louis XVI and Marie Antoinette were currently imprisoned. I recalled William Godwin's terror-stricken warning about the place, but fortunately, the decapitated head of the Princesse de Lamballe was nowhere to be seen.

I briskly rubbed my hands over my arms as a footman bounded up the stone steps and spoke to the butler. He wore no livery, but that made sense given the egalitarian stance of the solidly middle-class Filliettaz household. My French was excellent, but I frowned when I realized I could scarcely make out a word the butler was saying.

"*Excusez-moi.*" I stopped the footman. "*Je ne comprends pas.*"

The footman helped me alight from the carriage. "Theirs is a colloquial French, mademoiselle," he stated under his breath. "Not the academic French you speak. The master and mistress of the house were unexpectedly called out of Paris. You will be on your own for the next few weeks."

"*Merci.*" I frowned again and reminded myself not to fall into speaking English, no matter how much French might prove a struggle. Johnson had warned me that a French national might believe me to be an English spy. This could lead to imprisonment or, worse, a trip to the newly christened guillotine. I would have to be on guard everywhere here in Paris. And speak very little, unless I was among friends.

For the first time, I doubted the wisdom of traveling to France at the height of a revolution. I quickly shook off my worries; if Olympe de Gouges and those emboldened fishwives could look it all in the face, so would I.

Sapere aude. Dare to know.

It was my new motto, one Johnson had etched on an unchristened inkpot he gave me as a parting gift when I'd taken him my cat to care for. Blue silk overskirts in hand—Johnson had insisted I procure fashionable ensembles to fit in with the French philosophes, and I'd added *serviceable* to the criteria of the *robe à l'anglaise* I now wore—I climbed the imposing granite stairs to my new home. Unfortunately, as soon as the manservant spoke in his strange guttural language, all my fine French phrases flew away like startled sparrows. After much gesticulating, which was punctuated by the occasional phrase in French—I was able to communicate my name—he demonstrated through punctilious hand gestures that my trunks would be taken to my room.

"I'm going for a walk. To clear my head." I hoped the Parisians wouldn't throw me in prison for butchering their language.

Somehow, the butler interpreted my wishes and raised a finger, beckoning me to wait. When he returned, it was with an overlarge tricolor cockade that was the uniform of the revolutionaries, which he pinned to my bodice. "*Pour la sécurité,*" he said slowly and solemnly.

After only a few blocks I realized this was *not* the illustrious and renowned France I had anticipated. Instead, people scurried along the filthy streets while glancing over their shoulders. Statues missing from their plinths—marble royals, no doubt—scarred the city with their absence. One odious message scrawled in charcoal across a building warned people not to cheer for the king lest they *face the consequences.*

I had envisioned a glorious revolution of hopeful and bright-eyed people chanting in the streets as they snapped the reins of history. Instead, I'd entered a weary country terrified of its own shadow.

As I turned the corner and approached the Place de la Révolution, I gasped.

The French were rightly terrified.

A guillotine had been set up in the middle of the vast public square in front of the Hôtel Crillon, where Marie Antoinette had taken piano lessons and sipped tea. The once glorious square was deserted now, but I swallowed past the sudden vise around my throat to see the gleaming blade patiently awaiting its next victim. There was no mistaking the dark stain on the platform's wooden planks. *Blood.*

In that moment, my scalp prickled with fear.

Angry shouts approaching the square had me retracing my steps in haste.

Panic-hot blood thrumming in my ears, I arrived back at 22 Rue Meslée as the indignant cries behind me reached a fearful crescendo. Was it just my imagination, or was something momentous about to occur? Even with the language barrier, I was able to make out two words of the butler's rapid-fire form of French as he locked the door behind me.

Le roi. The king.

The manservant gestured for me to follow him up the richly carpeted staircase.

Up.

Up.

Up.

To the top floor, where he pulled down a hidden staircase

flush with the ceiling and pointed for me to ascend. Outside, a rhythmic booming rattled the attic windowpanes. At first, I thought it was canons. Then, I realized as I looked outside, drums. Great war drums whose reverberations I could feel deep in my bones.

All around me, Paris's citizens had flocked to their windows, but the casements were all shut. The red-capped revolutionary mob had fallen suddenly silent and not a voice was heard, not even an insulting gesture. The plainly dressed butler and maids surrounding me angled their gazes down at the square six stories below them, where I'd stood only moments ago.

The creaking donkey cart that passed beneath us was surrounded by armed National Guards in their blaze of cobalt-blue coats with white lapels and blue collars. The royal colors.

The lone inhabitant of the cart was a pale-faced and proud man any European would have recognized from his stamps and coins and the many sketches that accompanied articles about him and his crumbling monarchy.

King Louis XVI.

An all-powerful monarch who had once claimed that his right to rule came directly from God; now this man seemed irreparably broken to my wide eyes.

"On his way to the National Convention. He will stand trial for treason." I was thankful I could understand the maid who spoke between pursed lips, but I might have understood anyway when she spat down on the street. "*Connard.* May he meet the National Razor. He deserves nothing else."

I dragged my gaze back to the cart that was steadily passing from view. The king might still breathe today, but a rill of cold unease trailed its way down my spine.

Unable to sleep later that night, I used my new inkpot to write to Johnson in an unsteady hand.

I cannot dismiss the lively images that have filled my imagination all the day. I wish I had even kept the cat with me! I want to see something alive; death in so many frightful shapes has taken hold of my fancy. I am going to bed—and for the first time in my life, I cannot put out the candle.

As I stared at the flickering flames of that same candle with the hours carved into its side, my thoughts turned black.

I had dreamed of revolution in all its glory. Not until today had I considered it might possess a dark underbelly.

Weeks later, the city was again eerily silent, all of Paris's citizens ordered under penalty of death to remain indoors from fear that protests would erupt in favor of the king. The worry wasn't unfounded, given the many royalist revolts raging outside the capital. I'd promised Johnson eyewitness accounts of this revolution, but not even I dared breach the doorway and follow King Louis XVI to the guillotine.

So I gathered my accounts from sources available around me, namely newspapers. I reminded myself that Herodotus, the Greek father of history, had done the same during the Persian Wars, but that did little to assuage my feelings of failure.

Louis proclaimed his innocence and urged France to stop the guillotine killings, before mounting the scaffold. The eerie silence exploded into violent cheers of Vive la République once the blade crashed down. Jacobins who defied the order to remain inside soaked their hands in the king's blood even as the executioner held up Louis's severed head.

I couldn't go as far as one of the newspapers that proclaimed this moment of regicide as the start of a beautiful new epoch. Brute force had hitherto governed the world; I failed to see how something as luminescent as freedom could be born of the murky terror Paris currently wallowed in. I realized that until now I'd been spoiled by England's peace and civility while here in Paris vice was tramping on virtue.

My pen held in midair, I pondered asking Johnson to arrange passage for my return. I hated to admit that insufferable William Godwin had been right, but it was possible that conditions here in France would deteriorate further. If so, English nationals such as myself would surely become key targets of the newly formed Committee of Public Safety, especially if our own incompetent King George III declared war on France as Austria and Prussia had done.

Except . . .

I hadn't accomplished what I'd come here to do. I hadn't seen the women's revolution or made any notes on its progress toward equality and liberty. Here in France, even amid the trial and death of the king, divorce had been legalized and daughters were now allowed to inherit. The next step, argued writings by the renowned Marquis de Condorcet, was the right to vote.

Imagine!

A bolt of lightning electrified me at the thought of this promise of equality for women, and I yearned to see how far these radical ideas could take root in Paris. If in Paris, why not elsewhere?

In the days following the king's execution, word of my encampment in Paris spread and my two *Vindication*s garnered me invitations to upcoming soirees hosted by sympathizers of the Revolution. Also, Thomas Paine had arrived in Paris and expressed his hopes that I—plain Mary Wollstonecraft of Hoxton—would attend those salons with him.

As if I could say no.

In London, I had been a rare oddity—a self-educated woman

who cultivated a mind of her own and was determined to support herself while going toe-to-toe against the intellectual giants of the day. The intellectual *male* giants, that was. In the salons of Paris, I quickly discovered such Amazonian behavior was commonplace among the French *salonnières* and female revolutionaries. And yet, by nature of being foreign and known for my many published works, I still produced a sensation wherever I went.

"Mademoiselle Wollstonecraft," exclaimed the famed Marquis de Condorcet, that brilliant mathematician and moderate leader in the National Assembly who dressed like a common tradesman while possessing the sinister sort of sagacity common to the French. He had gathered alongside so many notable names of the Revolution in the small velvet-lined dining room of Thomas Paine's elegant hotel at Faubourg St. Denis. A merry fire danced in the grate, and I fluttered my fan against the overbearing heat—inadequately, I might add, given that the only fan a fashionable woman could use was a delicate and pointless lace contraption. My gaze constantly flicked around the room, for Olympe de Gouges was soon to make an appearance. Instead, a striking man with loose chestnut hair and the swarthy look of an American frontiersman snagged my gaze, but I was more interested in the ideas floating around the room than a handsome face. "I hope to see a plan drafted for the education of women, very similar to your *Education of Daughters*," Condorcet continued with aplomb. "I am of the opinion that by providing a secular education to all, France could adequately govern herself. After all, education of each citizen is the first and most important step in liberation."

I was so accustomed to having to defend my intelligence—even at Johnson's liberal dinner table—that it was a welcome, albeit bewildering, change to have my stance so readily supported. "Indeed. I strongly agree that boys and girls must be educated together in public day schools in pursuit of the same studies—reading, writing, arithmetic, botany, mechanics, astronomy." It was a radical idea I'd proposed in *A Vindication of the Rights of Woman*, one I hoped to see fulfilled by all enlightened nations. "If a woman is not prepared by education, she will stop the progress of knowledge and truth. We must be permitted—and encouraged—to turn to the fountain of light."

"I wholeheartedly agree. France simply cannot exclude half of the human race from participation in government." Condorcet was animated, the energy of his excitement scarcely leashed. "Mademoiselle Wollstonecraft, I would love to correspond with you further about this matter."

"I would be honored," I replied eagerly. After all, this was my favorite subject of contemplation—the future improvement of the world. "I look forward to our correspondence—I must admit I fairly devoured your most recent pamphlets denouncing slavery and advancing the cause of republicanism."

"Miss Wollstonecraft." Thomas Paine was at my elbow, dressed smartly in a frock coat embroidered in the French style with delicate snowdrop blossoms. Not for the first time, I noted the bright intelligence in his eyes and wondered what might have sparked between us had he been thirty years younger instead of past sixty and twice wed. "There is someone I'd very much like you to meet," he murmured. "A kindred spirit to the Revolution and women's rights."

Mouth suddenly dry as Paine led me to the entrance hall, I fully expected to come face-to-face with Olympe de Gouges. Instead, I gaped at the mud-stained masthead of a woman who bellowed about the violent downpour outside while shedding a severe white wool riding habit to reveal two dueling pistols strapped to her hips. *And* a sword at her waist.

I turned to Paine, eyes wide. "Is she goddess or highwayman? Or something else entirely?"

"Like you, Théroigne de Méricourt defies explanation. I believe the warrant for her arrest was recently repealed." His hand at the small of my back urged me forward. "May I present Mary Wollstonecraft," he said to his guest. "You both share many beliefs about women and their place in this new world. Citizeness Théroigne attends all the meetings of the National Assembly and Miss Wollstonecraft is the author of the recent *A Vindication of the Rights of Woman*."

"*Enchantée.*" I began to curtsy to the famed leader of the Women's March on Versailles, but suddenly, Théroigne guided me away from Paine—pistol bumping against my hip so that I hoped it wasn't loaded. Paine offered a helpless shrug when I glanced over my shoulder.

"Finally," she said in rapid French, "someone with ideas worth having."

Théroigne didn't walk into the dining room—she *swaggered*. Silence fell as Paine's dinner guests gaped. Ignoring the sword and dueling pistols, even her man's cravat and waistcoat were jarring and her wig might have been plucked from a statesman's nightstand—plain white curls gathered into a stark black ribbon at the back. I waited for the inevitable scorns of derision at seeing so uncommon a woman and was pleasantly shocked when everyone merely resumed their chatter.

I realized then that standing next to me was the very sort of female that all womankind should aspire to—a woman who saw the world as her stage and who dressed and acted and spoke however she desired.

Théroigne laughed when I said as much. "*Liberty is the mother of virtue,*" she said, slyly reciting the line from *A Vindication of the Rights of Woman*. "*And if women be, by their very constitution, slaves, and not allowed to breathe the sharp invigorating air of freedom . . .*"

"*They must ever languish like exotics, and be reckoned beautiful flaws in nature,*" I finished, feeling no small amount of pride.

"Indeed." She nodded with approval while helping herself to the salad of anchovies and *pigeons au gratin* that had been set at the edges of the table in preparation for the main meal. "I spent far too long bowing and scraping before men, first as a courtesan and then as an opera singer. I set all that aside when our glorious female compatriots marched to Versailles and seized the Revolution into their own capable hands."

"And have you always dressed this way?" I hoped she wouldn't take offense, but she only snorted.

"Since I quit the stage. It is far more comfortable, you see." Théroigne used her fingers to peel a bit of pigeon from its bone, then nibbled it daintily before licking her fingers. "No more will I be reminded of the days when I preened to please men. I ceased bathing and spraying myself with eau de toilette and learned how to use these"—a pat of her pistols—"against anyone who gets in my way." Indeed, there was a distinctly *earthy* smell emanating from Théroigne, who ran a hand down the front of her waistcoat, drawing more than one onlooker's attention to her prodigious curves.

"So, you've sworn off men?" I felt intense curiosity about this, especially given that my own physical experience with men was *inexistant*.

"Not at all." Her wink was devilish. "My body is strong and pleasing to anyone I care to share it with."

I didn't have the opportunity to blush before Théroigne directed me to one end of the long table. Thankfully, wine had already been poured and set out, giving me something to do with my hands.

Why am I so nervous? I realized that never before had I discussed such subjects with an educated, revolutionary *woman*. And I suddenly and desperately wanted very much to impress Théroigne de Méricourt.

"Tell me, citizeness," I said. "What are your thoughts on the king's recent execution?"

"*Très bien*," Théroigne answered. "If only we could revolt against the tyranny of all men instead of just the Bourbon one." Her voice rose, traveling over the gentle buzz of conversation. "Let us raise ourselves to the height of our destinies," she shouted with a salute of her glass. "Let us break our chains!"

Several guests raised their wine and a few even cheered. I gave a feeble lift of my glass, which had Théroigne arching a feral eyebrow at me. "You disagree with my passion?"

I hesitated. It wouldn't do to lie or dissemble. "I cheered Lafayette's passage of the Declaration of the Rights of Man and of the Citizen as a necessary step toward liberty and equality, and I shall cheer still louder when Olympe de Gouges's *Déclaration des Droits de la Femme et de la Citoyenne* is adopted." I set down my glass and tapped my fingers against the table. "But I fear that such rank violence shall not advance the cause of liberty, not when all I see is a once vibrant city now shrouded in fear and terror."

"Impossible to be vibrant when people are starving." Théroigne removed a pocketknife from her bodice and used it to pick under her fingernails. "You cannot argue that the king's government was corrupt. A true revolution demands that the streets run red with the blood of tyrants."

"Where does fear end and true freedom begin? I worry that the king's death shall whet the revolutionaries' appetites for still more blood, all while France's people cower." I thought of the family I'd encountered the day I'd met Johnson in London, on their way to the public hangings at Newgate Prison. "I'm of the opinion that executions, while meant to provide useful deterrents to the populace, instead have a contrary effect by hardening the hearts they are meant to terrify."

Théroigne stared at me for such a long moment that I feared she would aim one of her pistols at my head. Instead, she blew on her fingernails and replaced the pocketknife. "You may be right, my petite English philosopher. Perhaps at the next assembly meeting I shall caution against the overuse of the guillotine. Less revolution and more freedom, yes?"

I smiled in relief. *See, I did make the right decision in staying here in Paris.* "Indeed. Unfortunately, I doubt the Committee of Public Safety will take kindly to your critiques."

Théroigne scoffed. "I fight their fire with my own." She leaned back and kicked her heeled feet upon the table. Was there no limit to this woman's audacity? "From what I've read of your work, you possess that spark as well. You shall join me, *ma chérie.*"

"In the assembly?"

"*Oui.* I also give speeches on the streets, to the Jacobins and the Girondins. Your words could convince them to find common ground in this conquest for freedom."

"Are you sure?"

"Why? Have you succumbed to that very fear you claim has subsumed France?"

I swallowed. Every warning I'd heard—from Johnson and the French coachman and even that insufferable William Godwin—commanded that I keep my head down. *Observe and report*, I heard Johnson's voice say in my head, *nothing more.* I thought of King Louis mounting the stairs to the guillotine—if even a king was not safe, how could I guarantee my own safety?

I could not. But I felt something shift inside me as I realized some things were more important than safety. Courage meant looking fear in the eye and moving forward anyway, just as Théroigne had done when she led the women's march to Versailles.

I didn't have pistols and I'd never led a mob, but what I did have were *words*.

Words could elicit great change—one only had to look to the Magna Carta, Locke's *Two Treatises of Government*, or America's Declaration of Independence to see that truth.

Thus, there was only one answer I could give Théroigne de Méricourt. "It would be my honor to accompany you."

I would help blaze a path that other women might one day follow.

After all, someone had to light the way. Why not me?

CHAPTER 5

❧

June 1814

MARY GODWIN

Mary expected to find her sixteen-year-old self transformed, unalterably *changed* by the revolutionary kiss she'd shared with Percy. Instead, the face that stared back in the mirror was herself, and yet, not herself.

How much did people hide beneath the placid surface of their skin? What dark emotions heaved unseen within the swamp waters of their souls? For Mary, following that kiss with Percy Shelley, the answer was *so very much.*

"What have we done?" she'd asked as soon as they'd broken apart. Her lips had already felt bruised then, pleasantly so. Her conscience was more painfully marked.

"We've been marching toward this moment since we first met." Percy's eyes churned with an oncoming storm. "It was only a matter of time."

"You are *married*. And after this"—she'd gestured between them—"I can never see you again."

"This is only the beginning, Mary, not the end." Percy's tone had been feather-soft, his fingers even lighter as he'd tilted her chin so she caught the scent of citrus and wood that always clung to him. "Emotions reign supreme in a life fully lived. You know my marriage to Harriet is a sham, a mere piece of paper."

"And your children with her?"

Percy had the decency to look chagrined, but only for a moment. "Ianthe is still a babe and my parents are raising her. Well, their servants are, given my father's stance that this best befits an aristocratic daughter. And you've met Harriet—does she seem like the motherly type?"

"No, but still. Percy, this feels unhinged."

"It is, but I've never felt like this with anyone, like we're simply meant to be. You, Mary Godwin, are fairer than a garden rose among dark-leaved brambles."

Except theirs was a forbidden attraction. One that could come to nothing, unless . . .

Surely it was no error that this meteor of a kiss took place while standing amid the moss and decay of her mother's grave. And when she calculated the number of years left in her own life . . .

It was as if Mary Wollstonecraft had sent her a message today.

Live each day as if it were your last.

"Come away with me," Percy had whispered to her. "Say you'll be mine."

"You've already run away to Scotland with one woman, Percy."

It was a mistake to speak his name, but it felt so very *right*. Percy's eyes sparked with happiness at the sound, and he clasped her hands to his chest. "A marriage certificate means little when my heart insists that I belong with you. Tell me you don't feel this, and I'll leave you alone forever. You only have to speak the words."

She wanted to say them, truly, but she couldn't. And Percy saw it.

"We'll take a trip together while we figure things out," he said, the words coming fast. "We'll travel to Paris and beyond, perhaps even trace your mother's footsteps. Say you'll come with me. *Please*."

And suddenly, that was the one thing Mary wanted most in the world.

To escape the feel of London closing in on her, and Jane's expectations that she marry, to not constantly second-guess her father's standoffish manner, all while learning more about the mother she desperately missed.

And she wanted to do it all with Percy Shelley by her side. To what end, she wasn't sure, but they could figure that all out later.

Now, staring at the mirror back in her room above M. J. Godwin & Co., Mary had no idea how to explain this next decision to her family. Jane and Claire would recover—they were made of stern stuff. And, given her father's unconventional courtship with her mother, Mary was sure he would support her.

Once the scandal fires were reduced to embers, anyway.

But Fanny . . .

Mary carefully ignored that eggshell worry, lest it crack and ruin everything.

From the bureau she shared with Fanny, Mary shook out her second-best dress—a soft gown the color and feel of spring bluebells—and was folding it into a leather traveling valise alongside her copy of Mary Wollstonecraft's *A Vindication of the Rights of Woman*, where two of Percy's purple pansies had been carefully pressed between its pages. She nearly dropped the entire valise when her door suddenly banged open. "Mary Godwin." Claire blocked the exit. "What is going on with you? You've been fairly twitching since the cemetery today."

Mary dropped the valise to the floor, where she kicked it under her bed. She would pack her journal and a few books after Fanny had fallen asleep tonight. "Too much coffee," she said to Claire. "I fear it makes me jumpy."

She fiddled with the wooden hairbrush on the bureau, wondering whether to pack it. What did one care for something so mundane as hairbrushes in moments like this?

"I never thought you'd lie to me." The door snicked shut behind Claire, and the hellcat growl of her voice made Mary's skin prickle with gooseflesh. This was a side of Claire—who was usually so silly and effervescent—that Mary had rarely glimpsed before. "I heard you and Percy in the cemetery. I heard *all of it* and I know what you're up to."

Mary's body went bloodless. Of course Claire had overheard them.

"Please don't try to stop me, Claire. My mind is firmly made up. And so is Percy's."

"My mind is also made up. I won't tell a single soul."

Mary felt such a swell of gratitude that she nearly launched herself at Claire for an embrace. Only Claire's stony expression stopped her. "Really?"

"On one provision."

Mary set down the hairbrush. "What provision?"

"Take me with you."

Mary actually laughed out loud. "You cannot be serious."

Claire sat on the bed, shuffling her feet back and forth in their black half boots. "I am, deathly so. If you leave, you taint us all with your scandal—I'll never be able to show my face outside this house again. Fanny is content here between these four walls, but you and I . . . we're destined for bigger things. If you leave me behind, any hopes I had of ever escaping this house, of being an independent woman, will be destroyed. And that's not fair."

Mary balked at the truth in Claire's statement. Never before had she heard Claire speak so harshly. Even if she spoke true about the brush of scandal they would all soon be painted with. "Why?"

Claire cocked her head like a curious kitten. "Why what?"

"Why do you want to come? You told me yourself that you were half in love with Percy." She narrowed her eyes. "Why come with us?"

"It's true that I was infatuated with Percy, but we were never meant to be. Still, you can't deny we three are much the same—eager to drink fully from life's cup and see all this world has to offer."

"You are your mother's only daughter—she'll miss you terribly."

Mary didn't have to say the rest: *And she won't miss me at all.* Claire stood and shrugged. "And your father will forgive you, but he scarcely notices me unless I've done something wrong. There's nothing here for me except waiting to be tarred by scandal. Why not seize the opportunity to hitch my star on the adventure of my sister's elopement?"

"It's not an elopement," Mary muttered, needing to stall Claire and work out her own options. "Percy is already married."

Claire had noticed the valise sticking out from under the bed and now removed the bluebell dress to refold it properly. "I don't know what else you call a man—married or no—running off with an unmarried woman. Especially given how *familiar* you both were with each other at your mother's grave today."

Again, Mary's cheeks heated. She wasn't accustomed to having to explain herself. "Percy and I are traveling to France to learn more about my mother." It was at least partly the truth. Mary had always wanted to travel the Continent and walk in Mary Wollstonecraft's footsteps. Percy's offer solved the issue of her lack of funds *and* provided an ideal partner. Still, she hadn't anticipated Claire being part of the equation. Although perhaps having her sister along would soften the scandal, as well as provide an opportunity for Claire? "Retracing my mother's steps is why we're going to Paris."

Claire's lips went sideways. *Liar.* "I need your answer."

Mary hesitated. Then: "How much pin money do you have saved?"

Claire's smile was a flare of the sun. "At least enough for part of a ticket to Le Havre. I'm sure Percy can cover the rest, especially since he promised to pay off our debts. He *is* fulfilling his promise if you're running off with him, right?"

Inwardly, Mary cringed, even as she gave an outward nod. She didn't want talk of money to cheapen what she felt toward Percy, but after the cemetery he *had* made good his promise to pay off her father's debts, whether they went to Paris together or not.

Claire picked up the wooden hairbrush and dropped it into Mary's valise. "I'll see you downstairs tonight, just after midnight. What an adventure this will be!"

As Mary watched her go, cold dread pooled in her belly.

"I wasn't sure you'd come." Percy's hands were chilly around Mary's, despite the uncommon July heat of the predawn hour. Everything felt especially clandestine at four o'clock in the morning—Mary had only ever seen this candlelit hour when a book had kept her engrossed far into the night. Percy's feverbright eyes dimmed as he peered over Mary's shoulder. "Now, *this* is an unexpected surprise."

Mary looked over at Claire, who was clambering into Percy's carriage where it waited at the corner of Hatton Garden to carry them to Dover. For once, Claire was dressed in somber navy, sans her usual frills and ruffles. "She made a very persuasive case to join us."

"I see. And Fanny?"

Mary winced. "We crept out while she was sleeping." She'd wanted to inform her older sister of her destination—truly, she had—but a niggling voice in the back of her mind whispered to keep her silence. Not necessarily because Fanny would have tattled, but because Mary couldn't bear her older sister's reaction.

Better to explain once the act was done. Mary couldn't afford to doubt herself, not when she wished to follow in her mother's footsteps—to travel and be her own woman. To leave England behind and finally *breathe* again. She hoped that Fanny would understand and forgive her.

"And your father?"

To assuage her conscience at abandoning her dear, eccentric father, Mary had scrawled a note for him in Latin and left it on his dressing table outside his bedchambers, right next to the envelope Percy had instructed her to leave for her father. In running away with Percy, Mary was surely causing a scandal but so, too, was she rescuing her father's finances. William Godwin would be sure to see both her letter and Percy's in the morning.

After their ship was already halfway across the Channel.

Vale, Pater.

"Fortune favors the bold," Percy assured her after she told him. "You'll see."

Then he held open the door to the carriage. Claire motioned impatiently from within.

One moment. One choice.

Mary drew a steadying breath and gathered her skirts before climbing inside. Percy settled beside her; his thigh against her leg made her breath hitch. Across from them, Claire turned her nose up, gazing outside, where the constellations were still winking down at them. "Will it be a long journey to France, do you think?" she asked.

To which Percy only glanced at Mary and smiled. "The journey of a lifetime."

Mary had thought herself immune to seasickness—her own mother had boasted of a sturdy constitution in her Swedish travelogue—but instead Mary found herself mortified as her stomach lurched with each frothy wave that crashed over the bow of the fishing boat Percy had hired to whisk them to France. She managed to speak only once. "Don't come near me," she commanded Percy. "I can't bear you to see me like this."

"This salty tempest shall forge us anew," he hollered over a crash of thunder. As much as the journey threatened to overcome her, it seemed to revitalize Percy, who whooped and hollered as the sea sprayed his face and water sloshed overboard.

When they finally landed at Calais, Mary was a pale wraith of her former self, but Percy's every step burst with barely contained vim. "Look." He stood behind Mary—lending her his steady strength—and framed the stormy sky with his fingers just as the sun broke from behind water-heavy clouds, steady and glowing fire-red over the pier. "The sun rises over France, just as it shines on our future."

How could any woman resist someone so intoxicating?

Especially when Percy revealed that he'd booked the most expensive rooms at Dessin's. "It's the best hotel," Percy said sheepishly while she and Claire gaped. "Everyone from England stays there. I hope it's not too much."

"It's wonderful," Mary whispered. "Thank you."

Her head hurt and she was thankful for the well-appointed room and its luxurious down bed surrounded by thick bed-curtains. "I could just live here, it's so beautiful," Claire said as she pulled back the velvet drapes from the spotless windows and grinned as she peered onto the street. "Another new experience, since this will be the first time you and I share a room. Percy is just down the hall."

Suddenly, Mary found herself terribly unsure. Of course, she understood about certain relations between men and women, and she'd agreed to travel with Percy, which meant that she'd had certain *expectations* that most decidedly did *not* involve her sister.

Had she entirely misread the situation?

Exhausted from the journey, both girls had fallen asleep—perhaps for several hours, perhaps for half the day—when someone knocked on the door. Mary expected to see Percy, but it was a hotel butler at the entrance, looking rather harried. "*Une grosse dame est en bas,*" he said. "*Elle demande à voir sa fille.*"

Mary had always considered Jane more stout than over-weight, but there was only one *fat lady* who might be down-stairs, demanding to see her daughter.

Mary whirled on Claire, then wobbled on her feet, still weak from the crossing. "Is this your doing?" she asked as the edge of the bed caught her fall. "Did you tell her where to find us?"

"Of course not. My mother is likely to murder me." Claire's face had gone as pale as a January moon, and she beckoned with a gloved hand. "Come downstairs with me. *Please.*"

Still feeling poorly, Mary considered leaving Claire to fend for herself, but she wished to know whether Jane planned to drag Mary back as well. And whether William Godwin had accompanied his wife.

If so, would Mary return with them? Or would she stay with Percy, unsure though she was about their entire plan?

When the girls reached the foyer, a purple-faced Jane took Claire by her arm. "To my room, *now*," she ground out, using her body to shield Claire from curious stares as she marched down the hallway. "Ruining your reputation *and* your chance at respectability and happiness. Over my rotting corpse."

Jane attempted to bar Mary's entrance into the ground-floor hotel room. "And *you*," Jane snarled under her breath. "You'll pack Claire's things immediately. I'm taking her away from here—"

"Only Claire?" Mary didn't know where the words had come from. Did she truly want her stepmother to drag her back to England's shores?

Yes, a tiny voice inside her head whispered. Because that's what any mother would have done.

Except Jane was *not* Mary's mother.

Still, Jane cocked her head at Mary, arms akimbo. "If I said I was here to retrieve you, would you come? Instead of traipsing around the Continent just as your mother did, chasing after a man who will inevitably leave you, just as men have done to women since time immemorial?"

Mary cringed at the insult to her mother, but didn't hesitate. She wanted to live and to see the world, and to do so with an equal—with Percy Shelley—at her side. "No."

"Then you are a lost cause, Mary Godwin." Jane was breathing heavily. "But with my intervention, Claire might still escape the scandal you've wrought upon all our heads."

A man cleared his throat behind Mary, stopping them all.

Percy stood there, an oasis of calm likely alerted by the butler to the drama unfolding on the first floor.

"*You*," Jane nearly hissed at him. "Have you any idea what you've done? What about your wife, sir? And the children you've abandoned?"

"My wife and children are hardly your concern," Percy answered, his voice level despite his clenched jaw. "Given that I will always maintain their upkeep, they've hardly been abandoned."

"And yet, here you are with Mary and my daughter." Jane stomped a foot. "Claire, you'll return with me this instant. After all I've done for you, to throw it all away . . . If you return now, we might still salvage your future."

"I have no intention of leaving," Claire announced in a tight voice. Mary admired the hard-grained tone Claire took. "I will stay with Mary and Percy."

"You will do no such thing—"

"Mrs. Godwin." Percy gestured for her to open the door, then ushered Mary inside before shutting them all within. "Miss Clairmont's desires are quite clear, and Mary and I support her decision. Please allow me to make arrangements with the hotel for your departure in the morning. I believe the money I left Mr. Godwin should cover the expense."

Jane turned her full ire upon Mary. "Did you know Percy Shelley here purchased the two of you for fifteen hundred pounds? As if that could ease the scandal of two daughters running away with a married man?"

"I believe the money that exchanged hands was discussed even before I met Miss Mary." Percy gestured Mary and Claire toward the exit. "I promise your daughter will keep you apprised of our movements about the Continent."

Jane's glare heated even further so that Mary feared her step-mother would eviscerate them all. Mary forced herself not to shrink back. Instead, Jane retreated. First one step, then two.

"I've failed both of you." She lifted her palms before her gaze flicked to Claire. Her eyes had taken on an extra shine, perhaps a trick of the light. She straightened, and cleared her throat. "Just as you've failed me, and your father."

Was that true? Had William Godwin refused to travel to France because he had disowned her? Mary's mind couldn't make sense of a world in which she wasn't her father's favored daughter. Surely Jane's retaliation came from spite.

"Why did you come?" Mary dared ask. "And not my father?"

Jane paused. "I wished to save him the embarrassment. I've failed him in that too."

Then she was gone.

Neither of the sisters spoke until they were upstairs. Mary murmured something to Claire's retreating back, then followed Percy to his chamber.

Somehow, he'd already poured two glasses of wine.

"Why did you stand up for Claire?" Mary held the wine, but didn't drink. Suddenly, she wished it were just she and Percy here in France. "Why not let her return home?"

Percy swirled the wine in his glass into a ruby-hued vortex. "Your sister is a sweet child who deserves to make her own decisions, as we all do," he finally said. "I wished to bolster her so she could live a life of her choosing. But you wanted Claire to go, didn't you?" he asked. "And now I've bungled things."

Yes, I did want her to go.

But that wasn't fair and Mary knew it. So she only set down her wine and framed Percy's beautiful face between her hands. The new sensation of his cheeks with their golden glow of evening stubble was intriguingly rough beneath her palms. "We're together," she said, willing herself to believe the words. "That's all that matters."

"Indeed." Percy's voice grew coarse. His thumb tracing the line of her jaw sent a delicious shiver through her. "I don't deserve you, Mary." His touch made her gasp as his lips whispered along the path his thumb had made. "But I promise to make this an expedition you'll never forget, while we enjoy every sublime feeling this life has to offer."

She was overwhelmed by the *feelings* in her body and merely managed a moan as she threaded her fingers through Percy's wonderfully disheveled hair. Except Percy pulled back at that sound. "You should return to your room," he said with a groan. "With Claire."

"What?" That was the last place Mary wished to be right now. "Why?"

Percy ran both hands through his hair so it stuck out in every possible direction. Mary resisted the urge to touch it again, instead busying herself with smoothing the front of her dress. She still seemed to be feeling her way in the dark around Percy. "You were ill today and your stepmother is downstairs," he said slowly, as if forcing the words. "And tomorrow promises to be overfull with excitement with our journey to Paris. You will walk in your mother's footsteps, *mon amour*."

Mary's heart thudded at the endearment's tiny beacon in the dark. Truth be told, she *was* exhausted and still a little lightheaded. She let Percy open the door and dared to lift an errant curl from his forehead before slipping down the hall.

For now, she would return to the room she shared with her sister.

Tomorrow would be a new day.

. . .

They departed from Dessin's shortly after dawn and made their way toward Paris—Jane had already left without a word of farewell, which Mary could see troubled Claire more than she was willing to admit.

"It's not too late," Mary had said when they'd donned their travel bonnets. "If you wanted to go home, that is."

Claire had looked overlong at the door, as if imagining herself following her mother. Her chin wobbled before she reached out and straightened the bow under Mary's chin. "No. I'll only look forward, from this day on. To Paris we go."

Except Paris was not at all what they had expected.

Indolent in the oppressive summer heat, the city was war-weary after Napoleon's failed experiment at empire, its thin-lipped citizens slump-shouldered and suspicious of visitors. All the Parisian women strolling the boulevards wore short jackets and high caps without any stray curls to decorate their temples, but Mary—and Claire, who insisted on parroting her sister—roamed the streets in search of French ideals that had inspired Mary Wollstonecraft while dressed in high-necked silk traveling dresses and matching ink-black bonnets. Mary had decided black was her new signature color, its lack of fuss something her mother would have approved of, although it may have marked them as dull English girls. Even with Percy and Claire at her sides, Mary couldn't stop envisioning her mother around every corner, thin arms weighted with books or jotting notes for the articles she sent home reporting on the Revolution that became the basis for her book *An Historical and Moral View of the Origin and Progress of the French Revolution*. However, Mary felt her mother's presence most strongly when Percy checked them into the Hôtel de Vienne at the edge of the

Marais, after she'd settled before the fire with a dog-eared copy of her mother's book.

The French Revolution is a strong proof how far things will govern men, when simple principles begin to act with one powerful spring against the complicated wheels of ignorance.

"Paris seems exhausted," Claire remarked after Mary had finished reading aloud the first chapter. The trio was gathered in the girls' room with the door cracked open for propriety's sake while they tucked into the plates Percy had ordered. The chicken vol-au-vent was delectable—the first true meal Mary had enjoyed since her last dinner at Skinner Street. Had that been only two days ago?

"Napoleon fought for so long; it was excruciating for the French to lose at Waterloo, especially after their ill-fated Russian debacle," Percy reminded Claire. "It might be worthwhile to explore outside Paris."

Claire yawned into her hand, and Percy chuckled good-naturedly. "It seems France is not the only one worn out."

"It's been a long day," Claire offered, to which Percy rose and offered a gallant bow.

"Then I shall retire and see you both in the morning."

Except Mary had already made her decision about this evening. It had been so long since she'd felt cared for or treasured—with Percy, she felt all those things, and more. It didn't matter where they were; with Percy she had found her North Star. And she wanted *more.* Thus, she only pantomimed readying for bed: loosening her hair, cleaning her teeth with a boar bristle brush, and slipping out of everything except her thin cotton chemise. Once Claire's breathing evened into the soft cadence of sleep,

Mary padded on silent feet down the hallway. There was no hesitation as she tapped at the entrance of Percy's room.

"Bad dream?" His eyes lit like brilliant meteors as he took in her dressing gown and loose hair. Then he held open the door.

An invitation, a decision.

Live each day as if it were your last.

In a reckless but also purely calculated move, Mary stepped over the threshold. "Far from it," she answered. "For the first time in as long as I can remember, I am too happy to sleep."

"Indeed." The door closed behind her. "I cannot recall a time the future has been so brilliant."

Mary spied the papers lounging lazily on his table, the open inkpot and freshly sharpened quill. One of the pages had been scrawled upon; Percy made no move to stop her when she began to read.

> *I felt the blood that burn'd*
> *Within her frame, mingle with mine, and fall*
> *Around my heart like fire.*

"It's far from grand," Percy murmured when she touched the words with her fingertip. "Certainly less illustrious than Byron's verses. But it's for you."

It took Mary a long moment to find her voice. His poem had captured exactly the celestial fire of each of their kisses. "When did you write this?"

"Last night. Sleep eluded me." Percy's voice shook as one finger trailed up her bare arm. Mary turned in the circle of his arms. "I couldn't help myself—you have become my muse."

The idea that she might have inspired such beauty, and that Percy had forever immortalized their feelings for each other with delicate words crafted like silken wings . . .

Any lingering doubts she might have had evaporated. Mary had never felt so sure of anything—of *anyone*—in her entire life. She and Percy Shelley were simply meant to be.

When they came together, their crashing storm of a kiss contained enough force to inspire poets and playwrights the world over. And when Percy carried her to bed . . .

Well, that was the stuff of legends.

In the days that followed, Mary cared little for food or sleep or anything else. Material comforts ceased to matter now that she had the one thing she needed . . .

Love.

Mary didn't care when they left Paris a week later not in a hired coach, but on foot with a donkey to carry their baggage as they trod the same serpentine path as Napoleon and Empress Joséphine. She wondered what had happened to Percy's seemingly endless funds, but she'd have followed him through the hellscapes of the Sahara without complaint. What did it matter whether they walked or rode on this expedition in search of revolution and romance?

Claire, however, was less enamored, with Percy or Mary or the mules. Or their entire adventure. Mary noticed the tears welling in her sister's eyes as thousands of sun-loving insects, the same white color as the road, infested their path. It *was* hot and France itself had been a terrible disappointment. There were no signs of the glorious Revolution, and it was nearly impossible to reconcile the scenes Mary Wollstonecraft had written about with the stark reality of this new France. Mary hadn't realized how difficult it would be to trace her mother's steps, given that she had only an impersonal history—no addresses where she'd lived or people who had known her—as her guide. Instead, it was all barren soil pockmarked by torn cottages with burned black beams and gaunt people still trying to recover from Austria and Prussia's counterattack prior to Napoleon's recent surrender. Those foreigners had retaliated against Napoleon's invasion of Russia by pillaging the countryside, burning French villages, raping women and killing children.

Mary had never seen war, but its remnants were far from glorious.

Still, Mary felt drunk as a honeybee on summer poppy nectar each time she glanced at Percy, her rapture with him growing the more time they spent together. While her spirits were buoyed up, Claire's seemed cast ever lower.

While Percy carried the portmanteau of books, Mary took one valise and handed the other to Claire. Her sister sighed and seemed to slump further into herself, even after they found a humble inn at Troyes at which to spend the night. "The beds are too uncomfortable to allow for sleeping," Claire announced, her eyes tight with fatigue.

Percy caught Mary's hand as they followed her sister into the main room. "And what about you, Mary? Do you hope to sleep tonight?" he asked under his breath.

To which Mary only blushed. "Very little, in fact."

Percy grinned as Claire called to them. The trio ate a simple repast of sour bread and goat cheese served with lemonade before Mary and Percy retired to read Lord Byron's most recent poems.

> She walks in beauty, like the night
> Of cloudless climes and starry skies;
> And all that's best of dark and bright
> Meet in her aspect and her eyes;
> Thus mellowed to that tender light
> Which heaven to gaudy day denies.

Mary was looking forward to another cloudless and starry night spent in Percy's arms . . .

Until, from the chamber next door, Claire started screaming.

Mary made it to the door first, but Claire was already pushing into Percy's room. The candles had been doused—their acrid scent still tinged the air—but there was enough moonlight to see Claire clawing at her face, her hair disheveled and nightdress torn. Percy's strong grip eventually calmed her, but even then, Mary's stepsister sobbed. "Rats," she gasped, hands covering her eyes. "On my face." Her expression was wild, grotesque even in the sickly light. "I hate this place—this inn, this terrible town, this country!"

"We need not stay in France one moment longer than necessary," Percy reassured her in such a soothing way that Mary wondered how often he'd had to calm fractious females—his mother, his sisters, perhaps even Harriet. Mary gave a practiced nudge to that last guilt-ridden thought so it faded into the shadows of her mind. "In the morning I shall arrange a change of course. Our merry band of travelers can make its way to the Rhine Valley."

"The Rhine Valley?" Claire hiccupped. "Why there?"

"Why not?" came Percy's effervescent response. "It will be a fine and unexpected detour on our continental idyll, don't you think? Floating down the castled Rhine before we return to England?"

"We're returning to England?" Claire beat Mary to asking the question.

"Not yet, but soon. My funds won't last forever, I'm afraid."

Mary realized their adventure wouldn't stretch into winter—Percy had confided that most of his allowance had been cut off long ago, due to his parents worrying that he'd use the money to support rebellions in Ireland—but she'd been living one day to the next. And now they were to leave France to travel the Rhine?

The only things in the Rhine Valley are crumbling old towns and drafty castles, Mary wanted to say. *I came all this way, Percy, to be with you in France. Not to travel the Rhine.*

Except Claire was heaving ragged sighs and Percy looked proud of himself for so masterfully solving their problems as Claire laid herself on what would have been *their* bed, and pulled up the covers to her chin. "I *cannot* stay in that room a moment longer. I'll stay here tonight. If you don't mind, that is."

"Not at all." Percy's eyes were kind as he shrugged at Mary in the moonlight. His thumb brushed her hip bone, a promise of pleasures to come. *But not tonight.* "I'm sure Mary doesn't mind either."

Mary gave what she hoped passed for a sweet smile, aimed first at Claire and then at Percy. "Not at all."

Perhaps France *had* been a disappointment, but leaving was still a bitter pill to swallow, no matter that Mary was doing it for her sister and Percy.

Floating the Rhine *was* more pleasant than riding by mule through the desolate French countryside, especially as the calendar turned to September and the weather cooled.

Unfortunately, the high deck of the small *diligence par-eau* was crammed with loutish German-speaking passengers who smoked prodigiously and belched out drinking songs by night while Percy read aloud to Mary from her mother's travelogue *Letters Written During a Short Residence in Sweden, Norway, and Denmark*. (Percy actually knocked down one shapeless animal of a passenger when the man insisted on rudely singing over Mary Wollstonecraft's paragraphs. Fortunately, the oaf was too addled with drink to remember the offence the next day.) Worse still was the fact that Mary couldn't shake Claire even for a moment.

Mary loved her sister, but Claire was always with them—giggling, flicking her curls over her shoulder, and continuously singing—from the moment they woke until they all retired to the hammocks of the shared cabin at night to read the third canto of Lord Byron's *Childe Harold's Pilgrimage*, which so beautifully described the Rhine and was so at odds with the cadence of drunken snores that surrounded them. Was Claire perhaps overly joyful to cover her regret over coming on this trip?

Mary and Percy dozed with their fingers entangled each night, but Mary felt as if she might burst from her skin if she didn't have a moment alone with him. She'd envisioned pushing Claire—and several of their drunken companions—into the circling whirlpools of the Rhine just to have a moment's peace.

Percy laughed when Mary admitted to the daydream. "I'm afraid you'd have to go in after your sister."

"Your dashing heroics don't include ruining your fine clothes or mussing your hair?"

Percy chuckled. "My concerns are more practical than that." And with a devious tickle of his breath against her ear: "I never did find the time to learn to swim."

On an afternoon gilded by a perfect sheet of autumn sunshine, the barge passed the village of Gernsheim and tied up. Claire had fallen asleep in her rope hammock. "Let's go ashore." Mary's whisper to Percy was full of promise. Soon, just the two of them were wending their way down Gernsheim's cobbled streets past picturesque gabled cottages. Percy stopped at the lone bakery and parted with one of his last guineas to procure a paper-wrapped loaf of bread and wafer of butter for their lunch. "A modest picnic for my fair lady," he said as he offered his arm.

In that moment, everything seemed utterly, flawlessly, perfectly *right* with the world.

At the outskirts of the village, a verdant countryside freckled with the mauve flowers of witches' money-bags unrolled beneath a castle that lounged like a coiled stone dragon atop the hillside. They broke away from the path to meander their way through the rippling grass and flowery bushes to an obliging knoll, their two sides pressed together as if they couldn't bear to be apart.

"Frankenstein Castle," Percy announced as he shrugged out of his jacket and spread it on the grass as a makeshift blanket. His hair ruffled in the breeze, as if even the winds loved to touch him. "A perfect spot for a secluded party of pleasure with my ladylove."

Mary felt a rush of joy that he called her his *ladylove*. It might be dangerous to let Percy hold such sway over her happiness, but she was powerless to stop herself.

"Stone of the Franks," Mary said, translating the castle's name as she examined its two towers and the crumbling ruins that joined them. "An apt description, although perhaps lacking in imagination."

"I agree. However, the legends the captain told me redeem the old place."

"Oh?" Mary plucked a few purple flowers of aromatic ground ivy scattered about the grass. She tucked her legs beneath her skirts, while sitting so close to Percy that their shoulders brushed. How could such a simple touch send fire embers swirling through her belly? She had to clear her throat before she could speak. "Do tell."

Percy's laughing eyes recklessly acknowledged that he knew exactly what his touch had done to her, but his voice dropped and took on the tone of a bard of old. "The castle was once the home of a notorious alchemist named Konrad Dippel, who was obsessed with finding a cure for death. To that end, each night he turned grave robber to steal body parts from the good residents of Gernsheim and tried to reanimate the corpses he exhumed. He even concocted strange sorts of potions mixed with blood and dust made from human bones."

Mary shivered as a ripple of anticipation rilled its way up her spine. She could get lost in Percy's voice. "And? Did he meet with success?"

The sweep of Percy's jaw fascinated her as he swallowed the last bite of bread, so she had to wrap her fingers in her skirt to keep from tracing the elegant line. She *did* want to hear the rest of the story, after all. "Sadly, no. He died an abject failure. Thus, the world may never know whether it is possible to breathe life into death. Can you imagine? Being able to cure death?"

Mary shook her head. Suddenly she didn't wish to speak of death, not when she felt so gloriously, wonderfully *alive* sitting there in the sunshine next to Percy.

She glanced about, confirming they were the only souls in that lonely field.

Moments later, she and Percy were stretched out in the grass, the autumn sunshine warm on their backs and the peppery scent of the ivy they rolled about filling her nose while she kissed him.

Kissed him and kissed him and *kissed* him.

It was just the two of them in all the world. And Percy was so easy to love.

What did it matter if they returned to the barge several hours later in rumpled clothing, a nosegay of flowers in hand as a keepsake of that field of love while laughingly pulling gold-tinged bits of grass from each other's hair? Or if Claire refused to speak to either of them for the rest of the day?

It mattered not at all.

However, it *did* matter a few weeks later.

Mary was unwed, in love, and about to return home to the scandal she had created. Just before their return to England, she realized her monthly courses were long overdue.

Above all, she was pregnant.

CHAPTER 6

❦

April 1792

MARY WOLLSTONECRAFT

With a steaming cup of black tea warming my hands, I nestled farther into a corner of Helen Maria's English teahouse—one of the few bastions of safety left for us British here in revolutionary France. The trees were filled with spring's expanding leaves, but nothing could shake the marrow-deep chill as Madame Guillotine continued her bloody work. The king's death had solved nothing—France's people were still destitute and hungry. God help us all if the moderate Girondins of the National Assembly failed in their attempts to bring freedom to France via diplomacy—the radical Jacobins would burn the entire country to the ground before they'd entertain a temperate idea.

In the days since Thomas Paine's salon, I'd planned to accompany Théroigne de Méricourt to the National Assembly, but England had declared war on France, so now British citizens were declared enemies of the state. Why, just yesterday I'd been spat upon by a bookseller when I'd requested a newspaper in my accented French. Even the famed *salonnière* Madame Roland had announced an end to her salons, citing safety reasons for her guests. Thus, the Marquis de Condorcet had persuaded me that an appearance at the National Assembly was currently too dangerous for an Englishwoman. It was clear that the movement for women's rights here in France was stalling, and Johnson sent a steady string of missives urging me to return to England, reminding me that equality would still need a standard-bearer after these dangers had passed.

His last letter had included a return ticket from Le Havre to London, one month hence.

I felt like a craven coward to entertain the idea of abandoning my new friends here in France to fight this battle without me. Which was why I was sitting in this teahouse mulling over Théroigne's latest speech ideas and striking through many of her longest-winded lines.

"Has your tea done something to offend you?" a man asked in distinctively accented English. *American.* "That's a terribly stern frown you're giving your cup."

I glanced up to find a familiar man staring down at me—he was dressed in the same unembroidered French vest and jacket that he'd worn to Thomas Paine's salon. Here was the frontiersman I'd spotted before Théroigne made her arresting appearance. There was a hint of wildness to his unbound chestnut hair, his head bare of the usual cocked hat that most French citizens wore these days, and his tanned skin was an intriguing shade, as if his bloodline had mingled somewhere with indigenous or African heritage.

"I fear my tea is forced to bear the brunt of my dark thoughts." I winced as a cheer went up outside, impossible to muffle even through the medieval bricks. Just blocks away was a guillotine—it didn't take much imagination to envision the scene there right now, some freshly severed head being pulled from a blood-drenched basket. "These are trying times, yes?"

"Indeed." My visitor glanced beyond the windows before turning inquisitive eyes back to me. "I believe we frequent the same salons, including the Christies and Madame Roland. I am Gilbert Imlay."

"Mary Wollstonecraft," I said.

"I know. Renowned writer of *A Vindication of the Rights of Woman*. May I join you?"

It was terribly forward of him to ask, and I said so. He only shrugged, a sly smile tugging up one side of his lips. "*Live in the present moment*. It's one of my maxims."

I nudged the chair opposite me with my booted toe, approving his maxim and feeling suddenly bold. "Then I'd be happy for the distraction."

Imlay stretched his long legs out in front of him as he lit a cheroot cigarette. It was pragmatic but also a shame that he wore the trousers of the sansculottes instead of the breeches of an aristocrat—I wouldn't have minded appreciating the cut of his calves.

He jutted his chin to the papers in front of me. "What masterpiece are you penning now?"

"Only helping a friend with a speech." I gestured to a stack of half-finished papers. "Amid penning reports to England about the bloodshed here."

"The latter must keep you quite busy."

"Indeed. And what is it *you* do in Paris, Mr. Imlay?"

"A little of this, a bit of that." At a puff of fragrant smoke and a wave of his hand, the matronly shopkeeper brought a fresh pot of tea and poured it for him. Her eyes lingered on the square cut of Imlay's jaw and the breadth of his shoulders, not that I could blame her. My visitor stubbed out the cigarette in favor of the tea. "Mostly I dabble in philosophy and writing. And smuggling."

I nearly choked, both from laughter and disbelief, but managed to recover my aplomb. Barely. "That's quite the dossier." I set my cup on its saucer. "I'm torn as to which to ask about first."

"Then I shall have to tell you about all three." Imlay sweetened his cup—an abomination of more cream and sugar than tea, which I scarcely refrained from castigating. "Which is perfect, given that I've had designs on how to strike up a conversation with a particularly lovely British authoress for some time. Unfortunately, last time I nearly worked up the nerve at Thomas Paine's dinner party, Théroigne de Méricourt monopolized all her attentions."

"Truly?" Shocked, I merely sipped my tea. I was so accustomed to having to explain myself to members of the opposite sex that I heartily enjoyed the anomaly of this conversation. And for once, I was glad that I'd donned a fashionable white Greek chemise gown with a tricolor cashmere shawl, no mothballed beaver hat or outdated mobcap to render me invisible to the opposite sex.

"Actually, I admit to having failed several times—when I saw you come in here, I told myself it was a providential opportunity I could not ignore."

I found myself flushing into my teacup this time. How could a well-spoken and well-built man such as this—who surely must have had countless female admirers—have found himself intimidated by *me*? "All right," I responded. "I'm terribly curious. What have you written?"

Imlay rubbed his chin. "Hmm . . . I'd planned to lead with the smuggling bit, but I should have anticipated you'd be more interested in books. I've written two—*A Topographical Description of the Western Territory of North America* and a novel, *The Emigrants*. They both pale in comparison to your brilliant volumes—I wish I could have seen Edmund Burke's face when he read your first *Vindication*. I'm sure he was nearly apoplectic."

"You've read *Vindication*?"

"Indeed. Both of them, in fact."

"And?"

I almost wished I hadn't asked. Somehow, I found myself hoping for this man's approval. "Your ideas would fit in well in America," he answered. "My home is the one place on earth where utopian dreams of equality can become a reality."

"Not here in France?"

Imlay glanced at the soot-stained rafters before cracking his knuckles and shaking his head. "This place drips with too much history. Inequality is woven into the very fabric of France. It's why this revolution has turned so violent—it will take far more upheaval to bring about real change in this country." He took another draft of his mottled tea. "You might be surprised to learn that several themes you wrote about overlap with ideas I explored in my novel."

"Such as?"

"The slave trade, strict divorce laws, and impositions on freedom. Especially marriage."

"You disagree with marriage?" My lips pursed in disbelief. I'd always viewed the institution as a catastrophe for women, but it was difficult to find a man who didn't embrace the antiquated arrangement. Who wouldn't, when it came ready-made with a drudge to perform a husband's every whim?

"I find marriage to be a state of degradation and misery for women."

Already intrigued by this man, that comment made me sit up straighter. "You've just earned yourself a friend in me, Mr. Imlay."

He smiled and I nearly forgot to breathe. *Damn me.* One man shouldn't have possessed such effortless power. "Excellent. Although I hope we shall become more than just friends, Miss Wollstonecraft. And I insist that you call me Gilbert—the American in me can't stand formality."

This man was an insufferable flirt. And, heathen that I was, I was *enjoying* every moment of it. Still, it wouldn't do to lose myself in flights of fancy.

"I think friendship shall have to suffice, Mr. Imlay." He may want me to call him by his given name, but that was far too familiar. "Given that I'm scheduled to leave France soon."

"Now, that's a real shame." Imlay gestured to the woman behind the counter and paid for both our teas before I could stop him. "Considering our limited time together, I insist that you take a turn with me around Paris. Today, in fact."

"You're very sure of yourself."

"I *did* warn you I've had time to plan this all out." He lifted his brows. "If you're leaving soon, we shall simply hasten the timetable."

There was no hiding the brushfire that spread from my cheeks all the way to my ears. This man was pursuing me. The question was, was I going to let him?

"I know all the best pastry shops and where to find the most spectacular view of the Seine at night." He was helping turn out my chair. "And I have plenty of stories about America to entice a traveler such as yourself."

"Let me guess—tales of smuggling?" I found myself rising from my chair and stacking my papers to tuck into my reticule. I should really return home and write to Johnson, but it was as if Imlay had cast a spell over me and I was powerless to resist. Had no desire to, actually.

If I was leaving France, what harm could an afternoon off possibly cause?

"Smuggling? Those stories may take a bit longer."

"Well, I'm not leaving for a few weeks."

"Good." His hazel gaze roamed over me as we meandered toward the door. And damn me, but I *liked* the feeling of it.

We strolled through Paris's cramped boulevards that afternoon, pausing for croissants and *chocolat chaud* when we felt like it and enjoying the city's views until the sun began to set amid the fragrance of clustering flowers. It was so freeing, just strolling with a man while surrounded by beauty. In fact, if I ignored the cockades and the guillotines and the angry set of the city's shoulders, Paris might have been a fairy scene that touched the heart.

"What is America really like?" I asked as we meandered to my address. I slowed my pace on purpose and breathed in the tobacco-and-sea scent of him. "Is it as magical as it seems?"

If I hadn't been looking askance, I'd have missed the wistfulness that softened Imlay's face before he turned playful again. "Even more so. The Kentucky countryside where I'm from is green and verdant, and there's plenty of hardy farms tilled by pioneer men and women."

"It sounds lovely."

He shrugged. "I think we all love the place we're from, don't we? Home gets under the skin, weaves itself into our sinews and bones."

I thought of dour Hoxton, its air filled with screams of the mad amid its crumbling Tudor ruins. *My* screams, when my father had turned violent. Part of me worried that Gilbert Imlay would find me lesser if he knew my crude roots. I had no wish to own that place, nor my own family. "I'm afraid the English and American countrysides must be quite different."

"Well, America is a land so fresh and new that anything is possible—the freedom of slaves, equality among all."

I chuckled. "You're an idealist?"

"The same as you."

"Oh?"

"Only an idealist would believe in the equality of the sexes, don't you think?"

"I hope for it *and* I believe in it," I answered.

"Then you're an idealist. As president of that particular club, I'd like to officially welcome you."

I laughed as we approached the steps of 22 Rue Meslée. "I expect a membership card in the post."

My breath caught in my throat as Imlay suddenly clasped my hand. "I'd like to see you again, Miss Wollstonecraft," he said. "If you're amenable."

I was entirely unpracticed in whatever *this* was, but I'd have had to be a withered old crone to reject Gilbert Imlay's attentions. Probably not even then—I'd need to be dead.

"I am indeed amenable," I responded. "Tea again tomorrow?"

"Coffee," he suggested. "I know a particularly enjoyable coffeehouse that is still serving, although who knows for how long. The Turk's Head possesses excellent conversation and not a cup of tea to be found."

"I *did* notice the destruction of a particularly innocent cup of tea back at Helen Marie's. Could you even taste your tea today with all that cream and sugar?"

Imlay's hands went up. "I normally never drink the stuff—tea reminds me of dirty water—but choking down a cup seemed a worthy sacrifice to make your acquaintance."

I shook my head and chuckled. "Until tomorrow, then."

I felt Imlay's gaze upon me until I was back inside 22 Rue Meslée. And smiled to myself.

"There you are!" Aline Filliettaz's bright voice made me jump. Despite the horrors outside, everything about my highly strung Parisian hostess was cheery as sunshine, including the lacy butter-yellow frocks she typically donned. I was surprised to see Théroigne sitting with her, dressed in her usual pirate attire while balancing a delicate teacup on one knee. "We were starting to worry."

"We thought you might have been seized by a mob." Théroigne tapped with one finger the pistols she'd placed on the table. Better the pistols than her muddy boots—I supposed she had *some* manners.

"You can't get rid of me so easily," I responded, although I worried I'd been seized by something far more insidious. Now that a door separated me from Gilbert Imlay, I was astonished at how carefree I'd acted with him. Brazen with my glances, encouraging him to take my hand . . .

I shook myself. Those were society's expectations pressing down on me—the ironclad protection of a woman's innocence, as female ignorance was courteously termed. I'd done nothing that Imlay himself hadn't done, and I refused to bow to social mores that demanded I blush and simper. If I enjoyed Imlay's company, so be it.

"Well, thank goodness you are safe." Aline wrung her hands. "Although I can't guarantee for how much longer."

Théroigne gave an exasperated huff and interjected, "Foreigners will soon be required to chalk their names on their doors, the easier for the Committee of Public Safety to identify."

The effervescence of my carefree afternoon dissipated instantly. "To identify and . . . ?"

Théroigne shrugged. "Possibly—probably—much worse. It seems we must postpone our outing to the National Assembly, perhaps indefinitely."

"You would be safer in the countryside. Until you return to London, that is," Aline fretted. "Our gardener has a cottage in Neuilly a few miles from the city walls. Please let me arrange for you to stay there. Paris just isn't safe."

Except I wouldn't be able to report on what *did* occur if I was languishing in the countryside. Surely nothing terrible would happen to foreigners over the next fortnight. "A few more weeks and then I'll remove myself from Paris. I promise."

Aline flew to her feet. "I'll make the arrangements. For the cottage."

As soon as she was gone, a sly smile spread across Théroigne's striking face. "Your decision to linger doesn't have anything to do with that handsome American who walked you home, does it? Gilbert Imlay, I believe?" She shrugged as my eyes widened. "That stallion looks like he knows his way around a woman."

I turned my back to stare out the window, the better to hide the secret smile that spread across my lips. "I only properly met him this afternoon—"

This time Théroigne shoved her way around me. One glance at my expression and she cackled. "A woman hasn't truly experienced Paris, *chérie*, until she's had at least one love affair." She stood next to me, bumped my hip with hers. Thank goodness her pistols were still on the table. "Life is short—enjoy it. And enjoy *him*."

To which I only rolled my eyes, wishing I were worldlier so I'd know what questions I might ask Théroigne about embarking on one's potential first love affair. Instead, I merely rummaged through my reticule and retrieved the set of ink-marked pages I'd been working on when Gilbert Imlay had walked into my life.

"Enough about me," I said. "Let's talk about this speech of yours."

Even as Paris—a city always cruel in panic and now in the throes of what was being called the Terror—descended deeper into madness, Imlay patiently and doggedly courted me, but I still hadn't decided whether to encourage anything more than our morning walks and afternoon conversations over steaming cups of tea or coffee. (We took turns alternating between the Turk's Head and Helen Maria's, which I found terribly democratic.) I had no intention of ever marrying, but even though women were forbidden love outside marriage—a stance that didn't apply equally to men—that didn't mean I was averse to experimenting with love. Or pleasure.

However, I did realize it was the woman who usually bore the brunt of such a scandalous decision—a ruined reputation or, heaven forbid, the raising of an illegitimate child—should the relationship turn sour. Still, women like Théroigne—not to mention countless French widows and mistresses over the centuries—had managed. So why not me?

I reminded myself that few women faced this freedom of choice that now lay before me, no father or brother or anyone else to dictate my decision.

Although I did request feminine assistance in the matter . . .

At my relentless urging, Théroigne grudgingly offered tips from her days as a courtesan—how to becomingly style my hair in loose curls and where to best dab perfume at the pulse points on my wrists and below my ears. Most importantly, how best to touch a man. Really *touch*. And how to *be* touched.

Between any other females, that conversation might have been mostly composed of awkward stutters or girlish giggles, but my radical friend Théroigne took her former art seriously. And just like with all knowledge, I craved facts.

Sapere aude. Dare to know.

"But what does it feel like when a man touches you there?" I asked after she'd discussed the mechanics of fellatio. I was ready to ask as many questions as Voltaire's Man of Forty Crowns. How had I made it thirty-four years on this earth and never heard of such a thing? As a woman, I knew I was supposed to be repulsed, but instead, I found myself intrigued. And undeniably curious. "Beyond just *fantastique*."

"I am not the writer," she said with a fox's sly smile. "But if I were, there are some things you cannot put into words, *mon amie*. Sometimes you must experience firsthand. Consider it a scientific experiment."

I wasn't sure Gilbert Imlay would appreciate being compared to a scientific experiment. Then again, if the experience was as shattering as Théroigne had described, I doubted he'd mind.

"You must bring your American smuggler to my political speech in the Jardin des Tuileries tomorrow," Théroigne demanded after she'd instructed me in the methods of preventing pregnancy, most of which seemed decidedly unscientific at best. "So that I may decide if this man is worthy to occupy so much of your time. Or whether he is a one-ride man. Do not waste your time on inferior lovers."

To which I had slapped her arm with a rolled-up newspaper—the Jacobin rag *L'Ami du Peuple*—which was best suited for the trash heap. Théroigne merely laughed herself hoarse.

Now my dearest friend here in Paris stood atop an overturned apricot crate—today she donned a jaunty sort of privateer's hat with two feathered plumes and a loosely tied cravat, although without her customary saber and pistols, as she claimed they were disquieting to Paris's working-class citizens—and addressed the patchwork crowd of red-pantalooned workingwomen alongside a handful of men who had gathered to listen. Imlay nudged me and gestured in the direction of a shaggy-haired man wearing the trousers of the sansculottes whose forehead seemed a trifle too broad for the rest of his proportions. The man itched at the angry rash up the side of his neck, one everyone knew had been earned during his years living in poverty in Paris's sewers. "That's Jean-Paul Marat."

The most radical agitator of them all, and the author of *L'Ami du Peuple*.

"His latest issue calls for violence against the Girondins," I whispered. "Apparently, they're not revolutionary enough for his tastes."

Imlay frowned. "I hope your friend chooses her words wisely today."

"She will." Or at least, I hoped she would, given the gentle modifications I'd suggested Théroigne make to this speech. I'd never seen the famed Marat in the flesh, but his presence here would be of great import to his supporters, many of whom muttered under their breath around us or chanted for *du pain et du savon*—bread and soap, the barest necessities of life.

"Women of France," Théroigne began, "let us raise ourselves to the height of our destinies; let us break our chains! At last the time is ripe for women to emerge from their shameful nullity, where the ignorance, pride, and injustice of men had kept them enslaved for so long!"

It was a radical and revolutionary message, but apparently not radical enough for these Jacobins.

"You consort with mealymouthed Girondins, the enemies of republicanism!" one shouted. A man with greasy hair made an obscene gesture and thrust his hips in her direction, making the back of my neck prickle. "Do they pay one hundred sous to part your legs," he shouted, "your one hundred lovers a day? Is that how you would finance the Revolution, with the sweat of your body?"

"Citizens, we must work together with the Girondins to effect real change." Théroigne projected calmly over the angry drone of the crowd. I could see my friend trying to gauge how best to reach this mob, like trying to catch a falling knife. "Divided among ourselves, we will never achieve equality!"

It was then that the rocks started to fly from the women's skirts and pockets. The stones were hurled at my friend, who cried out. Théroigne's raised arms made a flimsy shield of flesh and bone.

"Down with the patriots' whore! Down with the Girondins! *Vive la France!*"

This wasn't a protest; it was an *ambush*.

"We need to go. *Now*." Imlay's hand was on my elbow, but I couldn't leave my friend unprotected. Especially when the crowd of red-faced women surged anew around Théroigne.

Why, oh why didn't she wear her pistols today?

Théroigne gave one shout of surprise as the mob toppled her from her crate before they surged over her like fire ants on the attack. I elbowed the woman next to me in an attempt to push forward, but my knees turned to water when I saw the melon-sized rock poised over Théroigne's head. And heard it come down with a wet crack.

I screamed as I realized the women were tearing away Théroigne's clothes while jeering and shouting slurs. Shoving my way forward, I barely recognized that Imlay was still behind me until a male command barked over the shouts and yells. "*Arrête!*"

It was as if a puppeteer had jerked at the strings of his marionettes. The red pantaloons fell back, my friend's shredded dress and bloodied shirt still dangling from their fingertips. I glanced in the direction of the shout and saw Jean-Paul Marat there, clicking his tongue and shaking his head. "Citizeness Méricourt is indeed misguided in her message of reconciliation," he announced for the mob's benefit as I surged my way toward her. "But we have greater enemies to focus on."

I didn't hear the rest, too busy taking in the horrors wrought upon Théroigne. Clumps of her thick mane of dark hair had been ripped away to reveal bloody patches of her scalp, and she was bleeding from so many head wounds I didn't know where to stanch the blood. Some bit of white poked out from the carnage, and I nearly fainted to realize it was her skull lying beneath the bloody lattice of her flesh. Imlay was at my side then, shrugging off his jacket. "Hold her," he instructed with an eerie sort of calm. "So I can bind her head."

And then Marat was towering over us, his rodent eyes *leering*. For a moment I imagined he was my father, fists clenched as he stood over my mother, deciding where best to land his next blows. I knew then that Marat's choice of when to intercede was cruelly calculated, that he had allowed the mob to beat Théroigne until she was nearly dead. And that no one could be expected to survive these wounds. "I'll see to it that she is attended to," he said, as if soothing a small child over a scraped knee, then snapped his fingers at a waiting sansculotte. "Take Citizeness de Méricourt to the Salpêtrière Hospital. Immediately." Except the Salpêtrière was no medical hospital; it was an asylum where inconvenient women disappeared. I felt as helpless and weak as I had as a girl trembling before my father when Marat's lackey— armed with his own set of pistols—lifted Théroigne into his arms, none too gently. "How wonderful that our Girondin firebrand had such close—and unexpected—allies here today."

The threat was blatant. And implacable.

"*Merci*." Imlay helped me to my feet, kept me steady as I stumbled. A woman spat at me as we backed away from the Tuileries Garden, the glob of angry spittle staining the hem of my day dress. I wanted to stamp it away and scream at the injustice of what I'd just witnessed, while also wishing to simultaneously flee and run to Théroigne's side again.

"Don't look back," Imlay said, so I fought the urge to turn around for one last glimpse of my friend. I knew I'd forever see her battered skull and that bit of blood-slicked bone in my nightmares. "You can't help her now. Théroigne would want you to save yourself, to fight another day."

He was right, but one block later, my legs finally gave out. My teeth chattered so violently I feared they might crack, and I shivered despite my cashmere wrap. Imlay took one look and scooped me into his arms. "I can walk," I protested, but he merely made a sound deep in his throat.

"Like hell you can."

Two blocks later, we'd arrived at a modest apartment in the quiet neighborhood of Saint-Germain-des-Prés, with buildings set far back from the street dotted with flower gardens and horse chestnut trees in front that gave the sense that we were in the French countryside. The building was new and made of white stone with tall windows. Perhaps I should have demurred as Imlay unlocked the door to what I realized were his own accommodations, but such social niceties were beyond me now.

"I'm afraid I only have coffee," he said after depositing me on the settee of a cozy ground-floor sitting room. He wrapped a woolen blanket that smelled faintly of tobacco around my shoulders.

"No tea?" My teeth were still chattering, although intermittently. I'd never felt this untethered before, as if I couldn't control my own body.

"You'd have to be dying for me to offer you that stuff." He felt my forehead, checked my eyes. "You may be shaken, but you're still very much alive."

Damn me, but despite the horrific events we'd just experienced, this cocksure American still enticed a half smile from me, not that he could see it while he banged about his kitchen. When he arrived with two steaming porcelain cups of coffee dwarfed in his large hands, I felt a little less frantic. "I'm sorry for what happened today."

The feel of the warm cup between my hands was grounding, even as I sniffed the coffee's strong aroma. It was surprisingly sweet, but I managed only a sip. "Théroigne is a radical, yet still they turned on her."

"This revolution has begun to eat its own," Imlay answered. "Paris is no longer safe."

"You mean it's not safe for someone like me? A foreigner *and* a woman?" My questions came out acerbic—I hated feeling weak and exposed, but after today I could no longer deny the truth.

"I simply mean it's not safe." Imlay gently removed the cup and saucer from my hands, then surprised me by sitting so close his knee touched mine. "I know this is sudden—I had intentions to court you for months until you were dizzy with love for me, but if you marry me . . . well, then we could move to America and leave all this violence behind us."

Rarely have I ever been at a loss for words, but Imlay's unexpected proposal sprung open a box of mischief that stole the wind from my lungs. "But . . ." I grasped for something to say, *anything*. "You don't believe in marriage."

"I could," he said. "With you."

I merely stared at him, indulging in the rosy future that rolled out in my mind: a sun-drenched farm somewhere in America where we could breathe clean air of freedom and democracy and independence.

Until I remembered that no matter the country, my marriage to any man would mean the legal end of my own freedom.

No, I refused to be confined to a life of domestic concerns and placated by the paltry crown of marriage. Until men and women were equal before the law, marriage was too far removed from the sacred act it was meant to be. I refused to take part in that vehicle of legal slavery. To do so would make me the worst sort of hypocrite.

But I couldn't say that, not right now with Gilbert kneeling next to me, his expression so open and honest that my eyes stung with unshed tears.

However, there was one freedom I'd never explored, one thing I desperately sought after facing death today. And when I kissed Gilbert, I knew he would give it to me. I need only ask.

"Where is the bedroom?" My voice sounded deeper, throaty. The voice of a different woman, a *new* woman.

Live in the present moment.

Gilbert's eyes darkened as he took in my meaning. "Are you sure?"

"I can't think right now," I answered. "I just want to *feel*."

Gilbert needed no further urging. He swept me into his arms again and mounted the stairs two at a time.

This time I had no desire to look back.

I lay awake afterward listening to Gil's easy breathing while staring at the cold face of the moon outside the window. Worrying about Théroigne, even as I heard her voice urging me to enjoy my time with Gilbert.

There was nothing I could do to save my friend, but as I looked at Gil, I knew . . . this was no conventional love.

And I was no conventional woman.

"I cannot marry you," I said when he finally awoke sometime before dawn.

Already I saw his eyes shuttering as he withdrew from our drowsy tangle of limbs, rolling onto his back to stare at the ceiling. "So, what, then? We're over before we've had a chance to begin?"

I suppose most women in my situation would have demanded a wedding ring, which he'd already offered, or made claims to an egregious error in judgment and left as quickly as their feet could carry them.

Instead, I rested my forearms on his chest, the curtain of my hair brushing his skin. "Quite the opposite," I said. "Friendship or indifference naturally follows love. I cannot imagine being indifferent to you, but neither can I marry you, not without compromising my beliefs." I'd spent hours trying to puzzle out a way that I could be both a wife *and* myself, but one might as well ask night and day to share the same sky. "Beliefs you share, if I remember correctly."

"So, you desire our return to a state of friendship?" Gil's face darkened. "You know I cannot want that."

"Neither can I." The words felt dangerous, treasonous even, as if we were the first lovers ever to speak them. "Not marrying doesn't mean that this can't continue. In fact . . ." I swallowed and leaned closer, feeling a tiny surge in confidence as Gil's hungry eyes roamed over the exposed curve of my breasts. "In fact, I believe passions are spurs to actions. And there's an action I'd very much like to repeat."

Gil's kisses were soft as his lips worked such magic that I moaned with pleasure. "Several actions, I hope."

In this room, in this very bed, Gil and I were forging a revolution of our own, a relationship between equals.

"I'll accept Aline's recent offer of a cottage in the country," I said later that morning as Gil walked alongside me to 22 Rue Meslée. We had tracked down Théroigne at the Salpêtrière Hospital—her head had been shaved and the worst of her wounds bandaged—but while she still breathed, my friend was far from lucid. It had taken all my resolve not to flee at the screams of the madwomen housed there, the sound transporting me back to Hoxton and all I'd left behind. Paris was taking a step back when all I wanted to do was leap forward. "Her gardener's cottage is only four miles outside the city." I looked at

Gil through my lashes, still feeling somehow shy as this more forward version of me asserted herself. "You'd be welcome to visit anytime."

It was a solution to our arrangement that couldn't continue in its current form. Aline might be modern in her ideas, but I couldn't expect her to countenance Gil staying nights with me under her roof. Nor could I traipse about Paris to and from Gil's lodgings on my own any longer, not with the current resentment against foreigners and women. A broad-shouldered American smuggler would never be the target of the French radicals, but a slight and incendiary British female writer most decidedly would be.

"The sooner, the better." Gil's hand was loose on my waist as he dipped his head and kissed me one last time until I felt nearly drunk on it. "You'd best go inside now," he murmured, "lest I ravage you here on the steps."

Damn me, but I might have let him. Suddenly I could understand the midnight scenes I'd witnessed along the docks when Johnson's carriage returned me home following a prolonged dinner party—the men and women pressed up against darkened alley walls that lined the docks, heads thrown back in moments of sheer abandon.

With Gil, I suddenly realized that there was more to being a woman than I'd ever suspected. Being with him in a physical sense made me feel powerful and curious and courageous. And I wanted to revel in it *all*.

I took the cottage of Aline's gardener not a moment too soon.

On May 31, eighty thousand Parisians took to the streets to once again protest the price of bread and call for the removal of the Girondins, which happened one day after all resident aliens were forced to chalk their names on their doors.

It had been years since I'd lived in the countryside and at

first, I found the peace disquieting. However, I had plenty of time to write and the Filliettazes' gardener left me baskets of peaches and grapes and whatever other particularly fine fruit was in season. I soon discovered an inexpressible delight in the beauties of nature and took to wandering the nearby woods with those treats while I waited for Gil's evening visits. Only once did I venture into Paris alone, where I realized too late that my practical buttoned boots were stained with blood that ran down the gutters from the nearby guillotine. I let out an involuntary gasp and found myself hushed by a gray-haired woman wearing a tricolor cockade.

"Shh!" she whispered. "Smile at the blood. Else you'll be charged as a collaborator."

I pasted a smile on my face and hurried back toward the city gate.

Deciding Paris had shed its last vestiges of safety, I walked the eleven miles to Versailles one morning, the better to have something to report to Johnson and still feel mildly useful. Gil had informed me that the revolutionaries had auctioned everything inside—marble busts and gilded paintings, the king's furniture and draperies, even the queen's gowns and jewels that had been left behind.

The gates of the abandoned palace remained sprawled open. The estate hadn't been occupied since the king and queen had been forcibly removed to the Tuileries—compliments of Théroigne and her army of women—and my lonely footsteps echoed eerily as I strolled alone down the still-glittering Hall of Mirrors. Muted sunlight warmed the windows, but the light reflected from the crystal chandeliers seemed subdued, as if the entire massive palace knew that its glory was spent. The gigantic oil portraits of long-ago kings in the War Salon seemed sunk in embraces of death, and the dusty air in the queen's chambers shimmered with ghosts. The flower beds were choked with weeds, and the shrubs grew wild on the grounds of Marie Antoinette's infamous *petit hameau*, where she'd pretended to be a common shepherdess.

Chased away by an implacable chill of foreboding, I hurried home to find a note pinned to my door. Worried until I recognized Gil's handwriting, I faced a dark wave of despair when I read its contents.

Dearest Mary,

My apologies for my absence this evening. England has placed an embargo on trade with France and I must seize this rare opportunity. Providing common American wheat, soap, and iron raises me up as a hero here in France.

Brace yourself for the bad news I must impart— Olympe de Gouges and Thomas Paine have been imprisoned. There is talk of further violence against prominent women leaders and a possible rescinding of their hard-won rights. We should discuss registering you as my wife—in name only, if you prefer—at the American embassy to guarantee your safety.

When this is over . . . well, I promise the Ohio River is one of the most captivating places on earth. Can you imagine us together on a small farm there, perhaps with a flower garden and some cheerful poultry, writing and studying and reading to our hearts' content?

Yours,
G

My vision went cloudy to imagine both my dear friend Thomas Paine and the legendary Olympe de Gouges in dank prison cells, or worse, mounting the stairs to the guillotine. Every day's fresh horrors made me want to sail to Ohio with Gil on the first ship out of France. Such a happy, easy life it could be!

But I wasn't born for an easy life. Even this love affair was proving far from simple—I certainly hadn't anticipated how closely my heart would cleave to Gilbert's, so that his absence caused my very soul to ache.

"Buck up, Mary," I muttered as I let myself into the cheery cottage and set down the letter. "You're not one of those colorless women who mope when their lovers aren't nearby."

True, but the hours ahead seemed grayer than a cloudy January day. The summer sun came out only when Gil arrived the following evening.

When I made my decision, he was feeding me tiny wild strawberries, in bed, as we'd meant to have a picnic but hadn't made it out the door. We faced each other while propped on our elbows, both of our clothes thrown about the tiny bedroom. I knew I looked positively dishabille, which Gil thoroughly enjoyed, given that he was the cause of it. "I like the idea of your registering me at the American embassy," I said. "As your wife."

Gil paused, one dimpled red strawberry hovering midair. "Truly?"

I nodded. "I want to return to Paris. I need to be closer to the revolution for my updates to Johnson. And I can't live with Aline—I don't want to put her household in danger."

And there it was—my proposal that we live together, when honestly, my main motivation was to be close to Gilbert. However, this loophole skirted my concerns about giving up my freedoms—without a marriage certificate, I was legally still a free woman, in charge of my own destiny. Yet, I worried that my excuse was utterly transparent, especially when Gil didn't respond right away.

"My apartment in Faubourg Saint-Germain is quieter than the Marais where the Filliettazes live, but the revolution will get worse before it improves," he finally said. "*If* it improves. Are you sure you want to be in the thick of things?"

I was. And I also wanted this man at my side. Gilbert Imlay was my port in this storm.

"I'm not done witnessing this revolution." I took a deep breath, my heart thudding as I balanced on the precipice of utter happiness. "If you're amenable, Mary Imlay I shall pretend to be."

The strawberry came down, and I took a bite, then licked a drop of juice slowly from my lips, reveling in the light that flared deep in Gil's eyes as he rolled me onto my back. His kiss tasted of strawberries and tobacco. "I've never been more amenable to anything in my life."

After that, there was nothing more to say.

CHAPTER 7

❧

November 1814

MARY GODWIN

Mary might have pretended to be Percy's wife, save that he was already married.

While Mary didn't doubt Percy's passion for her, she had yet to ask his plans regarding his wife and child. *Children*, actually, given that Harriet had just announced the arrival of Percy's firstborn son. Percy had rented a separate house for himself and Mary in London, but would he visit Harriet? Even more troubling was Mary's worry that Percy would tire of her and return to his legally wedded wife, no matter how ill-suited they might be. Which meant she had to muster her courage to bring it up, nearly a full week after they'd arrived in London.

"Percy, I have to ask . . . Does renting a house for us mean you won't be returning to Harriet?"

Percy gave a startled bark of laughter, but fell silent as he realized she was serious. "My darling Mary, the Faerie Queene of my heart." She loved that his newest nickname for her had been lifted from Spenser's *The Fairie Queene*. He pulled her so close she could feel his heart beating. "Did you honestly think that I could ever return to my rash and heartless union with Harriet after I'd pledged myself to you?"

"I wasn't sure what to think. I've never done this"—with a gesture between them—"before."

"Let me put your mind at ease." He tilted her chin up and pressed a kiss to her forehead. "I will never, *ever*, not even if the earth were hurtling toward the sun and she were the last person on earth, return to Harriet. While I'm duty bound to maintain her and our children, *you* are my one and only love."

"You swear it?"

The kiss he gave her sealed the promise. "I give you my word as a poet and your Elfin Knight."

Which meant that Mary could plan for their future, even if it was so different from the future she'd envisioned for herself.

Regardless of Harriet, Mary expected that most of her former acquaintances in London would shun her—society would never condone an unmarried woman who traveled farther than Gretna Green and still didn't come back with a husband—but she held on to hope that her dear father would still welcome her home, and even that he might be proud that she and Shelley were living out the ideals of free love that he and her mother had once extolled. And that once he learned she was with child—just as her own mother had once been—he'd forgive her everything and rush to see her. Especially as she worried of perishing in childbirth as her mother had, living out less than eighteen years instead of Mary Wollstonecraft's thirty-seven. Surely the same worry would occur to her father and heal their rift?

Except, rather than a warm family reunion at the modest house on Margaret Street that Percy had rented, Mary received only a frosty reception from Jane and her sister Fanny. They deigned to speak to Claire and Mary from the safety of the front steps but refused to come inside.

"It's true, then." Jane's lip curled unbecomingly while one of her ridiculous little dogs bared its teeth from her arms. "You've returned."

"We have," Mary responded calmly.

"And is it also true you're with child?"

Mary's high-waisted empire dress hid the evidence, but she cut a sharp glance to Claire, who had always been a leaky sieve when it came to gossip. Claire studiously avoided her eyes, leaving Mary alone to answer her stepmother. "It is."

"Given that Percy Shelley remains with you, the scandal sheets are also correct that he has abandoned his wife and children."

Had he? Mary still wasn't sure, but she certainly wasn't going to discuss the topic with Jane.

"Where is our father?" Mary directed her question to Fanny, but her sister's gaze remained on the ground. Her lips were chapped as if she'd been biting them. "Is he ill?"

"Your father is sound of body," Jane snapped. Already she was opening the door of the hired coach and thrusting her yapping dog inside—apparently this interview was reaching its speedy conclusion. "But his heart is irreparably damaged. Did you know not even the butchers in Skinner Street will serve our household anymore? After all I've done to repair your father's reputation after your mother's death . . . you've dealt the final blow to our good name."

"Please don't leave." Claire actually reached for her mother before letting her arm fall. "Not even my old governess will come visit me."

Jane handed Fanny into the coach. "You've destroyed your reputation—and everything I ever built for you—by association. All my many sacrifices have been for naught. Lear was right: 'Tis sharper than a serpent's tooth to have a thankless child."

She looked as though she might spit at Mary's feet. "We won't return here again. You can count on that."

Claire stared at the coach as it clattered down the cobbles, her face pale. "We're ruined, Mary. Irrevocably ruined."

Mary threaded her fingers through her sister's, and Claire leaned her head against Mary's shoulder. The truth was, Mary *did* feel remorse for the scandal she'd rained down upon her family. However, even if she'd been able to deny the powerful love she felt for Percy, there was no going back now that she was pregnant. "Then it shall be us against the world, from this day forward."

Claire straightened and dashed a hand over her eyes before glancing at Mary and sobering. "Dearest Mary, this must be even more difficult to bear in your condition." She cleared her throat and brushed the front of her gown, seeming almost motherly for a moment. "Come inside and I'll make us a pot of tea. Then perhaps we can sing and outperform each other reciting scandalous poetry, just like when we were girls." The motherly visage disappeared as she waggled her perfectly arched brows. "Although I daresay whoever reads Lord Byron's latest verses will inevitably win."

"I'll write a letter to your father," Percy announced when Mary recounted the disastrous visit later that evening. Spending the afternoon with Claire had helped raised her spirits—the poetry recitations had them both in stitches—but they'd collapsed anew once darkness fell. "After all, we've done nothing wrong, only traveled the path of freedom and free love that both your mother and father championed."

"You must help him see reason," Mary pleaded with Percy. She had put on a brave face for Claire, but in truth, Jane's visit had shaken her. "I cannot imagine a future without my father."

Even if William Godwin no longer seemed all-knowing and immortal due to his poor judgment in publishing the memoir about her mother and his shunning of her and Percy, he was still her father and she loved him. Mary felt a resurgence of hope the following afternoon when a letter was delivered, addressed to Percy in a familiar hand.

"Your father says . . ." Percy's voice had shrunk somehow, until it was smaller than a frog. "Well, he claims he will have nothing more to do with you or your sister. Despite accepting my assistance in paying off his debts, he writes that he has ordered his family and friends to shut you out of their lives."

"*What?*" Mary's voice cut like broken glass across her throat. She snatched the letter from Percy and read the impossible words until they blurred and she could see no more.

She loved Percy tenderly and so entirely that her life seemed to hang on the beam of his eye. Her whole soul was wrapped up in him. But as he gathered her into his arms, for the first time, Mary wondered if she had made a terrible, horrible mistake in choosing love over all else.

The late autumn afternoons that followed were a beautiful blaze of red and russet, carmine and copper. Every day, Claire begged Percy for the small pleasure of a stroll to the pond on Parliament Hill. And every day, Percy relented and Mary accompanied them, even as her waistline expanded and her energy began to wane.

Still, it was good to get out of the house and leave most of their worries on its doorstep. In a troubling turn of events, pounds and pennies had grown scarcer than friends—Percy's illustrious father had cut him off from his inheritance following the scandal of his second elopement—and creditors often came knocking at the door. Percy suddenly eschewed meat—which he claimed was for his health, but that was merely one more symptom that money was in short supply. Mary had even cut sugar from their puddings, mostly because she didn't care to support slavery in the West Indies plantations but also because it was a horrendous expense.

Percy had brushed aside her concerns, although he agreed they could do without sugar. "I plan to battle my father's lawyers and we can always make a living from my pen. Yours, too, if you wish it."

She scoffed. Unlike her mother, she was a reader, not a writer. Still, their financial woes had unsettled her. For now, she forced herself to shake off her anxieties as she tugged closer her old tartan shawl around her shoulders and followed Percy and Claire into the fading autumn sunshine.

"How many boats today?" she asked Percy. Her step grew lighter when he presented two folded paper boats with a flourish, one from each pocket.

"One for you and one for me," he responded.

"I take it Claire already pilfered hers before we set out?"

"Claire is a sad, silly girl," Percy murmured as he pressed a kiss to the back of Mary's hand. She wished they were back in their bedroom, cozy in bed and dressed in only their bedclothes while rereading Spenser's *The Faerie Queene*. When they were alone, Percy was her Elfin Knight; when they were with Claire, especially on these serpentine walks, he sought to placate both of them. "And I've a surprise for this set of boats. Just wait and see."

As if she could sense her stepsister's budding happiness, Claire chose that moment to meander back to them. "I've decided to change my birthday," she announced.

"Oh?" Mary cocked her head in question. "I didn't know that was something one could adjust."

"Indeed. I've been reading your mother's *A Vindication of the*

Rights of Woman and have decided that I agree with Mary Wollstonecraft: women should be educated and avoid the outdated
custom of marriage. I'll never be shackled to some man, nor will
I keep his house like my mother. Thus, as one of Mary Wollstonecraft's true daughters, I shall adopt her birthday as my
own. From now on, we shall celebrate my birth on April 27."

"Let it be," Percy murmured gently in Mary's ear as she
gaped. One of Mary Wollstonecraft's *true daughters*? It was
likely that Claire felt abandoned by her own mother and was
casting herself in the most un-Jane-like mold possible, but what
was she playing at here? "She's asserting her own independence.
Just as you and I have."

Mary understood his logic, but still, annoyance thrummed
all the way to her very marrow, especially as Claire sauntered
away as if she'd somehow won an important battle. Mary found
herself aching for some time away from her sister—the three of
them had been living atop one another in the tiny house on
Margaret Street. It was suddenly too much.

"Let's just sail our boats, shall we?" Percy asked. "I've been
looking forward to this moment all day."

Mary forced a nod. Percy's eager way of drinking in the
simple joys of life—the man adored gingerbread in every season
and had a schoolboy habit of rolling dinner bread into pellets to
shoot at targets on the walls—was one of the reasons she loved
him. If Percy, who was beset upon by creditors and scandals,
could find a moment of pleasure in sailing a tiny paper boat,
then so could she.

And so Mary watched Percy—her dashing poet who loved
to study fire and electricity—as he set his craft on the sparkling
waters of the Parliament Hill pond, and placed hers to follow
suit. Only this time, Percy also lit a friction match from a small
emerald box he pulled from his pocket.

"Oh, Percy, no!" cried Mary when he touched the dancing flame to his boat. The fragile paper sputtered and caught, turning the tiny craft into a fallen filament of the sun, magically skimming the water's glassy surface.

When it bumped into Mary's boat, it set that one ablaze as well.

Two sparks, fallen to earth just like Icarus. And both burned themselves out, their paper masts and sails transformed to ash as the charred wrecks pitched to the murky depths of the pond.

Despite the warmth of the autumn evening, Mary couldn't help the shiver that rippled up her spine.

Back aching and ankles swollen, Mary was bent over her latest reading—a firsthand account of slavery in the West Indies—in the flickering candlelight while a winter snowstorm swirled outside her drafty windowpanes. It was past midnight and Percy slept peacefully beside her, but like so many nights recently, Mary had been roused by shooting pains in her legs. Her body might have felt the discomfort of the child she carried, but as always, she took solace in her books, this time reaching for her latest obsession.

Despite the 1807 Slave Trade Abolition Act, which forbid slavery anywhere on English soil, the abominable practice still flourished elsewhere in the Americas. The injustice made Mary crave a pen to defend the idea of abolition, but her nerve failed her each time she set one of Percy's freshly sharpened quills to paper. No matter what she wrote, her every word would be held to the light of her mother's works, or even her father's. Probably Percy's as well. And like a paste jewel next to a diamond, her prose would be found wanting. So each time Mary pushed away the quill and paper and instead contented herself by reading with the intent of cramming every corner of her mind with all manner of ideas. Despite all, England's abolition gave Mary hope that the world was moving closer to her mother's and father's visions of absolute freedom and independence.

Her father still refused to speak to her, but surely he'd change his mind once his grandchild was born?

Mary placed a hand on her ripe belly—the child was expected any day now—and strained to reach her arms overhead and ease the pain in her back.

But rather than ease her pain, an invisible knife dragged its whetted edge across her belly. She cried out.

"What is it?" Percy awoke in an instant, concern writ clear on his handsome face. Mary wanted to reassure him, but this pain felt different from any she'd experienced before.

"Fetch the midwife. And send Claire with word to my father," she murmured as she looked about the room, feeling woefully unprepared. In a few hours, she might be a mother.

Or, like her own mother, she might be preparing to quit this world forever.

Dear little Clara Everina entered this world just as the flurries settled, leaving all of London covered in a dusting of sugar snow. Their daughter was fairer than a pictured cherub, perfectly formed and already in possession of a fine head of hair to rival Percy's. As a peace offering, Percy suggested naming the baby after her aunt Claire, and while Mary agreed, she had insisted on changing the spelling. She knew all too well what it meant to live in a namesake's shadow; this daughter of hers would forge her own path, become her own woman.

Each day, Mary felt her own forehead, but the fever she expected never materialized. She was nearly eighteen; not even half her mother's age. Instead of growing weak with childbed fever, she regained more of her strength and started a new enterprise of writing in her journal each starlit night as she fed the child she insisted on calling by her middle name: Everina. Nothing Mary penned could ever compare with her mother's volumes, but setting down her thoughts each night was calming, soothing even. She wrote so that little Everina—the name sounded like the perfect constellation, one named after a delicate fae princess—might know Mary as she was in this moment, the same way Mary wished she could have known her own mother.

Today Mary had emerged from her room for the first time since her confinement and undertaken an expedition downstairs to enjoy the frosty winter sunshine streaming through the front window. At Claire's voice, she paused outside the sitting room door.

"I can't stand being housebound," Claire announced. "You and I should walk to the park, Percy. I'm sure Mary won't mind."

Mary glanced down at her sleeping daughter bundled in a white quilted gown and hollie point lace cap, her celestial eyes closed and her precious face so sweet and trusting. *I most certainly* do *mind*, Mary thought as she envisioned her sister strolling alone with Percy.

But Mary smiled at Percy's response. "No walk today, I'm afraid. Mary *did* just give birth to new life, Claire. I don't care to miss an instant with the little star that just came into being beneath my own roof."

A star that would be raised under that same roof, given that Mary and Percy agreed that they, not a nurse or governess or a boarding school, would raise their child. Mollified, Mary chose that moment to enter and avoided looking at her sister as Mary allowed Percy to fuss over her and their daughter. The room was a mess, but that was what came from leaving Claire in charge of the housekeeping. Only once they were settled comfortably at the window seat did she address both Percy and Claire. "So," she said. "Tell me all I've missed."

"You've missed nothing," Claire announced with a sigh from where she lounged on the worn Grecian couch. "Absolutely *nothing*."

"No callers or visitors?"

Because Mary still held out hope that her father would see the error of his ways. Surely blood would conquer gossip, in the end.

Percy only shook his head. He knew the true nature of Mary's question. "Your father still refuses to visit." He retrieved a letter from the top of his stack of correspondence. "Although he *did* write to ask that I extend him yet another loan."

Claire's snort of derision startled little Everina from her sleep. The poor dear mewed like an abandoned kitten, opening and closing her mouth while her arms flailed about. Mary glared at her sister and adjusted her bodice so her daughter might suckle.

"No matter." The brightness Percy forced into his voice was artificial as he folded away William Godwin's letter. Mary almost asked to read it herself, but she couldn't bear to see her father's rejection in his own familiar handwriting. "I'll write to him again. I'm sure he'll experience a change of heart when he realizes what he's missing."

"A squalling baby at all hours of the night, the stink of spoiled milk and soiled linen clouts, and an endless winter." Claire toed her shoes off and kicked her heels up on the table. There was a hole in her stocking. What had happened to the carefree spirit who flitted happily through life? "If anything, your father knows exactly what he's missing."

"Out," Mary ordered, pointing to the staircase. She was

weary from lack of sleep and couldn't condone another moment of such behavior from her sister. "Not another word, Claire."

Her stepsister had the gall to look to Percy for assistance. When he only eyed the stairs, she gave a loud huff. As Everina emitted a startled howl at the sound and Claire stomped upstairs, Mary could only grind her teeth.

"Patience," Percy murmured to Mary. "We have so much and your sister has so little." As always, Mary felt a stab of guilt, given that it was her and Percy's choices that had ruined Claire and the rest of the Godwins' reputations. "We can afford to be tolerant with her."

"She needs something to lift her spirits. We can't keep on with her acting like this." Mary said *we*, but she really meant *I*.

"I've been invited to meet with Lord Byron—he's taken an interest in my poetry and wants to compare notes." Percy rubbed his chin. "Perhaps I'll take Claire along. She's always been an enthusiast of Byron's."

Ordinarily, Mary might have been annoyed that Percy hadn't invited her, but an afternoon of peace and quiet at home was too enticing to turn down. And Percy was right—Claire needed something to look forward to. "I think Claire would enjoy that very much."

As late winter frost crowded the windows of the house on Margaret Street, all of London was abuzz with the scandalous doings of the wickedly handsome Lord Byron. The writer of the wildly popular *The Corsair* (set in, of all scandalous places, a Turkish harem), Lord Byron was cut from the same cloth as Percy—a radical who had traveled extensively and used verse in an attempt to bottle the beauty and pain in the world. In fact, the two men had corresponded since before the trip to Paris; after all, the pond of English poets was small and stagnant.

Except, where Lord Byron was a bestselling poet—*The Corsair* had sold ten thousand copies on its first day of publication—Percy was still struggling to publish his latest work, *Queen Mab*.

Percy and Claire's afternoon outing with Byron had been a success, especially given that he'd pronounced Claire a musical virtuoso when she'd offered to sing for him. Talented as she was, this led Claire to gush about Byron's brilliance until both Mary and Percy traded looks every time Claire mentioned the poet. The threesome's initial visit soon expanded into another tea, followed by a luncheon, and then, finally, a dinner. Mary demurred when Percy offered for her to join them—she'd been using the quiet afternoons to write in her journal while Everina napped, plus she didn't mind hearing secondhand stories of the famed writer. And their interludes had certainly brought a sparkle into Claire's eyes again.

Still, it was with shock that Claire pronounced one chilly afternoon, "I'm meeting Lord Byron tonight at his box at Drury Lane." The imperious tilt of her chin exposed the swan-white curve of her neck. "*Unchaperoned.*"

"Pardon?" Mary wasn't sure she'd heard correctly.

"He asked me to meet with him, alone." Claire shrugged. "And I said yes."

Mary wasn't sure whether she was supposed to shake Claire or take her stepsister under her wing and explain what an assignation with a man such as Byron—who had recently signed a Deed of Separation against his wife and been denounced by his jilted lover Lady Caroline Lamb as *mad, bad, and dangerous to know*—actually meant. Fortunately, Percy's interjection saved her from having to respond.

"You do know that a private rendezvous with a man like Lord Byron will cause tongues to wag, don't you?"

To her credit, Claire at least flushed at Percy's question. "Of course. Although I don't think it's fair, that a woman can't meet with a man without her honor being besmirched. Men suffer no such consequences."

"Do you have any idea what you're getting into, Claire?" Mary knew she needed to proceed with caution. After all, she'd run off with Percy and was living with him, unmarried. But that was Percy. And Lord Byron, well . . . "Byron is London's most notorious libertine."

"He's more than that," Claire protested. "You should meet him instead of hiding in this wretched house and reading the gossip rags. Did you know that Lord Byron donated a portion of his earnings to your father a few years ago? Byron told me he has a signed copy of *Political Justice*; he shares many of William Godwin and Mary Wollstonecraft's beliefs."

Mary didn't know about the donation, but she *did* know that Lord Byron was keen on her mother and father's ideals, since Percy was already acquainted with the poet. Percy had expressed Byron's curiosity in meeting *her* one day, but given her current state and their reduced circumstances, receiving such a famous visitor had seemed as likely as setting up house on the South Pole.

And if Percy hadn't introduced Claire to Byron . . . But then, Mary had encouraged the acquaintance, so this was just as much her fault as his. If only she'd been more patient with Claire.

"Be careful with him," Mary began, and was thankful when Percy picked up her argument.

"Are you sure you know what you're about, Claire?" he asked. "You might be meeting Byron for one thing while he may be planning this interlude for quite another purpose."

"I'm quite clear that Lord Byron has rather . . . *physical* plans for this evening." Claire looked as unruffled as if she were discussing Britain's current tax structure. "I informed him that I have no father or brother to cause any difficulties." She held up a hand at their shocked exclamations, and her eyes turned wistful. "I want to experience the love the two of you share for myself. I think—I *hope*—that perhaps I can have that with Lord Byron."

"Is this a good idea, Claire?" Mary empathized with her sister, but wanted to point out her own situation: barely scraping by while ostracized by all of polite society. Certainly not all she'd dreamed of when making plans with Percy Shelley amid breathless kisses in the St. Pancras cemetery. And she bit her tongue against pointing out that scandalous Lord Byron seemed quite capable of lust, but not necessarily love.

Claire merely pinched her cheeks and smoothed her dark chocolate curls. "If you can take up with Percy, then I can do as I please with Lord Byron. I *am* almost eighteen, after all, without a dowry and with no inclination to enter into so outdated a custom as marriage."

As if that were somehow supposed to placate Mary. Percy pressed a brotherly kiss to Claire's temple. "Mind how you go, Claire," was his parting advice.

Mary still felt somehow responsible for her stepsister, but reminded herself that Claire *did* deserve to make her own choices, just as every woman did, even if the gratification of those choices became a serpent's sting. So, Mary merely slanted her eyes at her sister. "Percy and I love each other and have pledged ourselves to each other for life. We will care for each other always. Will Byron care for you so well, even if you become pregnant?"

"You worry too much." Claire checked the state of her bodice, frowning as she adjusted her pale cleavage. When she glanced up, a wicked smile spread across her full lips. "I plan to live in the moment. And, according to my prognostications, my future in a few hours looks very enjoyable indeed."

Mary couldn't help it; she stayed up that night awaiting her sister's return.

She'd rocked tiny Everina to sleep before finishing her journal entry for the day and now sat downstairs with her legs tucked under her, not wanting to waste the expense of a candle. It was the dead of night when she finally heard the door open and the staircase creak. Mary examined her sister, but nothing seemed amiss. And yet, Mary remembered wondering after her first kiss with Percy whether people could see the difference in her. Mary cleared her throat and Claire gave a sharp exclamation of surprise.

"Bloody hell," Claire whispered when she saw Mary draped in shadows. "What are you still doing up?"

Mary rose, feeling suddenly exhausted. "I wanted to make sure you're all right."

"I'm fine," Claire answered, her voice tightly leashed. "Better than fine, actually. I slept with him. Lord Byron."

"And?"

"And now I'm no longer a child. Therefore, I don't need you to treat me like one."

Mary stepped back, stung at the rejection of her kindness. "Fine. Good night, then."

She passed her sister on the stairs, was almost at the top when Claire's voice stopped her. "I'm sorry. That was rude of me." Claire's voice quavered, but only for a moment.

"It's no matter." Mary felt herself softening. "You've had an emotional night."

"Byron wants to meet you, you know. I told him that you admired his work," Claire said to Mary. "And that you've been eager to make his acquaintance since you scribble Byron's lines on Percy's poems." She shrugged at Mary's sharp look. "I saw what you wrote inside the copy of *Queen Mab*."

Mary colored. Shelley had gifted her an early copy of the poem and she'd added her own declarations of love from her favorite lines of Lord Byron's:

> *Ours too the glance that none saw beside;*
> *The smile none else might understand;*
> *The whisper'd thought of hearts allied;*
> *The pressure of the thrilling hand.*

To which she'd added, *I have pledged myself to thee and sacred is the gift*.

She and Percy would never exchange vows in a candlelit church, but she had made a vow to him in the margins of his poem just the same. A vow that now felt cheapened by Claire's tittle-tattle to Lord Byron, of all people.

Mary could barely grind out the words to her sister. "That was private."

"I'm sorry. You did leave it lying around."

"I'm not interested in entertaining Lord Byron." Mary's tone was frosty as a December morning. She was exhausted from caring for an infant and hadn't expected her own sister to expose her private writings. "Not right now at least."

"Please, Mary," Claire suddenly pleaded. "I'm so overcome with emotion when I see him that I can barely talk. He makes me feel so awkward that I'm inclined to sit on a little stool at his feet and just stare at him. I need your help. *Please*. I was your accomplice with Percy."

Mary pressed her fingers to her eyelids, willing the gathering headache to disperse. Perhaps this tryst with Lord Byron might turn into something more and he might whisk Claire away to his own household, where she might be happy. "Fine," she said. "I'll meet him."

"Thank you." Claire pressed kisses to both of Mary's cheeks, giving Mary a whiff of her sister's rosewater fragrance and something decidedly male. "I promise to make it up to you."

The next day, Percy left at sunrise to deal with his father's lawyers about his inheritance from his grandfather. As the hours ticked by, Mary worried that he wouldn't return home before Lord Byron's arrival, when he suddenly came breezing through the door, laden with paper-wrapped packages and donning a wide smile. "The fight has ended and I emerge victorious," he announced as he dropped the parcels and swung Mary around so fast she became dizzy even as they chortled with shared laughter. It was moments like these when she was struck dumb by the force of her love for Percy. "The problem has been solved. Sir Timothy has promised to pay my annual sum of one thousand pounds!"

"A thousand pounds a year?" Mary nearly doubled over from spinning and the glorious news. "Why, that's more than enough!"

"I've agreed to pay two hundred a year for Harriet's upkeep." Percy's visage darkened slightly at that. "But still, we shall be quite comfortable on eight hundred a year." The kiss he gave her sealed the promise. "And now we shall celebrate our love. And our financial freedom!"

"So long as we are careful," Mary reminded him. When had she become so responsible? *Damnare*, but she almost sounded like her stepmother Jane for a moment.

"Indeed." Percy's sparkling sea-blue eyes and mischievous gaze landed on the packages he'd set down. "And so we shall be, after tonight, of course!"

It turned out Percy had stopped off on his way home and ordered a whole piglet for their dinner, along with a carafe of white wine and a delicate spice cake from the baker down the way. More food than they could eat, even with Claire and Lord Byron sharing the table.

Despite her relief in settling the Harriet question and Percy's celebratory mood, Mary was fully prepared to dislike the infamous poet, even while being unsure of what to expect from Lord Byron—the only person in all of London who would deign sup with them in their own scandalous house—when he finally arrived. Certainly not the quiet and unassuming young man who was so tall he had to duck to enter their house. True, George Gordon Byron was startlingly handsome in an almost feminine way—waves of dark hair framed a face with full lips and a cleft in his chin that Michelangelo might have chiseled—but he was deferential and soft-spoken upon Claire's introduction to Mary.

"Miss Mary Godwin." He offered her a deep and sensual bow. "It is my absolute honor to make your acquaintance."

I wish I could say the same, she nearly said as she curtsied, but she reminded herself not to believe all the dark rumors that swirled about him—among those that he's slept with his sister and his male classmates—even if Byron *had* availed himself of her sister. Instead she answered, "The pleasure is all mine."

Trailing her guest into their low-ceilinged dining room, Mary took note of Byron's slightly uneven steps. Eyes narrowing, she suspected that perhaps he was inebriated, until she realized he was limping, and doing his utmost to hide the fact. *Interesting . . .*

"You are a shrewd observer," he said when he caught her studying his right foot. Lifting his pants leg, he revealed a surgical boot that was cleverly crafted to disguise his withered calf muscle and make the foot fit in an ordinary shoe. "I call myself *le diable boiteux*, for the limp has been with me since birth. Fortunately, it doesn't stop me from being a competent boxer and excellent swimmer."

At dinner, Byron acted every bit the polished lord, discussing his love of Napoleon alongside the rules of poetry before asking Mary about weightier philosophical matters regarding equality and ideas of marriage. "I tried it once." Byron referenced his failed marriage after Mary claimed the institution to be an outdated construct, albeit one that society still held dear. "I'm afraid it didn't agree with me."

Exhausted from a late night with Everina, Mary chuckled and almost chose that moment to excuse herself, despite the fact that she found herself warming to Byron, simply because he was educated and easy to converse with. Had it not been for Claire . . .

"I'm sure Mary is delighted to agree with you," Claire said in a falsetto tone. Dressed in a gown hand decorated with military epaulets in the latest French fashion—ostensibly to impress the worldly Lord Byron—Claire had been silent throughout the meal, a rarity. "My sister had been aching to make your acquaintance for so long. She simply *gushes* about your poetry."

Any sympathy Mary might have felt for her sister's former tongue-tied state disintegrated. What had gotten into her? Mary turned her attention to Byron. "Is the food not to your liking?"

Easier to focus on the fact that Byron had mostly pushed his pork around his plate than on how Claire was threatening to snap Mary's last nerve. Byron actually tugged at his collar so it was possible to imagine him as a young boy caught in some naughtiness. "I'm unaccustomed to so rich a meal," he confessed. "I have a morbid propensity to fatten—I was teased mercilessly about my weight at Cambridge—and usually maintain a strict regimen of biscuits and soda water. Or potatoes with vinegar."

Percy reddened. "I had no idea. I'm sure we can find something—"

But Byron merely gave an affable shake of his head. "It's no matter, really. I especially dread two things in this world to which I have reason to believe I am equally predisposed—growing fat and growing mad. Thus, I'm content to subsist mostly on conversation."

Which they did for the rest of the evening. Mary's mood grew ever lighter, even as Claire became more despondent, especially when Lord Byron excused himself.

"I'm afraid my muse calls," he said with a twirl of his elegant fingers. "And I must heed her demands."

"I'll just fetch my cloak." Claire was already on her feet and halfway up the staircase, but Byron stopped her.

"I work best alone, Miss Clairmont. Perhaps some other time."

"Oh." Claire visibly wilted in front of them. Despite her sister's recent poor behavior, Mary felt true sympathy for her. Mary had guarded herself from her feelings toward Percy until she was sure he reciprocated; she couldn't imagine how she'd have felt had he rejected her. And had done so *publicly*. Mary frowned at Byron even as Claire sighed. "I'll leave you to it, then."

Claire trudged the rest of the way upstairs, leaving Mary and Percy to accompany their guest to the door.

"I envy your easy happiness," Byron said to them both after wrapping a red silk scarf around his neck with a flourish. "And you, Miss Godwin, have been a breath of the crispest winter air.

I'm such a strange mélange of good and evil that I'm accustomed to women shrinking from me due to my reputation, or trying to seduce me"—a glance above his head to where Claire was likely listening with her ear pressed to the floorboards—"so I find myself intrigued at your very existence."

Mary laughed and Percy smiled. A smile so easy, she almost wished it were a little tighter, as if to cover a hint of jealousy. But jealousy was not their forte. "Lord Byron, I guarantee I have no intention of seducing you." She threaded her fingers through Percy's. "My heart has already been soundly claimed."

Byron placed his well-made top hat upon his head, then hesitated at the doorway. "You know, I'm planning an exodus to Geneva in just a short time, to follow in Rousseau's footsteps now that the political troubles there have died down and the country has been incorporated into the mighty republic of Switzerland. You two should join me. With your child, of course."

"Thank you, but we couldn't possibly," Mary said. "Everina is so young."

But next to her, Percy's eyes suddenly lit like twin furnaces of excitement. "Geneva? There's nothing for fresh inspiration like a bit of travel, especially when London has been so disappointing." He turned to Mary. "It might be a nice change of pace, don't you think?"

Mary could read the hidden meaning there. *With your father disowning you and all of society shunning us.* What exactly was keeping her tied to London? True, travel would be more difficult with Everina, but not impossible. Mothers had been traveling with their children since humans decided to walk upon two legs. Her mother had done it, after all. And written about it too.

And Mary Wollstonecraft had wished to go to Switzerland and even documented that hope in her final chapter of her Swedish travelogue, but the movement of French troops had barred her way. She had died before that dream could be realized.

"It's something to think about," Mary admitted. Except, suddenly, she didn't want to just think about things. She wanted to *do*, not dream. To see everything her mother had wished to see. Mary cleared her throat and lifted her chin to address Byron. "If you're serious, then we would be happy to join you."

Percy's blinding grin turned her knees watery, even as Byron slapped him on the back. "We can work out the details in the weeks to come. This shall be an adventure like no other."

To which Mary could only wonder what exactly she had just gotten them into. Still, one only lived once.

Live each day as if it were your last.

"Have I ever told you how much I love you?" Percy asked her the moment the door closed behind Byron. The lopsided, astonished grin still dangled from his lips.

Mary leaned her head against the steadiness of his shoulder. "I wouldn't mind hearing it again."

Percy twirled a dark curl of her hair around his finger. "You never fail to impress, my Faerie Queene. In the span of one evening, you thoroughly charmed England's preeminent poet."

Mary touched her nose to his. "I did that some time ago, I think."

A toe-curling kiss was her reward. Was it terribly wanton that she imagined the press of their bodies together here in the moonlit parlor? Except she was barely out of confinement and Claire was upstairs. A hand on Percy's chest was a gentle reminder. *Not yet.*

"Honestly," Percy murmured as he reluctantly pulled away, "what other woman in the world could charm Lord Byron *and* agree to a Swiss adventure in one night? You, my dearest love, possess a philosopher's soul in the body of an adventurer."

Mary gave a meager smile. "Just thinking about Geneva already has me exhausted."

Percy pressed a kiss to her forehead as she stifled a yawn. "To bed with you. I'll lock up."

Mary could almost feel the soft cloud of a feather mattress under her as she climbed the stairway, wondered if she'd even get her dress off before she collapsed. Perhaps, if she was lucky, she might nab a few hours before Everina woke and demanded the first of several nightly feedings.

"I'm coming," Claire announced from her doorway the moment Mary's foot touched the upstairs landing. "To Geneva."

"What?"

"I have nowhere to go if you leave me here. I can't go home and I have no means of living on my own." Claire's eyes took on an extra gleam. "I think I love him, Mary. Byron, that is. I know he doesn't love me, not yet, but perhaps if we were together in Geneva, he might learn to love me too. Don't you think?"

That seemed doubtful, especially based on Byron's palpable lack of interest in Claire over dinner, but Claire's bleak expression reminded Mary of the times she'd left the Skinner Street bookshop hand in hand with William Godwin on their way to Mary Wollstonecraft's grave. The very same frown had sometimes darkened Claire's face then, as if Mary had stolen some precious hope of a loving father figure from her.

"Please let me go to Geneva," Claire pleaded, clasping Mary's hand between her cold fingers.

Mary realized something important then. For all her posturing and claiming to be an independent woman following in the footsteps of Mary Wollstonecraft, Claire wasn't happy on her own.

And Mary wasn't happy with Claire. Not anymore. It was a

quandary she wasn't sure how to solve, certainly not if they all moved and piled atop one another in Geneva. But at the same time, she couldn't deny her sister.

"You can come."

May all the gods help them.

CHAPTER 8

❦

October 1793

MARY WOLLSTONECRAFT

Moving to the rural neighborhood of Saint-Germain-des-Prés with its ever-present scents of lavender and baking bread was lovely, but despite the colorful palette of American, French, and Russian that I heard from Gil's window every day as summer turned to fall, it was no quaint farm on the Ohio River.

We've plenty of time for that, I reminded myself one crisp autumn afternoon while Gil was meeting with his French customers to arrange payment for American soap, wheat, and iron in Bourbon silver. Gil had promised that if this deal went through, he'd be richer than King Louis XIV and we'd move to the Ohio Territory. Apparently, love was not enough to float our wild sugar-spun dreams, but one of us had to be a realist if we were going to make this work, even if I didn't mind the idea of being drawn closer together by pinching blasts of poverty. Instead, I was alone in Saint-Germain-des-Prés more often than not.

The trees were tinged with every shade of red, russet, and gold when I finished writing my notes on the French response to the British victory at Toulon and their subsequent naming of young Louis XVII as the rightful king of France. I worried that this valiant effort on the part of my countrymen would further enrage Robespierre, the fiery leader of the Jacobins. Outside, I heard sudden yelling and crept to the window, stopping only to ensure the front door was locked and bolted. One couldn't be too careful these days.

What I saw nearly had me on my knees—uniformed authorities banging their fists on doors while revolutionaries in scarlet trousers marched from the ancient medieval chapel of Saint-Germain-des-Prés, their swarthy arms laden with golden candelabras, altar boards, and even a jewel-encrusted crucifix. Robespierre had recently declared the Catholic Church corrupt and had even gone so far as to rename Notre-Dame as the Temple of Reason. I wasn't religious, but still felt queasy to realize Robespierre's crazed followers were looting priceless religious artifacts. "Girondins! British nationals! Monarchists!" One looter passed off his treasures to join the men banging on doors. "Enemies of the state—surrender yourselves or face justice!"

I cringed as the door across the way was kicked open and one of my neighbors—a middle-aged man with a belly like a friendly pig's who had always tipped his hat when he encountered Gil and me returning from our morning walk—was yanked outside and heaved into a wagon. "Where are you taking me?" he demanded.

"To Luxembourg Palace," the revolutionary replied from beneath his tricorne. "Perhaps you might even fete the queen!"

A cruel joke, made by a special brand of monster. Marie Antoinette had been held in the converted prison for months. The specious poisons of the French *libelle* claimed she'd been governed by uterine furies during her time on the throne. The pamphlets also claimed that this new France should be like ancient Rome, where men made the laws, and women, without allowing themselves to question it, agreed in everything.

I didn't have time to worry about that or my neighbor as the looter turned brute swiveled toward Gilbert's door. His gaze snagged with mine from the other side of the leaded glass. I pushed myself away from the window and let the curtain fall, the drum of my heart beating in my ears. That sound was quickly replaced by his fist hammering on the door.

"Open in the name of Robespierre and the Committee of Public Safety! *Ouvre cette porte!*"

I couldn't do it. My hands were shaking too badly and my cowardly knees actually gave out as I swallowed back a surge of bile. Was this how it would end? Despite my letting Gil register me as his wife, would I join my liberal friends in some moldy prison cell, left to rot or, worse, face the guillotine?

The thought of my brave friends forced me back to my feet as the thunderstorm against the door intensified. I would not be cowed by this filth-faced bully. No, if my fate awaited me in the dark bowels of Luxembourg Palace, I would do as Théroigne de Méricourt—who had suffered permanent damage to her mind and still remained insensible at La Salpêtrière—and Madame Roland and Thomas Paine had done: I would face my future with both eyes open.

I had only two regrets: that I wouldn't be able to say goodbye to Gil *and* that I couldn't make a final report to Johnson.

Eyeing the paper and inkpot on the desk, I worked to shove them into my pocket and bodice. One regret was better than two, I supposed.

The hinges groaned beneath the revolutionary's fists until I smoothed my hair and unlocked the door. "Can I help you?" I asked.

It was a ridiculous question for a ridiculous moment. But the man's hungry grin revealed a chipped upper tooth. "Fuck me if

I haven't won a prize," he said. "Is that an English accent I hear?" His gaze roved over my dress—nothing ostentatious (I was no fool, given the current political climate), just soft cotton with plain lace at the sleeves.

Except I'd forgotten to pin the damnable tricolor cockade that the law required everyone to wear. I was sure that Robespierre even wore one to bed.

"A Royalist sympathizer, no doubt." The man gave a hyena's triumphant yip as he hauled me outside by the arm, his grip hard enough to bruise. It was the first time I'd been manhandled since that horrible night in Hoxton, and I found myself struck senseless, unable to argue or do more than trip after him. "A fine addition to our collection."

I saw nothing save the open maw of the prison wagon, where my poor neighbor already trembled inside. Could I save myself by claiming to be American, an ally of France? Would that be enough to save me? I was about to concoct a new identity, when I heard the most beloved voice in the world bellow from somewhere down the street. "Unhand my wife!"

Had it not been for Gil charging toward me, tails of his brown overcoat flapping behind him and the overlarge tricolor cockade pinned to the selfsame jacket, I'd have given up all hope. So many before me—Louis XVI and Marie Antoinette, Thomas Paine and even Théroigne—had been eaten by this revolution that I was resigned to following in their footsteps.

"Who are you?" the revolutionary snarled so, I thought Gil might be arrested, too; that is, until he removed a sheaf of official papers from his jacket and brandished them below the man's bulbous nose.

"I am Gilbert Imlay. You'll see my papers are all in order."

"The Imlay who supplies the revolutionary army?"

"The very same. And in case you can't read, that's Robespierre's signature authorizing my movements. You'd best unhand my wife. *Now*."

The brute turned a sickly shade of white and dropped my arm as if I'd contracted leprosy. "She should be registered," he said weakly.

"She *is*." Gil responded with a threatening crack of his knuckles. "Which you'd know if you cared to check. And Monsieur Blanchet from across the street has been helping strip the city of its religious names—I applauded his utility to Robespierre just yesterday."

The revolutionary narrowed his eyes at Gil, as if trying to determine whether he was being swindled, but eventually decided not to chance it. "Release the potbellied one," he commanded before turning and lumbering away.

"Inside," I murmured to Gil. "I'm going inside." The ground beneath my feet buckled as if I were on a swaying ship, and acid rose again in my throat, but I forced my spine erect and my feet to move.

Until I was inside the safety of Gil's apartment with the door closed—and locked—behind us. Then I collapsed into a chair far from the windows. "I thought we'd be safe here." The room spun—I had to clasp both arms of my chair and grit my teeth to hold it steady. "We must escape this insanity before it's too late. We could go to England, or even Ohio."

I expected Gil to jump at the offer of Ohio—I might have considered marrying him in earnest if it meant escaping France. Which meant I couldn't understand the furrow that formed between his brows. Or the way he took off his hat and ran a hand over his thick hair. "I can't leave, Mary. Not anymore."

"What? Why?"

"You heard what I told that Jacobin, about providing the revolutionaries with supplies? I just settled those terms with

Robespierre. The revolutionaries seized the royal treasury, and I'm rerouting all the Bourbon silver they're paying me through Scandinavia, the only place in Europe where it's still legal, given how the rest of the Continent's monarchies feel about ousting the Bourbons. I'm going to be a rich, *rich* man, Mary, but not if I run out of the country like a whipped dog."

Gil's eyes shone as bright as the Bourbon silver plates he intended to receive when he talked about his deal with Robespierre. I'd one day call this his "money-getting" face, but this was the first time I'd made its acquaintance.

Gil cleared his throat. Apparently, there was more.

"The queen has been condemned to die," he said quietly. "She's to be executed tomorrow. And the Marquis de Condorcet has also been condemned." I gasped, remembering the plainly dressed and brilliant man I'd met at Thomas Paine's dinner party, but Gil plowed ahead. "If I leave France, it will be seen as an admission of guilt. I would lose my commission, if not worse."

"And if I leave?"

He shrugged. "I'd be guilty by association."

The spinning of the room intensified, made more frenetic by a loud buzzing in my ears. "I need to lie down," I gasped.

I narrowly avoided fainting as strong hands arranged my feet on a worn leather ottoman and gentle fingers smoothed my brow. "Everything will be all right, Mary, you'll see."

It wasn't until my breasts began to swell and I missed my courses that I understood my recent faintness wasn't due entirely to the violent events swirling around Paris, but instead the everyday miracle taking place deep inside my body.

I might have panicked, but given Gil's easygoing acceptance of the situation when I informed him, I saw no reason why life couldn't continue as it always had. Certainly I'd soon need to let out the waist of my day dresses, but little else must change.

Thus, my pen flew as Jacobin leaders rescinded all the hard-won women's rights that Olympe de Gouges, Théroigne de Méricourt, and even Madame Roland had fought for, the same rights that I'd raised my battle standard over in *A Vindication of the Rights of Woman.* Inspired by ancient Rome and Jean-Jacques Rousseau—that pompous jackanapes whose narrow prejudices included a woman being agreeable to her master as the grand end of any female's existence—the French ushered back in the vision of women fully cowed and caged in their own homes.

The right to divorce? Gone.

Rights to inherit? Obliterated.

Equal legal representation between men and women? As if it had never been.

Then the Jacobins barred women from taking part in political demonstrations or forming their own clubs. With the stroke of Robespierre's pen, half of France's population had their tongues cut out. And we women of a certain age were erased from the public record now that only images of chaste young virgins were allowed in the public sphere; even the female image of Liberty was replaced with the male icon Justice.

I was no longer young or chaste, but I ached to scream against these injustices, especially when one day later, all the remaining Girondists still alive were put to death.

Alone when I read the news, I fainted in earnest. Gil was gone from Paris to Le Havre on another business trip—with promises to return before the month was out—and I hit my head on a table edge when I passed out. I woke up in a greasy slick of my own blood.

Johnson wrote me letter after letter, begging me to return to England. Except it was already too late. Olympe de Gouges—

whom the Jacobins now called a virago and a man-woman—was guillotined after being stripped naked and having her genitals publicly examined. Five days later, Madame Roland was executed, her last words—"O Liberty, what crimes are committed in thy name!"—guaranteed to echo down the ages. To honor both women—and Théroigne de Méricourt, my dear friend who was still insensible at the asylum in the Salpêtrière Hospital—I was determined to write of all I had seen. Perhaps then the world would never again repeat the horrors here in France.

Not in letters, which were no longer enough. No, this required a new book.

Months passed. I spent my days locked in Gil's otherwise empty apartment, filling every piece of paper I could find as I compiled *An Historical and Moral View of the Origin and Progress of the French Revolution*. Realizing I wouldn't flee France, Johnson had offered me an extremely generous advance for this volume. I was determined to follow my own admonition from *Vindication* that a woman must not be dependent on her husband—or in this case, a man who was like her husband—for subsistence during his life. I would remain financially independent with this project while also seeking to demonstrate how the revolution fit into the larger landscape of history and to show that the American constitution should inspire others with its reason and equality, for its liberty seemed to promise shelter to all mankind.

I touched my hand to my belly, feeling the gentle twitches of life there. I was no alchemist or fortune-teller, but I always imagined this little darling as a daughter. I wanted her to grow up in a world that was better than the one I currently occupied. But not even thoughts of her or my writing could distract me from the loneliness and mounting despair as I fell upon evil days, my head aching and my heart heavy, especially as Gil's absence stretched on and the revolution continued to roil unabated about me.

By the time late autumn rains pelted the apartment windows and flooded the roads, I needed to find my way back into the sun. To do so, I had to bid goodbye to Paris.

My best love,

The world appears an unweeded garden where things rank and vile flourish best. I love you fondly and have been very wretched. If you do not return soon, I would like to leave Paris and join you in Le Havre until the birth of our sweet darling.

Say yes and you will make me happy.

Yours most affectionately,
Mary

I didn't have to wait long—Gil's reply arrived just two short days later.

Darling Mary,

I love you like a goddess and imagine the two of us at our fireside, little creatures like the one you are carrying clinging about my knees, your head on my shoulder. Join me in Le Havre as soon as the roads clear.

Gil

I was already done packing when the rains finally stopped. I left in the morning, my latest manuscript buried deep in one of my travel chests. If discovered by the guards that now loomed before me, I'd be branded an enemy of the state.

It would have been safer to burn it, but I couldn't bring myself to feed the flames before setting out for Paris's gates. I could no more burn my manuscript than I could sever from my womb the child I now carried. The documentation of this hateful revolution was too important to destroy.

"You there!" one of the guards called down to me. "Wait!"

I cursed myself, seeing the end that was near. He'd open the trunk and paw through my camisoles and underthings before finding the rare stack of precious papers. One glance at any of the pages and I'd be condemned, as would the child I now carried.

Would they let me give birth in prison before they led me to the guillotine? Would that be a mercy to the child, or a worse sort of condemnation?

The guard *did* fling open my chest, and I nearly stopped breathing when he reached the manuscript. "What is this?" he asked, squinting at the scrawls of my pen before waving the top pages at me.

"A diary," I answered, forcing myself not to sway on my feet. "I didn't have a journal, just loose papers . . ."

His upper lip curled and he flung the pages back into the trunk, shoved the entire thing closed with his booted foot before gesturing impatiently for the farmer's cart of cabbages that waited behind me.

I realized that I'd never, *ever* been thankful for someone's illiteracy until that very moment.

The large and pleasantly situated house Gil arranged for us in Le Havre was owned by a soap merchant. There, amid the omnipresent scents of lavender, almond, and honey that had seeped into the floorboards, we could watch ships arrive and depart from the bustling port while listening to crying gulls through the windows. My love and I had reached a cozy sort of domestic arrangement—I spent my days writing and embroidering butterflies onto tiny baby bonnets I sewed with linen sent from Paris, and he arrived home to dine on the leg of lamb the maid had left smoking on the board. As I watched one white-sailed schooner depart, I daydreamed that someday soon, a similar ship would spirit us away from France.

The three of us.

Fanny's birth was surprisingly quick. Painful, but blessedly quick. (Thankfully, I had armed myself with foreknowledge about the event by forthrightly questioning the matronly housekeeper Gilbert had hired for the process. It is essential that women know about their own bodies—just like the mechanics of sex, this particular struggle of nature is surely rendered more cruel by women's ignorance.) Gilbert had headed to the waterfront that morning—he spent long days negotiating with ship captains about black market commodities along with the thirty-six illegal silver platters stamped with the Bourbon crest he was looking to unload. He returned home that evening to find an uncommonly healthy baby girl nursing at my breast.

"Our little damsel eats manfully." He spoke with great affection, one rough finger tracing the downy dome of her skull. I was sore and exhausted, but still managed to chuckle as I playfully swatted his finger away when it journeyed to my own pale skin. The light of his smile reached his eyes. "Is it possible for a father to be jealous of his daughter?"

"You'll have to be jealous awhile longer," I teased *de gaieté de cœur*. "These are hers for now."

"No wet nurse?"

I hesitated. Common wisdom dictated that mothers were

not to have relations with their husbands while they nursed, which led many women to hire out that particular service to keep their men from straying. However, I deplored the practice of parents abandoning the care of children to their servants. I already understood that I could best provide everything my daughter needed right now. Gil could be patient for a few months until she could eat solid foods. Plus, he'd taught me there was more to sex than the act itself—we could be creative. I shrugged, then pressed my lips to his knuckles. "We have everything we need right here."

Everything, including so much happiness I thought my heart might burst with its sunshine.

Robespierre lost control of his revolution that July when he was overthrown by his former followers in a violent coup. Unwilling to face the guillotine himself, his unfortunate attempt at suicide resulted in his shooting himself in the jaw. While he was unconscious and bleeding out on his floor, his detractors arrested him and then assigned Madame Guillotine to finish the job.

Just like that, the Terror was over.

France—along with Gil and me and the rest of the survivors—breathed a heavy sigh of relief as a moderate five-member committee called the Directory took control of governing.

I assumed this heralded our move to America and the start of our new lives, but Gilbert only shook his head. "I'll be busier now than ever," he said as he tied his cravat one morning. Some knavery on the part of one of his underlings meant he was off to Paris for who knew how long this time. "And the Bourbon platters haven't yet sold in Norway. We must have money, Mary. Plenty of it."

That damned silver. A family with a modest farm could live their entire lives on its massive proceeds, but only if Gilbert's middleman who had transported the ill-gotten silver to Norway's safe harbor could actually sell them. And *if* that man was trustworthy.

"We have plenty of money. If you could let go of this obsession with making your fortune, we could go to America. We could be happy." Where was my *épanchement de cœur*? What had happened to the gallant philosopher who had written a novel about freedom and courted me with heady discussions about equality? Perhaps it was the late nights spent rocking Fanny or all my bottled unease from the revolution that was finally free to boil over, or maybe it was the frequent sensation that Gilbert was more interested in his business than in the vibrant dream of America he'd once painted for me, but a persistent shadow darkened my earlier happiness. I narrowed my eyes at him. "I hope that you aspire to do more with your life than to eat and drink and be stupidly useful to the stupid."

Gilbert's jaw clenched in the manner I knew preceded hours of silence upon his return. "I'm sorry." I blinked against the nettles that pricked my eyes. I'd thought a child wouldn't change anything in our lives, but I'd been so exhausted and emotional since Fanny's birth—motherhood was a sweet toil, the careening highs and desperate lows of which I'd never encountered—that I feared I was pushing Gilbert away. It wasn't as if he neglected us by wasting the night hours losing at the debauched card tables of the popular faro bank gaming house. No, he was merely fulfilling his paternal duties. For *us*.

"We must all do what we are good at," Gil ground out as he picked up his bags—two meant a long trip. He paused to drop a kiss on Fanny's forehead. The gentle touch woke her and she whimpered, needing to be changed and fed. "We can't all while away our days thinking deep thoughts that those *stupid* people neither understand nor care about."

Then he turned and walked out the door, taking a fragment of my bruised heart with him.

I might have traveled to Paris to mend things with Gil or used a hundred letters to persuade him of the depth of my feelings. Except I hadn't the time, not after Fanny fell ill.

When the telltale red sores appeared first on her milky cheeks and then spread to the rest of her innocent little body, I knew the worst had befallen us.

Smallpox.

"Close her into an airtight room," our gray-haired housekeeper advised before I sent the woman away. "Swaddle her tight and don't bathe her unless you wish the pox to cover her." The woman squeezed my shoulder with a knobby hand. "Prepare yourself—I lost a babe myself to the pox. Send for a priest."

A priest would not save my daughter. But science and sound reasoning might. Johnson had published John Haygarth's *An Inquiry How to Prevent the Small-Pox*, which I had borrowed out of simple curiosity following one of his dinner parties at home in England, and I still remembered its advice. As it recommended, I opened the windows and administered cool baths to Fanny.

Still, I descended down a dark spiral of horror as my once robust infant shriveled into a fevered and listless child. I knew not how many days passed, only that I labored like a slave for her, endlessly nursing her until my nipples cracked and bled, warming her bath water twice a day, and washing her countless sores as they burst with a putrefying mixture of pus and blood. If she survived, she would be forever scarred. But I didn't care— Fanny's precious soul had sunk its fragile hooks deep into my heart, and when I walked without her, her ghostlike little figure danced before me.

I would not let her turn into a wraith. Not while I drew breath.

My watchful ministrations triumphed over the malignancy of the distemper, until finally Fanny's fever broke. Though disfigured, she would survive.

I wrote to Gil in an exhausted hand to advise him of the news, worrying already of how other children would treat our daughter as she grew up. I informed him that we were coming to Paris. I needed him and so did Fanny.

Days passed and no response came. Word finally arrived after nearly a week.

Gil was no longer in Paris.

He'd moved to London.

CHAPTER 9

❦

May 1816

MARY GODWIN

It may have been nearly summer, but snow was falling in stubborn clumps when Mary, Percy, Claire, and little Everina finally arrived in the foothills of the divine Alps. The immensity of the snowy mountains and their eternal glaciers so staggered the imagination that it was difficult to believe they did indeed form a part of the earth. Thankfully, Percy's monetary settlement with his father meant this trip had lacked mules, but Mary worried she'd never seen a landscape more desolate as she peered through the carriage windows. The vast expanse of snow was checkered only by gigantic black pines that frowned down upon them, as if questioning why the traveling party dared brave the unseasonable cold.

"Nature is truly a poet whose harmony holds our spirits breathless." Percy peered out the window, wide-eyed as a child. "Would that we could dine forever on this open air, surrounded by this scene."

His eyes sparkled with such life that Mary felt her spirits lift, even as Claire tugged her wool cloak tighter. "You can dine on all the air you want," she scoffed. "Just don't forget that the rest of us mere mortals prefer food with more substance."

Byron planned to catch up with them, but the little group settled without him into the imposing Hôtel d'Angleterre outside the beating heart of Geneva. Mary felt a subtle pang of some unnamed emotion when Percy informed the proprietor that Mary was his wife, and booked them a suite of rooms on the top floor with a view of gleaming Lake Geneva. She smiled a bit to see what he'd written in Greek in the guest book under his name—*Democrat, Philanthropist, and Atheist*. Once the snow stopped, she wished her mother could have witnessed the blue lake sparkling with lively golden beams shot straight from the heavens and the majestic view of towering Mont Blanc, ancient queen of the primeval Alps.

It was paradise, however fleeting.

Leaving an ever more despondent Claire to her own devices and Everina in the company of her new nurse, Mary and Percy amused themselves in the evenings by rowing across the lake to view Switzerland's wild forests that were fit for high adventure and heroic deeds, often not returning until the horned moon hung in the light of the sunset. For the first time in ages, Mary felt as happy as a new-fledged bird and hardly cared what twig she flew to so long as she could try her new-found wings.

Then one dawn, a terrible racket down in the courtyard awoke nearly every guest of the Hôtel d'Angleterre. "What in God's name?" Percy pushed aside the bed-curtains as he fumbled into his nightclothes. Mary keenly felt the absence of him as she, too, slipped her linen nightgown on.

Poking her head out the window, Mary blinked in disbelief at the appearance of an imposing war carriage emblazoned with imperial arms and gaudy iron candleholders. The wooden flagstones of the hotel's courtyard were meant to soften noises from incoming carriages but did nothing to ease the cacophony that erupted below. Eight Newfoundlands bounded alongside the carriage, all braying as if on a royal hunt.

"Has Napoleon himself joined us?" Percy muttered, except Napoleon was exiled to St. Helena.

Mary blinked hard, not trusting her eyes. "Is that a falcon? And peacocks? And *monkeys*?"

"Ho there!" A dark silhouette unfolded itself from the carriage, lifting a hand to greet them as a familiar voice boomed out. "Greetings, Shelley and Godwin! I bade farewell to the land where the gloom of my glory arose. Thus, in Geneva I am born again!"

Next to her, Percy let out a wild whoop of joy. "Byron, old fellow! It's about time you arrived!"

Quickly donning flannel dressing gowns over their night-clothes, Mary and Percy hurried downstairs, rubbing their arms against the unseasonable cold. Their appearances would have been scandalous in England, but they had both agreed to drink deeply from the cup of life here in Geneva. What did it matter if they scandalized people abroad when they would never see any of them again?

"You don't travel light, do you?" Mary asked Byron once they were in the courtyard. The menagerie of dogs and monkeys and birds had been joined by cats—five of them, by Mary's count—a badger, and a goat with a broken leg.

"Well, I did leave behind the bear. I daresay the poor chap will miss our daily walks, but he'll manage." Byron ruffled the goat's floppy ears. The animal responded by chewing some un-lucky flowers from a stone urn. The hotelier's frown softened only slightly as Byron passed him a thick stack of banknotes. "I never travel without my companions. They're my only constant friends."

Mary was struck by the loneliness of this, especially when

she took in the haggard lines of Byron's face and the tired flop of his thick hair. She recalled hearing that he had kept a tame bear when he was at Cambridge, mostly to spite the authorities who had forbidden allowing dogs in student dormitories. There being no statute against bears, Byron had prevailed and considered applying for a college fellowship for the bear. Did this man's audacity know no bounds? Was his loneliness the price of such audacity?

Despite Byron's weariness, his eyes brightened temporarily as he read Percy's bold line in the guest register: "*Democrat, Philanthropist, and Atheist.* Daring, eh, Shelley? You'll set proper British tongues wagging all the way from Switzerland."

Mary wasn't sure whether Byron spoke in pride or warning, but Percy grew an inch taller as they followed England's most infamous poet inside. "The shoe fits."

"Claire is eager to spend time with you." Mary's nudge was an attempt at smoothing things over with Claire. If only Byron would indulge her sister, perhaps they could all find happiness.

"I'm beyond exhausted." Byron punctuated that statement by signing into the guest register and adding a flourish under his age written there, *100.* "But I hope the three of us can take breakfast together in the morning."

The three *of us.* Mary suddenly realized this would not be the happy journey Claire had envisioned. Mary had suspected as much, but Claire was going to be crestfallen.

After exchanging brief bows and curtsies, Byron wended his way to his room. His limp was more pronounced than it had been before, possibly a result of the long journey.

"Where is he?" Claire chose that moment to fly downstairs in a flurry of candy floss pink ruffles, her hair still loosely plaited for bed. "Where is Lord Byron?"

Mary and Percy exchanged a glance. "The poor man is bone-tired after traveling," Percy explained. "We'll see one another in the morning."

Mary averted her eyes as Claire's eyes filled with tears. "Of course," her sister managed to say as she wrapped her arms around herself. "I'm sure it's been a long day for him."

As Mary and Percy made their way back to bed, she could only hope this expedition was the start of something new, for all of them. This trip to Switzerland was a perfect opportunity to seek out new experiences, to *stretch* oneself.

Mary was determined not to squander a moment of it.

A day of nothing can be a gift.

A week of nothing itches under one's skin, each day adding to a trail of nit bites.

A month of nothing? A prison of boredom.

What had been an idyll turned into dead dullness. The Swiss sun rose each morning and by midafternoon their quartet escaped the cramped hotel to seek out the same bland amusements: eating identical meals as those from the day before, rereading the same books, and stretching like indolent cats in the endless sunshine. The only break in the monotony came when Claire sang to them, a new local ballad every night, usually about shepherds, love, flocks, and the sons of kings who fell in love with beautiful shepherdesses. Even Byron was entranced when Claire began her sweet trilling, but their talented songbird was reaching the end of her vast repertoire.

"I shall go mad if I have to stay one more night at this bloody hotel," announced Byron one evening over dinner.

"There is nothing here to fire the imagination," Percy agreed before spearing a roasted potato from Mary's plate, twirling melted Gruyère cheese around it, and popping it into his mouth with a flourish. Mary had to agree—while she enjoyed the countryside, the walled city of Geneva contained no public building to attract the eye, merely uneven narrow streets and ramshackle buildings piled atop stilts along the waterline. "'Tis pleasant, sure enough, but poetry and art cannot feed on *pleasant*. Hence the reason why I've rented a chalet," Percy proclaimed proudly. "The Maison Chapuis on the opposite side of the lake. And the villa behind it—Diodati—is available, Byron, with more than enough space for your circus to spread out. We can even lease a sailboat and moor it in the little harbor in front of the house. Perhaps I can learn to swim, now that we'll finally be safe from all the prying eyes."

Their impromptu decampment added to the red-hot embers of gossip that swirled about them. Word of Percy's incendiary guest book entry had reached Britain's shores, so he was now denounced as an atheist, revolutionary, and even being a lover of men, compliments of the etymology of *philanthropist*. And Percy wasn't the only target—the most recent tattle claimed that the snowy sheets set to dry on Villa Diodati's porch were the Godwin sisters' petticoats, abandoned as Byron took his turns in bed with each of them. There were even rumors that Percy was now sleeping with Claire as well as her sister, which, given the amount of time she spent with both of them, Mary knew to be false. Mary knew she'd brought much of this upon herself, but she fretted that she'd never be able to face London—or her father—again.

Percy's plans for a sailboat were scuttled as the weather became foul, the afternoon winds akin to autumn's gusts as the skies turned gray and churned the quicksilver waters of the lake. News of red snow falling in Italy and a distant volcanic eruption set newspapers to calling this the year without summer. One mid-June evening, incessant rain poured down and lightning ripped apart the heavens, stranding the entire group at Byron's rented Villa Diodati. The wet, uncongenial weather and a ribald discussion on the nature of souls had dissolved into an argument between Claire and Byron, which left a red-faced Claire tripping over her words before she stomped upstairs to lie down. Mary was still constantly amazed at how awkwardly tongue-tied Claire became in his presence despite having scrambled eight hundred miles to unphilosophize Lord Byron—as he liked to characterize their nocturnal amusements.

This left only a pensive trio—and Byron's motley collection of dogs—seated before the fire. Mary craved the comfort of their own chalet, where Everina was safely ensconced with her nurse, but it was impossible to venture out with the rain lashing like incessant whips.

"If God did not create human beings," Shelley argued over the dying crackle of the hearth and the howling wind, "is there not a possibility that humans created the idea of God?"

"I find that idea terribly frightful." Mary loved these philosophical debates that set her mind to whirring. "I don't believe humans are quite capable of such powerful—nor such positive—creations. Why, just examine the war and death and destruction that humans have visited upon one another in recent decades."

"So, you believe in God, then?" Byron asked. Percy looked at her expectantly, so Mary suddenly felt as if her answer were very important.

She prodded the fading fire with the iron poker and tilted her chin. "I believe in something purer than humanity. The fear lodged in so many human hearts causes us to do evil." *Those who gossip about us*, she wanted to add as an example. *Or even my own father and stepmother.* "I marvel at the perfection of my daughter's tiny hands or the beauty of an unfurling rose, and I know that nature is superior to mankind."

Byron nodded. "I, too, embrace the principle that nature is the generative force of the universe."

"But think of all humans are capable of. Can nature create a perfect poem? Or the beauty of a painting or sculpture?" Percy leapt from his chair, more enthusiastic than Mary had seen him during the prior languorous weeks. "Women already create life—why not mankind? Just recently I read of how Dr. Darwin applied an electrical charge to a damp strand of vermicelli and, by some extraordinary means, was able to animate it. It *moved on its own.*"

Mary smiled. Of course science had jolted her beloved from his lassitude.

"My mother dined once with Dr. Darwin, you know," she said as she fed the fire and watched it surge with fresh life. "I believe they shared the same publisher in Joseph Johnson. But, having created life once myself, I can say firstly that I had no part in the design. And secondly, the creation of a human is far more intricate than a strand of vermicelli."

Byron laughed. "I believe this round goes to you, Mary."

Percy merely lifted his glass in salute, his gaze upon her warmer than an afternoon sunburst. "Indeed."

The conversation tapered off until Byron took to reading aloud from a dusty volume of ghost stories—translated from the original German into French—that he'd found in his rented villa. Mary's mind wandered—she preferred the local tale of a priest and his mistress who had died in an avalanche while fleeing persecution and whose plaintive voices were still heard on stormy nights, calling for succor from nearby peasants—until Byron suddenly halted midsentence.

"I've just had the most marvelous idea." The ensuing explosion of dust and noise as Byron threw the book to the wooden floorboard was loud enough to match the thunder outside. It certainly startled the Newfoundland who'd been dozing in front of the hearth. Tippet, was it? Or Teague? Difficult to tell all his dogs apart. "We must have a competition!"

Percy looked up from his papers. From where she sat, Mary could make out his ministrations—no poem this time, only sketches of boats in all shapes and sizes. She wondered what he thought about then, her Elfin Knight who could pass whole days alone on the lake in a little boat, watching the clouds and listening to the rippling of the crystal clear waves. "What manner of competition?"

"A writing competition. One of original ghost stories to put this dreary drivel to shame." Byron nudged the offending volume with the toe of his boot. "We shall each write something new and infinitely terrible. Then we shall select a winner."

Leave it to Lord Byron to choose a contest he believed he could win.

"I'm afraid your competition is rigged." Mary didn't care to insult Byron, but neither did she wish for Percy to plummet deeper down a sinkhole of doubt. He and Byron were friends, yet there was a constant undercurrent of rivalry that ran between them. Poor Percy had been plagued with doubt about his poetry since Byron had joined them this summer. Hence the sailboats tonight instead of stanzas. "For I am no writer."

"Well, we can't have a competition of beauty, dearest Mary, for you'd trounce us all. And you've already proven you can win any debate." Byron began pacing. Mary bit her tongue, annoyed that Byron discounted her. True, she was no writer, but still, it would be polite not to dismiss her so soundly.

"What do you say?" Byron spoke to Percy now. "Original stories, each based upon a supernatural idea?"

"Well . . ." Percy rubbed the back of his neck; Mary could

see shadowy fissures of doubt streaking into his brain and splintering his confidence. Lord Byron might be a renowned poet, but Mary had fallen in love with Percy Shelley. And he'd hooked her with his *words*.

"We'll do it," Mary answered. The statement came as a bit of a shock, both to her and to Percy, if his wide eyes were any gauge.

"Excellent!" Byron whirled to the desk against the wall. After much opening and slamming of drawers, he retrieved blank pages of paper and two reservoir pens, one of which he kept and the other he handed to Shelley. Patting his jacket pockets, he withdrew a nub of a pencil. "I'm afraid I'm out of pens, Mary, but fortunately, I always carry a pencil. One never knows when inspiration will strike."

The pencil he handed her may as well have been an asp. What on earth had she just agreed to?

"Isn't a woman writer already a brand of monster?" It was a critique she'd read once about her mother's works. Honestly, who was she to join a writing competition against Percy Shelley and Lord Byron? As the daughter of *two* persons of distinguished literary celebrity, Mary had thought of writing as a child before quickly discounting the idea, understanding that nothing she wrote could ever compare with her parents' works. Why was she now asking to be insulted? "I doubt I can conjure anything worth reading."

Byron shook his pen at her. "I demand an original story from you, Lady Godwin."

She refused to allow the nickname to sway her. "My skills are slender indeed."

Percy nudged her foot with his. "Mary, you are your mother's daughter. Your veins probably run with ink; you just haven't discovered it yet."

Armed with Byron's pencil, Mary stared at the pristine paper placed before her. One story, meant to curdle the blood and quicken the beatings of the heart. A silly scary story that would never be read outside of this villa. She could do this. Her mother had written scads of stories, entire novels, even.

Five minutes later, Percy had started scrawling something.

Ten minutes beyond that, and Byron's pen was flying across his page.

Still, Mary had nothing.

"How long do we have to write these stories?" she asked, but received only a silent twirl of Percy's hand in response. "Well, then, I shall sleep on it," she announced.

"You must all stay here tonight, of course." Byron barely glanced at the rain-streaked window, where the war in the sky continued with a crash of thunder. Mary missed Everina, but she feared they'd be washed away if they ventured outside.

Neither man looked up as she withdrew.

Once undressed with the candle blown out—how the wags would love to know she was clad in one of Lord Byron's spare nightshirts!—she placed her head on the pillow.

Later, she would claim it had all been a dream, but in truth she was caught in that liminal phase between sleep and wakefulness, a place where dreams and nightmares lurked half-formed.

This was both, and neither, all at the same time.

Unbidden, her mind unspooled a story from the events of the day and cobwebs of moments from the past.

Dr. Darwin's experiments. The debate over creating life. Then, while they picnicked in the shadow of Frankenstein Castle, Percy's retelling of an ill-fated alchemist reanimating corpses.

And when Mary stumbled from her bed and struck a flint to light the candle stub sometime in the middle of the night, her hand was trembling as she set Byron's pencil to paper. It was not the opening line, no, but instead the beating, bloody heart of the story that emerged fully formed in her mind . . .

> *It was on a dreary night of November, that I beheld the accomplishment of my toils. With an anxiety that almost amounted to agony, I collected the instruments of life around me, that I might infuse a spark of being into the lifeless thing that lay at my feet. It was already one in the morning; the rain pattered dismally against the panes, and my candle was nearly burnt out, when, by the glimmer of the half-extinguished light, I saw the dull yellow eye of the creature open.*

CHAPTER 10

❧

August 1794

MARY WOLLSTONECRAFT

How could Gilbert have left without telling me? And when would he return?

More often than not, I stumbled from bed each night and fell into anxious reveries that further agitated and fatigued me, even when the sun finally rose and I was left the arduous task of caring for our three-month-old daughter on my own. Before he'd gone to London, Gil had left instructions with an American friend to provide me with funds until he returned, but, despite having plenty of money, he failed to pay the rent on the house in Le Havre past September. For every stilted letter of Gilbert's—growing ever vaguer—I wrote two, then three, then five.

Did Gilbert expect me to greet him as a sultan when he eventually stopped chasing more money long enough to respond, perhaps after he'd enjoyed half a hundred promiscuous amours during his absence? Despair nipped at my heels, and in my darkest moments I doubted his fidelity. What could possibly keep him from his own daughter and me? My soul was weary and my heart heavy even as my temper flared that he dared treat us so abominably.

The final days of September trickled away still without word from him, so I had to secure new lodgings for Fanny and me. Devoid of friends to lean on now that my French acquaintances either were dead from the revolution or had withdrawn their associations upon the occasion of Fanny's illegitimate birth— my registration as Gil's wife had fooled only the government and not those who had heard me rail against marriage—I moved in with a German family just before the coldest winter on record set in. That season was so frigid that many Parisians burned their furniture to stay warm as wood grew prohibitively expensive. Bread prices skyrocketed as they had before the Revolution, and meat became rarer than diamonds.

Finally, a letter from Gilbert arrived. Its terse language informed me he sought more money before he could return to France. That was it—no apologies or explanations. As if he'd just gone for a summer jaunt down the lane instead of decamping to another country.

To which I responded:

> *How I hate this crooked business! When you first entered into these plans, you bounded your views to the gaining of a thousand pounds. It was sufficient to have procured a farm in America, which would have been an independence. You find now that you did not know yourself and that a certain situation in life is more necessary to you than you imagined. I know what to found my happiness on—it is not money.*
>
> *Perhaps this is the last letter you will ever receive from me.*

I sent the scathing rebuke, then immediately regretted my harsh words after I dropped them in the post. But there was nothing to be done for it, given that I promptly succumbed to the most violent illness I'd ever experienced.

Exacerbated by my exhaustion and the want of wood for our fireplace, a hellish fever devoured me, and a galloping consumption quickly infiltrated my lungs so I was unable even to write without stopping frequently to recollect myself. The physician called by the German couple instructed me to write to my husband and make final arrangements for my daughter.

Barely able to breathe or rise from my cot, I feared I would die and leave Fanny alone in this cold world. So, I wrote to Gilbert again, instructing him that should anything happen to me, I would leave Fanny in the German couple's care.

Did I hope to goad him into returning to me? Perhaps. Instead, Gilbert's brief response—more note than letter—could have persuaded me to swim to Calicut.

I'm sorry to hear of your illness. Business alone has kept me from you. Come to any British port and I will fly down to my two dear girls with a heart all their own.

I didn't yearn for London as I once had—I knew the social horrors Fanny would experience if people learned that Gilbert and I weren't truly married, and I understood that my girl would grow up freer in France—but how could I resist?

Once my hellish fever finally broke, I waited impatiently for winter to loosen its grasp for a smooth sailing across the Channel. Fanny and I were scarred from our recent bouts of illness—her skin would never recover and my left eye had acquired a slight but perpetual droop. Unaccustomed to worrying about my appearance, I fretted over what Gil would say when he saw us, but there was nothing to be done about it. In the meantime,

I focused on getting well, weaning Fanny on bread crusts now that her teeth had come in, and entrusting the good people of Le Havre to sell our furniture before we sailed for London on April 9.

It had been eight months since I'd last seen Gilbert. I knew not what to expect upon seeing him again.

However, when we disembarked two days later, I *did* expect him to be waiting for us in Dover. Once again, I was disappointed. Perhaps he had gotten the day wrong, or more likely, he was detained by some business dealing or other. Surrounded once again by Cockney and English accents, and taking in the sensible English fashions and plain shop signs, I took a deep breath as Fanny began to fuss.

The coach I hired came to a stop outside the elegantly furnished house at 26 Charlotte Street in Soho. My stomach swirled with nerves as the door opened and Gilbert strode down the imposing stone steps. His hair had grown a little longer in the interlude since I'd last seen him, but he looked vibrant and healthy. "There's your papa," I whispered to Fanny as I dandled my darling little squirrel on my lap, her intelligent smile making my heart soar. "There is our happiness."

Except the man who opened the coach seemed a wooden marionette compared to the man I'd known and loved. "I trust you had a pleasant journey," was his milk-and-water greeting. "I've had a room arranged for you and Fanny so you may lie down."

Damn me, but I scarcely stopped my jaw from dropping. Was this another fever dream? I'd envisioned Gilbert sweeping me down from the coach and tossing our daughter into the air in the way of fathers everywhere.

This cool stranger? He was a creature I had never imagined.

"We've waited more than half a year to see you, Gilbert." I searched his face and the way he held himself so stiffly, anything for a clue as to how we'd displeased him. "We can wait to lie down."

"I only wish to be of assistance." His gaze slid from mine. "Henceforth I shall try to do my duty to both you and Fanny. I have business to attend to this afternoon—"

"Neither Fanny nor I wish to be a burden." I recoiled at his cold manner and the revelation that he was already leaving. I had no need to be loved like a goddess, but I wished to be necessary to him. "Is it because of our disfigurement? If you don't want us here—"

"No, of course it's not that. We'll live here together, just as you wished." He touched Fanny's ruined skin with such tenderness that I nearly wept. "The ship that carried our Bourbon platters is missing." His voice had gone low. "I cannot ignore so grave a matter simply because it coincides with your arrival. I'm sorry. Please make yourself comfortable in my absence."

Then he jammed a black fur-felt top hat onto his head and strode stiffly away.

I understood that Gil believed our financial future hinged on that damnable Bourbon silver—he'd be unable to continue his current business ventures once we were settled in America, and thus, he craved the financial security it would bring—but still I visited Johnson to see if my old friend might offer an advance that would cover our passage to America and still leave enough to purchase a small farm. "That's a mighty sum," Johnson said after I'd told him my request. I'd refused his offer to sit and barely glanced around the office with its floor-to-ceiling bookshelves that had once been so soothing. "Are you sure that Imlay still wishes to move to America? From what I hear, he's made quite a name for himself in the smuggling business."

That was decidedly *not* what I wanted to hear.

"Never mind," I said to Johnson. "I'm sorry to have troubled you."

I ignored Johnson calling my name as I shut the door. Perhaps this was one situation where my writing couldn't save me.

Thus, the days turned to weeks and Gilbert still spent virtually all his time away from us. He missed Fanny's first word—*mama* and her parrot-word addition of *come*, which always had me hurrying to her side—plus her introduction to leading strings. When he began to disappear at night and refused to tell me where he had been, my dark moods lurched into a terrible paralysis. Whereas I had always been moved to action when confronted with an obstacle—my base upbringing, my desire to be published, even France's revolution—now I could only weep. I recognized Gilbert's refusal to spend time with me—much less visit my bed—for what it was.

Rejection. The wings of his passion for me had been clipped.

I felt almost as tormented as I had during long winter nights in Hoxton, lying outside my mother's door after my father had fled to a pub following his violent fits of temper. Sorrow over this realization cast a mildew over all my prior gilded hopes so that I yearned to escape from this hell of anguish I now endured. Our illnesses, the move, and raising Fanny alone had finally taken their toll. I'd entered that terrible realm of exhaustion where I was too weary even to sleep.

I craved peace. An asylum to rest in.

The laudanum left to me by the German couple's physician was still at the bottom of my travel portmanteau, the liquid inside the glass vial the same rusty color of the old blood that had stained the cobblestones of Paris. It was bitter, and I thought of my mother when I swallowed it.

So, too, was life bitter.

I knew not how much was a normal dose. All I know is I awoke sometime later to Gilbert's frantic, faraway voice and the wrenching pain of a black-garbed figure forcing my jaw open.

Something warm and viscous and tasting of ashes poured down my throat. Moments later, I was vomiting forcefully into a chamber pot.

"Thank God," Gilbert exclaimed when I collapsed back on sweat-drenched pillows. The physician had pronounced me out of danger and left. Gilbert's eyes were wide with concern. "What did you do, Mary? Can you imagine what would have happened to me if you'd taken your own life? And what about Fanny?"

My heart convulsed at the thought of Fanny. I'd never intentionally cause my daughter any harm.

"I only wished to sleep." My body was so burdened by sadness, yet my soul opened one exhausted eye when Gilbert touched my brow to move a tendril of hair from my forehead. "I imagined us a happy family, reunited here in London. Nothing is as I hoped."

"Surely I don't hold such power over you, Mary."

You do, I nearly said, but something held me back. I'd been called immoral and insane for flouting society's expectations, a hyena for my thoughts regarding women's rights, and a whore by my Parisian acquaintances when they learned I was unmarried and with child. It had been enough to make me wonder if I'd chosen the right path in refusing to marry Gil, yet I'd taken solace that I was standing by my convictions. I'd borne all that, but there wouldn't be enough laudanum in the world to ease my pain if Gilbert ever truly cast me off.

I refused to believe that my summer with Gil was over, only that a storm cloud had passed overhead and we could recover our happiness, if we tried.

"I can't go on like this," I said to him. "I *cannot*."

He rubbed his chin. "That is why I have something to ask of you." I thought perhaps he meant to revisit the subject of marriage, and found my traitorous heart eager to broach the one subject that might still prove his devotion. Could I stomach the hypocrisy of setting aside my convictions now, of subsuming myself to him in order to guarantee his lasting commitment to us? Then: "Something important that I cannot trust with anyone else."

So, not marriage. Still, I sat up straighter, to better give him my full attention. "What is it?"

"I require someone to travel to Scandinavia to locate our Bourbon silver. I'd go myself, but I'm needed here in London . . ."

I stared at him, unnerved by the monumental task suddenly laid at my feet. "But I have Fanny to care for."

"There's no one else I can trust, Mary. I know I'm asking the impossible . . ."

Indeed. No one traveled to Scandinavia—it was an obscure destination still marked with northern monsters in the seas of geographical grammars. No Englishwoman in her right mind would trek there alone, much less with a small child. My gut reaction was to refuse, except . . .

Perhaps this was just one more way of society keeping women fearful and in their place. What was stopping a woman from traveling to another country on her own? Especially if it was to secure her family's future happiness?

With that thought in my head, I touched two fingers to his lips. I hesitated, but somehow my heart told me this was right. Terrifying, but *right*. This was something only I could do for Gilbert. So I would. "I'll make arrangements as soon as I am well."

I'd do this for him, for *us*—hunting down the fortune that would bring us together and whisk us away to the dreamland of America.

I didn't say it now—not when my throat hitched as Gilbert kissed the tips of my fingers—but when I returned to England triumphant and flush with our fortune, we would move to Ohio. I would *insist* on it.

Then we'd be happy. Just as we'd always planned.

Gilbert would have been perfectly at ease in Sweden, given its morbid fascination with commerce—the entire city was obsessed with making money, whereas I only wished to procure us a small farm far away from Europe's many sordid problems.

Fanny had learned to talk in earnest and spent much of the rain-swept voyage—when we weren't being tossed about without going forward—calling for her absent papa to *come, come*. We didn't see any monsters, but the gray sky growled overhead when we finally disembarked among the iron-sinewed rocks of Gothenburg. My spirits lifted when we arrived at the house of Gilbert's business associate, Elias Backman, whose comfortable home was clean (although sprigs of juniper were scattered over the floor in a strange country custom) and packed to the ceiling beams with a menagerie of vivacious children. I felt a painful shard of longing. How could Gilbert not want this comfortable domesticity too? Perhaps the problem with our relationship was that I felt everything so keenly and constantly strove to be closer to Gil, whereas he had replaced his passion for *us* with a passion for more money.

It might have been best if I learned to temper the strongest of my emotions and appreciate the current joys in life, rather than always turn my eye to the future.

Thus, instead of writing to Gilbert, I spent my days eating

salmon and anchovies, devouring bowls of wild strawberries with cream, and sipping on sweet cordials. Given that the northern summer evening meant I could write until midnight without lighting a candle, I filled several notebooks with my observations of life in Sweden and Norway: the strange child-rearing practice of giving brandy to babies (which I refused for Fanny's sake), the bucolic banks of wildflowers whose sweetness was overridden by the stink of putrefying herrings that were used as manure, and even my trip to the town of Tønsberg in Norway to track down one of Imlay's former employees. That was a day's ferry ride north and I went without Fanny, leaving her with the Backmans' nursemaid.

Tucked deep into my gray woolen greatcoat, the boisterous sea and briny air braced me as I traveled through a wild fjord filled with seals sunning themselves and colorful starfish thickening the water. Upon arriving in the town, the mayor—who had been alerted by the affluent Backmans as to the nature of my journey—assured me he would make inquiries on my behalf. "Please," he insisted in serviceable English, his teeth spoiled early by an overabundance of rye and coffee and spices, "leave everything to me. You can take in the sights while you wait. Visitors to our town often find the church with its mummies of great interest."

That was how I found myself inside the stone church and staring at a macabre display of embalmed bodies of the nobility in their coffins, my stomach churning at the human petrifications meant to remain until the Day of Judgment. Their names had long since scattered to the winds of time, but the teeth, skin, and nails were whole without the black appearance of Egyptian mummies.

Ashes to ashes, I thought as I recoiled from the sight. *Dust to dust.*

Nothing is so ugly as the human form when deprived of life. How I would hate to see a form I loved—embalmed in my heart—so sacrilegiously handled.

It was natural that our bodies would decay, but it was the soul that mattered. And having had plenty of time on this journey for reflection, I understood now that the garden of my soul needed to be watered by freedom and enriched with love. The only question as I fled those ruined bodies was whether I could keep both in my grip with Gilbert—we'd once had love, but I had rejected marriage on account of losing my freedom. Now I had my freedom but feared I'd lost Gilbert's love.

The Bourbon silver was the key to my happiness, I knew it.

Imagine my dismay when Mayor Wulfsberg approached, a downcast expression on his face. "I'm afraid that Captain Ellefson, whom Mr. Imlay had entrusted with his silver, has long since traveled south to Risor," he said in heavily accented English.

"Risor?"

"Indeed. That is the last place anyone has reported seeing Mr. Imlay's ship."

"And you believe I'll be able to recover the silver there?"

Mayor Wulfsberg sucked his rotting teeth, then shook his head. "It is my opinion that Ellefson has stolen the silver. I doubt you'll be able to recover any of it," he informed me somberly. "Although I wish you the best of luck."

I pondered whether to admit defeat and return to London then—I was certainly out of my element in Scandinavia, where I didn't even speak the language and was forced to rely on the kindness of strangers, most of whom were intensely curious about a woman traveling alone. But if the Bourbon silver was my last hope for salvaging the dream of America with Gilbert, then I'd hike my way to Timbuktu to find it.

I collected Fanny from the Backmans and set forth once

again by sea, sailing along the wild coast until arriving at Risor with its rustic white houses crouched along what might have been a charming harbor, had I not felt so bastilled by nature. Ellefson met Fanny and me in a smallish sort of inn. Imlay's associate seemed a regular type of seaworthy man, unkempt hair bleached from the sun and his skin leathered like a man soaked too long in brine. "Now, that's a pretty little lass you have there," he said once we were seated at a table in the corner, the thick fug of pipe smoke making my eyes water. Two glasses of brandy and a loaf of rye bread were set out, but I couldn't stomach the foul slices, so hard they might have been baked only once a year. "Reminds me of my Bonnie at home, plus her two sisters."

"Fanny and I have become quite the traveling companions." I bounced her on my knee and gave her a spoon to play with, which she promptly put in her mouth. Eschewing the practice of giving girls dolls to play with, I instead encouraged my daughter to sport in the open air and had noticed the positive effects of exercise in nature upon both of us during this expedition. I'd gained more confidence after learning that I could travel the world with this small piece of me in tow. Fanny and I could rely just on each other. "Of course, we came all this way from England to reclaim our silver. I assume you still have it, or at least the payment you meant to send to Mr. Imlay?"

Ellefson's gaze slid from mine. "I'm afraid the expenses I ran into with the ship, and with the silver as my only raft . . ."

A cold grip seized me. "What are you saying?"

"It's gone." He set down his brandy and tapped two fingers on the table. "I'm sure you understand, ma'am, the need to settle accounts and take care of one's family. I only did what any man would have in my situation."

My God, I thought. *We've lost everything.*

"I'll bring charges against you." That cold grip turned into a fiery furnace stoked by rage. I had no understanding of the legal system here in Sweden, but surely admitting to swindling someone out of a king's fortune in silver would lead to some sort of restitution. Not enough to buy a farm in Ohio, perhaps, but a start . . .

Ellefson cleared his throat. "You'll never be able to bring forward sufficient proof to convict me—I covered my tracks well. And the expense in doing so would be prohibitive."

"I'll write to the foreign minister and demand a legal settlement." My voice clotted and spoiled around the words. My hands were shaking so that Fanny noticed and started to fuss. "Imlay and I trusted you, Ellefson. And you betrayed us."

Ellefson had the gall to tip his hat at me. Had we not been discussing the very future of my happiness, he might have been mistaken for a polite Sunday churchgoer. "I'm sorry, ma'am, but I'm afraid I don't know anything about the silver you mention. You've mistaken me for a different man."

With that, he stood and strode away. I wanted to scream at him until my voice turned raw, but a hysterical woman never gains any ground. Instead, I turned that night to my most powerful weapon: my pen.

I wrote to the foreign minister as I'd threatened, demanding assistance in the matter.

His response? That I had no proof, and even if Ellefson was guilty—which he was—he'd be sentenced to only forty days' confinement on bread and water. However, no court of law would find in my favor without evidence. Aside from Ellefson's confession, which he would surely deny in court, I had nothing.

I'd come all the way to Sweden and lost Gilbert's silver.

And my dreams too.

I did not write ahead to Gilbert with the dour news. No, instead I hoped to convince him that the evaporation of the silver didn't mean the disappearance of our future in America, except that wasn't the sort of thing one could be persuaded of via letter. All the way to London, I rehearsed a litany of plans to persuade Gil to move to Ohio.

Such a slave I'd been to hope and fear. I needed to be pragmatic—there was a solution, if only I labored enough to find it.

Despite his earlier concerns about Gil's financial endeavors, I knew I could convince Johnson to offer me more advances for any book I chose to write. Readers would be interested in the Swedes' strange habits and customs, especially those mummies I'd recoiled from. I'd turn my notes on Sweden into a travelogue, the likes of which were starting to become popular. That was a start.

Except, upon arriving in Gothenburg, I received several letters from Gilbert, each one a spear to the heart. Apparently, he had learned from his associates in Sweden that the silver was gone. Without our fortune, he coldly claimed we had no future and implored me—for the sake of my own happiness—to see how different we were, then informed me he'd do his duty to Fanny and that he'd still try to cherish tenderness to me, which was why he'd rented us a house in London, the address of which he'd enclosed in his final letter.

Try to cherish tenderness to me? After all our shared history?

Had I not known Gilbert to be rational to a fault, I'd have believed his pessimistic letters to be caused by the news of his loss of fortune. More so, I was irked that he used the excuse of *my* happiness when making these decisions for *us*. Who made him—or any man—the exclusive judge of what would bring me—or any woman, for that matter—happiness? I contemplated writing to Johnson and asking him to procure me alternate lodgings, but I held out a final hope, especially for Fanny's sake, that Gil would realize the error of his ways by the time we returned home. Regardless, I was determined that we come to a permanent solution, either to come together or, much as it might sink me, part forever.

Fanny and I arrived in England during the first week in October. A pale lavender dusk cooled the heavens by the time we arrived at the address Gilbert provided. I expected him to be there, but there wasn't even an umbrella or well-worn jacket on the hall rack; not even his books lined the empty shelves in the front room.

Instead, a dour-faced housemaid—one of three liveried servants who greeted us in the tiny hall—conveyed Gilbert's cold instructions. "Mr. Imlay said that you're to let him know via a letter to his offices if there was anything else you or the child require."

"And when will Mr. Imlay return home?"

The ruddy-cheeked kitchen maid tittered behind her hand. "Mr. Imlay doesn't live here, ma'am."

"This house is just meant for his former mistress," the housemaid muttered as her lip lifted in revulsion. "And his bastard daughter."

I reeled back in shocked outrage, then quavered on my feet as the horrible realization crashed into me: Gilbert hadn't even had the decency—or courage—to sever the ties between us face-to-face. He had abandoned me, but worse, he had abandoned his daughter.

And in giving up the charade of our marriage, he had condemned us.

The kitchen maid shifted from foot to foot. "Ma'am, is there anything else you need?"

I let my kiss on Fanny's forehead linger, praying I could keep my composure stitched together long enough to avoid falling apart in front of these women. "I need to know where Mr. Imlay resides."

No one responded. The cook pushed a graying tendril of flyaway hair back from her wide forehead. "We don't know his address." The way her gaze slid to the side told me she was lying.

These women obviously condemned my own moral turpitude, but to condemn Fanny too? A swell of emotion threatened to overwhelm me; I diverted that intensity of feeling into my argument. "I have a young daughter who is not being treated honorably by her father. It isn't fair or just that a man can cast off a woman and her child with merely a note. Please . . . I must speak with Mr. Imlay and persuade him to do right by us."

The haughty housemaid sniffed again. "We're under strict orders not to tell you anything. Mr. Imlay pays our salaries, not you."

"I can't lose this post, ma'am," the cook said, but I felt her wavering in the way she glanced at Fanny, who had laid her rosy cheek upon my shoulder, blissfully unaware of the war I was waging. For her, for *us*.

"I won't mention you." My voice remained surprisingly steady. "In fact, it's quite likely that Mr. Imlay's business associates in Sweden let his new address slip in conversation."

The woman rubbed her hands on her apron. "I don't know, ma'am. This is all so irregular—"

"Please."

Like a spinning coin, I could see she tilted from side to side before finally heaving a sigh. "Mr. Imlay is living with his current mistress. All the way across town."

And there it was. My steadfast devotion had made me blind, and I felt a fool for not seeing that Gil's passions had finally gone cold. Rather than discovering the bedrock of our friendship, his feelings had turned to indifference. I had been duped by my own sincere, affectionate heart into believing that we would be happy together.

How wrong I had been.

The kitchen maid's airy blathering about the shows that Gilbert's actress performed with a strolling company of players became a dull droning buried somewhere in my brain, its reverberation turning my skin bloodless.

"Do you need to sit, ma'am?" The cook nudged a stool my way. "You look quite pale."

Pale from the force it took to restrain my rage. My voice came out a whisper. "What is the address?"

Fortunately, the woman didn't argue this time—she must have realized I could easily procure the address of some actress. "I'll mind your daughter while you visit Mr. Imlay, ma'am," she said. "No child should have to hear her parents argue."

Thankful for that small kindness that I hadn't been afforded as a child, I kissed Fanny one last time before halting in front of the sniffy housemaid. "I expect you to be out of this house before I return," I said to her. "No one calls my daughter a bastard."

Then I was out the door and flagging down a carriage.

I know not how long the trip took. When I finally arrived, I banged on Gilbert's door and called his name—once, twice, thrice—in a voice loud enough to wake the heavens. What did I care about making a scene? For too long women had allowed men to run roughshod over them. My happiness and Fanny's were at stake. I would not let Gilbert go peacefully into the night.

Gilbert's face appeared in the glass pane to the side of the entrance. His eyes narrowed as he swung open the door.

"Get inside," he commanded.

I considered remaining where I was, but my aim in persuading Gilbert wouldn't happen with both of us arguing from opposite sides of his doorstep. My resolve was further fueled by the appearance of a woman with a cockatiel's painted cheeks and a tigress's fierce glare. The *actress*. I noted then her black dress and Spanish hat with its yellow satin lining and three ostrich feathers and also that Gilbert was dressed in tails, his cravat freshly tied. Probably readying to attend an opera or symphony. "I won't have her in my house, Gilbert," the actress declared. "Send her away."

Gilbert ignored her. "I should have known you wouldn't leave well enough alone," he said to me once the door closed behind us. "Haven't I done enough, Mary? You claimed you needed freedom and refused to marry me, but now you deny me my own freedom? Has the philosopher turned hypocrite?"

I reared back, for I was not the villain here! Yet some dark part of me writhed as Gilbert's words hit their target. I *had* refused Gilbert's hand and espoused ideals of independence, which now wounded both Fanny and me. But so, too, had I written of duty and responsibility.

Remember Fanny. Your daughter needs her father.

"You assume that I still want you as my lover, Gilbert, which I do not," I lied, refusing to so much as flick my gaze in the direction of the cat-eyed—and far younger—woman who now shared his bed. "No, I'm here to remind you that you are no longer a fresh young man who can flit through life without taking care of his responsibilities. The choices you've made resulted in the creation of your daughter, who loves you very much." My voice trembled. Children often forged a more permanent connection between a couple than love; I prayed that bond would return Gilbert to his senses. My daughter needed a father who was part of her life. "Fanny calls for you constantly, asking where her papa is. You should live with her, with *us*." I swallowed the bile rising in my throat. *For you, Fanny.* "Keep your mistress if you want, but in a separate house. Come home to your family, Gilbert. Do right by your daughter."

Do right by me, I wanted to add, for I was no better than a poor moth fluttering around the candle that singes its wings. Gilbert tugged at his cravat and I knew he wavered then—he wasn't a bad man, just a restless one who chased whatever caught his attention. Once, it had been me he chased, but I hadn't realized that gift for what it was.

Gilbert crossed his arms, that stoic facade cracking. I saw it, but so did his mistress.

"I will not have you live with her, Gilbert," she said. "You belong with me."

"Would you separate a father from his daughter?" I felt myself unhinging and gave a wild little laugh. "Would you prefer we all moved here together?"

The chit only turned up her pert nose at me. "I'd sooner slit my throat. What sort of woman shows up on another's doorstep and demands her lover back? Where is your self-respect? My father walked out on my mother and never sent us a farthing—you should be grateful that Gilbert provided a household for you. Many women would kill for such generosity."

How I wished we women could see that allowing men to pit us against one another only weakened all of us! Would that we could buoy one another during the worst of our personal storms. But I'd never receive any succor from Gilbert's actress, not as she glowered at me from beneath her face paint and feathers. "And when he casts you off as well?" I didn't blame this woman, merely wanted to prepare her to stand in my shoes one day. "What then? Do you have an education to fall back on?" *Of course not, because we women are so rarely educated. No, society keeps us cowed and in our places.* I waved a hand to Gilbert's well-appointed house. "Perhaps a profession besides the stage to pay for all this?"

"If you don't send her packing," the woman growled to Gilbert, "I will."

Instead, I opened the door myself. Then: "You're not the man I thought you were, Gilbert."

"That was always the problem," he answered. "As I recall, I'm only 'stupidly useful to the stupid.'"

I didn't fully understand his throwing my words back at me as I emerged into darkness. Gilbert had always been all I'd ever wanted, even if I'd sometimes wished he were less focused on business and pecuniary interests. I understood only one thing as I felt my moth's wings burn away in the flame of his words.

I'd *failed*.

My daughter was doomed to a pitiful life of censure, culminating in the day she discovered her own father had rejected her. She would forever be called a bastard by housemaids and the like.

Already exhausted from my illness and Fanny's and then traipsing all over Sweden for Gilbert, my grief was such that I couldn't think straight—I knew only that I could never overcome the shame Gilbert had heaped upon Fanny and me, that I would not force myself on him again. I'd loved him with my entire being, but I had no other recourse—Gilbert and I had never married, and he could treat me as he wished. However, I knew that beneath his harshness he would always do right by Fanny, at least financially. So long as I was alive, Gilbert was content to leave me to raise her. Alone.

But if I were gone . . .

Gilbert would claim Fanny, I knew it. He wasn't so cruel as to abandon her to an orphanage and, much as I railed against the unfairness of it, society would be kinder to a child raised by her father than her unwed mother.

My little girl would be better off without me. And I would rather encounter a thousand deaths than face another night like this.

My cloak snapping in the breeze, I hurried as if chased by a sharp-fanged monster down the lamplit street to the river. As I hired a man to row me west to Putney and listened to murky waters lapping at the hull beneath a black and comfortless sky, I felt suddenly serene.

Tonight, I'd be set free. So, too, would Fanny.

When the boat arrived at the landing, rain lashed down in a perfect mirror of the sentiment of my soul. "You're sure this is right, miss?" the boatman asked from beneath the gutter of his cap, eerily reminding me of the coachman who had once deposited me in front of St. Paul's Square, my first unpublished manuscript in my bag and my eyes wide with dreams of the future.

"Yes, I'm sure." I paid the boatman six shillings before setting off along the deserted banks to the hill to Putney Bridge. Another halfpenny in the toll box, and the arched stone structure yawned before me. Rain streamed into my eyes—what need had I of tears when nature would furnish them—and my sodden skirts made each step heavy, meaningful. I stopped halfway across the rain-deserted bridge.

The corrupt monster that had nipped my heels silently fell back as I climbed over the railing. My soul settled to see the gray waves churning before me, their whitecaps big with promises of sleep and rest and peace. It seemed impossible that I should cease to exist, that the restless spark of my spirit could ever entirely go out. No, something that resided in my heart would always watch over my daughter.

My last thought was of Fanny's vibrant future unrolling like the verdant fields of Ohio.

Then I stepped over the edge.

CHAPTER 11

❦

July 1816

MARY GODWIN

His yellow skin scarcely covered the work of muscles and arteries beneath; his hair was of a lustrous black, and flowing; his teeth of a pearly whiteness; but these luxuriances only formed a more horrid contrast with his watery eyes, that seemed almost of the same colour as the dun white sockets in which they were set, his shrivelled complexion, and straight black lips.

The words rolled so fast into her head that Mary's pen could scarcely keep up; the vision brought to mind her mother's descriptions of the embalmed bodies she'd viewed in Sweden and her visceral revulsion at seeing such a treason against humanity. Mary had risen before the sun, the next scene buzzing in her head, and the words swarmed to the paper as if they were just as eager for creation as the monster roaming her imagination. Except who really was the monster in this story? Mary could *see* the pale student of unhallowed arts kneeling beside the soulless thing he had stitched together. In her mind's eye, the hideous phantasm of a man was stretched out and then, on the working of some powerful engine, showed signs of life, and stirred with an uneasy, half-vital motion.

The story had transported her out of this world, but now,

back in her own rented house with a breakfast tray set before her in the dining room, Mary reread her most recent sentences. Instead of having her inventor regard his completed work with pride—as she was sure Shelley and Byron would have done—she planned to have him abandon his creation of human petrification in horror. Mary understood all too well Frankenstein's creation, his anger and abject sadness at being abandoned. Her own life informed his deepest fears and loneliness.

No father to watch my infant days, no mother to bless me with smiles or caresses . . .

She set aside the pages, needing a moment to breathe and separate herself from her words. The tale of Frankenstein's creature had taken on a life of its own. She could as easily stop writing it as she could tell her lungs to stop breathing.

"Ugh!"

Claire's exclamation from her side of the table wasn't the first of the morning, nor did Mary believe it would be the last. However, given that this was the latest in a long litany of exasperated utterances, Mary forced herself to look up reluctantly from her writings. "Yes?"

"When will you be done? If I stay cooped up much longer, I swear I shall go mad."

"You could try your hand at the story competition," Mary said patiently.

To which Claire responded with a giant huff of air and clambered from her chair, her breakfast of baked eggs and clotted cream untouched before her. "I have no talent at writing. I didn't realize you had a passion for it either. In truth, I'm impressed that you have the mettle to compete against Byron and Percy."

Mary wasn't sure it was mettle so much as madness. And she

supposed she *had* been neglecting Claire in favor of writing. So: "What would you like to do?"

With a gamine smile, Claire claimed the seat closest to Mary and rested her elbows on her knees. "We could go shopping."

Mary bent back over her writing. She'd cared little for shopping in England, still less now that they were in Geneva and their every venture out of the villas was fodder for gossip. "Need I remind you of our budget?"

"You sound like my mother." Claire's lower lip jutted out in a pretty pout. "I need a few things: tiny white cambric dresses and perhaps even some little pantalettes. Of course, I won't need them for another nine months. Less, actually."

Mary's head snapped up. "No, Claire. Say it isn't true . . ."

Claire's grin might have cleft her face in two as she leaned back and pressed a hand to her still-flat belly. "It *is* so. I'm carrying Byron's child."

Damnare. Mary rubbed the bridge of her nose and forced a deep breath. Byron's interest in Claire had been fleeting indeed; she wasn't sure he'd visited Claire's bed at all in the past two weeks, although he *had* become overly friendly with one of the handsome stable hands at Villa Diodati, lending credence to the stories of Byron and his male schoolmates. This did not bode well, no matter what cozy domestic scenes Claire was already envisioning.

"How did Byron react when you told him?"

Claire cleared her throat. "That doesn't matter. I'm sure he'll come around to the idea. After he's had a chance to think on it for a while."

Mary dropped her tone an octave. "What did he *say*, Claire?"

Claire tried to tilt that pert little nose of hers into the air, an effect marred by her wobbling chin. "He claims he can't be sure whether the child is his."

"What?" Was there more to Claire's nocturnal adventures than even Mary knew? Surely not—Claire would have told her. "Is the child his? Or not?"

Claire scowled. "I've shared no other man's bed. It's his."

"Then he's trying to shirk his duties." Even Mary was taken aback by the violent swell of emotion that carried her up and into the corridor, her story momentarily abandoned in the face of this real-life monster.

"Where are you going?" Claire called, but Mary ignored her sister, and Claire didn't seem inclined to follow.

While Mary and Percy weren't married, there had never been any doubt that he would provide for their daughter. Byron had more money than he could ever spend, and yet he would circumvent his duties? And insinuate that Claire was no better than a prostitute who bedded a different man every night?

Some people might have feared lofty Lord Byron. But Mary was ready to give the self-centered poet a drubbing he'd never forget.

"Mary?" Percy poked his head out from the sitting room as she passed. Despite being clad only in his slippers and dressing gown, Percy had no qualms about following her, his hair still disheveled from sleep. "Where are you going?"

"Claire is with child," she ground out from between clenched teeth. "Byron is the father, but he refuses to acknowledge his role in the whole fiasco."

Percy blanched the color of curdled milk, and Mary thought he would surely retreat, unwilling to face down the friend he revered. Instead, he matched her pace. "Byron will be in his gardens at this hour. Feeding his menagerie."

Percy was correct. Mary didn't care when the monkeys

outside Villa Diodati shrieked and scampered away at their sudden appearance, leaving Byron alone and holding a basket of strawberries. Ever vain, his burgundy Albanian jacket was crisply pressed and his hair was perfectly coiffed this morning, a result of the curl papers Mary knew he wore each night. Byron merely raised an eyebrow as he took in Percy's footwear and disorderly appearance. "Well, well," he said. "To what do I owe this early pleasure? Come to update me on the progress of your stories?"

She clenched and unclenched her hands. "How dare you."

Byron took a rabid bite of strawberry. "I'm afraid you'll have to be more specific. How dare I what?"

"You get my sister with child and then abandon her?" She shook her head as he opened his mouth. "Don't try to deny it—Claire told me everything."

Next to her, Percy crossed his arms over his dressing gown. "You'd better start talking, Byron."

Byron stared at them, then made an exasperated sound lodged somewhere between a growl and a groan. "And just the other day I dared to write down in my pocketbook that I was happy. I should have known better than to believe it would last." He sighed. "I'll admit it's *possible* that I'm the brat's father. Claire might be a talented singer, but I never loved that odd-headed girl nor even pretended to love her. Still, a man is a man, and if a girl of eighteen comes prancing to you at all hours of the night—there is but one way . . ." He flung the remaining strawberries to the ground. Geese came honking and running in search of an easy breakfast. No matter where Byron went, chaos always followed. "However, for all I know," he added, with a finger pointed at Percy, "*you* might be the father."

"*What?*" Mary could barely form the word over the sudden roaring in her ears.

Percy's neck had turned a violent shade of scarlet. "Watch yourself, Byron."

Lord Byron merely fluttered a long-fingered hand, the sun hitting the thick gold-and-ruby ring he wore like a sunburst. "It's what everyone says, you know, and Claire told me that she was once infatuated with you. God, if you could hear her, droning on and on and *on* about your greatness."

Mary held up a trembling hand. She couldn't believe Byron would give credence to the rumormongers, not when they crafted such horrific tales about his own life. "Not another word. You are the father, and by God, you *will* support your son or daughter."

"I will not."

Mary gaped. Byron was a grown man acting the part of an ill-behaved toddler. "You claim to be a revolutionary and espouse the ideals of equality? Yet you'd abandon your own child and leave its mother to do both your jobs?"

"If it means severing my connection to that ridiculous stepsister of yours, then yes. Claire is not your equal, Mary, but surely she can figure things out. God knows many other women before her have walked the same path and lived to tell the tale."

"No one is asking you to marry her, Byron," Percy said. "Just own up to your responsibilities. As a man of honor."

"I have no intention of resuming my dalliance with Claire Godwin. It's been nearly two weeks since I've done so. There is no need for me to maintain any connection to so silly a woman, ad infinitum."

"Then I'll settle an allowance on Claire, for her and the child." Percy's fists were at his side. "It's the least I can do, given that I condoned this *dalliance* with you. And Mary and I will help her raise your child."

Mary stared at Percy, her heart swelling with simultaneous

pride and horror. They could scarcely afford what Percy was proposing, but he was doing the noble thing. And she loved him for it, even if she wished they might have discussed such a decision privately.

"You will do no such thing." Byron's eyes narrowed. "I'll not have it said that others had to step in and take care of my responsibilities."

"Then do your duty," Percy said. "Enough of this infantile tantrum."

Mary barely swallowed her exasperation. Byron wanted nothing to do with said *responsibilities* until Percy made him feel small. He was no better than a dog, marking his territory. She wondered if Percy had known this would be his reaction all along.

"No kin of mine will be raised by Bohemians." Byron's continued declaration had Mary wanting to scratch his eyes out. How had she ever deluded herself into thinking this man was their friend? "I will take the child to be raised by my sister. In England."

"Your half sister?" The same that he was rumored to have slept with?

Another wave of his hand. "Like me, Augusta is an aristocrat. I can be assured the whelp will be raised properly in her care."

"Unlike my Everina," Percy growled. "Whose *Bohemian* upbringing is apparently no better than being raised by wolves."

Mary's hackles were up, too, but she forced herself to focus on this new conundrum. "You would take a child from its mother? And then leave it to be raised by neither of its parents, merely to assuage your colossal conceit?" She nearly spat at his feet. "I thought better of you, George Gordon Byron."

She *had* thought better of him, but Byron right now was like a lawless planet, careening from its proper orbit. It was one thing to be eccentric, but *this*? Still, for her sister's sake, Mary threaded her next words with a softness she didn't feel. "Claire will never agree to letting a stranger raise her child."

"She'll have no say in the matter." Byron had the audacity to pick at his nails, his tone offhand as if they were discussing the clouds gathering overhead. "The law is on my side."

"You're an ass." Percy's tone was exasperated. He so often believed the best of humanity that he couldn't comprehend someone falling so morally short as Byron was doing right now. Mary wanted to scream, mostly because Byron was right—the law *did* favor the father in all cases regarding children. "Acknowledge the child and leave Claire to raise it. Provide an allowance for her and to ensure your son or daughter is educated and maintained in a proper manner."

Byron gave a bark of laughter. "That's rich, coming from the lofty Percy Shelley. Didn't you abandon a wife with two of your brats back in London? I don't see you taking care of your *responsibilities*."

Mary winced inwardly, but Percy remained unruffled. "I maintain Harriet and my children in a manner befitting their stations." Mary recognized the sudden edge to his voice. Byron had hit a nerve few people knew existed. "Be a man, Byron, and do the same."

Mary was sure Byron would hold his ground, but she couldn't allow him to maintain it. Aside from bombast and pride, what could possibly be motivating him?

Fear? Perhaps a craving for power? Byron had left behind a daughter—little Ada Lovelace was scarcely older than Everina—when he'd separated from his wife; was this his attempt to right that wrong?

These were all strong emotions, to be sure. Regardless, Byron was playing the villain here, and Mary had only one opportunity to appeal to his better nature. She thought of the real villain in her story, a scientist turned cruel, and prayed that Byron wouldn't become his mirror image. "It is better in moments like this not to be ferocious or hard of heart toward others," she said to him, "but instead to be kind, compassionate, and soft. Your first instinct may be to abandon both Claire and your child, but there is more humanity and goodness in you to outweigh the pressure of this moment. There is no need to be cruel to my sister, nor the child that you've created together."

She worried that she'd missed the mark and that Byron would cling to his irrational stance. Instead, the sun glinted off the golden hoop in his ear as his lips lifted into that calamitous smile of his. "As always, Miss Godwin, I am defenseless in the face of your arguments. But the child will be raised in England. I will depart immediately and I expect Claire to follow."

Percy exchanged a glance with Mary; she gave a tiny nod. "Thank you," she whispered.

And just like that, summer was over.

Percy had neglected to pay the creditors for the house on Margaret Street before their departure to Geneva, so they were stuck in Bath upon their unhappy return to England. Byron, despite his insistence on Claire's following him, had uprooted once again and was now in Italy. Without Claire. Thankfully, Claire's condition was still secret, although that couldn't last much longer, and the gossip pages already reported that Percy Shelley—poor, noble, misunderstood Percy—was keeping a harem of Godwin women.

First of all, two women does not a harem make, Mary wanted to protest. *Second, Percy isn't* keeping *Claire, only trying to shield her from the worst of Byron's behavior.*

A letter home with the news and the flinty silence that followed had confirmed that neither Jane nor William Godwin were willing to entertain their daughters. It was Fanny who broke that silence, and then only to write a steady string of increasingly morose letters to Mary, including one that asked whether Fanny might come live with them. And whether *Percy might love her too*.

Mary didn't respond. What was there to write if even her own sister believed them so debauched?

The mail horn sounded down the street one afternoon as Percy napped upstairs, so Mary used the excuse to put on a shawl and bonnet—a short jaunt to the post office offered a much-needed opportunity to set aside *Frankenstein* and stretch her legs. Claire didn't look up from her reading—she'd taken to heart Mary Wollstonecraft's line that it was as wise to expect figs from thistles as that an ignorant woman would become a good mother. Percy and Byron had ceased their horror stories after their falling-out, yet Mary had continued writing her tale of the scientist who dabbled in playing God but instead manufactured evil in himself and others. (That part was inspired by Byron's fit of temper, although she hoped reality would have a happier ending.) She had also added an explorer, Walton, and his sister—Margaret Walton Saville—who remained off the page. It was an echo of the role women were usually forced to play: one step removed, so often at a distance from the action of life. Mary thought her mother would have approved of the symbolism.

And she'd given Walton's sister the initials she wished she might herself have—MWS. Mary Wollstonecraft Shelley. Her own name, linked with the two most important people in her life.

Mary smiled even as she took the post directly from the scarlet-liveried Royal Mail guard, his blunderbuss and tin horn polished to a high sheen, and waited for him to record the time of the transfer. She wished she could have asked her mother's advice on her story. She'd shyly told Percy he must wait until it was finished before he could read her progress.

"From Byron." Mary handed Claire one of the letters after she'd returned and taken off her bonnet. She recognized Fanny's handwriting on the other, although it had been mailed from Bristol, which was unusual.

Like a starved bird of prey, Claire captured Byron's envelope—she sent at least ten letters for every one of Byron's rare responses—and tore into it as Mary lifted the flap on Fanny's message. Mary's lips pressed together as she read the labyrinthine message, its tone darker and more despondent than usual.

"We should visit Fanny soon," she announced to Claire without looking up. "She claims she wishes to depart immediately to the spot from which she hopes never to remove. What does that mean?"

But Claire leapt to her feet, crumpling Byron's letter in one hand with the back of the other pressed to her lips. The sudden movement startled the tortoiseshell cat and its two kittens that had been curled under the settee. "Don't worry, puss," Mary murmured as Claire stormed away. She picked up a kitten and touched her nose to its fuzzy forehead. "We can't help whom we love. If we could, there would be no novels. And far fewer love songs."

Claire's every emotion was easy to parse out—*too* easy—but Mary was still mulling over Fanny's cryptic message as she used a freshly whetted knife to cut new quills from the motley stack of raven feathers Percy had bought her. Difficult to get one just right—some were too long, too short, too weak.

A sudden pounding at the door caused her to nearly stab her palm. Ink-black feathers floated and swirled through the air in a macabre waltz.

"Mary! Percy!" The pounding continued, but the speaker's familiar voice caused Mary's heart to lodge in her throat as she ran to the front door.

"Father?"

William Godwin stood bent over on her stoop, ashen-faced with his cravat half-tied and his violet jacket askew. She reached out to steady him. "What are you doing here?" she asked.

"Is your sister with you?"

"Claire is upstairs—"

"Not Claire." Her father glanced frantically past her. Mary heard footsteps and turned to see Percy descending the staircase, his ocean-deep eyes still foamy with sleep. "*Fanny*," Godwin exclaimed. "Is she here?"

"No. We haven't seen Fanny since before Geneva. Isn't she in London?"

"I knew she'd been writing to you. I thought she might have come here." Godwin swayed on his feet, his face like a waxwork. "Oh God . . ."

"I'm sure Fanny will be fine," Percy said soothingly. He guided Godwin inside and lodged the door firmly shut behind them. Mary's moment of triumph at finally having her father across from her again was short lived.

"She disappeared yesterday and today I received an alarming letter from Bristol." He grasped Mary's arms. "She's your mother's daughter," he added cryptically. "And I can't find her."

"There must be a logical reason for her going to Bristol." Mary tried to direct her father to a chair, but he remained standing even as she heard the hollowness of her own words.

"You don't understand." Godwin clawed Mary's hands. "Your mother, she was chased by dark moods."

"I know." Mary felt a sudden need to sit. She recalled a passage in her father's memoir, when he'd admitted that her mother had once tried to drown herself while mired in melancholia. "You taught me that I should never give in to those moods because it would invite the darkness to stay."

"But your mother, she couldn't shake that darkness." Godwin collapsed into the chair and buried his face in his hands. "She nearly took her own life, first with laudanum, then by trying to drown herself. Fanny takes after her. And now . . ."

The calamity of the moment was so heavy that Mary couldn't speak. Mary had read the truncated versions of those terrible incidents in her father's memoir, but now wasn't the time to reveal that knowledge. Her mother had both felt and thought deeply—perhaps *too* deeply, as it had nearly claimed her life, but never had Mary considered that she or Fanny might have inherited such bleak inclinations. Mary wrapped her hands around her father's fluttering fingers, but Percy had already moved to action.

"I'll ride to Bristol." He jammed his hat over sleep-mussed hair. "I can trace Fanny from there."

Godwin buried his face in his hands with a moan. "Oh, Mary, I've failed you again." Mary moved to embrace her father, but stopped at his next words: "And now your daughter . . ."

William Godwin wasn't speaking to her. No, instead he spoke to her dead mother.

"We'll find her, Father." Chagrined, Mary squeezed his forearm. She'd wanted her father returned to her, but not like this. "I swear it."

Percy was gone the rest of the day. Claire came downstairs, and the two of them sat with their father in a quiet vigil. If tears were only eloquent when they flowed down fair cheeks, then Claire's tears were quite the opposite, as were her red-rimmed eyes and blotchy cheeks. "I'm pregnant, you know," she announced to Godwin after too long a silence.

Mary cut her off with a sharp look, made sharper by her father's sudden lack of color. "Now is not the time," Mary's father said.

"Of course not," her sister muttered. "There's never a good time for me, is there?"

Mary didn't have the energy for Claire's challenge, not when her every nerve was stretched taut with worries for Fanny. She had nearly given up hope of Percy returning before nightfall— Claire had retreated upstairs, and Mary's father paced the small measure of their front room—when Percy's message arrived.

> *Tracked Fanny to Swansea. Will follow her to coast of Wales.*
>
> *—P*

"What now?" Godwin asked. Her father had aged at least a decade since she'd seen him last.

Mary touched his shoulder, Percy's letter tightly in hand. "Now we wait."

Three long nights passed before Percy's steps finally sounded outside.

Despite his protests, Mary had insisted that her father stay in Bath, although they'd spent the time as two magnets with opposite charges. Godwin had refused to lodge with them and instead stayed at a nearby inn, only coming to the house to check for news before drawing away again. He was sitting silently with Mary, waiting on the evening post that third night, when Percy burst through the front door. The stale indoor air was suddenly infused with the smell of rot and spoiled autumn mushrooms.

"What news?" Godwin commanded, but Percy, still covered

in a fine layer of dust from the road, only went to the side cabinet and poured himself a fortifying glass of port.

Mary sat down, unable to stomach the look on his face.

"I tracked Fanny to Bristol, then Swansea," he rasped out as he held the glass but didn't drink. "By the time I arrived, the worst had already happened." Percy's eyes were bleak as he glanced first at her, then at her father. "A young woman had been found dead in her room at the Mackworth Arms."

Mary couldn't stifle her gasp. Next to her, her father moaned.

Percy's eyes glimmered with unshed tears. "Fanny had told the chambermaid she didn't feel well, and locked herself in her room. They found two empty laudanum bottles next to her; she wore the gold watch we sent her from Switzerland and your mother's stays," he said to Mary. "Embroidered with the initials M. W."

Unlike their bold and daring mother in life, perhaps quiet and timid Fanny had sought out a connection with her in death. With her sister gone, Mary felt the frail bond to her mother slip ever more.

"I should have invited her to live with us when she asked." Mary's eyes brimmed with tears that slowly slipped their moorings. "I should have *begged* her."

"She left this." Percy retrieved a pale slip of paper from his pocket. Next to her, Godwin moved his lips silently as they read the letter together, her sister's last words.

My intention is to end the life of a being whose birth was unfortunate and whose life has only been a series of pain to those persons who have hurt their health in endeavoring to promote her welfare. Perhaps to hear of my death will give you pain, but you will soon have the blessing of forgetting that such a creature ever existed.

"It's not signed," Mary said when she was finally able to look up. Her sister thought her own birth *unfortunate*? That her life had been only a *series of pain* to everyone who knew her?

"I removed her signature," Percy admitted. "She signed only her first name, but I didn't want her—or her family—condemned."

Of course. Because suicide was seen as a sin. More than that, it was a crime.

"I let them bury her in Swansea." Percy's face had gone hollow. "I didn't know what else to do."

"I must go to Swansea." Mary stood suddenly. She would leave first thing in the morning. "To say goodbye."

To her surprise, her father clutched her wrist. "You will do no such thing." Authority crackled through his grief-stricken words. "Do not disturb the silent dead. Do not destroy the obscurity your sister so much desired."

"But—"

"Fanny passed of a severe cold on the way to visit her aunts," Godwin said. "That is what we will *all* say about her death. Fanny would not have wanted to involve our family in further scandal." Godwin clasped Percy's fingers. "Thank you, my boy."

Mary wanted to argue, but she knew her father was right. Quiet, unassuming Fanny, who had always felt herself a burden. Who had traveled all the way to Swansea to die among strangers so as not to *inconvenience* her own family.

"It's preposterous that people would look down upon Fanny for ending her own life," Claire interjected. Mary hadn't even noticed her entrance, but her remaining sister stood at the doorway now, dressed for bed, with her hair in a loose braid over her shoulder. Her face was pale and tears streaked her cheeks. Despite their difference in age, Claire had always protected Fanny, just as she did now. "Suicide is an honorable option—Fanny shouldn't be condemned for refusing to be dependent any longer. It was her life to live, and thus hers to take."

"Perhaps, but that brings us little solace." William Godwin gazed through gray eyes like stagnant pools of water at the mantel portrait of Everina that Shelley had sketched and framed. "'Tis a heavy burden, bringing a child into the world." He glanced at Mary and then visibly cringed as Claire touched her belly. "As your sister is about to learn."

Mary winced at the pain that streaked through Claire's expression at Godwin's dismissal of her before her sister turned on her heel and went back upstairs . . . *Your father will forgive you, but he scarcely notices me unless I've done something wrong.*

Fanny had died believing she was a burden; Mary didn't want any of her loved ones ever feeling that way again. Not even Claire, whose current predicament *was* a burden. Mary made a fresh promise to be more patient with her sister and her father, to try *harder*.

Mary took the handkerchief Percy offered, and dabbed her overflowing eyes before following her father's gaze to her daughter's charcoal portrait. "Everina would like to spend time with her grandfather. We'd *all* like to spend more time with you."

Because Mary craved her father's forgiveness, for them to comfort each other in their grief.

Except William Godwin shook his head. He was already gathering his things, preparing to retreat into the night. Not to retreat—to *flee*. Mary recognized his wild eyes, the tight purse of his lips as he tried to keep his emotions leashed within. "No, I don't think so. Not right now. No, I must go."

Mary moved to stop him, but Percy's gentle touch on her

hand halted her. He shook his head. "Let him be, Mary. Let your father grieve in private."

The weather soon turned to winter, but death stalked them like a swarm of summer insects.

Mary felt Fanny's absence keenly, and their father still refused to visit, citing his grief. Ten days before Christmas, a letter with further ill tidings arrived, followed in quick succession by newspaper articles that roared Mary's and Percy's names in condemnation.

Whereas Fanny had been able to die in obscurity, Percy's wife Harriet thrust herself into the stuff of legend—and Percy and Mary into further infamy—by jumping to her death off Serpentine Bridge. To make matters worse, according to the newspaper reports, she'd been heavy with child.

Not with Percy's child, given that he hadn't been with her since his elopement with Mary. Which merely made the news even more scandalous as rumormongers whispered that Percy's wife had been forced into prostitution to support herself and her children. A blatant lie, given her family's wealth, but truth never mattered to the scandal sheets.

"My God." Percy's face blanched white as the December snow outside when he read the news from the warmth of their kitchen. The rest of the world went suddenly cold, trapped forever in an unending winter. "I didn't think . . . certainly I never thought . . ."

Mary wished she could comfort him, but she could only stare, realizing how precariously she, too, was balanced on the knife-edge. Percy had rejected Harriet only because of his love for Mary. Which meant Mary was complicit in Harriet's—and her unborn child's—death.

"What have I done?" Mary whispered that night after she'd

stolen into Everina's nursery. After receiving the news about Harriet, a wild-eyed Percy had raced to London to take custody of his children—three-year-old Ianthe and two-year-old Charles, who he'd learned were with Harriet's parents. Mary lay alone in their bed, and black wings of guilt had chased away the possibility of sleep until she had felt the sudden urge to behold something pure and unsullied.

Her daughter. No matter the circumstances, Everina was her contribution to the world. Not the only one she hoped to make, but in her daughter, she'd created an innocent new life. A blank page yet to be written.

Except Everina was illegitimate, a *bastard*. The stark word was too black a stain to describe the perfect child nestled beneath the frothy cloud of blankets. Too young to understand the crime she'd been born into, would Everina one day walk the same path as Fanny? Mary's breathing became panicked, and she had to touch Everina's downy head to steady herself.

And now her husband was about to return with his *legitimate* children in tow. Children by another woman, a woman Mary had wronged so horrifically.

"I'm sorry," Mary whispered into the night, just in case Harriet could hear. "I swear I'll do right by your children."

She stayed awake until Percy finally returned, sitting sentinel in her place next to Everina's crib. "Where are the children?" she whispered.

But he only shook his head, his eyes rimmed with shadows. "The Westbrooks said we're nothing but a flagrant scandal, that I ruined their daughter's life and I have no right to ruin her children's." His voice broke. "They refused to give them to me."

Mary's hand went to her throat. Those cruel words cut and would leave scars, even as she recognized their roots in grief and anger. "What can we do to convince them? Can our friends write letters attesting to Everina's comfort and happiness?"

Mary had no idea which friends they could lean upon in such matters. Perhaps Byron, not that his word would carry much weight. Or Claire? Maybe even her father?

Percy only shook his head. "It won't be enough, at least not to convince a judge." His expression was cloaked, inscrutable. "There's only one thing we *can* do." A pause. "We must marry, you and I. Immediately."

At his words, a tiny flame of something fragile sputtered and then died in Mary's heart. For all her adherence to Mary Wollstonecraft's beliefs and her own reticence to relinquish her few rights as an unmarried woman when she became the property of her husband, some small part of Mary had always nurtured the fledgling hope that she and Percy might one day wed. And that perhaps in doing so, she might regain her father's love.

It wasn't supposed to happen like this.

Most young women considered their wedding days the happiest of their lives, but days later, as Mary walked down the aisle of St. Mildred's Church on Bread Street and took in Percy's storm-tossed eyes, her mind twisted back to their first kiss that damp afternoon in the St. Pancras cemetery. The moment Percy's lips had touched hers, a fierce explosion of joy had rattled the marrow of her bones. *That* had been the wedding of their hearts, the eternal vow their souls swore.

This ceremony and its certificate that would officially make them man and wife?

They were scarecrows, devoid of all life.

Mary wanted to care about the vows, truly. But she and Percy had been forced into this, and deep down, Mary was terrified that by taking his name, she was following Harriet's well-trod path. Percy hadn't married either of them because he was overcome with love—he'd felt backed into a corner. Would he become disillusioned with Mary? Set her aside as he had Harriet? At losing his freedom, would he lash out like a cornered animal?

Worse, would she?

With each step, she came closer to becoming his *wife*, a word her mother had written equated to *chattel*.

Mary's steps faltered. Only a few feet from the altar, but it might as well have been miles.

Their family members would pick up on her hesitation like hounds on a hunt. When her gaze met Percy's, she knew he could read the question writ clear on her face. Yet he only lifted his eyebrows in silent question.

She could leave him standing there, and somehow, she knew he'd understand. They could go on living just as they had.

But then Percy might never be reunited with his children. Also, Everina would soon feel the sting of her illegitimacy, a sin this marriage would absolve. Mostly, at least.

You're braver than this, Mary reminded herself as she assumed her place next to Percy.

Even her mother had married and been happy, for a while at least. This was Mary's choice.

"I'm so proud of you." William Godwin embraced them both after the ceremony, and even Jane offered a smile that reached her eyes. William Godwin's vibrant lemon waistcoat was a joyous splash of color in the otherwise austere church. Mary herself had worn dove gray, as had Percy. "Such a good marriage to finally come of all this."

That was the only allusion to Mary and Percy's prior elopement. As the tiny wedding party poured out of the church into the watery winter sunshine—only Claire was absent, given the imminent birth of her child—no one so much as mentioned their travels to France or Switzerland or even little Everina. It was as if the past two years had never happened.

Perhaps that was why Mary sniped back at her father. "Percy and I have been married since we went to France, at least in our hearts. I assure you that our prejudices against marriage remain the same."

Even without the gentle squeeze of her hand—Percy's callus from holding a quill matching the one on her third finger—Mary would have known from the softening of his expression that they hadn't abandoned their ideals or themselves, merely bent a little to accommodate society's gusty demands. Even if part of her *was* relieved to know that they had forged a new bond today, one that would last until death parted them.

The wedding may not have been what either Percy or Mary had envisioned, but at the inn where they stayed that night, Mary whispered her newfound desire into Percy's ear.

"I want another child," she breathed to him once they lay side by side in bed with warm bricks at their feet, the words feeling so terribly, wonderfully right. Her gauzy nightgown had hitched up, its fabric as insubstantial as spider silk while his thumb rubbed lazy circles along her hip bone. "Another perfect little pixie created from this magic between you and me."

Their dance in the dark that followed was fierce, impassioned. Afterward, Percy fell to his knees at her bedside. He dipped his head to brush her lips. "I will always worship the brilliance of your mind, Mary, the goodness of your spirit. You and I exist on some sort of higher plane, our souls like two exquisite lyres that vibrate as one."

Staring at him there on his knees like a fallen demigod, his bare flesh lit by a divine kaleidoscope of living gold firelight and the witching hour's silver moonlight, Mary wondered how she ever doubted him.

The next morning, Mary frowned over her journal. She'd written little about her wedding day and that mostly out of obligation. It wasn't as if anyone would ever read anything she wrote.

The thought had her avoiding looking at her traveling case, where the manuscript for *Frankenstein* awaited its final pages. Before the wedding, she had finished the creature's rampage, pouring all her anger and dismay from the past weeks—from Fanny's death and her father's continued rejection of her family to Harriet's suicide and their forced marriage—into the terrible bloodbath of a scene. Men could go to war, she supposed, to excise their baser emotions. Women weren't allotted such a luxury, but there had been something cathartic about the destruction she'd wrought on the page.

"I'll miss you while you're in Bath," Percy said. He'd just finished breakfast and they were about to part ways, Mary to assist Claire with her upcoming birth—Byron was still in Italy—while Percy remained in London and worked to secure Harriet's children. Now that he was a respectfully married man again, he was optimistic about his chances of success.

Mary closed her journal and tucked it into her valise. "I wish we didn't have to part. Not so soon."

He kissed the tip of her nose. "Sometimes I imagine we could return to those days in Switzerland. Everything was simpler then."

"If we were in Switzerland, we could go back to bed right now." Mary placed one hand on Percy's chest, the other hand roaming . . . lower. The upcoming weeks away from him loomed large and lonely. Percy uttered a deep-toned oath that strummed the back of her throat.

"God, woman." His voice was thick. "I ache for you. You are my Faerie Queene, my own heart's home."

Mary nearly missed her coach to Bath, and when she finally clambered on board, she was keenly aware of the stray tendrils of her chignon and her rumpled skirts. She was also keenly aware of Percy's citrus scent on her and the cheerful disarray of his hair as he handed her up over the drifts of dirty snow and December mud, holding her gloved fingers overlong so he could press a chaste kiss onto the back of her hand. However, his laughing eyes were far from chaste as he latched the door and pounded twice on the coach with the flat of his palm. "Go well, Mrs. Shelley," he said. "And keep up your writing—I can't wait to read this *Frankenstein* of yours."

Mary turned and craned her neck as the coach clattered down the cobbles, bound for the next London stop, where Jane would deliver Everina to her after keeping her for the night. Technically, Mary was a newlywed, but after two years with Percy, she hadn't expected to feel this giddiness the morning after their marriage. As she settled back into the meager coach cushions, dutifully ignoring the knowing smiles of the rest of the coach passengers, she was heartsick to realize this would be the longest she and Percy had ever been separated.

She'd use this time to finish *Frankenstein*. Once her monster of death and destruction was complete, she and Percy would be together again and able to start anew.

Then perhaps they could put the darkness of this past year behind them.

CHAPTER 12

❧

October 1795

MARY WOLLSTONECRAFT

"This one's still breathing, Ernst!"

Death was big with promises. Those promises were denied to me.

After falling into the black and frigid river, I forced my head beneath the churning waves time and again until the violent urge to breathe came as a bitter surprise. I'd scarcely started to drift toward unconsciousness when a pair of strong hands heaved me from the embrace of the Thames and deposited me like some scaled prize on the floor of a modest fishing vessel.

"I told you tonight was a good 'un for jumpers. The king himself'll buy us a pint. Maybe two."

Was I dreaming? I could scarcely see the men who spoke—rain still lashed down, and my eyes were waterlogged from the river. "Excuse me?" I managed to grind out from between chattering teeth.

A dank-smelling wool blanket was wrapped around my shoulders by hands that reeked of bait. "The Royal Humane Society has a new policy, miss," a kindly voice informed me. "For every jumper we pull outta the Thames, they pays us a reward. See, Putney Bridge 'ere be a popular spot for men and women at the end of their rope. But surely things aren't so bad—once you're warm before a fire, you'll soon find a way out of yer difficulties."

My thoughts sputtered so I couldn't formulate a response. Never in a thousand years would I have imagined I'd be plucked from the Thames by two fishermen paid for their kindnesses by aid societies. And my difficulties did *not* seem better once I was bundled in front of a crackling fire in the back room of the Duke's Head tavern, the innkeeper's wife studiously drying my wet dress while a doctor pronounced my traitorous lungs clear and my fickle heart steady.

I did not thank him; I felt inhumanely brought back to life and misery.

Except perhaps the fishermen were better philosophers than I'd realized. With a dented tin mug of steaming tea between my hands, it occurred to me that I'd been living in a terrible fantasy.

The Gilbert Imlay that I'd envisioned welcoming Fanny and me home, of sailing off to build a new life in America . . . he was an imaginary being created from my own fancies. The Gilbert Imlay I'd known since Fanny's birth was a far weaker being—a man who chased money and the chimera of some elusive fortune. When he was younger and in love with me—and I was sure he had been at one time—Gilbert Imlay had been inspired to higher ideals, but since then he'd sunk deeply into base motivations of commerce and money. I never wanted anything save his heart; with that gone, he had nothing more to give.

Society seldom feels much compassion excited by the helplessness of females—unless they are fair; then perhaps pity is the soft handmaid of love or the harbinger of lust. I could admit my guilt in this sphere, just as I now admitted that I *had* been helpless when I'd allowed my love of Gilbert Imlay to consume me. To *define* me.

Never again.

I'd written once that love's nature was transitory, and my recent experience taught me that was true; my seeking to keep Gilbert's love constant was as wild as a search for the philosopher's stone. I could not change Gilbert and I was not responsible for his choices. I could only scrub my own heart clean. And that I was determined to do.

The beginning is always today. So, today I would begin anew.

As soon as I was able, I hurried back to the house Gilbert had rented for us, scooped Fanny (whom I embraced as my only comfort and swore I would never stray from again) into my arms, and packed our things. I paused only long enough to send off a message demanding that Gilbert return all of my letters.

I'd claimed in *A Vindication of the Rights of Woman* that whether a woman be loved or neglected, her first wish should be not to rely on other fallible beings for her happiness. It was time to take my own advice, for both my sake and Fanny's. It didn't take much effort to find my own rooms to rent at 16 Finsbury Place, a quiet neighborhood close to both the famous bookshop the Temple of the Muses and Johnson's house.

"I'm writing a new book, a travelogue and reflection based on my notes from Scandinavia," I informed a very surprised Johnson when I arrived with Fanny in tow at his offices at St. Paul's the very next afternoon. Imlay had returned my letters, along with a note that I should maintain the fiction of being his wife—for Fanny's sake—and also that he'd reconsidered my offer that Fanny and I move in with him and his mistress. I'd burned his response before *I* reconsidered, and instead reorganized the letters I'd sent him from Sweden. There was definitely something there—a book that would chart my travel observations and honestly examine my struggles even as I found my footing in Sweden. "Will you publish it?"

"I'll publish anything you write, Mary, even just your lists for the butcher and fishmonger." Johnson rose and stole my breath away in a dust-and-ink-scented embrace. He was the same as ever, save for a slightly choleric constitution, but then, we were all getting older. "God, it's good to have you back."

I made a show of switching Fanny from one hip to the other and felt my face flush that I hadn't kept up our correspondence. "I came to see you when I first arrived in London, remember?"

"That wasn't you, merely an automaton with your face and voice. It makes this old man's heart happy to see you've broken free of the dazed thrall that held you captive then. Also, this means you can finally take back your ill-behaved cat. I hadn't wanted to trouble you with her when you seemed so out of sorts, but now . . ."

The silt of some unnamed emotion clogged my throat as I chuckled. "I'm happy to be back. And Fanny will be pleased to have a pet."

I wasn't entirely renewed—a broken pot will always bear the scar where it was glued together—but I'd hit the bottom of the Thames before I could come up to breathe fresh air and leave my melancholia behind. Now, with each page my pen filled and every time Fanny reached out her arms to me when she awoke from her afternoon nap, I ruthlessly cut away bits of the gangrene that had taken over my life.

That determination to make one more effort for life and happiness grew even stronger when my Swedish travelogue sold briskly and was translated into Swedish, Dutch, German, and Portuguese. *Letters Written During a Short Residence in Sweden, Norway, and Denmark* meant that Fanny and I were now financially independent once again. It wasn't enough to move to America, but I was no longer sure that dream was for me.

For now, this was enough.

Writing had vanquished my monsters, and my latest literary success meant that I could ignore anyone who dared speak against me or my situation with Fanny, if they dared speak against me at all. I had sunk my claws firmly back in the land of the living.

And I was determined to stay.

The January outside was gray, as if the world couldn't be bothered to put on a show, but inside Mary Hays's home, a glittering party gathered. Still, I wanted to scream when I discovered my hostess—who had invited a ridiculous cunning-man to cast attendees' fortunes and already forced me to observe the mundane tricks of her furry lapdog—had matchmaking in mind during that particular afternoon tea.

"A widower named Thomas Holcroft would like to make your acquaintance, Mrs. Imlay." I'd continued using Gilbert's name out of necessity, playing the estranged wife to confer some amount of respectability to Fanny. An unmarried mother was too scandalous to be borne, yet my matronly suffering not only was acceptable but somehow rendered me exotic. So exotic that even that little troll Henry Fuseli—creator of the sexualized *Nightmare* painting that had so scandalized me at that first dinner with Joseph Johnson—had crafted a fresh story that I'd pursued him determinedly until he'd soundly rejected me before I traveled to Paris. I didn't deign to respond, especially after he'd claimed to hate clever women because we were too troublesome.

Ah yes, because we troublesome women didn't simper and bat our lashes before letting him lead us to bed. We were too clever for that.

Still, it appeared a married woman—regardless of her cleverness—could be propositioned in a way that no unmarried girl could be. My meddlesome hostess didn't allow me to demur, only forcibly directed me to where an unremarkable man stood by the windows. He'd attempted to position himself to his best advantage—one foot forward, a fist at his waist, and a smile on his lips. The arrangement was lackluster at best.

I had no desire to take up with any man ever again. I still maintained my position from *Vindication* that it was better to be disappointed in love than to never have loved, but cupid's honey-tipped arrows had made me wretched, and thus I had no interest in a second serving.

Unfortunately, Mary Hays performed the necessary introductions before abandoning me to the bespectacled widower, whose fly-eye gaze paused overlong at the sweep of my neckline. "I believe it is customary to look a woman in the eyes when addressing her," I muttered crankily.

Holcroft offered a rigid bow, then shocked me by grasping my gloved fingers in a most violent manner. "You are a scintillating specimen of female, one I know is well versed in the ways of men and women." I reared back, appalled at the innuendo, but Holcroft tugged me so close I could smell the sour-cheese stink of his breath. "I've never touched your lips, yet I have felt them, sleeping and waking, present and absent. I feel them now and ask why I am forbidden to fall on your bosom and dissolve there in bliss such as I have never known, except in reveries like this."

Holcroft must have expected his declaration to cause a cattish affection that would induce a woman of six-and-thirty to purr to any man who fed and caressed her. Instead, I was repulsed having this raw country lout proposition me into a sexual adventure involving my lips and bosom. Why did society equate an understanding of sex on a woman's part with licentiousness? And why couldn't men think more often with their minds than with the equipment hidden within their trousers?

Well, mostly hidden, in the case of Holcroft's tented breeches.

Predictably, the widower's gaze had once again strayed lower than my eyes even as he continued to grasp my gloved hands.

I exhaled in utter exasperation, prepared to surrender my favorite satin gloves—or scream if necessary—in order to extricate myself from the attentions of this mutton-headed oaf. Holcroft still refused to release my hands. "Please excuse me," I said, "I think it's my turn to have my fortune read."

I tried to turn and nearly collided with a beautifully dressed woman chuckling behind her folded fan. "My apologies, Mr. Holcroft," she said in an airy accent before taking my arm. Freedom, at last! "I simply must claim Mrs. Imlay."

"I owe you my next-born child in gratitude," I whispered as the stranger led me into the adjacent sitting room. Thankfully, it was sparsely populated at that moment.

The woman's laugh was neither the usual forced feminine simper nor a hoarse guffaw, but something plain and honest. "No infant required." Her eyes shimmered with hoyden playfulness. "Although I'm not averse to sharing a bottle of East Indian madeira."

I didn't often indulge in spirits—my father was a cautionary tale—but I'd make an exception for this savior of mine. "Well, I owe you the finest bottle of madeira money can buy. For I was about to cause a scene."

My rescuer offered me a plate of biscuits from a table filled with confectionaries. The cardamom and cinnamon brought to mind the spice markets of exotic locales. "It wouldn't have been the first time a lady needed to escape Holcroft's pungent clutches. You'll want to be on your guard—all London's eligible bachelors, and even some scoundrels who aren't, crave a glimpse of the brilliant and beautiful Mrs. Imlay. And some of them—like Holcroft—desire more than just a glimpse."

My skin crawled. "Well, I'm grateful for your speedy extrication." I set down my plate of biscuits. "I don't believe we've been properly introduced."

She gave a succinct curtsy. "I am Maria Reveley." I waited for the conversation to turn to the inevitable—I'd already been asked four times where I'd purchased my gown, a high-waisted white muslin confection cut in the fashionable French style and adorned with a scarlet sash. Instead: "I enjoy painting and possess a neglectful husband who is rarely around and a young son named Henry whom I dote upon. But I believe you were about to have your fortune told?"

I glanced across the hall to where the ridiculous cunning-man was seated behind a velvet-draped table, currently absorbed in scrying our hostess's bared palm. "I'd sooner have a canker treated by a magnetizer."

Maria laughed. "Agreed—a priest of quackery if ever I saw one. Though our present company doesn't appear to concur."

I glanced at the long line of partygoers forming down the hall, then turned my back on the entire farce. If everyone here was akin to Holcroft, then a pox could take them all. Yet this Maria Reveley reminded me of a toned-down version of Théroigne de Méricourt, who still wasted away in the Salpêtrière Hospital asylum, her daring mind ruined beyond repair. "Where is your accent from?" I asked her. "I can't place it."

She waved an elegant hand. "I was raised in Constantinople and Rome—my wandering merchant of a father kidnapped me from my mother. Thus, I speak enough languages that they've all left their stamp on me."

"You were kidnapped?" One read about such plots in novels, but never in real life. "Truly?"

"Not so glamorous as it sounds, but yes. Sadly, I was left to run wild, although my father—God rest his weary soul—did hire the best tutors money could buy in both Constantinople and Rome."

"I've never been to either city." In fact, despite my travels, Maria's worldliness made me feel positively provincial. Still, how wonderful it was to converse with someone who knew more of the world than I!

"No, but you just returned from a trip to Sweden." Maria shrugged at my silent question. "I read your book. It's garnered you many admirers, including my friend here."

I glanced up from my biscuit to see a reed-thin man standing at the doorway, a porcelain teacup dwarfed by his large hands while he scowled at the fortune-teller. The vague familiarity of his cleft chin and stern visage itched at the corners of my mind. I reared back in sudden recognition tinged with revulsion. "Why, it's William Godwin!"

The same William Godwin who had mocked and belittled me at Johnson's dinner party when I'd announced my intentions to travel to revolutionary Paris. He now looked as startled as I felt. I'd read his book *Political Justice*—which lashed out against the conservative government of England—and had found it an angry tome designed to provoke authorities and institute reform. Normally, I'd have approved, but instead I equated the author of those screeds with the conservative dinner guest who had fretted over me like some sort of medieval lord well into his dotage. Even if he *had* been correct about some of the dangers that had awaited me in France.

Godwin's pivot upon my undignified exclamation was slow, his dismayed expression a mirror image to my own. "Mrs. Imlay," he said with the barest incline of his head. "It's been a long time."

Not long enough, I could tell he wanted to add, to which I concurred. I was going to require a second excuse to flee, and quickly.

Godwin nearly beat me to it. "I was actually just looking for the sugar," he mumbled with an awkward lift of his cup. But Maria ignored the way we were studiously avoiding looking at each other and merely motioned him over to the table.

Godwin had cut what I recalled to be his unfashionably long hair, and I smothered a smile to see the sharp-toed red morocco slippers that matched his green coat and scarlet waistcoat. No more was he a fusty old minister; now he looked the part of a radical revolutionary. Albeit an eccentric one.

Maria passed Godwin the flowered sugar pot, but he ignored it. "I take it you two have met?"

"Indeed," I answered as Godwin said, "We have."

"At a dinner party," I added with a wave of my hand. "Ages ago."

Lifetimes, even.

He scowled. "A terribly awkward dinner party where you talked too much."

"I did no such thing!"

"Indeed. You dominated the conversation and left me twiddling my thumbs at the end of the table." Godwin sipped his sugarless tea, making it impossible to read his hooded expression.

"My apologies," I said. Perhaps I *had* talked too much, listened only to respond rather than to understand. "I was quite swept up in the excitement of my plan to move to Paris."

"A most unsuitable plan, if I recall." Godwin looked me over, but not in the way Holcroft had. Maria was watching this exchange with the rapt interest of a handball spectator. "Fortunately, you must have evaded the worst of the violence. At least, your head is still attached."

I had survived the revolution, but so many of my friends had not. "If it's any consolation, you were correct about the violence," I admitted. "Not that I'd have listened to caution then."

"Well, I wished several times that night that I'd succeeded in persuading rather than enraging you."

"Admit it—you wished you could have shaken some sense into me as well. Discreetly, of course, but all the same." Godwin's eyes crinkled at their edges, and I found myself wanting to change the subject. "So, you read my Swedish travelogue?"

"Not yet, I'm afraid, although I've heard many positive accolades. I admit to visiting the bookshop and finding it sold out."

"However," Maria interjected solemnly, "we were both impressed by your independence and fortitude after your recent troubles. Godwin here has been kind enough to listen to my own marital woes."

I found it difficult to believe that William Godwin was a sensitive listener. However, Maria appeared to be one of those honest and friendly creatures who possessed shrewd good sense joined with worldly prudence. "Well," I responded to Godwin, not wanting to discuss Imlay, "your kindness to my new friend has raised you in my esteem."

To which Godwin harrumphed. "A small compliment, given that you did not esteem me at all after our first introduction."

I blinked. This version of William Godwin eschewed social niceties in favor of blatant honesty. For some reason, I found that refreshing, at least in small doses. "I am no longer the woman I was then, just as I expect you are now a different manner of man. I propose we move beyond that first meeting."

"One would not wish to remain static over these intervening years," Godwin agreed after an overlong silence. "Perhaps it would be best if we erased from our memories that most unfavorable encounter."

Indeed, where I had once found Godwin pedantic, overbearing, and annoying, now standing across from me in an eye-bleeding waistcoat was a man whose pen argued that he might even be a bit of a genius. An awkward sort of genius, but still . . .

Slightly less pedantic and overbearing. And scarcely annoying at all.

Had he been a woman, I'd have welcomed his friendship immediately. I'd argued for equality between the sexes time and again—it seemed hypocritical to reject him simply because he was a male of our species.

I thrust out my gloved hand. "I'd like to begin again, Mr. Godwin. I am Mary Wollstonecraft and I am most pleased to make your acquaintance."

His brows lifted in surprise, and it was only after he'd bowed over my hand that I realized I'd dropped Gilbert's name from my introduction. And that I'd missed the question Godwin had asked me.

"Pardon?"

"I merely wondered what you're working on now. Your pen is rarely idle. More politics?"

I shook my head as Maria had linked her arm through Godwin's, which he didn't seem to mind. I noted what a perfect pair they'd make, much better suited intellectually than Imlay and I ever were. "While I'm still intrigued by the machinations of government," I said, "I'm currently more interested in internal struggles, specifically how nature can heal the human spirit and whether imagination can triumph over a mundane sort of life."

"Godwin here is too humble to say it, but you should read his novel *Caleb Williams*," Maria interjected over her fan. "I found the psychological effects of the tyranny depicted there to be fascinating—certainly an internal struggle worth studying. Wouldn't you agree that was one of the novel's themes, Godwin?"

Godwin gave a long silence, which I was beginning to recognize as one of his many foibles. "I may not have the experience of a grayhead, but I believe that words can help us make sense of the human condition. If we can understand the thoughts of the victims and oppressors, surely we can decipher the vast sum of history and politics?"

"Quite so." I groaned to see our meddling hostess enter the room and beckon me with an impatient wave. How long would be acceptable before I could plead sudden illness and fly my way home to Fanny? "I'm being called away, but I will endeavor to find a copy of *Caleb Williams*."

"You may borrow mine," Maria said, "so long as you don't mind my notes in the margins. And, Godwin, you must read Mary's *Letters Written During a Short Residence in Sweden* before we meet again."

"*If* we meet again, you mean," Godwin said. "Mrs. Imlay here may find herself too much in demand to associate with the likes of dusty philosophers."

"We move in the same circles, you daft man." Maria rapped him on the wrist with her fan. "Recluse that you are, we're still bound to run into one another time and again."

I moved to join our matchmaking hostess, but some impish impulse made me turn back, a wide smile on my face. "I'd have avoided you after our first meeting, Mr. Godwin, but I heartily approve of the changes time has wrought upon us both."

Godwin's eyes widened, but I caught his smile before he offered a polite bow. "As do I."

The cottage I'd rented for Fanny and me came with two woven skeps of honeybees that I was learning to tend and a wide-open hay field that was perfect for a romping dog. The only thing missing?

The dog.

I hadn't had a dog since the one my father had hanged in a drunken rage, but a week after the Hays tea, Fanny and I trekked to a nearby farm to acquire the requisite canine. No lapdogs for us; no, I wished for Fanny to have a sturdy companion who would induce her to romp in the fields—exercise had been a healthful boon for us in Scandinavia and so, too, would it be here—and also teach her how to be kind to smaller creatures. (My cat Bet was an aged old lady now and had taken to dozing all day atop my highest bookshelf in order to avoid Fanny's enthusiastic embraces.) We returned from our excursion red-cheeked from the cold and exhausted, and with a wiggling black-and-tan bloodhound pup in tow. Merryboy—the farmer had already named our new pup—was an energetic fellow with wise eyes and a wrinkled visage who lived up to his name, licking Fanny's face eagerly when she tied one of her yellow satin hair ribbons around his overlarge ears. Once home, she ran to the kitchen and splashed milk into a saucer—well, *some* of the milk made it to the saucer— to make her new friend feel welcome. Less than an hour later, I found the two curled together asleep in her bed, both worn out from the excitement of the afternoon.

"Ma'am, you had a visitor while you were out," the maid, Marguerite, informed me as I ate my solitary bowl of vegetable soup in front of the kitchen hearth. She was a pleasant and efficient country girl—I'd left Gilbert's servants behind when we'd fled his house.

I savored the warmth of the soup as it heated me from the inside out. "Oh? I wasn't expecting anyone."

"A gentleman caller—William Godwin. He didn't have a card to leave, said he didn't carry them."

I was flattered that Godwin had sought me out, but wondered why he had come calling. Surely his intent was platonic.

I'd noticed the comfortable familiarity he shared with Maria Reveley—I wouldn't have been surprised if they had a liaison on the side in the French style. But such speculation was unseemly—what they did or didn't do behind closed doors was their business, not mine. Now the question was what to do next.

If Godwin were a woman, I'd probably have returned his visit the next day. But he was *not* a woman and I was perfectly happy alone in my cottage.

Thus, days passed, Godwin failed to repeat his visit, and I most certainly did *not* seek him out. Instead, I delighted in teaching Fanny how to calm the bees before inspecting their straw skeps, reveling in the sweet smell of beeswax and wood smoke, the taste of new honey on our fingertips. My daughter's patience when it came to insects was prodigious—she was often single-minded in her pursuit of grasshoppers and could wait an eternity for a lone honeybee to land on her outstretched hands. Once night fell and we were tucked inside our cozy cottage, we laughed at the puppy's evening antics until our sides ached.

Still, I found myself craving the intellectual vertigo that a conversation with Godwin heralded. "Perhaps it wouldn't be so terrible to call on him," I muttered to myself one afternoon while Fanny napped. I was attempting to write a dramatic play, but was stymied by the emotions of my characters. Straightforward philosophy was so much easier to write. Much as I loved reading stories to Fanny and singing children's songs with her, perhaps a riveting discussion about weightier matters than the Bogey Beast and the Lambton Worm would shake loose some sort of necessary brilliance.

One problem, aside from the glaring issue that respectable women didn't hunt down single men: I didn't know where William Godwin lived. However, I'd been meaning to visit Maria Reveley for some time. Perhaps she might provide the inspiration for my play. If not, I suspected she could tell me where to find Godwin.

"Take Merryboy?" Fanny asked—although it came out *Mewy-boy*—as I buttoned her into her linen jacket. The April weather was divine and the air hinted at spring phlox and freesia. Our pup whimpered as geese honked their way down the lane and sheep shaggy with spring wool brayed in the distance, but I shook my head.

"Next time," I instructed as we set off. "We have a stop to make that Merryboy won't like."

Along the way we dropped into the Temple of the Muses bookshop so I could pick up a copy of *Caleb Williams*. Perusing the shelves for other treasures, Fanny and I heard the familiar voice at the exact same moment. Her scarred little face lit like a firecracker, and she squealed with glee as my heart gave a painful twist.

"Papa!"

There was Gilbert, thankfully without his actress, browsing the section on finance and economics. When Fanny ran toward him with her arms outstretched, he bent down and enveloped her in a brief hug. "Hello, sweeting," he said before straightening and tipping his hat to me. "Good afternoon, Mary."

I waited for the blow to land at the stiffness in his voice but felt . . . nothing.

It was freeing, that emptiness where I expected pain and sadness to make their presence known. My love for Gilbert had finally gone to weeds after keeping me so long under his feet. So I merely tipped my chin, feeling the egret feathers on my fashionable day bonnet sway with the movement. "Gilbert."

"Are you here for books?" Gilbert asked Fanny, who nodded. "Yes."

"And what is your mama reading?"

The question was kind, but distant. I didn't want to share the title of Godwin's book, as if Imlay's notice would color my views or cheapen the adventure I anticipated within its pages. "Oh, a little of this and that," I answered.

"We have a puppy!" Fanny nearly exploded with the excitement, rocking on her toes. Only Gilbert didn't understand her muddled toddler talk, leaving me to translate.

Gilbert smiled at the both of us. "A proper guard dog, I hope."

I thought of Merryboy with his overlarge paws and ears. He'd actually tripped over his feet this morning. "Hardly."

"See the puppy, Papa."

I didn't want to decipher, but this was Fanny's father, who was looking at me expectantly. "She'd like you to meet her dog."

Gilbert cracked his knuckles—how had I never noticed how irksome that habit was? "I'd be happy to meet your new pup." He tugged Fanny's thin plait. "Tomorrow, perhaps?"

At least he lifted his gaze in some semblance of asking my permission. I didn't relish the idea of Gilbert intruding on our quiet cottage, but neither would I deny him the opportunity to visit his daughter. So I merely shrugged, noncommittal. "If you'd like."

Again, I waited for the flutter of *something*, but there wasn't even an echo. Gilbert—the placid, staid man in front of me who preferred to read Adam Smith and the financial papers—could no longer offer me the passion or intellectual stimulation I craved. I was suddenly thankful that I'd rejected his long-ago offers of marriage—better to go without companionship than settle for something inferior.

Once I'd made my purchases and he his, I said in parting, "I wish you peace, Gilbert." And I meant it.

I didn't wait for a response, merely ushered Fanny outside and in the direction of Maria's house.

We would keep moving forward, not back.

Except that's not how it felt when Maria wanted only to discuss men and matters of the heart a scant few hours later.

"William Godwin declared in *Political Justice* that he doesn't believe in marriage," she announced amid the din of the outdoor carnival we'd taken the children to. Maria had demurred on the subject of human emotion, claiming she felt only two emotions these days—disappointment in her husband and love for her son, who was attempting to toss rubber balls at painted wooden placards of clowns and kings. Neither he nor Fanny was hitting the targets, but they still squealed and clapped their hands amid the scents of grilled meats and cheesy pastries. "Godwin lives alone—the perfect candidate for a discreet affair."

I'd never been keen on gossip, but the way she said it—and her familiar banter with Godwin during the Hays tea—made me wonder anew just how close the two really were.

She tapped a gloved finger against her chin. I knew that paint rimmed her nails beneath the kid leather as if she'd dipped her fingers into a rainbow—I'd interrupted her today while she was painting a portrait of her son, and had been pleasantly surprised to discover her vast talent. "Some of us wonder if Godwin has ever had an affair," she continued. "However, he's just turned forty, so of course he has. But then, he did seem embarrassed that one time when I tried to kiss him."

I handed Fanny and Henry each a new ball and glanced at Maria through my lashes. A better time to satisfy my curiosity might never come. "I assume you made more than one attempt?"

Maria pressed her fingers to her breast, eyes wide. "What exactly are you insinuating?"

I suddenly worried that I'd offended her. "Well, the two of you seemed very close at the Hays tea . . . And you and your husband have difficulties . . ."

Maria's eyes widened before her laughter allowed me to breathe again. "You think Godwin and *me* . . . ? God and the blue heavens above, no! That silly man is like a brother to me." She and I both clapped as Henry hit one of the clown targets. "I will admit to once aspiring to belong to the Fairs, but not anymore."

"The Fairs?"

Maria smirked. "A group of nonsensical women who are considered quite handsome, at least by those who don't miss the mind when the face is plump and fair. They consider Godwin quite a catch with that brooding, rebellious streak of his. He, of course, is oblivious to their wiles." Maria bumped her hip against mine, a devious sort of smile on her lips. "In fact, I have a confession to make."

"What sort of confession?"

"What if I told you that I invited William Godwin to Mary Hays's tea in order to meet you?"

I gaped. "I'd say that's utter nonsense, especially since I'd never met you until that same day."

"Yes, but your fame precedes you. And I suspected you might be just what my dear friend needed."

"Now I know you jest. Godwin loathed me on sight and never would have deigned to join the Hays tea on my account."

Maria chuckled. "Godwin *did* respond to my invitation by saying you had frequently amused yourself with depreciating him. Still, he *did* show up. All that aside, he seems quite taken with you. And since you're separated from Mr. Imlay . . ."

I sighed. I'd hoped to keep the charade of my marriage going, but I didn't want to lie to Maria. Not now that I recognized a kindred spirit in her. "I've never been married. Imlay *did* propose," I hurried to explain, suddenly glad for the din of shouting that broke out over a nearby game of skittles, "but I refused. Then Fanny came along and we had our falling-out."

"Then you're entirely free to embark on an *affaire de cœur* with William Godwin!"

Not quite the reaction I was aiming for. Maria didn't even blink an eye at my revelation. "William Godwin would just as soon have spat at me had he seen me on the streets before the Hays tea."

"Godwin would never be so crass." She held her hands up at my arched eyebrow. "I'm not saying he wouldn't have wished it, only that he wouldn't have done it. Well, I have it on good authority that William Godwin procured a copy of your Swedish book—even before I could lend him mine—and enjoyed it immensely."

"Oh?"

"Indeed. I believe his exact words were 'If ever there was a book calculated to make a man love its author, this appears to be the book.'"

"Surely you jest."

"I have never been more serious."

I flushed, a hot and uncomfortable sensation. Godwin seemed a man of sense, but now I worried that he was addled. "I'm sure he didn't mean anything by it."

"Just as you don't mean anything by asking for his address."

"I am not visiting William Godwin with the intention of starting an *affaire de cœur*," I reminded her, somewhat exasperated. "I merely wished to return the favor of *him* calling on *me*."

"Of course." Maria gave me a meaningful look as the children dragged us over to where the pins had just been reset for a fresh round of skittles. "Just as you'd do if Thomas Holcroft left you his card."

I grimaced as my ball went wide. "I'd sooner instruct Merryboy to bite Holcroft's ankles. I just want to converse with people—men and women—about ideas and thoughts and philosophy as I did in those early days in France." I sobered to think of how many of my friends had met untimely—and bloody—ends during the Revolution. So many were just memories now, or echoes of history captured forever in their writings. "I miss the matured fruit of profound thinking. We should be free to think and discuss ideas with all members of humanity, regardless of gender."

Maria turned serious even as our children squealed when a costumed fool waddled past on stilts, their games suddenly forgotten. "Indeed we should. There is no doubt in my mind that you and William Godwin will make excellent confidantes about all things cerebral."

Thus, two days later, I stood outside the lodging house on Chalton Street in Somers Town and smoothed my hair with my palms, wishing for a mirror while simultaneously chiding myself for such superficial concerns. Except I *was* rattled.

On the afternoon walk from my cottage, a foulmouthed tradesman had recognized me, ostensibly from a sketch of me in the latest edition of *A Vindication of the Rights of Woman*. "Whore," he'd spat at me. "The only education a woman deserves can be had against that alley wall. I could make you beg, you know, see how *vindicated* you felt after I was done with you."

I had ignored him, just hurried my pace. That wasn't the first time I'd rued the decision to include that sketch of me in *Vindication*. People generally maintained a veneer of decorum, even if they disagreed with my platforms, but it took only one ignorant blockhead to ruin one's day. This one had probably been rejected by every woman of his acquaintance and thought me an easy target for his anger and frustrations.

Fortunately, I doubted whether eccentric William Godwin with his crimson morocco slippers would notice my mussed hair or the spittle on my hem. I'd received Godwin's address from Maria and rationalized this visit because I desperately needed to discuss something, *anything*.

If that was true, why did I feel so nervous now, shifting on my feet outside his lodging house? Part of me wished Godwin would step outside in a pure moment of serendipity, but as dour-faced passersby streamed around me, I forced myself to shake off this irritating spasm of shyness.

When I entered the lodging house, the frowning proprietress asked whom I sought. "You may only meet with a gentleman in the common area," she instructed me with a strident glare. "No chicanery or corrupting influences in the gentlemen's rooms."

This low-ceilinged commons with its smoking hearth was already occupied by three other men, two arguing loudly over a chessboard while another sucked tobacco through a long clay pipe shaped like a bearded mariner. I didn't like the way they all fell silent at my entrance, so I hurried my way to Godwin's attic abode.

I was about to knock on a man's door. Unchaperoned. I hadn't done such a thing since France, but there was no crime in this, no matter what the gossips might claim.

Sapere aude. Dare to know.

Thus, I knocked.

Upon opening the door, Godwin blinked behind his spectacles, which led to the least celebrated response I could possibly have uttered. "Why, you wear glasses!"

Damn me. Where was the well-spoken writer of *A Vindication of the Rights of Woman* when I needed her? My thoughts had always been more eloquent on paper, but this was dredging the basest levels of conversation.

Godwin touched the wire rims of his spectacles. He hesitated before taking them off. "Indeed, I do. At least when I need to see."

"Don't take them off on my account." I suddenly felt all angles. *I shouldn't have come.* Unable to read his expression while words snarled on the tip of my tongue, I tried afresh. "My maid told me you called, but then you didn't return—I've undertaken a new writing project and thought perhaps we might have a discussion, you and I. To jar loose some half-formed ideas that have been rattling around my skull."

If Godwin seemed to judge my behavior unorthodox, he didn't show it. Instead, he opened the door a fraction wider. "Would you care to come in?"

I bit my lip. "The proprietress informed me quite sternly that I am allowed in the common area only. She called me a *corrupting influence.*"

Godwin's smile was gentle. "I hardly think you're here to corrupt me. But we can shout across the common room if you'd prefer."

Touché. Enough of society's silly edicts. I stepped over the threshold and let him close the door behind me. That damnable nervousness frothed inside me again. "Do you invite all the Fairs into your rooms?"

He coughed, a sound designed to cloak his surprise. "I see Maria Reveley has given you a thorough education. No, none of the Fairs have ever sought me out here. I find privacy a necessary ingredient to write."

"I can leave," I said. "If you're writing and don't wish to be disturbed."

"I wouldn't have invited you in if I found you a disturbance."

Stepping inside, I saw that Godwin's was a space meant to be used for work, but not as a home. Books were stacked on every possible surface. Godwin may as well have been living in a bookshop.

I admit to being distracted by the titles—some new but many, such as Voltaire's *Dictionnaire Philosophique* and Locke's *An Essay Concerning Human Understanding*, were old friends— long enough that Godwin interjected again. "So," he asked, "what else did Maria tell you about me?"

I traced a finger along the spine of a familiar volume—*Letters Written During a Short Residence in Sweden, Norway, and Denmark*. Maria hadn't been jesting—Godwin really had read it or, at least, had purchased it. I resisted the urge to ask what he thought of it, to see if my prose really had made him love-sick.

"Just that you have a tendency to doze off during dinner parties when the conversation bores you."

Again, this was met with the surprised cough. "Time is limited. I sleep little as it is—my hours are sometimes better spent napping than listening to people prattle about things they don't understand."

"Duly noted."

"Not you," Godwin sputtered. It was then that I realized he was nervous. *Why?* If word got out that I was in his rooms, it was *my* reputation that would suffer, not his. Such was the unequal lot of women, always being forced to bear the brunt of such nonsense. Was he always this jittery around members of the fairer sex?

Godwin offered me a chair, which I took, before sitting himself, crossing first one leg and then the other. "What questions bring you to the doddering philosopher's door today?"

"Pardon?"

"I cut a rather dull figure next to the likes of dashing Gilbert Imlay." He gestured to himself. The morocco slippers were on display again, although his waistcoat was a subdued shade of moss green. I neglected to mention that his cravat was loose, given that I rather liked it that way. I also neglected to mention Imlay's afternoon call to see the puppy yesterday, which had been tepidly uneventful, save for Merryboy's growling at him. "However," Godwin continued, "my mind is at your service should you wish to philosophize on the meaning of freedom or the nature of man."

"Actually, I wanted to discuss something infinitely more fragile." I ignored his slight to himself and perched on the edge of the worn velvet footstool that had seen better days. "Human emotion."

"Indeed." Godwin leaned forward, then back, as if unsure what to do with his limbs before finally crossing an ankle above his knee. "What manner of emotion?"

"The worst of them—fear, rage, control. It's for my latest writing project. Mr. Imlay always dreaded my displays of feeling." I bit my lip, unsure how much of my darkness I should reveal. William Godwin was known for his rectitude and honesty, plus I'd come here seeking authentic conversation. Even if it meant continuing the subterfuge that I'd been married to Gilbert Imlay. "I admit to a certain propensity for melancholy, as you may have heard."

A melancholy so deep I had jumped off Putney Bridge.

Godwin's coffee-brown gaze met and then held mine. I dared not look away during his silence—it felt like he was plumbing to my very core. Like he truly did *see* me. "I believe such displays of feeling are evidence of a person's depth, Miss Wollstonecraft. You have an artistic soul, and we artists, well, sometimes we feel and ache and *yearn* more deeply than those who have an easier time of this life."

My eyes smarted so I had to look at the rafters for a moment. "That's very kind of you. However, I recall Edmund Burke claiming it was masculine for a woman to be melancholy. If that's the case, I'm more male than Burke himself."

"First, Edmund Burke is a pompous ass, a fact that was clear even before you took him to task with your initial *Vindication*. Second, my statement is not kindness, only my honest thoughts." Godwin cleared his throat. "You should know that I don't prevaricate, Miss Wollstonecraft. It's a character defect that has lost me many acquaintances over the years."

I smiled, but then my stomach gave a rumble so loud it was impossible to ignore. I cursed myself—in my preoccupation with flouting society's rules and coming here, I'd forgotten to eat when I'd set Fanny's porridge in front of her this morning. Godwin sprang to his feet, so I worried I'd offended him somehow. "*Damnare*," he cursed in Latin as he fumbled around the stacks of books, searching for something. "I am a horrible host, not even offering you tea or a biscuit. I'm sure I have something around here, an apple perhaps, or maybe a tin of crackers . . ."

"Actually . . ." I hesitated only a moment. "Would you join me for supper? There's a clean-looking chophouse around the corner that claims to serve a decent plate of bangers and mash."

"The Black Horse?" Godwin straightened. "Their chine of mutton is the best item on the menu. Well, it's the only thing edible, at least."

I waited with bated breath until Godwin nabbed his coat and hat from its hook and opened the door with a flourish. "I'd be delighted to join you for supper, Miss Wollstonecraft, and discuss this new writing project of yours. Please, lead the way."

CHAPTER 13

❧

March 1817

MARY SHELLEY

"You really think I can publish this?" Mary asked Percy. They were breakfasting outside in the mild spring weather of the newly leased Albion House. Mary had taken one look at the house's impeccable stables, sprawling garden, and cozy library with its sunny window seat and fallen in love. And being thirty miles outside London was just enough distance that she could ignore *some* of the scandal sheets about their household, at least on a good day. The birth of Allegra—and Claire's constant presence alongside Mary and Percy—had hatched vicious rumors that Percy was the child's true father, ridiculous gossip that Mary wanted to crow to the world was untrue.

However, no one would listen to her—another woman painted by the brush of scandal—so right now, Mary did her best to ignore the broadsheets. London and its viciousness seemed far away while Claire and Allegra slept upstairs and Everina darted like a little squirrel among the garden topiaries.

"I don't just think you can publish *Frankenstein*." Percy tapped the pages with his knuckle before popping a handful of sultanas into his mouth. The story was still rough, but Percy had persuaded Mary to let him read a fair copy after dinner last night. He'd burned through several candles to stay up the entire night to finish. "I *know* it."

"I feel like I've birthed another child," Mary admitted as she buttered a thick slice of bread. It was true—the book had taken nine months to write and another six weeks to copy into a readable draft. Just shy of twenty years old, Mary had created a child *and* a novel, both of which she hoped would outlive her.

"Now all that remains is to find a suitable publishing house. It's unfortunate your mother's old publisher isn't still in business in St. Paul's Square. Joseph Johnson would snap this up quicker than you could blink."

Mary had hazy childhood memories of accompanying her father to visit Joseph Johnson on St. Paul's Churchyard, where the grandfatherly publisher had always plied her with peppermints hidden in his desk drawer. But his passing seven years ago had led to the closure of his revolutionary press.

"I'm not sure anyone will want *Frankenstein*. Especially when they realize a woman wrote it." Mary was familiar with her mother's publishing woes, that only Joseph Johnson had been bold enough to take a chance on a visionary female writer. And what Mary had written . . .

"There's never been a story like this. This *Frankenstein* of yours is brilliant."

"Or *The Modern Prometheus*," Mary amended. The second title was a nod to the classical Titan who stole fire from the gods and gifted it to man, just as her Victor Frankenstein placed the spark of life in a creature he knew not how to control. However, the name was also a nod to Percy, given that his latest work—which Mary was sure would be heralded as a masterpiece—was a lyrical drama about doomed Prometheus. After all, Percy was *her* Titan, who had lit the flame of so many of her passions. "I haven't decided on the title yet."

Everina ran to them, opening her mouth for the sultanas like a baby bird. Instead, Percy lifted and swung Everina in a circle, eliciting her wild shriek of laughter before he bent over in a coughing fit. Percy's health had deteriorated over the winter until Mary finally summoned a doctor after Christmas. The physician had made a grave pronouncement—*consumption*. But many people lived long lives with the condition; Percy just needed fresh air and to refrain from overexertion. Unfortunately, neither was likely here in England. He waved away her frown and cleared his throat as Everina climbed into his lap, fingers in her mouth and head leaning on his shoulder. "*Frankenstein* must be the title. This book of yours stands on its own."

"*If* it ever becomes a book. Right now it's just a pile of pages."

"It will line bookshop shelves for years to come, I guarantee it." He took a bite of bread and chewed thoughtfully before handing the rest to Everina. "We'll go to London this spring. Publishers will trip over themselves to print the words of this monster tale and your journals from our trip to Switzerland. You'll see."

It had taken another nine months, but Percy had been right. Of course, he'd also been right because he'd refused to drop the matter until *Frankenstein* found a publisher willing to print it.

Now Mary's novel would join the library's shelves at Albion House, a lone copy from the meager print run of five hundred. She tried not to be disappointed—Lord Byron's and her mother's works had sold tens of thousands; even Percy's sold in the thousands. But they were *real* writers.

Despite Percy's many enthusiastic assurances that she'd written a masterpiece, she was merely a pretender. She had dragged her heels on traveling to London to find a publisher, but Percy had insisted until she'd grown hesitantly excited about the idea. Now her father held her nascent creation open to the dedication page that bore his name. "*Gratias tibi ago*," he said. They sat in the library of Albion House, with its view of the garden that was just beginning to bend from winter to spring. "This is a precious gift, Mary, one I shall remember in perpetuity." He ran an ink-stained thumb over *Frankenstein*'s cheap paper cover.

Mary forced her hands to remain clasped in her lap, no matter how she longed for her father to ignore the cheap cover with its binding that threatened to split at any moment, and sweep her into a sage-scented embrace. The hope that he would be *proud* of her had motivated the dedication she'd written:

To
William Godwin
Author of Political Justice, Caleb, *&c.*
These volumes are respectfully inscribed
By
The author.

She'd written a different dedication—to her mother—before throwing it into the fire, unable to find the words to adequately express herself. Perhaps Mary had imagined it, but she felt as if her mother was urging her to use the dedication to send a message to Mary's father. This final version was an olive branch of ink and paper, the only language William Godwin sometimes understood.

Except her father didn't blink back stubborn tears or clear his throat of excess emotion, instead merely browsed the much-loved volumes lining the many shelves. Mary knew his usual lack of emotion shouldn't matter—after all, he was here and holding *her* book—but her heart turned leaden as she realized this moment was not going to unfold in any of the myriad ways she'd envisioned. No happy shouts of joy or bone-crushing embraces, just the same stoic coldness. Why could her father not tell her he was proud of her, that he loved her? Was she truly so unlovable?

This need for her father to envelop her in some warm blanket of love and praise—and the crushing disappointment that always followed when he did not—was a monster of her own making. And unlike Frankenstein, who abandoned his monster, she could not let it go.

"I'm glad the dedication is to your liking," she said, but her father merely paused his perusal of the shelves to frown at her.

"I do wish you'd been able to include your name on the book. Surely you can find a more prestigious publisher for the second run." *Frankenstein* had been published by Lackington, an undistinguished house of hack writers but one that owned the famous bookshop the Temple of the Muses, which Mary's mother had frequented. "Was anonymity truly necessary?" he asked. "Your mother was always able to claim her works."

"Unfortunately, I am not my mother." Mary's tone was more peevish than she liked, but William Godwin was giving voice to her own doubts. Her publisher had mandated that the public wasn't ready for a woman writing of such difficult themes as sublime nature, dangerous knowledge, and man as a monstrosity. They persuaded her that anonymity was better both for the book's sales *and* for Mary's already tarnished reputation.

It was the latter that had made Mary capitulate. That, and the impact she worried it would have on Percy, who had bowed to the publishers' demands that he publicly write the introduction to the book. Now people assumed Percy had written *Frankenstein*, and the bulk of the criticism against the book's dark and weighty themes fell on *his* shoulders. He claimed it didn't bother him, but his writing on *Prometheus Unbound* had stalled as a result, and his health continued to deteriorate. Her noble Elfin Knight had become fragile. *Breakable* . . .

To make matters worse, the usual gossip about Percy intensified immediately after they learned that he was not to receive custody of his children with Harriet.

The trial had been swift and brutal. Percy had tried to capitalize on facts shaken loose after Harriet's death—that she had taken up with a soldier and been abandoned first by him and then her family when they learned she was carrying a child not her husband's. There was a six-week gap from when her father turned her away from his doorstep until she had washed up dead in the river; rumor claimed she had been living as a prostitute.

However, none of that mattered. Shelley's infamy had only grown with Harriet's death. Even his marriage to Mary, meant to convey a veneer of respectability, had fanned the flames of scandal, and his previous walks about London with dark-haired Claire led to revived whispers that he was living in a harem. The judge ruled that due to Percy's immorality, young Ianthe and Charles would be raised by Harriet's parents, the Westbrooks.

In the wake of the failed custody attempt, Percy had grown morose and despondent, and his bleak mood only plumbed to new dark depths when the Westbrooks decided Ianthe and Charles would never be allowed to see him. To add insult to injury, reviews of Percy's latest poem, *The Revolt of Islam*, trickled in, all negative. The poem was set in the Far East, and Percy had tackled political and sexual reform, even daring to ask: *Can man be free if woman be a slave?* His idol, Mary Wollstonecraft, would have cheered from the rafters—her daughter certainly did—but critics crowed that Percy's vile political views promoted anarchy and scandalous behavior that had broken Harriet's heart and caused her suicide. Then he was diagnosed with rapidly worsening consumption and his appetite had declined until now he subsisted on a single lump of bread for days at a time.

Mary shook herself as her father cleared his throat. With weightier matters to attend to, it didn't matter that her name wasn't on *Frankenstein*'s cover, nor that her travelogue on their time in Switzerland—really just an edited compilation of her journals—had recently been published under Percy's name. For propriety's sake, of course. Name or no, she had still created two books that would outlast her, even if they would never compare with her mother's or father's or husband's works. She had manufactured entire worlds from ink and ideas, even if no one would ever know they were hers. That would have to be enough.

"Where is Percy this morning?" Godwin fiddled with the timepiece in his vest. "I thought he'd be down by now."

"He departed at sunrise for the British Museum. The marble ruins Lord Elgin brought from Athens are being displayed and Percy likes to visit the statue of Pharaoh Ramses as well. He's started a sonnet about it, actually." The lines Percy had toiled over last night still danced like spindrift in her mind:

> *I met a traveler from an antique land*
> *Who said: Two vast and trunkless legs of stone*
> *Stand in the desert. . . .*
> *"My name is Ozymandias, king of kings:*
> *Look on my works, ye Mighty, and despair!"*

Her father merely grunted. Poetry had never caught his interest. "With treasures like the British Museum, I cannot fathom why you two are choosing once again to traipse around the Continent like common vagrants. Worse still, you're allowing Claire and her daughter to join you in this madness! Far safer to sink your roots deep in English soil and not drag my grandchildren around where they might catch all manner of illness."

Except it wasn't the children that were ill . . .

"We must leave, Father. Surely you can see that, given Percy's health. Not to mention the scandal sheets."

"Even if I live to be one hundred, I will never fathom why you all associated with Lord Byron. I read about his Venetian orgies—Claire should be ashamed that she fraternized with such a man. Much less that she produced a child with him."

"Please," Mary pleaded. "Don't mention any of that to Claire. She gets so upset when Byron is mentioned." Which was why Mary and Percy doggedly kept the latest gossip away from her.

A change of scenery would do them all a world of good, especially as Mary spent countless nights staring at the ceiling after reading about Percy's relationship with Claire. She'd been able to think of little else, couldn't chase the dark shadows from under her eyes.

Monsters, indeed. She was becoming a victim of the gossip pages in more ways than one. Percy thought of Claire as a sister, nothing more.

"Mary?" Her father was looking at her pointedly. "I asked when Claire and Allegra are joining you." He buttoned his aubergine-toned jacket, a sign that their visit was drawing to a close. Mary had no idea when they would see each other again; given England's treatment of Percy, she had a mind to stay in azure Italy's pure air and burning sun indefinitely.

"Immediately. Lord Byron is currently in Italy, and Claire is hoping they can live together as a family."

Godwin's sniff matched Mary's own disdain, but for a different reason. Mary knew that Claire hoped Allegra's famous father would extend enough financial security for them to live the life of leisure she'd always imagined for herself. Not only that, but Claire still waxed poetic over Byron, which was unfathomable to Mary, given his high-handed treatment of her.

"You should call upon Maria Reveley when you're in Italy," her father suddenly said. "Although I suppose she's Maria Gisborne now."

"My old nurse?"

"Maria was far more than your nurse. She was a dear friend of your mother's—she painted the portrait of her in my study."

Mary hadn't realized that. "I'll write to her before we leave."

"I hope you find what you need in Italy, *corculum*." Her father squeezed her shoulder as she showed him out. Mary hated herself for lapping up the crumbs of that sparse touch and the return of her childhood endearment. "And that you then return home, where you belong."

As Mary watched him walk away, his aubergine waistcoat gaudier than a summer dragonfly, she wondered if she'd ever live up to his expectations.

Italy was beautiful.

So beautiful, in fact, that after clearing the Alps and arriving in Turin, Mary declared she was never leaving. "The very air is different," she effused to Percy as they meandered down a green lane sprigged with buttercups and bluebells to see an ancient triumphal arch that had been erected in honor of the Roman emperor Augustus. Delicate dove-colored cows lowed in the distance as she and Percy swung young Everina between them.

"Health, competence, tranquility." Once away from London's smoke and its chilling fogs and rain, Percy had floated about in a haze of happiness. "All these Italy permits and England takes away."

Mary smiled. "I feel like we can finally breathe again."

Claire scowled from behind them, carrying little Allegra on her hip. "The air is the same everywhere." Her chiding sounded like a younger version of her mother. Gone was the carefree songbird of their younger days—even Claire's lips possessed Jane's same wry twist. Mary felt a pang of regret, wishing she could go back to guide Claire to make different choices. At least Allegra's smiles could coax a gleam of happiness to Claire's eyes—nothing else did these days. "You're not immune from your worries just because the Italian climate is warmer."

Except Percy's lungs *did* clear in that clean Mediterranean air. Eager to secure lodgings for their party and Lord Byron—who surprised them with an announcement that he would join them from Venice—Percy signed papers on a half-ruined old villa, packed with tapestries and paved with marble, that offered a blinding view of Lake Como. Mary fervently hoped that Byron would come and claim Claire and Allegra, so they could work out this mess between them and she might burrow deeper into these precious moments with her own little family.

That had been her greatest hope, until Percy received a scathing letter from Lord Byron that caused his face to turn a sickly shade of white. "He refuses to see Claire," he whispered, not wanting Mary's sister to hear from the other room. "And commands that I play courier to all communication between them."

Mary set down her copy of Homer—she and Percy had been reading the classics since passing through the Alps. "Enough is enough. Claire must cease contact with him."

"But his demands . . ." Percy handed Mary the paper, as if unable to speak the details.

Insatiable, incorrigible, indomitable *demands*.

With the slash of his pen, mercurial Lord Byron had donned

a tyrant's full mantle. "Claire will die before sending Allegra to live with him in Venice," Mary whispered.

"Will she? Better to be the bastard-born daughter of Lord Byron, rather than the illegitimate offspring of plain Claire Clairmont, don't you think?" Percy's parrot of Byron's words were despairing rather than cruel as he cradled his forehead in his hands. "This is rich, given Byron's recent proclivities."

Mary winced. She and Percy had tried to keep from Claire the rumors of the sex-and-alcohol-drenched bacchanalia that Byron reputedly put on in Venice. Mary knew from experience that the scandal sheets could lie and exaggerate, but she also knew Byron. By now, Claire had likely heard of the sinful revels, although she had yet to mention them.

But she certainly heard Byron's current demands, given that she had crept her way on cat's feet to the doorway. Mary and Percy could only stare as she held out a hand for the paper and read it with ever-widening eyes. "What sort of beast does he think I am, that I could abandon my child?" Tears slipped down her cheeks as Allegra cooed from the next room. "Does he truly think so little of me?"

"Write to him." Mary ached for Claire as she stood and squeezed her shoulder, truly she did. Yet she also understood that Lord Byron was a powerful man with a volatile temper. And the law was on his side, especially since Byron had acknowledged Allegra as his own—one snap of his beringed fingers and Claire would never see her daughter again. Mary wanted to rage against the still-standing injustice that her mother had railed about decades ago; instead she went to the next room and plucked Allegra from her cradle, pressing a kiss to the still-soft depression on the baby's crown. To refuse Byron entirely would incite violence; to compromise had the greatest chance of success. "Tell him of your love for this sweet girl and demand in no uncertain terms that you be allowed to visit her." She stood in the doorway, swaying slightly to rock Allegra to sleep. "Cite my mother's words—Byron will have a difficult time arguing against Mary Wollstonecraft."

"Will you help me?"

There was no hesitation in Mary's answer as she handed Allegra back to her mother. "Of course."

Thus, Percy played with the children that afternoon while Claire penned her letter to Byron—with Mary's guidance. Claire's tears splashed all over the paper until it was scarcely readable. "Mail it for me, won't you?" she asked Mary once they were finished. "I've wept so much tonight that my eyes seem to drop hot and burning blood."

Silent days passed. Dejected and seeking to appease Byron so he would agree to her visitations, Claire sent Allegra to Venice and then fell into a deep morass of sadness.

"I received an invitation from Maria Reveley," Mary announced to Percy over breakfast after several weeks of tiptoeing on eggshells around Claire. Her sister's melancholy was bottomless, and Mary found the excuse of her mother's old friend both convenient and alluring. Mary had wandered the streets of Paris hoping to find her mother's spirit; here in Italy she hoped to do the same. "Maria Reveley—Gisborne now, since she's remarried—took me into her house and raised me while my father learned to manage his grief. I'd like to hear what she remembers about my mother. I think you'd enjoy meeting her as well."

"We can all go," Percy said while Claire stared dejectedly out the wide window. "An expedition will put the color back in all our cheeks again."

Mary instantly regretted extending the invitation, then felt guilty for wanting to spend an afternoon alone, or perhaps just with Percy. Not even Livorno's picturesque coast, russet-roofed villas, or the fragrant jasmine that cascaded off the town's many stone walls could shake her sister's despondency after they'd all piled into the hired coach together. "I'm afraid I'm not fit for company," Claire announced in a quiet voice once they'd arrived at the Gisborne villa in Livorno. "I'd like to return home."

"I'll pay my respects to Mrs. Gisborne and accompany you back," Percy said. True to form, he could never resist a helpless woman, but his eyes beseeched Mary: *Can't you see she's miserable?* "The coach can return for you, Mary, or perhaps the Gisbornes can spare their hackney?"

Mary's responsibility to her sister was strong enough that she nearly canceled her rendezvous with Maria Gisborne and turned around with them. Only the reminder that Maria held the key to many remembrances of Mary Wollstonecraft had her agreeing, albeit hesitantly. "If you don't mind . . ."

"Certainly not. This is important."

Claire had already closed her eyes to the world, her head leaned against the coach's wall.

"My word, if it isn't Mary Shelley and her husband!" Maria Gisborne answered her own door, despite the austere front garden and well-appointed drawing room. Nearing fifty, she was far past the springtide of youth, but the concise elegance of her carriage drew the eye back time and again. Or would have, had not an enormous black-and-tan bloodhound bounded out the door, barking cheerfully at Mary and Percy. "You could pass for your mother's younger sister," Maria added to Mary as she reined in the hellhound with a commanding whistle that could have stopped an entire regiment in its tracks. "Even Jupiter here recognizes the friend in you—he's the grandson of your sister Fanny's pup Merryboy, you know." Mary could see the sudden resemblance, even though Merryboy had died when she still wore plaits. "I'm pleasantly surprised—we didn't expect you for several weeks."

"There was a change in plans." Noting the easel set in the front parlor and the colorful smudges on Maria's fingers, Mary suddenly doubted her arrival here. "But I'm happy to return another day if my appearance is an inconvenience."

"Not at all." Maria glanced behind her, but the parlor remained empty, save the easel. "I was just finishing a project and readying to take Jupiter here out on his lead, but I can arrange for some biscuits and madeira instead."

"I'd be happy to walk," Mary admitted. Jupiter had sprawled at Maria's feet and was actually drooling through his many jowls onto her fashionably heeled court shoes. "The coach ride from Lake Como was overlong."

Maria patted her hand, as if understanding there were hidden strata to that innocent statement. "Let me just inform Mr. Gisborne that I'll be longer than expected. We have much to discuss."

"I'm afraid I must depart immediately." Percy gestured to the waiting coach. "Mary's sister is feeling poorly. However, I couldn't leave without meeting the woman who raised my beloved wife as a child."

After Percy took his leave—following Maria's exhortations that he must call again one day soon—Mary and Maria strolled along Livorno's seawall under twin striped parasols, only the occasional shrieking gull and Jupiter's excited barking sometimes punctuating their conversation. Mary had very few memories of Maria, but just walking and talking with this sage woman who had known her mother felt like a homecoming of sorts.

"Mary Wollstonecraft was the most courageous woman—nay, the most courageous *person*—I've ever met," Maria admitted with a bittersweet smile. "Your mother faced down the lion's maw on more than one occasion, for both you and Fanny." By now Maria had threaded her arm through Mary's and had set their pace to a leisurely stroll. The waves today were calm, the waters dappled like a sultan's jewel chest—glittering sapphires and emeralds, with a foam crafted of pearls. "I was terribly saddened to hear of your sister's passing. And I'm even more heartsick that your mother isn't around to meet your little one you wrote of. A daughter, yes?"

Mary nodded proudly. "Percy and I hope for a nursery full."

Maria's chestnut-brown eyes sparked with genuine joy. "Well, I hope you'll stay in Italy long enough that I can meet all the grandchildren of Mary Wollstonecraft. I still miss the sound of her laugh, not to mention that wit that pilloried so many people. All of them deserving, of course."

That was a side of her mother that Mary had never heard mentioned. To hear her father tell it, Mary Wollstonecraft had been one step short of sainthood. Feeling like a much younger girl, Mary leaned her head toward Maria's. "Do tell."

So, Maria did.

Wonderful tales of Mary's mother skewering William Godwin during their first meetings and how she took to task Henry Fuseli and Thomas Holcroft and even godly Edmund Burke. Those anecdotes had Mary both chuckling and beaming with pride while the waves crashed into the seawall beneath them. But there were also stories of Mary Wollstonecraft walking through the blood of the guillotines and fleeing for her life during the Terror. And of holding Mary for the last time before she finally slipped the tethers of this life.

Maria Reveley—it was difficult to think of her as Gisborne— dabbed her eyes with an embroidered handkerchief. "Your mother wrote like a woman possessed before the fever finally claimed her."

Mary blinked at that. "Difficult to imagine writing at such a moment."

"She wanted to commit her life's story to paper." Maria looked to her. "She'd started in the final weeks of her pregnancy, at my urging, actually. She wrote for you, Mary, and for Fanny—an entire journal's worth. So that you girls—and the rest of the world—might know the truth of her."

"Are you saying my mother wrote an entire book no one has ever read? About her *life*?" Such a treasure would be finer than a chest of pearls. Mary felt as if she were shaking loose cobwebs within her skull. "But I've never heard of these writings."

Maria stopped walking, one fist on her hip and a fierce frown beneath her lace-trimmed parasol. "Your father never gave you the manuscript?" Mary shook her head vehemently. "But I'm sure he kept it safe all these years."

"Are you quite sure he has it? He's never mentioned it."

"I gave it to him—your mother always intended the pages would go to him, just not right away. She worried he'd be too full of grief and raising you girls, and she didn't want him lingering in the past. I cannot believe he didn't give it to you. Nor the letter I wrote, explaining the volume?"

Mary shook her head again. Then: "Why did you feel you needed to explain?"

"I wanted you and Fanny to understand your mother before you started reading. So you weren't shocked." Maria drummed her fingers on her arm. "Mary Wollstonecraft led a most unorthodox life. Your father truly never mentioned it?"

"My father never gave me anything."

"Damn you, William Godwin," Maria muttered before apologizing to Mary. "No woman was ever more happy in marriage than your mother was with your father, and no man endured more anguish than your father after her passing. But your father can be quite . . . trying."

A fact Mary was all too aware of. "I had to sneak the memoir he wrote about my mother."

Maria's scoff was an indelicate sound coming from such a stately woman. "*Memoirs of the Author of A Vindication of the Rights of Woman*? That rubbish never should have seen daylight. Your father's mind was so clouded by grief then that he couldn't think straight. For years, actually, including when he proposed to me."

Mary gaped. "My father . . . *proposed*?"

Maria's face softened with her wry chuckle. "A mere month after my first husband died. William Godwin didn't want a *real* wife, only a mother for his daughters, and I'd already been caring for you, as you know. Your father is a brilliant man—undoubtedly eccentric and sometimes cantankerous but undeniably brilliant—yet he didn't understand that, after my first marriage, I wouldn't settle for anything less than a love match. However, he found what he needed in your stepmother, and I met my talented Mr. Gisborne. I gave your father the journal shortly before we decamped to Italy."

That meant that not long after Maria had rejected his proposal and left their household, Godwin settled for Jane Clairmont. Their lack of suitability made sudden sense—not a love match or even one with much affection, but two people who required partners to raise their children. Mary recalled the tiny kindnesses Jane showed her father—darning all of his waistcoats with precision, serving his favorite venison stew at least once a week, making sure his slippers were always laid by the fire. The lack of affection certainly seemed more one-sided in the case of Mary's father. Still, how different all their lives would have been had Maria Reveley accepted William Godwin.

But to marry for convenience instead of love . . . Well, Mary wouldn't wish that on anyone.

Once back at the Gisborne villa, Maria embraced her mother's old friend while Jupiter nudged her hand with his damp nose. "I have a strong feeling you and I will be fast friends, just as your mother and I were." She insisted that Mary return to Lake Como with a tin of sugar biscuits for Percy and Everina, then offered one final piece of advice. "Since you mentioned Mr. Shelley's illness, be sure to avoid Florence and Rome and Venice, at least until the weather cools. Italian cities are cesspools for all manner of dreadful summer diseases."

Allegra was already in Venice, but surely she'd be safe in Byron's villa. Wouldn't she?

Mary's restless return journey to Lake Como was soothed only by the knowledge that there was an unknown trove of her mother's memories safe in her father's keeping. She disembarked early, wanting to walk the last mile, the metal tin of biscuits under one arm while her sunbonnet dangled down her back. The decadent silence felt like a return to something from which she had long been absent. Upon approaching the secluded three-story Villa Bertini, Mary spotted Percy inside the thick hedge that guarded the house. Storm clouds gathered on the western horizon, but Percy sat on the rocks with his back to her, sunning himself like a king upon some secret throne near the burbling woodland stream that dropped into a succession of pools and small waterfalls, dappled daylight sparkling like the rarest of diamonds on the water's surface.

A volume dangled in his hands—Herodotus, Mary guessed as she drew closer—but otherwise . . .

Otherwise Percy was entirely nude.

Mary paused for a breathless moment, absorbing the scene

as Percy lifted his sun-kissed face to a skylark that landed on an overhead branch and merrily chirped away. He seemed so vibrant in that moment, so healthy. Seeming to sense her gaze, Percy turned, a slow smile lighting his eyes before he cocked his head in question.

A question she well knew the answer to.

Mary was already untying her straw bonnet as she approached, the sight of him giving wings to her soul. The sun and fresh air had finally chased the shadows from under Percy's eyes. He looked strong, healthy.

> *Teach us, Sprite or Bird,*
> *What sweet thoughts are thine:*
> *I have never heard*
> *Praise of love or wine*
> *That panted forth a flood of rapture so divine.*

"What's that?" Mary murmured, dropping to her knees beside him.

"Lines that came to me just now. Inspired by both the skylark and my Faerie Queene."

Heat rose to her cheeks, especially at the scene his final line inspired. Pursuit of another child or no, in that moment, there was only one person Mary wanted. And he was right before her.

"How is my fair wife this afternoon?" Percy's hair was still damp from a prior dip, delicate beads of moisture clinging stubbornly to his skin. Mary yearned to touch and taste them. To taste *him*. That muse of a skylark paused its song, seeming to sense their need for privacy, and fluttered away.

"Your fair wife is missing her husband," Mary responded with a glance toward the house.

"They've all gone into town." Percy answered the question as he took the bonnet and bag from her hand so they could join the abandoned volume of Herodotus.

Mary threaded her arms around her husband's neck and tilted her head to soak up that glorious sun as Percy's deft fingers undid the buttons at her back, baring her shoulders to the summer breeze. She practically purred with pleasure as his lips added to that decadent warmth.

And she knew one thing as Percy laid her out on that sun-warmed rock: they could be happy here in Italy.

For seven weeks Mary and Percy swam together in that warm sea of happiness, worshipping nature and each other. They read the classics and explored the tangled wilds around their villa, then made love nightly until they were drunk on it while hoping Mary's womb would fill. Everina thrilled Percy by saying, "Father," and raced around their hilltop retreat on sturdy legs like a tiny Amazon, chasing birds and pointing at butterflies that flittered past. The only dark spot among them was Claire, who first twisted her ankle and then injured her leg while riding with Percy. It seemed that Claire's happiness always decreased in response to Mary's own joy; the only time she smiled these days was when she was with Percy, although even then, hers were always sad and wistful smiles. As if envisioning what might have been.

In the days after her visit with Maria Gisborne, Mary also sent off a carefully worded letter to her father, regaling him with anecdotes about their recent happiness along with a concise postscript about her visit with Maria and a query as to the whereabouts of Mary Wollstonecraft's missing journal. There was no answer yet, but it wasn't unlike her father to let the post sit for days—or weeks—before finally responding.

Everything was idyllic. Until it wasn't.

Percy returned to the villa one humid afternoon in a spray of gravel as he reined in his horse and dismounted in a blur. Lazy from the heat haze, Mary had been wandering through the overgrown gardens, imagining them as a scene in a new novel when Percy ran to her.

"Where's your sister?" His eyes were frantic. "Where is Claire?"

"Inside, lying down," she answered, her heart starting to pound. "What's happened?"

"Disaster." Percy's chest heaved as he pressed two letters into Mary's hand. "Allegra's nurse wrote begging us to rescue her and Allegra. Byron has forced her to move out, and the nurse claims that he wants to raise Allegra to be his future mistress."

"What?"

"I don't know the truth, but surely something terrible happened for the nurse to write so desperately. Perhaps Byron's debauchery has finally ruined his mind. The nurse fears for her own safety, and for Allegra's. We must go to Venice. Immediately."

Mary glanced around their magical villa, the wild sunlight streaming down on Percy while his horse pranced behind him, and felt their perfect idyll retreat into the afternoon shadows. Her Elfin Knight, always willing to ride to everyone's rescue.

"Of course you must go, and quickly."

"I'll have all our bags packed immediately."

Mary placed a hand on Percy's forearm. "I can't leave Everina, and taking us both will only slow you down. Maria warned me about the cities during the summer—it isn't safe for children. You've only just recovered your health."

Percy hesitated before pressing a kiss to her forehead. "I've never felt stronger. But you're right about Everina—Claire and

I will leave immediately. We'll be there and back before anyone notices we're gone."

Mary bit her tongue as Percy rushed into the house, wondering whether she might persuade her sister to remain at the villa with her. But Claire was Allegra's mother. And if Mary's child were in danger . . .

No, she would let them go without an argument.

A scant hour later, Mary and Everina waved to Percy and a frantic Claire as they departed with promises that he would write the moment they arrived in Venice.

Mary barely waited until they were out of earshot before she turned to face northeast, the direction of Venice. "Damn you, Byron," she muttered under her breath. "Damn you to hell and back."

The fever started a week after Percy and Claire left for Venice.

Everina woke Mary from a troubled sleep with her whimpering—as if it were too hot for her to rouse fully and cry out. "You poor sweet thing," Mary murmured as she untangled her daughter from the blanket, alarm growing as she felt the heat roiling off that tiny little body. She recalled the story of how her mother had nursed Fanny through smallpox, and panic jangled through the marrow of her very bones—there were no telltale pox on Everina, but everyone knew fevers in the very young were dangerous. Especially summer fevers.

Unsure what to do, she woke the housemaid, but the girl shook her head in the candlelight. "I don't know, *signora*. Maybe she is teething?"

Mary knew this was more than teething. She motioned for the maid to dress. "Ride for Maria Gisborne in Livorno. If you leave now, you can bring her back by noon."

It was a long wait, made longer still by Everina's fitful whimpers. The poor mite couldn't be parted from Mary's side, so they lay together in bed with the windows and doors flung open. The meager breeze did little more than shuffle the hot and humid air while Mary pressed cool compresses to Everina's blazing forehead. Mary was as fretful as her daughter by the time Maria arrived.

"You poor dears," Maria tutted as she felt Everina's forehead with the back of her hand, eyes widening at the tiny furnace contained within the girl's skull. Mary felt the start of tears and plumbed some hidden well of strength to push them down.

"The compresses aren't enough," Mary whispered, throat constricting at the fear she refused to voice. "I don't know what else to do."

"A cool bath would be a good start. Not too cold," Maria instructed, "but enough to lower her temperature. Your mother taught me that."

"Will Everina be all right?" Mary asked as they slowly dribbled the cool water over her daughter. Everina had cried when they'd tried to submerge her feet and legs, reaching out for her mother. Mary couldn't stand it and had proclaimed that they'd bring the water to Everina instead.

"The young are stronger than they look," Maria affirmed, but Mary knew that was no real assurance. "So long as the fever doesn't develop into anything further, she can rally."

Between the two of them, they managed to calm Everina enough that she settled into a restless sleep. Maria had gone down to the kitchens to fetch some tea when the maid clomped up the stairs. Mary motioned for her to be silent, but the girl only held out a creamy envelope. "A letter from Signore Shelley arrived."

Mary read the letter, then reread it. By the third reading, she had sunk onto the stairs. She hadn't moved when Maria found her there. "Percy needs me in Venice," she said, still dumbfounded. "He says I can be there in five days if I leave tomorrow."

"You can't go," Maria announced. "Not until Everina recovers."

And that was what had kept Mary sitting on the stair, desperate to glean some direction from Percy's note.

"*Damnare,*" she muttered, then looked up at Maria, wondering if anyone else could feel the cracks that suddenly streaked like lightning through the ground beneath her feet. As if hell itself were sending her a warning. "Percy lied to Byron," she finally got out, her mind winging ahead to scan the gauntlet of disasters suddenly placed before her. "He told him that *I* was waiting to receive Allegra in Venice instead of Claire. If I'm not there to take Claire's daughter, Byron won't hand her over. And Percy can't stay alone with Claire for much longer without the world finding out."

My husband courts scandal, she wanted to say. *While my sister opens the door and ushers it in with promises of warmth and sweets. And only I can save them.*

"I need more time to decide." Mary held her head in her hands. "But instead I must either pack or send Percy my refusal."

"Everina seems to have settled somewhat." Maria spoke slowly. "Pack a bag and decide in the morning. Rest and make a decision with a clear head in the light of day."

Mary felt her vision blur with tears and she berated herself for the weakness until she realized its source: she'd never had another woman to lean on in times of need. Maria had just acted as Mary's own mother *would* have, had Mary Wollstonecraft lived to this day.

Maria seemed to understand her thoughts. "I'll stay through the night. In case you need me."

The offer made Mary weak-kneed with relief. "Thank you. I'm not sure I could do this on my own."

"You surely could, but you don't have to. That's what friends—and family—are for." Maria pressed her forehead to Mary's. "You *are* your mother's daughter. Remember that whenever you doubt yourself. The blood that runs in your veins is fierce enough to make even Napoleon tremble."

Mary's view of the world had narrowed until it contained nothing more than the pinpoint of a restless infant. Everina's hair remained matted to her fevered forehead, and her cheeks flushed ever brighter as she struggled to sleep.

The hours crawled by, each one seeing Mary vacillate on whether she would attempt the journey to Percy. After spending every moment either tending to Everina or packing her bags, it was only as dusk settled and Maria called her down to the kitchen that Mary even remembered what day it was.

"Happy birthday, Mary." Maria held up a tiny glass of grappa in a celebratory toast. She had whipped up a simple *sbrisolona* cake dotted with almonds, a sweet luxury during such a trying time. "One-and-twenty, isn't it?"

Mary pushed her bedraggled hair from her face and used a hand to fan her damp bodice. When would this infernal heat dissipate? "I feel twice that."

"Time is the cruelest of tricksters. When you reach my advanced age, you'll feel half your years, that is until you look in a mirror." Maria pressed a plate of cake into Mary's hand. "Which is why I removed most of the mirrors from my house."

Mary broke off a piece of cake with her fork and savored the rich flavor of the almonds and lemon and sugar. Just like life—the sour with the sweet. "I'm glad we were able to spend these past days together," she said wistfully to Maria. "I only wish we'd had more time."

"You've decided, then?"

"Percy is waiting for me. I can't let him down—Everina and I depart at dawn."

"You must love him very much."

"My heart is his and his is mine." It was a simple and unalterable truth. "One of us cannot live without the other."

"Then you are lucky, especially to have found such a match so young. Your mother waited too long for a love like that."

Mary thought of her father. If Mary Wollstonecraft and William Godwin felt half what Mary did for Percy, then it was no wonder that her father now floated through life in a daze, lost between one moment and the next. Mary would be unmoored without Percy.

"I sometimes think my mother might have brought Percy to me." Mary had never spoken that truth out loud. "That we were meant to be."

She waited for Maria to scoff, but her mother's old friend only smiled. "Your mother possessed a formidable will. It wouldn't surprise me to learn that she had found a way to watch over you."

Mary could only hope that her mother would continue to do so.

And especially watch over Everina.

CHAPTER 14

❧

May 1796

MARY WOLLSTONECRAFT

That daring supper at the Black Horse was the first of many between William Godwin and me.

By the end of spring, Godwin began frequenting my dinner table on a regular basis. I'd worried about introducing him to Fanny, but then, I'd had no qualms introducing Maria Reveley to Fanny, so why would I fret over a different friend?

To my delight, Godwin was patient with my daughter's childish antics, and Merryboy's too. While Merryboy begged shamelessly under the table, we ate wholesome meals made from ingredients I purchased from the surrounding farms—Cheshire cheese and mutton, omelets and gooseberry pies, fish custard and pea soup—and discussed philosophy. I enjoyed the food and conversation so much that Godwin jested I'd have made a fine acolyte of the pleasure-seeking ancient Greek philosopher Epicurus, to which I retorted that at least Epicurus would have allowed me—a woman—to join his school. (Which led Godwin to point out that Epicurus also allowed slaves to join his school, which would have been revolutionary in any era.) Once the table was cleared, Godwin and I went on evening ambles down the lanes—often taking Merryboy, who tore through fields chasing hapless geese—while Marguerite readied my daughter for bed. Our cheerful conversations on those walks were often the highlight of my days.

One early June evening, I found myself distracted while Godwin and I strolled into the dusk. Over the course of the past month, we had exhausted an expansive list of topics ranging from Gothic architecture to slavery in the West Indies, Napoleon's current campaign against Austria to the best breeds of English dogs. (I claimed bloodhounds in solidarity with Merryboy; Godwin added foxhounds in honor of a beloved pet he'd had as a boy.) I worried that soon we would run out of topics and that Godwin would grow weary of me as Gilbert Imlay had. But there was something between Godwin and me that Imlay had mostly abandoned before he met me—our love of the written word. Words had sustained my long friendship with Johnson and so, too, might they fortify this fledgling acquaintanceship. Thus, I finally worked up the courage to set free the trapped bird that had long been fluttering about my mind.

"I was wondering, if you have time, that is, if you might be interested in reading my latest writing project. It's a play, which I've never attempted before." I fiddled with the fringe of my shawl and avoided looking at Godwin. I was asking too much of him; surely he was too busy to read something so ill formed. "It's quite rough and I understand if you're unavailable."

"I'm flattered," Godwin said. "However . . ."

I waved a hand. "I shouldn't have imposed. Of course you're not interested—"

To which Godwin grazed my elbow with his fingertips, as if to gain my attention. That initial contact felt heavy, important somehow. His eyes were kind—how had I never noticed the flecks of green around his pupils, like tiny chips from some sultan's emerald? "I was only going to say that I'm a stiff critic.

If you can bear up under stark criticism, I'd be honored to read your play."

All the fine words I might have said flew away, the trapped bird suddenly soaring skyward. I cleared my throat, both excited and terrified at the same time. Why had I asked him to read my work, especially when it was in such coarse form? What if he thought me a fraud after reading it? *Of course* he was going to think me a fraud. I swallowed, hard. "Let me just retrieve the manuscript."

I hesitated as I bound the slim stack of pages in twine. Never had anyone other than Johnson read my work before publication. Still, I found myself craving Godwin's feedback, knowing instinctively that his quiet prodding would further buttress my ideas.

He was still standing on the front step watching lazy insects buzzing drunkenly in the warm air when I returned with the pages. "The gloaming has always been my favorite time of day," he said. "The world seems so at peace."

"It *is* lovely." I tilted my chin ever so slightly so our gazes met and he stepped forward, reaching for me. In the dying light, I might have almost believed that Godwin would kiss me.

More surprisingly, I found I wanted him to.

Except he wasn't reaching for me—he aimed for the manuscript I held between us.

"Is this it?" he asked. "The play?"

I cursed myself for my feminine flight of fancy. I *must* stop reading novels and writing plays if this was a side effect of fiction. Only dull factual treatises from now on.

I might want William Godwin to kiss me, but I doubted very much that the feeling was reciprocated. And my craving certainly wasn't wise.

"I apologize in advance if your eyes bleed," I said. "I'm no playwright, but this has been an enjoyable experiment."

"I'll read it straightaway and organize my thoughts before next we meet."

"Take as long as you need." I wanted nothing more than to reclaim the pages, but I'd felt the same inclination when I'd left *Education of Daughters* with Johnson. That had ended happily—this might too. "Or burn it, if that's easier."

"Trust yourself, Mary," he said. "We push ourselves to accomplish something new every time we set our pen to a page. That's something."

I liked that Godwin didn't assure me that he'd enjoy my play. Honesty from William Godwin, always.

And I realized something as my new friend strode off into the gloaming . . .

Tonight was the first time he'd called me Mary.

"It's crude and imperfect."

Godwin paused as he tucked away his spectacles and slid the manuscript across the table to me, probably waiting to see if I'd fly into hysterics. I didn't—I knew my play was crude and imperfect. And certainly a lot of other things, none of them good.

I'd never tell Godwin, but I didn't care if the play was ever published. It was a cheap scarecrow that I planned to develop into a living, breathing novel dramatizing the plight of abandoned and abused females. I found fiction more difficult to write, but this topic required plumbing the depths of humanity's darkest emotions—fear and horror and the desperate need for control and power.

I sometimes wondered if I was the right woman to write such a story.

"Indeed," I said over a bite of mutton, pausing only to admonish Fanny—whom Godwin had taken to calling Fannikin—to stop kicking the table leg. "That's why I asked you to read it."

A smile quirked the corner of Godwin's mouth. He scooted his chair nearer, so close our knees brushed under the table. I expected him to draw back, but he only leaned closer, flipping through pages with single-minded focus. "The ideas are good—especially the bits about women needing to stand on their own, but the punctuation and grammar are wanting."

I dabbed the corner of my lips with a serviette, forcing myself to focus. It was true—I'd always leaned on Johnson when it came to the finer points of commas and syntax for final versions of my work. And this was the earliest, messiest sort of draft. "Well, perhaps you could teach me."

Godwin reached over and cut one of Fanny's pieces of mutton, which she promptly popped into her mouth, smiling around it before taking a healthy swallow of milk. "T'ank you," she said to him. "Man."

"You're quite welcome, Fannikin."

I smiled—Fannikin and Man, they were now my favorite dinner companions.

"I find it ironic that the theme of the play is that men shouldn't be seen as rescuers of women, yet you're asking me to save you from an injudicious use of semicolons."

My laugh deepened at Godwin's mock high-handedness. Correcting grammar might seem like a strange basis for a friendship, but there it was.

"Perhaps we can go over the manuscript tomorrow?" It was already late—we'd gone for our walk before supper, and Fanny had yawned several times into her milk cup.

Godwin shook his head. "I'm headed to Bristol tomorrow. I'll be gone several weeks, actually."

"Oh?" I couldn't explain the shadow that fell across my mood then. I reached for my cup of cider to avoid looking at him. "I shall miss our suppers together."

Godwin's hand moved toward mine, but then he merely straightened the serving platter. "Then I shall write to you, which will be infinitely better. I've been reminded many times that my character is far more palatable on paper than in person."

There it was again, that self-deprecation.

His hand still on the table, I leaned over and grazed his knuckles, surprised at the surge of energy that went straight to my beating heart. His startled gaze locked with mine. I had to clear the emotions from my throat and infuse lighthearted sunshine into my voice. "I expect a letter every other day. No artificial compositions either—just a bird's-eye view of your innermost thoughts."

He gave a madcap grin. "I promise you nothing less."

I had just finished checking my honeybees one morning when the post finally arrived. It was still early, before the heat of the day set in. After the first rush of summer nectar, my bees were now in a dearth, which I empathized with all too much. Godwin's visits had been sweeter than honey; his absence would have left my days empty and listless had it not been for my writing of *The Wrongs of Woman*, which occupied all my rare moments not spent with Fanny. Still, I missed the timbre of his voice and the sound of his laughter entwined with Fanny's.

Fortunately, there was a post road directly from Bristol to London, which meant I didn't wait more than a few days for a scarlet-liveried postboy to deliver Godwin's first letter. I didn't even take off my bee veil when it arrived, just removed my kidskin gloves and read through a hazy cloud of buzzing bees and white gossamer.

The letter began with a brief discussion of his journey and

his impressions of Bath, including the lack of proper dining establishments and how he preferred our suppers together. It was the very end of the letter that struck me senseless:

> *Now, I take all my gods to witness that your company infinitely delights me, that I love your imagination, your delicate epicurism, the malicious leer of your eyes, in short everything that constitutes the bewitching tout ensemble of the celebrated Mary.*

I read and reread the words. Had he spoken them over dinner, I might have guessed that he was courting me. Did William Godwin *court*? More to the point, if he *was* courting, did I want him courting *me*?

The immediate response in my mind? *Yes.*

Godwin and I were both writers—the emotions and questions and statements that flowed from our pens were the dearest truths that our lips weren't brave enough to utter. Yet, I wasn't entirely convinced of the ardency of William Godwin's feelings—perhaps he was just pining for the comfort of the familiar. Still, his letter begged a response.

Thus, I abandoned my bees and hummed my way inside, where I took up my quill.

> *You say that I am bewitching, but you mention only a few of my finest qualities. Do not write back, kind sir, unless you honestly acknowledge yourself bewitched.*

I knew William was sharp enough to read those lines for what they were—an invitation for *more*. While also an opportunity to withdraw.

His response arrived mere days later:

> *Curse the icy mechanical medium of pen and paper.*
> *Shall I write a love letter? May Lucifer fly away with me*
> *if I do! When I make love, it shall be in a storm, as Jupiter*
> *made love to Semele and turned her at once to a cinder.*

I shook the damnable labyrinth of a paper. William's riddle mentioned love letters but then rejected them, all in the same paragraph before raising the subject of making love. My cheeks would have flushed were I not so flustered. My past experience with love had been straightforward, dull even; I should have known things would be different with a man as layered and intelligent as William Godwin.

And yet, despite William's latest message, the strength of my emotions had scared away Gilbert Imlay. I had no desire to repeat history, even as I recognized Godwin was made of sterner stuff than business-minded Imlay. Our friendship was too dear to me.

So I held myself back from any further flirtation, merely queried when he was returning. Of course, upon receiving his reply I began counting down the days. When Godwin didn't appear on the day he claimed, I paid little attention. He was likely unpacking and weary from the journey. I made further excuses on the second day—the summer downpour outside was cataclysmic—and distracted myself by reading to Fanny my first collection of children's tales. (I'd never imagined when writing *The Ant and the Bee* that I'd one day be reading the pages to my daughter.) On the third, I went to Godwin's lodgings—despite the comfortless rain, which had yet to let up, only to be informed by the proprietress that he had yet to arrive.

Damn me. Was this a repeat of Imlay? Had I read more into

Godwin's feelings than actually existed? When I went to Maria Reveley's in an anguished state and poured forth the entire story over biscuits and tiny glasses of madeira—never tea with Maria—she could barely restrain her glee. "You and William Godwin?" She clapped her hands over her grin, oblivious to my anxieties until she noticed I'd broken an unfortunate biscuit into tiny crumbs. "Trust me," she said as she rushed to my side on the overstuffed settee, "William Godwin has never paid more than a moment's notice to any woman, myself included. The fact that he spent every other night trekking to your dinner table in Pentonville is proof enough that he is besotted with you."

"I don't know about that." What I *did* know was that over dinners with my daughter and storms of ink and paper—and despite my best intentions—I'd become quite attached to William Godwin.

"You'd best take your furniture out of storage and find lodgings closer to Somers Town," Maria said with a sly smile. "For I suspect you'll be spending your near future in London. Which will also mean you'll finally be close enough that I can paint your portrait. And to think, all this because I invited Godwin to meet you over tea!"

I wasn't convinced. I *wanted* a romance with William Godwin, truly I did, but I'd left behind forever the naive young woman I'd been in Paris. Was it worth the inevitable heartache to experience the soaring heights of love?

On the fourth day, the rain finally broke, leaving the air perfumed with many delicious scents. I took advantage of the fair weather to trim the roses while Fanny napped and my bees visited the buttercups lining the road. A familiar lean figure caught my eye—actually, his sky-blue waistcoat and the afternoon sunshine glinting off his spectacles caught my eye—as he strolled up the lane.

William Godwin lifted a hand, and I swear my soul soared straight into the sun.

I forced myself not to fly toward him and instead calmly set down my shears. Calmly, save for the way my hands shook as I wiped them against my apron. I had envisioned this moment from its every facet, had even written it when I couldn't sleep last night, but every time I went to write William's dialogue, my mind went blank.

Perhaps it was best if I said nothing about the letters. We could always continue as we'd left off. Yes, that could be enough.

After all, friendship was the most holy band of society; as rare as true love was, true friendship was still rarer. Our friendship would be enough, simply because the alternative was unthinkable.

I removed my embroidered straw bonnet, some perfectly inane greeting on my lips while my heart performed a series of wild pirouettes. I expected William to bow in greeting, but he only halted and held so still I nearly reached out and touched him. The breeze carried the heady scent of his sage soap.

"You are late," I managed.

He swept his hat from his head and crushed that poor beaver tricorne between his hands. "That post road is a disgrace to the entire country."

He stood so close—as if he craved my nearness—and his eyes went dark when his gaze met mine. Then he leaned even closer, the distance between us suddenly charged, like the air before a lightning storm . . .

I was no longer an artless young woman who had needed lessons on flirting and courting. No, this time I recognized the signs, knew exactly what William wanted. What *I* wanted.

I touched my fingers to his, stilling them. "I missed you."

I hadn't planned the words, teetering dangerously on a precipice of something powerful and important.

Except: "I missed you too." Then William Godwin, professed introvert and awkward intellectual, bent from his height and *kissed* me.

His peppermint-spiked lips were hesitant, questioning. Then he tried to step back, to make space between us. "I'm sorry," he murmured, running a hand through his hair. "I've wanted to do that for so long that I'm afraid the sentiment quite overcame me."

I merely wove my fingers into the dark hair at the nape of his neck and tugged him down so I could see the green flecks scattered like emerald dust in his irises. "I certainly hope there are similar sentiments where those came from. *Many* more."

Relief came off him in waves as he kissed me back. Kissed me until I was dizzy and wanted nothing else in this world.

Yes, my own lips responded. Because sometimes writers have no need for words.

This was where I belonged, where *we* belonged. William had been right when he said that we artists felt and ached and *yearned* more deeply—and I could no more stop feeling the riotous emotions lifting me up right now than I could cease breathing. "You set my imagination on fire, Mary," he finally murmured, pressing his forehead to mine to ground us both. "For six-and-thirty hours I've been able to think of nothing else except the inexpressible longing to have you in my arms."

"Only six-and-thirty hours?" I teased. "I shall have to work harder."

He laughed, a full bark of giddiness that had me grinning. And feeling a bit mischievous. Aware that we were still standing on the lane outside my cottage and also that I wanted, perhaps *needed*, more of him in that moment, I pulled him into the nearby shed among a helter-skelter of rakes and shovels and sickles.

Did I stand on my tiptoes and pull William Godwin closer to kiss him again? Yes, I certainly did.

He was the one who finally broke off the kiss, but I could see what it cost him. "By all the gods, if we don't stop now, I'll have you pressed up against that wall. And I won't stop there."

My hands were still in his hair, his hands at my waist and the small of my back. "I won't want you to."

Except he still set me back, tugging at his cravat as if it were suddenly difficult to swallow. "I want to take this slowly. *Court* you properly."

I colored, suddenly glad at the dimness within the shed. Here I was, wanting all of him, when he wished to woo me. I straightened my bodice, which had gone askew. "I never took you for a romantic."

"Can you fault me for wanting to savor every moment as I feel my friendship for you melting into love?" William cleared his throat and removed his glasses, pretending to clean what I knew were pristine lenses. "As easy as it is for you to talk about your emotions, it's equally difficult for me to *act* on mine."

I chuckled. "Recent events claim otherwise."

Did William Godwin actually *blush* then? "I'm not accustomed to feeling this way about anyone. Yet, I fear your feelings may be too fragile to withstand the force of my idiosyncrasies."

"Perhaps *your* feelings are too fragile to bear *my* foibles. Have you considered that?"

He scoffed. "If you knew how ardently I felt, you would never propose such a thing."

I felt so safe there with him that I laced my fingers through his and directed his hand to my waist. "Then I shall strive to be patient. Remind me—how slowly do we need to take things?" I nudged his hand so his thumb brushed a little higher, and reveled in the way his breath hitched.

"My father was so puritanical that he considered the petting of a cat a profanation of the Lord's Day." I felt the low rumble of his chuckle against my throat all the way to my toe tips. "But perhaps not *that* slowly."

His words had just the effect that he intended—I chortled with laughter and the spell was broken. Just as well, as I heard Fanny and her nursemaid somewhere near the house—she must have woken from her nap.

We emerged separately, and William made a show of bringing me a rusty hive tool I couldn't possibly have needed, not that Fanny or her maid knew that. I wasn't sure how to harness my emotions around William now, but a slow progression was likely the wisest course of action, even if my body protested the thought. After all, I had Fanny to think of, plus a love affair between two well-known radical philosophers would provide ample fodder for the scandal sheets.

I smiled as William retrieved a wrapped caramel from his waistcoat and offered it to Fanny, who squealed in excitement. Perhaps it would be safer to live a life without love, to never take chances. But then, that would hardly be living.

William and I would be discreet, that was all.

I fully intended to enjoy every moment of it—our discretion *and* our indiscretions too.

Our romance was delayed by the last possible culprit I could have imagined: disease.

Poor Fanny fell ill once again, this time with chickenpox.

Once again, my darling was blighted with spots, the new red welts taking up residence atop her smallpox scars of old. My heart ached as she itched and whimpered while submerged in medicinal baths. Although Fanny's nursemaid helped boil water and replace compresses, I constantly carried my daughter about the house—forcing her to cling to me so she couldn't scratch her face. I read to her while she was awake, and stroked her hot forehead while she slept ever so fitfully. I slept not at all.

When it was finally over, William came calling with a nose-gay of wildflowers for me and a colorful atlas for Fanny. "She appears much better," he said after helping Fanny page through the atlas. She had finally yawned off into a contented nap, thumb in her mouth.

It was my turn to yawn. How I wished I could go upstairs and transform myself—at least wash my hair and pinch some color into my drawn cheeks. Instead, seated on the parlor's up-holstered settee, I merely leaned my head against Godwin's shoulder, drawing immense comfort from the small intimacy.

"Come away with me," William said suddenly. I jerked up-right, but he only chortled and nudged me deeper into the nook under his bent arm. "Just for the day. You could use a change of scenery—Marguerite can look after Fanny. I'll arrange every-thing."

I wanted to shake my head in protest—my daughter had just recovered from a second dreadful illness and still had the raw scars to prove it—and I'd fallen behind in my writing during the interim. Without its proceeds, Fanny and I could anticipate a long and cold winter. Yet so, too, did I desperately want to say *yes*.

William must have sensed my train of thought. "Let me take care of you, Mary."

With Godwin sitting there, brows raised in expectation, I wondered what it would be like to have a true partner instead of struggling against life's every storm on my own.

Except, I had sworn after Gilbert that I would be an inde-pendent woman. Did it make me a hypocrite to allow this man to help me? But wasn't *choosing* romance and happiness a sign of independence? Or was that just my trying to justify my hypocrisy? Only I'd been unhappy for so long and every moment with William Godwin ushered in sunbeams of joy.

Finally, slowly . . . "Yes."

"Yes, what?"

"Yes, I'll let you steal me away. Just for the day."

"Really?"

I nodded. "Truly."

His eyes lit with a potent happiness, all created by my utterance of one simple word. Such is the responsibility of love, to hold such power over another being. And perhaps this was also the obligation of love—to take care of each other. I realized then that I was indeed falling in love with William Godwin. And that scared me speechless.

He pressed a kiss to my forehead—I might have demanded more had I not been so weary and astounded by the revelation of my fledgling feelings. "Rest tonight," he murmured before rising and tucking a blanket around my shoulders. "And tomorrow I shall sweep you away."

I'd fallen asleep before he even let himself out. When I woke several hours later, it was to a cup of tea—now cold, but then he knew that was my preference—and a carefully folded note.

If you let me, I will always take care of you.

William kept his promise, arriving early the next morning with a basket packed with apples and fresh cheese, plus two tickets for the coach to Ilford. He'd even thought to ask Marguerite to ready my tea before his arrival, knowing I required it to lift my eyelids.

"What are we doing in Ilford today?" I asked once we were bouncing down the road. I didn't care about our destination, only that the entire glorious day stretched before us.

"Whatever you wish."

I pondered that for a moment. Strolling the town all afternoon would be easy, but . . .

Sapere aude. Dare to know.

"I'd like to walk to Hoxton."

"That's a long trek. More than ten miles."

"I've always been an advocate of robust physical exercise. Especially with a man such as yourself."

It was blatant innuendo and I reveled in the strain in William's voice when he responded. "And what draws us to Hoxton? I haven't been back since I attended the academy there."

I clasped my hands primly in front of me, smothering a secret smile before falling serious. It was time to confront the demons of my past and let William see that dirty part of me that I'd kept secret even from Gilbert. I wanted William Godwin to know *all* of me so I could lay to rest my fears that I would be too much for him. Surely my heart—and his—was strong enough for this. "My family home. I haven't been back since I was a girl. I'm afraid I didn't have an easy time of it."

William's hand over mine was solid and reassuring. "Whatever you wish."

Once in Ilford, we paused at a tartman's stall to purchase two apple taffety tarts—William's favorite—and then walked to Hoxton, saving the paper-wrapped tarts even as we enjoyed the basket William had brought along. Upon our arrival, I was surprised to see how unchanged the village was. Aside from the students outside the academy that William had attended—my brief time in Hoxton had indeed overlapped with his, so I often wondered how things might have been different had we met earlier—most of the people seemed wary and dirty and old before their time, especially the women in the marketplace with their motley assortments of children underfoot. And everything was so *small*. My old home was there, abandoned now but still the small and cramped cottage with the leaky roof where I'd listened to my mother stifle her cries as my father's fists landed, and where I'd fallen victim to his violence myself. Across the way from my mother's tiny garden in its wild and ruinous state were the empty green fields I'd run through and beyond them, the Clares' library, where I'd finally escaped all this.

"Are you all right?" William asked when I stared at it all, my eyes brimming with tears. "Were we wrong to come here?"

I shook my head as I wiped away the tears. "No, this is just what I needed." For the first time since going to London those many years ago, I spoke of it all: my father's drunken rages and my mother's excuses, even how my father had hanged our family dog and how I'd escaped and never looked back. It was only to William that I dared unburden myself.

"It was a terrible childhood," I admitted at the end. "But its hardships informed my views on the necessity of education. For boys *and* girls." I waited for William to respond, but his eyes only swept over the mean streets and crumbling houses.

"We should head back," he said, making a show of examining his timepiece. "I don't want to overtire you."

With that, he raised his hand to a passing farmer who had just enough room for us on the back of his cart of chickens. Had my base upbringing so disturbed him? Did the debaucheries of my family change his opinion of me?

We were quiet on the ride back to Ilford, not a word between us as we ate our taffety tarts. I usually enjoyed the peacefulness of my time with William, for we were as easy together whether engaged in fiery debate or silently slinking about our own thoughts. This silence, however, did *not* feel easy.

Contemplative and of great import, but not *easy*.

Just outside of town, William wordlessly helped me down from the cart. He scarcely waited for the farmer to drive on before his hands cupped either side of my face and he kissed me.

And kissed me.

And *kissed* me.

He tasted of apples and sugar and desire. My mind could hardly form a coherent thought by the time he was done—I wasn't sure how I was still standing. "Damn *me*." My voice came out husky. "What happened to our necessary restraint?"

One strong hand still cupped my cheek, and I leaned into it. "Seeing your home today and hearing what you went through . . . I have never encountered anyone, man or woman, with your strength." His voice came out rusty. "We were so close when I attended Hoxton Academy, and then I think back to that dinner party at Johnson's all those years ago—I can't help but imagine the years together we lost. I don't want to waste any more time, not when we could share every minute together."

My knees grew weak with relief. "I want to do more than kiss you right now," I admitted under my breath. "*So* much more."

A long silence. Then: "There's an inn."

A glance over my shoulder revealed a well-appointed building with a painted sign of a trumpeter swan hanging over its door at the edge of town. The White Swan. Despite William's brash words, I could feel his shyness. "We could stay the night," he added, his gaze studiously avoiding mine, "and tell Marguerite the roads were bad."

Anticipation lanced my belly, but I gestured to the cloudless sky. The weather had been mild all day, perfect, really. "She'll hardly believe that."

"Your maid likes me and she wants you to be happy. Marguerite won't gossip."

I was a woman in love, being asked to spend the night with

a man I desperately wanted. I yearned to run to that inn and claim their nearest room, but things were more complicated than that. "I can't," I said.

I hated the sudden hurt in his eyes as William stepped back. "My apologies." He cleared his throat. "I'm worse than the village idiot—we said we would take things slowly and I shouldn't have assumed—"

"I want to," I reassured him, filling once again the space between us. "I want nothing more than to stay the night with you, here. But the veneer that I'm Gilbert Imlay's estranged wife is all that keeps Fanny from bastardy and ignominy."

"Mary, know this—I love you." William drew a shaky breath, and my heart swelled like a tidal wave at those penultimate words. "However, I'm a practical man who understands that someone like me could never capture your entire wild heart. Just know that I'll cling to the hope that one day, you'll feel half of what I feel for you."

I stared at him, unraveling the layers of his words. The silly, foolish man! He still believed that Gilbert Imlay held part of my heart. Despite my being a wordsmith, nothing I could say or write would ever convince William Godwin of the depth of my feelings for him.

No, I had to *show* him.

Fingers tangled together in a knot I hoped would never come undone, I raised on tiptoes. This was my choice, and suddenly, it felt so *right*. "I will follow you to the ends of the earth, William Godwin. Or, better yet, to the White Swan."

His eyes widened, but then he shook his head. "No, you're right. We can't—"

"We *can*, and we will." I smiled, feeling my dimple emerge. "The roads weren't bad, but the coach *did* break an axle just outside town. Remember?"

I tried to calm the anxious fluttering in my stomach with the reassurance that I had maintained a watertight fiction to protect Fanny from scandal; my work would not be undone by one night. One fiction protected by another. Godwin's thumb stroked the back of my hand so I nearly erupted into flames then and there on the main street of Ilford. "Fortunately," he said slowly, "a replacement was found in the morning."

The proprietor of the White Swan scarcely looked up as William checked us in—paying for two rooms—but I felt a surge of pure happiness to read William's entry in the guest ledger.

W. G., besotted with Mary.

"Go this way, Mama, I wants to see Man."

Fanny tugged my hand so hard down Chalton Street that my reticule—which contained the first rough half of *The Wrongs of Woman*—slammed into the stick legs of a passing courier, who cursed at me. Then Merryboy started barking, which prompted Fanny to pull the dog's lead even as she yanked me in the direction of William's lodging house.

Chaos. That's what my life was these days—pure, unadulterated chaos.

Marguerite had barely batted an eye over the broken axle story after William and I returned home, even as we maintained our secret affair. Only, I quickly learned there weren't enough hours in the day to cram in all I wanted—and needed—to accomplish.

Caring for Fanny and her education.

Keeping the house.

Paying bills.

Writing *The Wrongs of Woman*.

Spending every spare hour—and the occasional night when Marguerite went home—with the man I loved.

I'd have hired more servants to tend the house, but I could barely afford cheese, much less a cook or housemaid. I'd asked Johnson for an advance on *The Wrongs of Woman*, but he'd informed me over coffee that it was unfair that I paid for the entirety of Fanny's upkeep, and insisted that I write to Gilbert Imlay and demand his portion of pecuniary assistance. I'd only ever sought Imlay's heart; with that gone, I wanted nothing more to do with him, but Johnson turned my own arguments about the need for gender equality against me and made my next advance contingent on my writing Imlay.

Add that to the list.

William noticed my exhaustion one evening—how could he not when I dozed off in the middle of a conversation?

"Hmm?" I'd blinked when he nudged my foot from under the table.

"We were talking about your progress on *The Wrongs of Woman*. You nodded off midsentence."

"I'm sorry." The last thing I recalled was promising to let William read my latest chapter. "I stayed up writing last night."

"How late?" William's voice made me feel like a child caught reading by illicit candlelight.

"Until dawn," I admitted.

"This can't continue, Mary." I bolted upright—my sluggish mind thought he meant this thing between us—but he only gestured me back to my seat. "You can't keep working yourself to the bone. Bring Fanny to me for a few hours in the afternoons once I'm done writing." As a rule, William wrote every day from nine until one o'clock. "I'd be happy to entertain her, truly. Then you can write by daylight instead of furtive moonlight."

"Oh no, I couldn't." I shook my head. "Fanny exhausts even Merryboy. The other day I found him napping in the shed—I'm sure he was hiding from her to steal a moment's respite."

"She's a toddling girl whom I enjoy. And I think she rather likes me."

I smiled because it was true. Sometimes I worried Fanny preferred William to me.

"I appreciate the offer," I said. "But I still can't."

"Why? Because of some silly notion that I don't share Fanny's blood?"

My minute nod was enough to narrow Godwin's eyes and launch him out of his seat and into the chair next to me. "She's part of you, Mary, and I'm rather fond of her. She has Imlay's name, but no father. She deserves more and you know it."

Chagrined, I glanced at my lap. What had I done to deserve this man whose every utterance possessed a lightning flash of genius, and who loved me and my daughter too? Sometimes when I thought of it, I wondered that my heart might truly burst from happiness. That rapturous moment was always followed by a dark shadow of worry that such joy could never last.

"It's settled." William tilted my chin to press a kiss to my forehead. "Bring Fanny—and her hellhound—to me tomorrow at one o'clock. You'll get your drafting done and I'll ply Fanny with sugar before sending her home to you. We'll have a grand time, I promise."

I poked his ribs in play, but in truth, I was grateful.

I'd proven I could stand on my own two feet, but right now, I didn't mind letting this wonderful man help me. If the tables had been turned, I'd have done the same for him.

"Good luck," I told William the next day after Fanny and Merryboy had bolted into his room. I could see the table already set with tea and jam tarts and lemon biscuits, hoped that Merryboy's fiercely wagging tail wouldn't upset the entire production. "You weren't jesting about the sugar bit, were you?"

William winked, then checked the hallway before pulling

me in for a kiss that fizzed with phosphoric passion. "Leave the book, the beast, and the babe to me. Go write."

I spent the afternoon engrossed in writing, so much that I sent Marguerite to fetch Fanny and her dog. William would come to us this evening for dinner.

He arrived with my manuscript in tow. I was proud of *The Wrongs of Woman* and knew it was destined for Johnson's desk and then the printer's shop. So I was taken aback when he handed it to me and pronounced, "There is a radical defect in your writing."

"Pardon?"

"Not a terminal defect, mind you. Your grammar is still slapdash and the ideas lack coherency. I marked the places that need improvement."

I flipped through the pages, eyes bulging to see copious notes crammed into what felt like every margin. There were many about my grammar, but also spots where my ideas needed further polishing. Finally, I dared look up, unsure whether to scream, cry, or hurl the manuscript at him. Instead: "It seems I must either disregard your opinion, think it unjust, or throw my pen down in despair."

A smirk settled briefly on his face. "I cannot imagine you ever giving up your pen."

I sighed, resigned. This man knew me well. "That would be tantamount to resigning existence. I suppose you *did* warn me of your honesty."

Godwin seemed wholly unaffected. "You asked for my opinions and I gave them. I only sought to give lift to the wings of your ideas."

It was true. William wasn't cowed by my intelligence or my emotions, but instead urged the roots of my ideas deeper while nudging the vines of my prose to amble higher, something not even Johnson did. It didn't matter if we were acquaintances, friends, or lovers—William Godwin pushed me to be better.

Still, I knocked a fist against my hip and managed a smile. "Giving lift to my ideas while correcting my sentence structure? Apparently, I am a far worse grammarian than previously suspected."

William chuckled under his breath. "My offer of grammar lessons still stands. For every correct answer, you can earn a kiss."

"I might accept that intriguing offer, your sapient Philosophership."

Godwin nuzzled my ear. "I'd like that. Almost as much as I'd like to take you to the theater next week. What?" he asked when I pulled back and smoothed the bodice of my gown, suddenly discomfited. "Isn't that what couples do?"

"Regular couples." I busied myself with straightening the cushions on my settee. It was good to have my own furniture again, now that I'd decided to settle here for the foreseeable future, although I wasn't sure Godwin even noticed the change. *Absentminded* sapient Philosophership was more apropos. "Except I thought we planned to keep this"—I pointed between the two of us—"secret."

Because while this love affair was my choice, I feared so many things if our feelings were to be made public. I'd scarcely come to terms with my own private emotions; I wasn't sure I was strong enough to bear society's scrutiny, nor did I want to.

"It's merely the theater, Mary. I'm at your table nearly every night for supper—there's no rule that two friends can't enjoy a performance together."

I bit my lip, listening to Fanny giggling upstairs with Merryboy and her new barn cat, Puss, who was decidedly friendlier than Bet. My decisions had to be guided by Fanny now. A single clandestine interlude at the White Swan was one thing;

publicly owning my lie about Imlay and my new relationship with William was quite another. "I can't. I dare not tell even Maria Reveley the full truth about us."

The sag in William's shoulders made me hate that decision, but he straightened as soon as he caught me watching. "You're right. And I'm not even particularly fond of the theater."

I sought a solution. Wasn't that the trick to a relationship, each person trying to keep the other happy? Via compromise? "We might both attend the theater, but separately. Then we could discuss the performance afterward and no one would be the wiser."

"Don't you think that will look suspicious, both of us attending on our own?"

"No, it will be perfect. The entire idea is to throw people off."

"You forgot one thing." At my lifted eyebrow, he closed the space between us. "I won't be able to keep my eyes off you."

I spread my hands across his chest, fingering his lapels. "Keep your wandering eyes in check, Mr. Godwin. Bring someone else if you like, to throw the hounds off the scent."

William threw his hands in the air. "*Damnare*, woman. I'll think twice before asking you to the Epsom Derby."

I felt somewhat smug. Until the next day, when I went to the theater and saw another woman at William's side.

Despite her unfortunate name, Elizabeth Inchbald was one of the Fairs—a gossipy widow in her forties who was still passably pretty and acted if she were a long-lost duchess rather than the author of several poorly written novels. I hadn't cared for her since I'd critiqued those novels for Johnson ages ago—they were some of the dullest and most ridiculous drivel I'd ever read.

She would never be my intellectual nemesis, but she was certainly fairer than I, with her spaniel-like affections and endless coils of blond hair. A widow, she was a vapid woman of comfortable means who could afford the box she and William now sat in, whereas I was frantically trying to rewrite *The Wrongs of Woman* to keep Fanny and me in coal and mutton over the winter.

From my cheap seat on the floor, I watched Inchbald murmur in William's ear and felt a wave of something volcanic sweep over me. *Jealousy*, peppered with a healthy dash of anger at myself. Once the show began, I couldn't focus on the drama unfolding on the stage, not as I sank deeper into the abyss of my own melancholy.

I cringed when Inchbald caught me watching them and winked my way before placing her hand on William's arm.

A hollow victory, that our subterfuge should have fooled her so completely.

"I should have invited John Opie to join me," I taunted William when he next came over for dinner, referencing the brooding portrait painter we'd both met at a recent party. "Perhaps he might have painted me afterward."

"I thought Maria Reveley wished to paint your portrait?"

Of course my attempt at making William jealous fell flat—my brilliant philosopher was oblivious to women's wiles. "I found the play rather dull," he continued, "although I appreciated the character arc of the shepherd in the second act. What did you think?"

"I couldn't care less about the silly play." I stood abruptly but sat down quickly as spots exploded before my eyes. Godwin's voice retracted as if down a long tunnel, and then shattered into a hundred sharp and tiny shards. "I need to lie down," I managed to gasp.

"Sitting is better," I heard William say before he gently bent me over my knees. His hand rubbed over my back in calming strokes. "It's no wonder, as busy as you've been. Deep breaths."

After some time, my hearing and vision stabilized well enough for Marguerite to press a mug of chilled water into my hand. "Drink," William commanded, and I did. "And now to bed with you."

I shook my head, feeling as if I were moving through something thicker than air. "I need to tuck Fanny in. And read to her."

"I'll do both," William insisted as he led me to my bedroom. There was nothing sensual about the way he disrobed me, just tenderness as he folded me into bed and tucked in the warmed bricks Marguerite brought at my feet.

"Dearest Mary," I heard him murmur after he'd blown out the candle. His hand smoothed the hair from my brow before he pressed a kiss there. "Working yourself into such a state. As if I cared for Elizabeth Inchbald—I only have eyes for you."

Perhaps William wasn't as oblivious to women's wiles as I'd believed. Still, tears stung my eyes as I curled into myself. It wasn't due to gossipy Elizabeth Inchbald that I was filled with foreboding.

The fainting spell had been my first clue, followed by my tender breasts and upset stomach. When I couldn't keep food down and missed my cycle, I knew for certain.

And I was terrified.

Terrified that history was about to repeat itself. Terrified that in having a child with William, I would be dooming him to leave me. Except William wasn't Gilbert Imlay.

I trusted him with my heart. And I'd trusted him with Fanny. Now I would trust him with my future and with this new babe I carried. And pray my faith hadn't been misplaced.

It wasn't quite one o'clock. William would still be writing at his lodging house, but I didn't wish to wait any longer.

"Is everything all right?" he asked when he opened the door. As he ushered me inside, his brows drew together with the question. "No, I can tell it's not."

But then I opened my mouth and turned our world upside down.

And William . . . He only blinked before wild sunspots of joy exploded across his face. "Truly, Mary? You're going to make me a father?"

I swallowed, then nodded. "Truly."

His eyes widened even farther before something shuttered in his expression. "But you look positively grim. Is it the nausea? Are you feeling weak? Here I am, a fool, making you stand. Mea culpa—you must sit and put your feet up. I'll put a kettle on for tea."

"I'm fine. Really," I added when he plumped a cushion on a tattered settee and ushered me to sit. "I just don't want this to change things. Between us, I mean."

He clasped my cold hands in his warm ones, folding them over his heart as he kissed my forehead. "I love you and you love me. And that love has created a child. Nothing will ever change that."

His words were reassuring, but unlike when I'd been pregnant with Fanny and believed I could continue down life's path unchanged, as he pulled me into a tight embrace, a thought came to me unbidden.

This child will change everything.

CHAPTER 15

❧

September 1818

MARY SHELLEY

It took Mary four days on the road to regret her decision to leave Livorno.

From inside their coach, the heat ratcheted up with each passing mile as if they had unwittingly passed through the nine gates of hell. Fortunately, Everina slept through the heat haze of most of the journey, both in the coach and in the mediocre inns where they stopped. But on the last day, Everina's fever returned with renewed vigor until she slipped in and out of consciousness, seeming not to recognize her own mother when her eyes did flicker open. Mary's panic banged on the walls of her chest even as she willed the horses to sprout wings and fly her to Percy, anything to get there faster.

Late in the afternoon on the fourth day, Mary nearly wept when they finally reached the villa Byron had lent Percy, a mansion that was ten hours outside of Venice. She was surprised to see Claire—with Allegra in her arms—join Percy as he rushed into the courtyard to greet her. *Was this journey even necessary? Byron must have fallen for Percy's lie. Perhaps my sister's happiness will make our travels worth it. And surely Everina will recover here.*

As it was, Mary's legs had lost their bones somewhere along the way, and she collapsed when she stepped from the coach.

"Oh, you poor creatures!" she heard Claire exclaim.

Percy lifted Mary and their daughter into his strong arms. "Oh, Mary." The voice she'd longed to hear was sweeter than a harp. "As sunset to the sphered moon, as twilight to the western star, thou, beloved, art to me."

His voice was a balm to her weary soul, but now wasn't the time for prepared poetry. "Everina is ill, Percy. She needs a physician."

"Of course." Percy understood the granite in her voice. "I'll ride for one immediately."

Claire carried Mary's bags to Percy's room. "I'll fetch cool compresses for Everina and a tray for you," she said soothingly before squeezing Mary's hand. Tears limned her eyes. "Thank you for coming."

Owls and bats flitted beneath a sinking crescent moon by the time Percy arrived with the country surgeon. The ancient and bent-backed man unwrapped little Everina and prodded her heat-drenched limbs with all manner of cold metal instruments before giving a grave nod. "A summer fever. There is little we can do in one so young. It is in God's hands."

Mary wanted to rage at the old man, but Percy gave her a knowing look and handed the man his coins. "Byron's personal physician lives in Venice. At sunrise, I'll ride to him," Percy said to her. "I'm sure he can help us." When Mary didn't respond, his hands kneaded away the tension at her shoulders as he pressed his forehead to hers. "Everina is well protected with you as her mother, my Faerie Queene."

Mary couldn't respond as tears of exhaustion spilled from the corners of her eyes and Percy gently kissed them away.

. . .

As promised, Percy left with the dawn. Hours ticked by and Everina grew steadily weaker, but still there was no response from Percy in Venice. In her thoughts, Mary pleaded with each passing hour—with her mother, with the Supreme Being, to anyone who would listen—to make her daughter whole again.

Finally, a message appeared that Percy had arrived outside Venice and was locating the doctor. Everina fell so motionless that Mary found herself checking whether her daughter still breathed. She could stand it no more. The candle markings heralded the time as three o'clock in the morning, but Mary bundled Everina into a traveling basket and ordered Byron's footmen to ready the coach. Claire and Allegra were still sleeping. "We travel to Venice." Mary's voice trembled with fear. "In great haste."

One of the grooms grumbled as he walked away, but the driver merely bowed his head as he took in Everina's pallor and listless form. "I have a daughter the same age," he said in Italian. "And I would drive through the flames of hell if it meant saving her. I will do the same for your little angel, *signora*."

"*Grazie*," Mary eked out, willing the tears not to come. She'd always exalted emotion over reason, but she needed to be clearheaded and rational right now. For Everina's sake.

After ten hours of travel, with the skyline of Venice in sight, Everina started convulsing. Hot tears streamed down Mary's face as she kissed Everina's burning forehead and dribbled lukewarm water from her metal canteen between her daughter's parched lips.

Life and death hung on their speedy arrival in Venice.

But Mary felt her daughter's death rattle as the driver rushed her to the inn where Percy waited. One look at her had him racing for the doctor. "I thought we had more time. We planned to leave in a few hours," he said by way of apology, his eyes frantic. Then he was gone.

Mary clutched her daughter in the darkened back hallway Percy had ushered her into before running for the doctor. "Please don't leave me. Stay for me, sweeting. *Please*."

Perhaps she imagined it, but she felt Everina's grip on her finger tighten. Then her soft hand with those tiny pale fingernails fell limply to her side.

Mary counted to ten—ten seconds, ten hours, ten minutes, ten *forevers*—as she waited for her daughter to draw breath.

Nothing. How could there be *nothing*, when just moments ago there had been *everything*?

With a broken sob, Mary crushed her daughter's listless body to her chest, but Everina's gleaming soul had already fled like a butterfly slipped from its chrysalis. And like a wild wolf that suddenly finds itself pinned in the sharp teeth of a trap, Mary *howled*.

She howled as her heart fractured and splintered and shattered. And knew that she would never be able to piece it together again.

That was how Percy found her, crumpled on the floor in the back hallway of that terrible inn, her dead daughter pinned to her chest as if she would never—*could* never—let her go.

Mary could not speak, had lost the ability to think or to form words. Percy only wrapped his body around both of theirs, the three of them rocking and swaying and sobbing on that filthy floor.

Mary refused to give over her daughter's frail body until long after Everina's skin had gone cold. Only then could she bear for Percy to gently remove their daughter, to bury her.

He took their baby to the Lido, a place neither Everina nor Mary had ever been. Percy told her it was a place of crashing surf where Everina would enjoy an eternal view of the sun-drenched sea and the yawning expanse of the Venetian sky. Mary couldn't bear to see it, didn't want to imagine her baby buried in any stretch of earth, no matter how lovely it might be.

The cup of life was poisoned for her, and would forever remain so.

Byron arrived at the inn the next day, shoulders bowed and his countenance grimmer than a battlefield lord of death. Mary tried to summon one iota of fury at him, to bellow her anger and hurt and despair at the man whose childish games had called her from Livorno and led to her daughter's demise.

Only there was nothing. Not even an ember of anger remained. Just numbness.

And guilt.

If Mary had been stronger, she'd have refused Percy's summons. If she'd been stronger, she'd have stared down Byron's demands.

Instead, she'd been weak. As a result, Everina had perished.

Byron sat next to her and crossed one leg over the other, a polished gesture that would have sat easily upon a turbaned raja or perfumed Turk. Mary's emotions flared slightly then, feeling as if her skin had been sewn piecemeal over some monster that had once been human but now hid a snarling horror of hurt and guilt. "I came to offer you work."

Mary blinked, unsure she had heard him correctly. "Work? My daughter just died, Byron. I am not in need of *work*."

Byron had the decency to look discomfited, even shifted in his seat. *Fidgeted.*

"The thing about grief, Mary"—he spoke slowly around the words—"is that it can eat you alive. It starts with the heart and devours you from the inside, until there's nothing left of you save a raw, bleeding mess. I read your *Frankenstein* and it's bloody brilliant. Work—*writing*—will keep your heart beating. It will keep you from losing your mind."

Mary wanted to garrote Lord Byron where he sat, to demand as he gasped his last breath what he knew of grief. Nothing could have prepared her for this feeling that her very bones had been shattered and hastily reassembled.

Still, she said nothing. Merely stared straight ahead.

Byron cleared his throat and removed a folded packet from his jacket pocket. "My two latest poems," he informed her as he placed the papers on her lap. "In need of transcription before I deliver them to my publisher." He paused, waited for her response that didn't come. "Words will distract you from the pain of living, Mary, I swear it. Start with mine and then let them give way for yours. But be prepared: once the deluge begins, you may find yourself powerless to stop them."

Mary managed to churn up some of the vitriol she wished she could hurl at him, funneled it into a filthy glare. "Anything else?"

Byron merely shook his head. "Only that I'm sorry, Mary. Well and truly sorry."

That made two of them.

Their world would never recover.

Percy thought the scarlet leather-bound journal a secret, but Mary knew where it lay nestled beneath his poetry notebooks. She'd never cared that he kept a hidden journal, but in these days following Everina's death when they were hardly speaking to each other, her eyes craved the sight of his thoughts. As if somehow that would make up for the lack of his voice in her ears, the feel of his touch on her skin. Her husband's latest entry—written last night in front of the fire when he'd tried and failed to cajole a rare smile from her—seared black scorch marks into her soul when she'd read it.

> *Wilt thou forget the happy hours*
> *Which we buried in Love's sweet bowers*
> *Heaping over their corpses*
> *Blossoms and leaves instead of mould?*

She recognized herself in his lines, the happy hours they'd spent in Livorno's summer sunshine, memories now turned to rotting corpses. Percy's stark words had nearly scattered the guilt and grief that plagued her, and prompted her to seek him out. Nearly, but not quite.

She deserved the omnipresent mildew and rot, the biting pain and stinging sorrows. Her daughter had died because of *her* choices. That was a regret she would have to live with until the end of her days.

It went against the natural order of things for a daughter to die before her mother. Everina's death was a far crueler tragedy to Mary even than being denied her own mother. She'd never thought her mother lucky before, but at least Mary Wollstonecraft had been spared the horrors of Fanny's passing.

A physician who'd come to see Mary had murmured to Percy that giving her another child would surely cure her ills. Mary felt part of her die even as Percy ushered the man away. They had wanted another child, but the idea of mothering a new baby ripped the soft pink skin from her never-healing wound. Without Everina, she was no longer a mother.

With each passing day, she drifted from Percy.

That's all she did now—drift.

Once back in Livorno, she and Percy had taken up separate

rooms, Mary because sleep had fled so that she wandered her room each night like an evil spirit, and Percy because he rose at seven to read in bed for an hour before eating breakfast and ascending to a glassed balcony on the roof where he wrote until two o'clock, baking in the sun. After convincing Percy that the rumors about Allegra were patently false, Byron had taken his daughter back to Venice—Mary no longer possessed the ability to care for the child—and Claire had returned to Livorno to manage the household as Mary floated in a state of detached paralysis. Her sister and Lord Byron had become almost amicable following the tragedy of Everina's death, which should have roused Mary from her melancholy, but she couldn't bring herself to care. The sound of Claire sloping about the house typically roused Mary around noon, but most days, she couldn't bring herself to leave the four-poster bed she'd once shared with Percy.

Days passed. Weeks, maybe months.

"Get up," Claire demanded one afternoon when Mary hadn't yet risen. It was after two o'clock, for Mary had heard Percy descend his stairway and pause at her door before his footfalls moved to the dining room, where he often ate with Claire. Mary envisioned the two dining together, their heads bent close, Percy talking about poetry and Claire humming her favorite songs.

Except now Claire was flinging open the curtains and windows, letting crisp air pour in with its painful shafts of light that stabbed Mary's eyes. She dropped an envelope on Mary's bedside table. "The mail came. You have a letter from Father."

Mary gave Claire a view of her back, but her nest of warm blankets snapped away with a flick of Claire's slim wrists. Warblers and orioles chirped happily outside, oblivious to Mary's suffering. "You've wandered the hellscape of grief long enough," her sister announced. "It's time to rejoin the land of the living."

"You don't understand what I'm going through." Mary loathed the way her eyes filled with hot tears, the feel of her heart with each beat fauceting out the last of its lifeblood. *You don't understand that I deserve to die.*

"You're right—I can only imagine the hell you've been living." Claire opened the wardrobe drawers; Mary felt clothes being deposited unceremoniously onto her bed. "But you haven't been living, Mary, and if I have to drag you back to us kicking and screaming, I will. You're going to get dressed, and then you're going to eat a proper lunch with us downstairs."

Mary slitted an angry eye at her sister. "You're just here because you've always been in love with Percy."

It was cruel, but Mary could see that she'd hit some tender underbelly of truth from the way Claire flinched. The reaction passed quickly, replaced with silver fire in Claire's eyes that nearly set Mary to trembling.

"Because you are grieving, I am going to forget that you ever said that," her sister ground out. "I am here out of love for you. Just yesterday I wrote Byron that I can't make my scheduled visit with Allegra because you are in no state to be left alone. No matter what feelings I may have harbored for Percy eons ago, I cannot believe you would think I might try to steal your husband away, especially after the death of your child. But I will say this—a bad wife is like winter in the house. And this house—and Percy—have had enough of your winter."

Claire left without so much as a backward glance. Mary still didn't rise, not even as dishes clattered downstairs amid the low murmur of Claire's and Percy's voices. Mary merely listened to the corn rustle in the nearby fields and the drumming of her still-beating heart. Sometime later, she mustered the strength to read her father's letter.

There was no word of her mother's lost journal, only a message of condolence upon hearing the news of Everina's death. One that quickly turned to admonishment.

> *Though at first your nearest connections may pity you this state, human nature and our abhorrence of death and grief will turn them from you. I fear that if you do not return your attentions to your husband, he will abandon you. Above all, you must guard against your mother's tendency to despair and despondency.*

Her father didn't understand. No one did.

Mary couldn't rouse herself because it was *her* fault Everina was moldering in the ground among the grave-worms of the Lido instead of running through the sunlit fields outside.

My fault. I *ought to have died.* My *fault.*

Twilight had gathered, and Mary was still abed when another knock sounded at her door. She didn't answer. What need did she have for sustenance or company when her aim was for the grave?

Everina would be waiting for her on the other side. And her mother.

"Mary."

Percy's voice as he opened her door cut deep. Just her name, but those two syllables were a microcosm of swirling planets, stars being born and dying, grief and fear, anger and love.

Above all, *love.*

Illuminated by the candle he held, Percy knelt at her bedside, worry and concern leaking from his eyes, his very soul. His voice was less than a whisper, as if he were afraid a sudden sound would cause her to shatter into a thousand jagged pieces. "My dearest Mary, where have you gone and left me in this colorless world alone?" His lips feathered against the cold stone of her fingertips, her wrists, the delicate skin of her arms. Finally, he pressed her palm to his cheek and leaned into it. "Thy form is here indeed—a lovely one—but thou art fled, gone down the dreary road." More whispers against her temples and her closed eyes. Beseeching, *begging*. "For thine own sake I cannot follow thee. Do thou return for me."

"I can't," she managed to respond. "I *cannot*."

Tears flowed freely from Percy's eyes. He'd never been afraid to show her his true self. "This life is empty without you in it."

"There's nothing left of me." Her whisper was hollower than a winter breeze. "It's all died and withered away."

Percy shook his head, that gloriously thick hair she'd loved to run her fingers through trembling in the meager candlelight. Together, they'd once basked in the full light of the sun, but now all that golden warmth had fled. "Your heart still beats and my soul still answers your call. The love between you and me exists on a higher plane," he reminded her. "It can never die, not even after we've turned to dust. Our love will be remembered so long as there are people alive to read our words. But, Mary, we're not gone yet. And I need you to come back to me."

With that, Percy pressed something between her unresponsive fingers. "I want you to open your journal," he said. "Write the first words that come to mind."

Mary stared as Percy opened it and flipped beyond her last entry. Its final words seared her soul, written in the hours after little Everina's departure from this world.

This is the Journal book of misfortunes.

She'd vowed never to write again after she'd concluded that entry, to never let herself love again—too scary, too painful, and always doomed to end—but here was Percy. *Begging* her, as if his own life depended on *her*.

She owed it to Percy to try. Once, at least.

The heft of the pen was a foreign weight in her hands that had done nothing, touched nothing, for so long. It wasn't her words that emerged from the fog of her mind fully formed.

Instead, they were Percy's words, a scrap of poetry written in the despair and anger just after Fanny's and Harriet's deaths:

> *We two yet stand, in a lonely land,*
> *Like tombs to mark the memory*
> *Of joys & griefs that fade & flee*
> *In the light of life's dim morning.*

She dropped the pen, exhausted. "Don't you wish you could forget it all?"

Percy pressed her hand to his chest above his heart, where it beat true and steady. "Never. I never want to forget a moment with Everina, nor how you were with her. No, I want to remember our little girl, Mary, to celebrate her life. And one day, when you're ready, I want to make a brother or sister for her and tell them stories of how she once chased fireflies like a tiny sprite and how the golden peal of her giggles shook the blackened rafters of this house."

Mary felt the firedrake of grief within her lift its weary head and shudder at the force of her memories, then shake itself free with a pained roar that matched the terrible sobs that racked her very bones. Dimly, she became aware of Percy climbing beside her, cocooning and shielding her with his body. "Let it out,

Mary," he crooned to her. "When winter comes, spring is never far behind."

Read—work—walk—read—work.

Such was Mary's schedule and her journal entries after they moved to Florence. A fresh city for a fresh start. She could not cheat her way back to happiness, but step by step, day by day, word by word, Mary was painstakingly determined to live again. Claire remained with them long enough to ensure that Mary could withstand the gusts of everyday life, then left for her delayed visit with Allegra.

"You and Percy have always been fools for each other," were her parting words. A decided coolness had settled between them since Mary's outburst. "He'll take care of you, if you let him."

And he did.

Together they spent quiet afternoons practicing their Italian and translating verses from Dante's *Purgatorio*. While Percy began penning a new play, he encouraged Mary's own writing projects. She started with Byron's poems as a first step toward forgiveness and a way to ease herself back into the creative world of words. After Byron's poems were transcribed—simple work that reminded her of her mother's work transcribing for Joseph Johnson—Mary began sketching out a new novel. The initial pages cracked open a stone dam she hadn't known existed—the trickle of words turned into a deluge. *Mathilda* was a gloomy story of desolation and death, but so, too, was it a purging.

In the meantime, Mary forced herself to seek out the quiet joys in this life.

Including, some months later, telling Percy he was to be a father again.

Mary had cried quiet tears when she realized the truth, but just as the flow of words in her manuscript had been healing, so, too, were those cleansing tears. Although her soul ached to think of rocking another baby in her arms when she would never again rock Everina, Mary knew she could not make an idol of her grief. That living, pulsing mass of sorrow in her heart would never be fully excised, but it must be set aside. This child would not suffer because of Mary's sins.

One starry November night, Percy Florence—named for his overjoyed father and the city of his birth—was born. Sound and healthy and with a nose that promised to be quite as large as his grandfather's, he revived Mary's spirits each time she held him, which was often. The feel of the new babe in her arms was pleasure laced with the finest pain—reminding Mary of the joys and responsibilities of motherhood.

"I wrote to Byron and asked him to join us," Percy said one evening as the threesome sat under blankets beneath Pisa's fading sun, listening to the downy owls call to their mates in the cypress trees. Claire had come to Florence to assist with the birth, but had remained in the Renaissance city when the rest of their little family had decamped to Pisa once Mary and the baby were well enough to travel. Here Mary partook the healing waters of the Bagni di San Giuliano each day and tracked the progress of Venus across the sky each night. Just like that golden planet, her sacred friendship with Percy would always endure.

"And did the mighty Lord Byron deign to respond?" The poet's name in Mary's mouth tasted bitter, for she was still crawling slowly toward forgiveness.

For Byron, for Percy, for herself.

"He's keen on the idea. He's taken up with an Italian contessa, even mentioned setting up a literary society."

Mary nodded her drowsy acknowledgment, but Percy had more news. "Byron sent Allegra to a convent in Bagnacavallo. It's renowned for raising chaste, good Christian girls."

Mary sat up. The rustic conditions and immodest practices of raising indolent girls in convents had led to her own mother railing against the custom in *A Vindication of the Rights of Woman*. Allegra was only four years old; to lock her up until she was sixteen seemed a cruelty. "Does Claire know?"

That she was to be denied raising her own child and then forced to sit idly by while Byron handed their daughter off to be raised by strangers? That was vile, even for Byron.

Percy's nod was accompanied by a sigh. "She'd already written to him a letter so scathing he refuses to hear her name spoken. Or so he informed me."

So the truce brought about by Everina's death had failed, and Byron was back to his old games. Mary didn't care to know the rest of the details. "Can you persuade Byron to release Allegra to Claire? Permanently?"

"That's why I invited him."

"He's a bullheaded villain when it comes to Claire. And she has no rights." Mary felt a familiar anger boil to the surface.

"I know. She suggested we help her kidnap Allegra."

"What?" That was shocking, even for Claire. Although Mary empathized with the wild emotions that could drive a mother to madness for her children.

"I disabused her of the notion." Percy idly twirled a lock of Mary's auburn hair around his finger. "Claire could live with us, you know. If she did, there's a chance I could convince Byron to give us Allegra."

"I love Claire. However . . ." Mary chose her words wisely. Her recovery was still fragile, and she wasn't sure she could bear to see Claire with Allegra every day. Not only that, Claire filled every room she entered and made it impossible for Mary to breathe. "Perhaps we could stay in Pisa and find somewhere nearby for Claire."

Percy understood, but then, he always did. "Claire can remain in Florence while you and I work on Byron."

Mary felt the furrow between her brows ease as she settled back against Percy's shoulder and cuddled their son's warm body between them. She recalled a saying of Mary Wollstonecraft's that her father had once told her, although she'd never found where her mother had written it: "A little patience and all will be over."

A little patience and Mary would put Byron in his place, once and for all.

Lord Byron arrived with his usual panache, but the spectacle left Mary unmoved.

The winter air felt heavy as carts rolled into Pisa laden with the poet's worldly possessions, just as they had done in Switzerland several years ago, this time including his cavernous bed with the Byron coat of arms—complete with mermaids and chestnut horses surrounding the motto *Crede Byron*—carved into its colossal headboard.

Crede Byron. Trust Byron.

The very idea made Mary roll her eyes. Much as she often wanted to strangle the man—with his brain from heaven and his heart from hell—even she had to admit he was a Midas when it came to his Spenserian stanzas and heroic couplets. His latest had set her to thinking:

> *He first sank to the bottom—like his works,*
> *But soon rose to the surface—like himself;*
> *For all corrupted things are buoy'd like corks,*
> *By their own rottenness . . .*

Again, that feeling that his bombast was meant to cover some crippled and cowering creature that clung to the shadowy corners of Byron's blackened soul. Except Mary no longer cared to plumb Byron's dark depths, not when he'd hurt her family so. Best to skim along the surface lest they be dragged down with him.

"Oh, the stories that bed could tell," Mary murmured under her breath, earning a scoff from Percy as the onslaught of geese and dogs and goats and donkeys and peacocks and monkeys continued. The entire city suddenly seemed to bray and honk and bark and screech.

Where Lord Byron went, chaos followed.

His lordship's eccentricities had appealed when Mary had first met him; now she pursed her lips at his extravagance, especially when he emerged from his coach swathed in silks and furs.

"The tight little island of England has already dubbed us the League of Incest and Atheism," Byron proclaimed as he drew both Percy and an unwilling Mary into his sandalwood-scented embrace. A pencil mustache topped his full lips, and he'd grown plumper since they'd seen him last. She recalled his telling her at their first dinner that he'd been ridiculed as a schoolboy for being overweight, so he often resorted to fasting or eating only potatoes in vinegar. Perhaps his love of excess now extended to his table as well. His limp was slightly more pronounced as he pressed kisses to Percy's cheeks, then hers. "I propose we tell them that I'm sleeping with both of you and we've taken up atheism and enjoy dancing naked on the full moon. Nothing less will do."

Mary blinked. She was accustomed to Percy's mercurial moods and he to hers, but Byron's flamboyance made them both look downright prosaic.

"I don't think Percy and I are up for such full moon revels."

"I've missed that calm gray gaze of yours, Mary. That's why I've come to join you, far from the hustle and prying eyes of Ye Olde England. It shall be like old times again. And I've brought more poems for you to copy, if you want them, that is."

Mary did not, for she'd just finished copying her latest novel to send to her editor. Percy had read *Valperga* and proclaimed that she'd composed something unequalled of its kind, a work that would add renown to her name. She'd scoffed; no one knew she was the author of *Frankenstein* so her only renown was her illustrious parentage and her connections to Percy and Byron. And while this latest novel would be published by a more esteemed house than Lackington, it, too, would be published anonymously, credited only to the author of *Frankenstein*.

But at the same time, she'd allowed herself to ask, *What if?*

Still, Mary tried to see Byron's offer to transcribe his masterpieces for what it was—his own brand of kindness. Beneath all that bluster and in spite of his treatment of Claire, Byron *could* be kind, when he wished it.

Byron's desire to avoid the cities and their crowds didn't last long, and within weeks—during which Mary *did* transcribe his poems, simply so he would stop bringing it up—he procured an invitation to a masked ball for the Pisan carnival on all their behalf. As always, his bidding was their command.

"I've missed us all being together, laughing and enjoying one another's company," Byron announced as they climbed into his obscene Napoleonic carriage. His Italian contessa, Teresa Guiccioli, was seated on the cushion next to him, an apple-cheeked girl several years younger than Mary who was costumed—rather uncreatively—as Madame du Barry, the last *maîtresse-en-titre* of France's King Louis XV. Mary had forgone her usual black gowns tonight to don a Turkish costume with silk bloomers complete with tinkling bells and tiny mirrors at her wrists and ankles, plus a full-sized saber attached to her hip. She'd heard that one of her mother's French friends had regularly worn such attire—Mary had to admit to a certain feeling of invincibility with the blade strapped to her side.

She'd been patient long enough. Right now, while she felt powerful and had Byron's attention . . .

"I've missed my niece's company," she announced as the coach lurched forward. Now was the perfect moment—Byron was full of good cheer and would be on his best behavior in front of his mistress. Percy wasn't impressed with Allegra's education—he'd ascertained on a recent visit that the child knew her prayers but little else—but Claire's daughter had seemed safe enough. "When shall we expect Allegra to be released from the convent?" asked Mary.

Byron huffed a laugh—proof he was in a good mood tonight. "You sound as if my daughter is being held prisoner."

"Isn't she?"

Byron turned a face of nightmares on her, his good mood forgotten. Mary forced herself not to shrink into her seat—she knew how quickly his emotions could transform. "I will not release my daughter to the conniving bitch that whelped her," he growled. "Claire may sing like an angel, but she is insolent and unchristian, and Allegra will *not* turn out like her mother. My daughter is being raised properly, I assure you. Do not speak of her again."

The last sentence came out a snarl, and Mary felt her own fury frothing up inside her. Byron preferred simple women like the contessa at his side—a pretty thing with the social stature to serve as his glittering accessory by day and spread her legs for him at night. Despite their differences, Mary could easily concede that Claire—a talented musician who adhered to Mary

Wollstonecraft's ideals of female independence—was too much for Lord Byron. That the small-souled Byron—a notorious rake accused of sleeping with all manner of men and women—could legally condemn Claire and separate her from her daughter made Mary want to tear her nails down his face.

Shelley's hand on hers urged restraint. "Let us discuss only happy things," he said.

Byron dismissed the conversation with a twirl of his swollen and beringed fingers. Mary was so furious she might have spat at him. "This isn't over," she said, to which Byron gave a tight smile.

"My new boat is to arrive this week, Percy," he said as if she weren't seething directly across from him. "The *Bolivar*."

Mary scarcely listened to Byron's persiflage. Until Percy announced, "I have plans to build a schooner of my own. American in design."

Mary frowned, recognizing this unexpected proclamation for what it was—another attempt to best Byron. When would Shelley stop comparing himself to Byron and realize that he was the better—and nobler—man?

She ignored the talk of sails and midden masts, and made no attempt to draw the bland contessa into conversation. The moment they arrived at the ball, Mary burst from the coach, leaving Percy to scramble after her. She'd crawl home before she had to spend one more minute in Byron's infuriating company.

The ball passed in a riotous swirl of music and colors, laughter and dancing. Mary waltzed several times with Percy and then found herself shocked when the hostess interceded to invite her to a soiree the following week. "I fear you have been much maligned," the overly perfumed woman murmured to Mary over tiny bowls of *zuppa del duca*, a sweet pudding that was also believed to be an aphrodisiac. "But I've watched you tonight—you have the prettiest ways and figure. I'd be happy to ease your entrée into society."

Perhaps Mary had been too long *out* of society, but she wondered at the woman's ulterior motive, especially as she eyed Lord Byron—wearing a wax carnival mask of an elderly man with a luxuriant gray beard—and his flock of followers across the way. It was suddenly too hot, and the liquor of the *zuppa del duca* custard made her stomach roil; Mary longed for her quiet villa with its call of the owls across the garden, and the cool air of her library.

"Excuse me," she said before dashing through the crowd, praying she would make it to the garden in time . . .

She did, bursting into the cool air before emptying her stomach into a nearby hedge.

Percy must have seen her streak across the ballroom, for she felt his warm hand on her back as he crooned calm words in her ear. Byron's chuckle came from behind them both; his monogrammed handkerchief fluttered next to her ear. "I never took you as one to overindulge," he chortled, his mask dangling from his wrist so he might sip a tiny glass of ratafia—its almond fragrance making her stomach heave anew—before sniffing up his nose a pinch of snuff from the enameled box he kept in his jacket pocket. "Although I, too, often enjoy a thorough purging after too large a meal."

"I didn't overindulge." Mary wiped her mouth with Byron's handkerchief as she straightened. Save for her predilection toward seasickness, she had a stomach of iron; the only times she was sick had been . . .

The last time she had been ill, she'd been pregnant with Percy Florence. And before that, Everina.

She struggled not to vomit again.

Mary didn't mind the idea of more children, but something

about being pregnant again right now felt *wrong*. Perhaps it was because Percy Florence was still so young. His birth had helped her heal after Everina's death, but there were still moments when she fought back terror at the thought of losing him. Was she strong enough for another child?

Panic rising in her throat, Mary choked back a fresh wave of bile.

Byron had the good sense to return to the party, leaving Percy to cradle her head in his hands, the steady gaze of his blue eyes grounding her. Somehow, he *knew*. "If we're to have another child, Mary, I'll be counting the days until I get to welcome into our family another tiny pixie with your soft gray eyes."

Panic stilling somewhat, Mary let Percy bundle her up, first in his arms and then into Byron's carriage, which he commandeered to take her home. As he did so, Mary forced herself to breathe.

And she held that breath as the future barreled toward them.

A little patience and all will be over.

Her new mantra became a daily—sometimes hourly—recitation. Mary *was* with child, and from its very first day, this pregnancy was fraught with difficulties.

Because Mary was exhausted and often too ill to rise until evening, Percy made two decisions for her benefit. First, that they would move from landlocked Pisa to the Gulf of La Spezia, where the cerulean waters and salt-kissed breeze could lift Mary's spirits. Second, that Claire would join them to help care for Mary, Percy Florence, and the new baby, when it came.

Mary was actually relieved to see her sister. "Percy asked me to secure a house for us all in La Spezia," Claire informed Mary after her arrival. "You and Percy can join me in a few days after

I send word." It was unusual for an unmarried woman to assume such responsibility, but Claire didn't realize this was Percy's tactic to keep her separate from Byron and his new mistress. Mary was beginning to doubt whether Claire continued to harbor tender feelings for Byron. Still, there was no need to parade the contessa under her nose.

As Mary watched Claire's quick departure from where she sat wrapped in a chair in the garden, she realized it was a relief to allow Claire to shoulder some of her burdens. Until Byron's contessa arrived not long after, flush-cheeked and wide-eyed. "I saw your carriage pass." Her English was thickly accented, like a favorite dish overpowered by summer spices. "Has Signore Shelley just left?"

"That was my sister Claire you saw." Awkward that Byron's two mistresses were now living within a half mile of each other, but there was nothing to be done about it, save keep Claire in La Spezia. Mary prepared to plead exhaustion and escape this unexpected and unwelcome visit.

"She is here?" Teresa's long-fingered hands flew to her lips. "Such terrible timing."

Mary nearly smirked. "There is no good time for Claire to be near Byron, I'm afraid."

No good time for any of us to be near Byron.

"No." Teresa shook her head, pearl earbobs gleaming with the motion. "I bring ill news. Claire's daughter, Allegra . . . she is dead."

Mary stopped midmotion, hands holding on to the back of her wicker chair. The world slowed then, that dread moment narrowing into a tunnel that contained only the heart-shaped face of Byron's mistress. "What?"

"The child—Allegra—took ill at the convent and never rose from her bed. She is no more. Byron is inconsolable, so I came to speak the news." Teresa seemed to reach for Mary, then thought better of it. "I am deeply sorry."

The guilt over Everina's death that had loosened its garrote around Mary's heart tightened again, made it difficult to breathe. All the things she could have done, *should* have done to force Byron to release Claire's daughter assailed her at once. *One dead child and now another . . . We never should have come to Italy.* She knew what it was to lose a daughter, but Percy and the birth of Percy Florence had reminded her what it was to live. Claire was alone and would lose *all* with Allegra's passing. How could a woman survive such loss?

"Claire will be devastated." Mary leaned against the chair for support as she glanced at Teresa. "Being in such easy reach of him"—a jut of her chin toward Byron's mansion, which could be seen through the trees—"is not a good idea. For either of them."

In grief, the havoc Claire and Byron might wreak upon each other would be the stuff of nightmares. It wasn't outside the realm of possibility that Claire would seek revenge—Mary had contemplated all manner of harm for Byron after Everina's passing, but Claire's temper ran hotter.

"I will lure him away," Teresa said. "But when she returns . . ."

"She won't." Already Mary's mind was skipping ahead. She had failed Claire with Allegra, but she would protect her sister now. From herself, at least. "Percy and I will ensure she remains in La Spezia."

As Mary slowly wended her way inside and shut the door behind her, she looked around at the place where she had been happy, for a while at least.

And felt the door of something else close behind her.

CHAPTER 16

❦

February 1797

MARY WOLLSTONECRAFT

Men have sung songs for millennia about wartime heroics, yet battle-hardened soldiers shrink in fear and dread from the twin campaigns of pregnancy and childbirth. It is women—everyday, ordinary women—who are truly courageous.

However, our combat is made worse by the fact that women are kept in the dark about our own unruly bodies: left first to stumble through adolescence, then navigate our initial romantic encounters in the dark, and eventually watch in horror as we are subsumed by the small creature we must inevitably expel from our own body.

I will not prevaricate, nor hide my difficulties as many women do, given my belief that womankind should be aware of what will happen to their bodies at all stages of life. My severe nausea during my second unexpected pregnancy made it impossible to eat, which also meant that not collapsing from exhaustion was a herculean task. Not to mention the swelling ankles, crushing headaches, and even the pain induced by simple walking that came in the middle months. Just running out for a fresh pot of ink in the harsh winter weather was enough to knock me into bed for the rest of the day. Or I should say, make me wish for my bed, given that Fanny was constantly underfoot.

No one tells women how difficult it is to raise a child while being *with child*.

All this meant I was too exhausted to write, which made me irritable in the way of a storybook dragon whose treasure has been looted from beneath it.

With icy cold feet and petticoats clogged with muddy snow, I arrived home one February afternoon from purchasing new boots for Fanny—an expense I could ill afford, but her toes had burst through the seams of her others—to find William in my parlor before a merry fire, smoking a pipe while reading a book with his feet kicked up on the ottoman. "Oh, good," he said, taking his feet down. "I made much progress on my writing today—I'm almost done with the new edition of *Political Justice*—and thought I'd come early. I've been waiting for you nearly an hour."

"Isn't that lovely." I struggled out of my sodden wool coat and batted William away when he came to help. The fire in the grate irked me—I didn't want to know how much precious coal he'd used to stoke it.

"What's wrong?" he asked.

I stared at him. In my mind, I knew he was just trying to be helpful and pleasant. But the storm surge of my emotions made quick work of the driftwood underpinnings of that understanding. "What's wrong is that my feet are frozen solid and I spend my days entertaining Fanny instead of writing." I also couldn't control that my voice gained an octave with each word any more than I could control the squall howling outside. I flung down the paper package containing Fanny's boots. "What's *wrong* is that I'm struggling to get through each day with one illegitimate child and cannot imagine how I'm going to manage with two. What's *wrong* is that I wrote to Gilbert Imlay for money as Johnson demanded, but he didn't respond and I haven't more than a pound to my name after buying these boots. Oh, and the roof started leaking last night, so that's another cruel thing to look forward to."

I paused, eyes stinging in a way I couldn't control. *No. I am stronger than all this.*

It wasn't just the sodden petticoats or my exhaustion then, but the dam against all my worries for the future suddenly caved in and I was helpless against its onslaught. I sobbed in such a manner that William should have run from my cottage without ever looking back. Gilbert Imlay had done just that, and I feared William would be driven away from me as well.

Instead, he merely gathered me onto his lap and stroked my hair until I could breathe again. My darling William, who had been beside himself with joy when I'd informed him that we had created the child I now carried.

"My fierce, independent Mary," he murmured once I'd calmed. "No one should bear so many burdens. Let me help you."

I merely used his jacket to mop my cheeks. I didn't want to accept help—didn't want to admit that I *needed* it—but . . . perhaps William could watch Fanny more often. I could let him do that.

"First," he said, "I'll borrow fifty pounds to get you through the winter."

"Absolutely *not*." I dashed a sleeve over my eyes, which felt filled with river grit. William calculated his living expenses down to the penny, and I had no desire to be merely the graceful ivy clinging to his sturdy oak. "I can't let you do that. You once wrote that financing a family blighted the freedom of a male intellectual."

Difficult to argue against that particular inconvenient truth, given that my current circumstances—and languishing manuscript—proved it also applied to a *female* intellectual.

"Circumstances change." William gave a pointed look at my slightly rounded belly. "So, too, do ideas. I now perceive there are other pleasures in the world than my philosophy, and I have you to thank for that. I'm not a man to shirk my responsibilities, Mary. If it makes you feel more productive, I'm sure Johnson can also provide you some review work. Or even a few pieces to translate."

I sniffed and rubbed my nose. "I suppose. I *did* write to Imlay as he asked. I even thought it was a good idea."

"Forget Imlay." William's hackles always rose at the man's very mention. "I'm your family now, Mary, not that cavalier. I'll take care of you, I swear it."

It *would* be a huge relief not to fret over food and clothes for the next few months. Heaven only knew how I'd find time to write once this new baby was born, but that was a worry for a different day.

"Now, as for your next concern, that of Fanny and this new child . . ." William stared at the fire overlong, but I was accustomed to his odd silences. "I was content to carry on with the way things were, but that was simpleminded of me. So . . . marry me."

I blinked like a lackwit, then shook my head—this couldn't be happening, not when I knew how William abhorred marriage, and not when I'd already experienced once how attaching myself to a man—even if it was legally only on the French registers—could end so horrifically. But William merely wore a lopsided grin as he gathered my hands into his. "Mary Wollstonecraft, I'd be honored if you would make me your husband, and a true father to Fanny and this new child."

"You don't believe in marriage and neither do I." I shook my hands loose to knock away the fresh tears that were forming. My eyes were already puffy and my nose was undoubtedly the unattractive color of a summer radish. "You don't want to marry me, William. Look—I'm a disaster. You'll tire of me eventually, and your affection will turn to loathing or, worse, indifference."

I heard echoes of my old self and felt the frigid waters of the Thames closing over me then. But I couldn't break loose or paddle my way to the sweet air above, no matter how I wished it.

"Bah." William clasped both my hands between his. "You can't hide from me, Mary, not when I know you inside and out. Did you not write yourself that *personal attachment and esteem can forge a friendship which only death can dissolve?*"

"I did—"

"And we are the best of friends, are we not?"

Grudgingly: "We are."

"And do you think I could be content knowing that I had the power to solve all your worries—and those of my children—and chose not to? What sort of friend would you take me for then?"

But he was the best sort of friend, given that he was offering to reorder his entire life for me. I loved him for it, but even more I loved him for the two words he'd just spoken: *my children*. For he truly was father to both Fanny and this child I carried. And in my heart of hearts, I wanted him to claim me as he'd just claimed them.

But I loved him too much not to give him one more opportunity to rescind his offer and preserve his freedom.

"A life with me will be messy." I sniffled into the handkerchief he'd pressed into my hands. "Two children underfoot. *And* a dog and two cats. You may even have to adjust your writing schedule."

"Let's not be hasty." William's tone was serious, but his eyes sparkled—he knew I was caving. "We're intelligent individuals— we both have a right to work, and I'm confident we can create schedules that accommodate all our needs. While also finding a way to leash that hellhound."

I smoothed the furrow between his brows. "People will laugh at us," I whispered. "They'll call us hypocrites and say we've compromised our beliefs."

"Hang people. I never cared for them anyway." I laughed and William fell serious. "Say you'll do it, Mary. Say you'll marry me."

So . . . I did.

On March 29, William Godwin and I walked hand in hand to St. Pancras Church, the old country church in Somers Town, and exchanged our vows.

The ceremony was small; we had no party or celebration. Only one of William's friends witnessed; even Fanny stayed behind at the cottage with Marguerite and Merryboy.

Marriage has never been about speaking vows in front of an officiant—those merely benefit the curious onlookers. One day I hoped my children would understand that. A true marriage is the little moments you build together every day . . . The feel of William's thumb brushing the back of my hand when he slipped the gold band on my finger . . . The tiny apple cake he insisted we buy to share with Fanny after dinner . . . The first edition copy of Olympe de Gouges's *Déclaration des Droits de la Femme et de la Citoyenne*—which I'd once mentioned that I regretted not bringing with me from France and which he gave me as a wedding gift . . . The signed copy of Thomas Paine's *Common Sense*, gifted to me by the author, which I tied with a navy ribbon and left for William on our bed.

Our bed . . .

The same bed that would soon find its way to our new shared lodgings at No. 29 in a new neighborhood called the Polygon. Close enough to London to call on friends or attend an evening play, but with a country house's high ceilings, large windows, and an expansive garden. "A garden is important," William had said. "So you can keep your bees." I'd readily agreed.

For the first time, I had a season of calm in my stormy life, while William was stirred by real passion in an otherwise staid life. While this was a season of change, some things would stay the same.

"You should rent a room nearby so you can write every day," I'd instructed, recalling his telling me that his privacy was a critical ingredient for writing. He hadn't objected, merely rubbed at the cleft in his chin and nodded.

"We'll keep Marguerite and hire more help when the baby comes. Then you'll have time to write as well."

We might need to turn highwayman—and highway*woman*— to steal the money to hire more help, but any female who allowed her household to fall into disrepair was deemed a failure.

Wife, mother, writer . . . could I manage them all?

Anxiety flapped its bleak wings, but I refused to allow that vulture a perch. Not tonight when I was so cozy and content.

"Can we set Merryboy to sweeping and Puss to dusting?" I prodded William playfully as I snuggled into his warmth. This was only the second night we'd spent together, and I eagerly anticipated waking up next to him, no stealth or subterfuge required.

"It's worth a try." William pulled the cozy counterpane over us both. "Although if the beasts prove as indolent as I suspect, I believe I can find my way around a broom and rag."

It was an extraordinary concession—growing up, I'd never seen my father so much as wash a dish. In fact, no men that I had ever encountered—Johnson included—knew their way around a broom or dustpan, much less a kitchen. But William was open to the idea, just as I was determined to remain the friend of my husband and not become merely his humble dependent.

With Fanny sleeping soundly next door and William's hand on my expanding belly, I, too, was beginning to perceive that there were indeed other pleasures in the world than my philosophy.

I blew out the candle and plunged us into moonlight as I pressed a kiss to the back of his free hand. "This may prove a most fruitful experiment, husband."

I felt William's chuckle against my back as he tugged me closer. "Indeed, wife. Indeed."

"Mr. Godwin, author of a pamphlet against matrimony, has married the famous Mrs. Wollstonecraft, who wrote in support of the Rights of Woman." William glanced at me while I read the paper over breakfast about a week after our wedding. Having informed our family and friends of our new marital arrangement—Maria Reveley burst into joyous tears upon hearing the news, while other acquaintances caused me a transitory pang by scorning me upon the revelation of my former unmarried connection to Gilbert Imlay—we'd also received responses that we were *extraordinary characters with sublime theories* about equality in marriage that we'd never be able to put into practice. I folded up the paper. "I'd expected worse from the *Times*."

"Patience," he commented as he finished off his final bite and urged Fanny to take another. "The eggs from my mother are good."

The gift from William's mother—a simple country Method-
ist widow—was as heartfelt as her message congratulating her
son for giving up his stance against marriage. However, I understood the underlying symbolism of the eggs—and the feath-
erbed scented with dried thyme and mint that she'd also sent.
She wanted our union to be fruitful, which the waistline I'd let
out last night already attested to. "You didn't tell her about little
Master William, did you?"

We'd played a game—all three of us with Fanny included—
to guess whether the baby was going to be a boy or girl. William
and I both guessed boy, hence Master William. Fanny, however, desperately wanted a sister and now carried with her everywhere the rag doll I'd stitched for her last birthday.

"My mother is nearly seventy and possesses a weak heart."
William carried his plate and mine to the sink, where he kept
up his end of our household arrangement by washing them. "I
feed her one tidbit of news at a time, given that I don't wish to
be the cause of her demise."

I smiled. There was time enough to inform William's mother
that she was to be a grandmother. At thirty-eight years old, I
felt in some ways that my life—our lives together, with Fanny
and our soon-to-be child—was just beginning.

The dishes dutifully set out to dry, William shrugged into
his coat and pulled his black tricorne onto his head. For all his
simplicity in hats, today's waistcoat could only be described as a
scorching shade of marigold. "Are you sure you don't mind my
going?"

Fully unpacked and officially settled in, William would
make use of his lodgings down the street today for the first
time. We were determined to prove that a husband and wife
need not lose their identities after marriage—William and I

would still write and publish our work, no matter how society scoffed.

Still, I appreciated William's extra checking and sought to reassure him.

"I wish you, for my soul, to be riveted in my heart," I responded in an officious voice while beckoning him to bend down for a kiss. Getting up expended too much energy until I'd been braced by a second cup of tea. I poked his rib as he kissed me. "But I do not desire to have you always at my elbow."

He grinned. "Duly noted."

"Bye, Papa!" Fanny offered from her place. No more *Man*—she had easily made the transition to an even sweeter endearment.

He laughed and ruffled her sleep-mussed hair. "Send Marguerite with a note if you or this little animal needs anything."

That was how the notes began. And they soon became the highlights of my mornings.

In all honesty, it started with rather dull, often serious notes—sometimes there were simply things that needed to be communicated to one's husband over a four-hour absence—and Fanny actually requested I send the first one after I'd dressed her for the day.

> *My dear love—*
>   *I have ordered some boiled mutton. You will, perhaps, have no object to eating at four while I am writing. Fanny is delighted at the thought of dining with you—but I wish you to eat your meat first, and have her end with her pudding. And whatever you do, do not give Fanny butter with her pudding.*
>
> *—M*

To which he responded:

> *I am scandalized that you think me so irresponsible as to ply our daughter with butter in her pudding. What sort of wild heathen do you think I am?*
>
> —*W*

William seemed suited to jests on paper—there was a jokester's side to my husband that he kept hidden from all save Fanny and me. My eyes still welled up to read *our daughter*—I'd been so emotional of late—but I kept my response lighthearted:

> *W*—
> *Fanny believes you a pirate. Do pirates eat butter? I thought it was all hard biscuits and rum.*
>
> *M*—
> *I cannot give Fanny rum. And you call yourself the responsible parent.*

I laughed and bade Marguerite to wait for my response. Our poor maid merely pursed her lips; her cheeks were flushed from all the traveling back and forth to William's rented office. "Surely it would be faster if you and Master William spoke face-to-face?" she asked, hands fisted on her hips. "I've a piecrust to make, and the kitchen maid says the sink is blocked."

I shook my head, barely containing my mirth. "I must abide by the rules of our contract. I cannot face Mr. Godwin until one o'clock when he departs his office."

By then I'd written my next missive, which Marguerite grudgingly took.

W—

The maid will tell you about the state of the sink.
Also, I have a design to keep you quite to myself this
evening. (I hope nobody will call!)

—M

When Marguerite arrived some minutes later—still frowning and this time without waiting for a response—Fanny seized William's folded letter and wouldn't let it go. "I miss Papa," she informed me, so I let her open the message and then read it aloud in my best impersonation of William's voice.

M—

I cannot wait to find out about the state of the sink.
Such anticipation!
I find I am regretting my past, when I ranked philosophy
more important than love. We seem to combine, in a
considerable degree, the novelty of the lively sensation of a
visit, with the more delicious and heartfelt pleasures of
domestic life.
We love as it were to multiply our consciousness, even
at the hazard of opening new avenues of pain and misery
to attack us.

—W

Except in those moments, as Fanny clapped with glee at my impersonation and I eagerly awaited the return of my husband, I couldn't fathom the idea of pain or misery.

Not during such a glorious summer as this!

. . .

Thus, the months of my pregnancy dwindled away. I did my best to keep the exact same schedule—breakfast with William followed by a morning with Fanny, writing through tea, and then our little family reuniting for vigorous walks to the book-shop in Sadler's Wells or to visit Johnson for supper. Every so often, Maria Reveley stopped by for a visit, including several to paint my portrait and one mid-August to take the children hay-ing. It was too bright to see it that sun-dappled afternoon, but a comet—or as some called it, a strange star—had appeared in the night sky, bewildering most and leading me to hope that little Master William would be born soon.

"I can barely keep up with you," Maria laughed as we walked down the lane. Henry had run ahead, pulling a reluctant Fanny with him—instead of hoops today, Henry had brought toy rakes and pitchforks so they could make hay in a nearby field. I was enjoying these days with my introspective daughter, trying to soak all my love and attention into her before her sibling arrived. "And I'm not the one expecting a baby any day."

"Not quite any day," I reminded her, although my girth cer-tainly made it feel that way. I'd made the concession of shorten-ing our usual three-mile walk to just a mile. "I still have a few weeks yet. Although I'm eager to regain my activity and reduce to some shapeliness this portly shadow of mine."

Maria laughed. "I recall at this juncture being instructed to nap and engage in nothing more strenuous than needlework. Of course, leave it to the great Mary Wollstonecraft to eschew so-ciety's advice."

"Being outside in nature is invigorating. I aim to be in prime health for both the delivery and the work to come."

"And your writing?"

"Stymied," I admitted. My aim in *The Wrongs of Woman* was to showcase the misery and oppression, peculiar to women, that arose out of the partial laws and customs of society. My main heroine awoke in a mental asylum where her husband had committed her not because she was insane, but because he sought her fortune. She was attended to by a former prostitute—my characters were two women from different social classes, both tyrannized by the men in their lives. The story drew distantly from my experiences in Hoxton and with Gilbert Imlay and Théroigne de Méricourt; it was grim and gritty and scandalous, which was precisely what I wanted. After all, sex and violence had intrigued humanity since before the days of the Coliseum; why not use those tools to teach modern society of current evils?

The problem was that I had no idea how to end the novel. But time and persistence always unraveled even the trickiest Gordian knot of writing, so I just had to keep at it.

"I press forward, but thus far, no breakthroughs are being made."

"Set it aside."

"What?"

Maria shrugged. "That's what I do. Take a break from an obstinate painting to work on something else. Then return to it with fresh eyes. Not that your portrait was obstinate, of course."

"Of course not." I smiled. Maria had just finished my portrait the day before, and it was truly a good enough likeness that its unveiling had brought tears to William's eyes. "Except I have nothing else to work on." I shook a finger at Maria. "And don't you dare suggest I take up something so foolish as trimming hats."

"I would never dare propose something so horrific." Maria laughed as Fanny jumped out from behind a haystack, startling Henry into a game of tag. "Why not write about your life?"

"No one would want to read about that." Really, such an idea was beyond mundane.

"Not necessarily to publish, just to record. You *have* led a rather interesting life, you know. Fanny and her sibling may one day wish to know about their famous mother and her wild adventures."

"They weren't *so* wild." At Maria's questioning eyebrow, I amended: "Not all of them, at least. I suspect my children will crave a different sort of story before bed."

Still, Maria's words niggled me the next day when I sat down to *The Wrongs of Woman*. Perhaps my friend was right—I *had* led an interesting life. And writing of the past decade might be cathartic *and* help me determine what I most wanted from the years to come.

A loving husband to grow old with, brilliant children to challenge and enjoy, more books to write, and perhaps even another expedition to foreign lands . . .

The words flew from my pen, and before I knew it, I'd written of my final days in Hoxton, coming to London, and even Johnson offering to buy *On the Education of Daughters*. Then my two hours were up and Fanny was rapping on the door, asking me to come outside and look for grasshoppers.

Two weeks later, my labor pangs began.

"I'll have just enough time to finish the chapter I've been revising before we meet this new little animal of ours," I announced to William as I fluffed the pillows of our bed. Maria Reveley's portrait of me hung on the wall at William's side of the room, where he had insisted it take pride of place, despite my protests.

It was August 30, just two weeks after Maria had brought up the subject of my memoir, and I'd made great progress on the secret project. It seemed silly to be writing my memoirs, given they were absent any deep philosophy that I hadn't already mined in my prior books. But the memories and words flooded my every thought so I could scarcely keep up with them, and I planned a return to heftier prose once the baby was born. After all, what were midnight feedings for if not candlelit writing sessions?

"I'll fetch the doctor." Poor William looked frantic as he shoved his long legs into his trousers, but I merely tiptoed in my nightgown behind him and rubbed the knots of his shoulders with ink-spotted hands.

"No doctor." I reminded him of the argument I'd already won, having procured the services of a respected midwife. I'd refused to employ an accoucheur—one of those supposedly educated men who assisted women in childbirth—given that no man could understand a woman's body as well as another woman, and I had no plans to observe the usual monthlong lying-in required of new mothers. "And there's no need to fetch Mrs. Blenkinsop until there's something for her to do."

"But you said Fanny's birth was brisk. Surely *someone* should be here."

I pressed William's jacket and coat into his hands, along with a jaunty canary-yellow waistcoat that perfectly matched my mood. "Go to your apartment and write," I commanded. "I'll send for you when you can meet your son."

"But I wish to be useful. Please, Mary. I *need* to be useful."

I stood on tiptoes and kissed the tip of his nose. "Send over some light reading after you take Fanny to Maria for the day. I'll need a distraction."

"I'll send every book and newspaper I can find." William jammed his hat on his head and sailed out the door, leaving me wondering if I should inform him that he'd put his jacket on over his sleeping shirt. I decided against it. Years from now, I could laugh with our son while telling of how I sent his father out into London half-dressed on the morning of his birth.

Over the course of the morning, I received a flood of newspapers and books—William must have emptied the bookshop at Sadler's Wells along with every other on the way—accompanied by an urgent message inquiring as to our progress. I responded back with a happy note:

> *I have no doubt of seeing the animal today.*

That effervescent happiness waned as the hours stretched on. By midafternoon, I summoned the midwife and sent Marguerite to ensure my husband dined with Maria Reveley—otherwise he'd forget to eat. I sent William a final note as the pains grew deeper:

> *A little patience and all will be over.*

I paced when I could manage, got down on all fours and moaned when the pains streaked across my abdomen like shooting stars. I was too exhausted to speak and would have traded my soul to every demon in the underworld for five minutes' rest. Fanny had been easy, but *this* . . .

My babe was finally born just before midnight on that August eve, the fragrance of summer jasmine swirling with the copper tang of blood as the midwife caught the child and lifted the new life I'd created onto my hollow belly. As twilight-blue eyes met mine, that precious, fragile soul crashed into mine.

My midnight daughter, her quiet spirit full of stars and darkness.

When the midwife finally allowed William into the room, I

felt the sacred sensation of his soul entwining with hers and mine, its warmth caressing and questioning.

"Meet your daughter," I managed to whisper, holding up the precious bundle of our child. I already loved her in the most brutal manner. I'd never seen William's eyes so wide as when he held her for the first time. I took in his harried expression and the lines etched deep around his eyes, and knew that he had fretted the day away.

His eyes were twin moons when he finally looked at me. "She is the shrine into which our two lives have been poured," he whispered, "never to be separated."

We stayed that way, a midnight portrait of our little family, until the midwife shooed William away. "There's women's work still to be done," she announced as she shut the door behind him. Assuming her place on the stool at my feet, she prodded about my abdomen. "The afterbirth must be delivered. I shall press here and you must bear down."

We struggled like beasts of burden in their harnesses for nearly three hours until sweat streaked down Mrs. Blenkinsop's arms and I had been sapped of the last of my strength. Whereas the birth of my daughter had filled me with such incandescent joy, now a sense of foreboding crackled like hoarfrost down my spine. The midwife's white face and grim expression told me something was terribly, horribly wrong, but I couldn't muster the energy to ascertain what it was.

She didn't have to call for William—he'd been waiting outside the door. "Fetch a surgeon," she commanded. "Immediately."

I recall in a haze the midwife urging me to allow the baby to suckle, but my swaddled daughter was swept back into her basket when William and the surgeon arrived. "Out," the physician commanded dear, helpless William.

Somehow, I found the strength to lift a hand, which my

husband clasped even as Mrs. Blenkinsop urged him from the room. The sour smell of his fear settled like ash upon my skin. "Don't worry," I whispered weakly to my love. "I am determined not to leave."

Except when the surgeon went to work—without anesthesia— I screamed at the fiery claws of agony that gored my abdomen, barely registering William pounding and shouting on the other side of the door.

Before I fainted, my nostrils filled with more than the sunny scent of jasmine and the sharp tang of blood. There was no mistaking the black stench of death that stalked the room.

CHAPTER 17

❧

June 1822

MARY SHELLEY

Casa Magni, the house that Claire secured for them, was a pale-faced, tragic villa.

Fitting, given that Claire became its ashen idol upon learning of Allegra's death. Mary's worries that her sister might seek revenge against Byron for their daughter's death never materialized; her sister proclaimed that her relationship with Byron had produced only a few minutes of pleasure and a lifetime of pain and that their experiment in free love had transformed one of the finest poets in England into a monster of lying, meanness, cruelness, and treachery. Then she simply fell silent. To look into Claire's red-rimmed eyes was akin to viewing the wreckage of some biblical storm. Unwilling to leave her sister alone for fear that she might walk into the sea and never return, Mary accompanied Claire on long walks through the nearby chestnut grove. She may as well have been walking with a woman already dead.

The house was approachable only by water and exposed to the sea's capricious moods, and its seven arches that faced the bay were buffeted by wild winds and constant sea spray. To keep her sister safe, Mary had taken to sleeping with Claire at one end of the house, Percy on the opposite side with their son in a makeshift nursery in the middle.

Only a few weeks after they moved in, Mary woke to a silent house and an oily, dark feeling of desperation at her throat, as if some terrible creature traced a claw up the knobs of her spine and now held her pinned to the bed.

Her stomach cramped, in fear she thought at first. Then in pain.

Her fingers touched her legs, the warm dampness there.

She pushed the blanket back. And screamed at what she saw in the sickly moonlight.

Stumbling from her own bed, Claire rushed to Mary's side, then blanched at the torrent of blood staining the shroud of sheets tangled around Mary's legs. "I'll get Percy," was all Claire said before her footsteps pounded away.

By the time he arrived, an insidious and comfortable heat had seeped into Mary's soul and dulled the edges of her terror. If only she could lie down and sleep, she would wake from this horror and all would be well . . .

"I don't know what to do." Claire's voice seemed distant, underwater perhaps. Mary could no longer see, but surely they were submerged somehow. "There's so much blood."

"We must keep her conscious," Percy seemed to say. "Rub her brow with brandy or cologne, something to revive her until the physician arrives."

Mary wanted to laugh and tell them all would be well, that the physician would never make it to this far-flung, sad little house. Percy said something else, but his words faded away before they could fully form.

Was this how her mother had felt as she slipped slowly into the comfortable warmth of oblivion? Was it finally time to join her?

Even that thought failed to land; Mary's consciousness was already dissipating into a thousand bewinged fragments that fluttered into soft and silent darkness.

Until she was plunged into waters so frigid that a thousand—no, a million—tiny fanged teeth tore at her very flesh.

Mary must have screamed—she imagined she thrashed in some reverse parody of a fish so cruelly caught—until she felt Percy's voice reverberate up the shell of her ear. "An arctic ice bath for my Fairie Queene, to tether you to this life with me." The waters splashed and rearranged themselves against her waterlogged nightgown.

"You'll kill her in there," she heard Claire cry. "Her last moments on this earth will be hell, Percy, and it will be your fault that she suffered so mightily."

"The ice will stanch the blood flow until the surgeon comes. Tell the servants to fetch a steady supply from the icehouse. And get that damned doctor *now*." Mary felt his hand at her brow even as something splashed and his warmth formed a solid wall behind her. "Stay with me, Mary. Please, just stay with me."

Together they floated between this world and the next. Whenever Mary drew too near to that shadowy realm that beckoned her with its promise of rest, Percy's murmurs and a fresh wave of cold hooked her to this side of darkness. Finally, the surgeon arrived, and Mary felt herself lifted from the bath. Her eyes cracked open and her soul cringed at the wreckage she saw there—bloodstained waters like the site of some ancient massacre, a war-torn Percy whose ruined trousers were likewise streaked with carnage.

Her blood. And their child's.

"There will be no baby," she heard the surgeon say once she was warm in Percy's bed, a fire roaring in the hearth and a composing draft on the sideboard. Strange to be warm, when in the bath the very marrow of her bones had seemed to freeze solid. "*Signore*, there is no doubt that you saved your wife from a fatal hemorrhage with that ice bath."

Mary didn't hear the words of Percy's response before she drifted to sleep, only its muffled cadence that seeped into her ears like the intonation of a funeral bell.

After her miscarriage, Mary closed her eyes each evening to find herself haunted by nightmares more relentless than the monster she'd once written about. One particularly humid night, she set aside her journal and padded on bare feet down to the kitchen, intent on finding something cool to drink. Percy had never been in better health prior to the loss of this most recent child, but now he stood outside on the portico, his sodden form illuminated by untethered surges of lightning, the wild sea and sky crashing together while a gale-force wind tore at his hair and whipped his nightclothes.

"Percy!" Blades of rain lashed at Mary as she flung open the door so she had to shield her face and eyes. "What are you doing?"

Her husband's silhouette was illuminated again by a flash of lightning; he looked like a madman as he flung out an arm. "Don't you see her?" he yelled, but Mary saw only his new schooner—the *Ariel*—thrashing in the black and turgid waves where he pointed. White surf broke upon the shore, as if Neptune himself were stirring the sea to a vicious peak. "There she is again!"

"*Who* is there?" Mary strained to see what he saw. Her skin rippled with gooseflesh at his answer.

"Everina. Can't you see her, Mary? In the waves, her hands clasped? Right next to Allegra!"

A ghost passed through Mary and racked her body with a violent shudder. "There's nothing, *cor cordium*." *Heart of hearts.* She guided Percy—her heart of hearts in this world, no matter how he set that organ to pounding in horror right now—toward the door, but barely avoided looking back at the ocean's fury. "Your mind is playing tricks—you only wish you could see Everina and Allegra again."

His wail was that of an animal whipped to its breaking point. "I should have saved her. I should have saved them both."

Only once Mary had the doors closed behind them did Percy slump to the floor. Water pooled in the flagstones and dripped from the ends of his hair, seeping into Mary's thin nightgown as she crouched at his side. "I killed them both, Mary," he sobbed. "I'm a monster. And now we've been punished anew. I should never have called you to Venice, I should have pushed Byron harder, forced him to return Allegra—"

Mary pressed two fingers to his lips. "There was nothing you could have done, my love. *Nothing.*"

The truth of the words did little to soothe him. Mary helped her husband to his bed and doused the candles before arranging her own battered body around his. She recalled the purple bruises beneath her husband's eyes since her miscarriage—his lack of appetite and his offhand remark about needing laudanum to ease the rheumatic pain in his side. After so many tragedies, the loss of this child had finally snapped his indomitable spirit, like a wild oak torn asunder by a crack of lightning.

After Everina's death, it was Percy who had pieced Mary back together, who had taught her to forgive herself. Now it fell to her to hold Percy together. Mary only hoped she had the strength.

"Save me, Mary," Percy intoned. His entire body shook with the force of his sobs. "For the love of God, save me from this."

Mary nested closer until they were fused as close as skin and bones would allow. Then she began weaving together her mother's words and Percy's poetry and snippets of her own writing, braiding together visions of their future together until Percy's breathing leveled and he sank into an ocean-deep sleep. Exhausted, she could only lie there, her mind whirling.

A little patience and all will be over.

Percy's boat sketches were everywhere.

His obsessive mind, once turned on poetry, on his children, on *her*, now turned toward the *Ariel*. The overflowing font of his stanzas slowed to a trickle and then ceased altogether, as if blocked by the magnitude of his grief. First, he'd lost his children with Harriet, then Everina, then Allegra, and then this child—it was simply too much. Numb and hollow-hearted, Mary knew only time would sand down the jagged edges of their shared pain.

Byron fed the flames of Percy's latest nautical obsession—unwittingly or not, Mary didn't know—by sailing the gaudy *Bolivar* into the bay, its letters emblazoned on the sails and his contessa's shell-pink pennant flying from the mast. The teeth-shattering blast from the ridiculous war cannon mounted on its deck set a headache throbbing in Mary's skull.

The ship was obscene, a reflection of its owner. But somehow, Percy had gotten it into his head that he could beat Byron at this game.

"I've lengthened the masts on the *Ariel* so she'll sail like a witch." He pointed first to his latest sketch and then to the austere boat tethered next to the *Bolivar* that Mary could just see from her vantage in bed. Her head still pounded following Byron's arrival; even Percy Florence was exceedingly fractious, given that he'd missed his nap over Byron's fanfare. "I added extra sails and stored over three tons of pig iron in the hull to give her more ballast. Can't you see it, Mary? *Me*, besting Byron on the high seas?"

Normally, Mary would have tempered Percy's insatiable appetite to outshine Byron, but she merely nodded her absentminded assent, wishing she could steal a few minutes of sleep with Percy Florence.

"I've packed her with supplies. My friend Williams and I are sailing her across the bay tomorrow."

The fog cleared from Mary's vision and she sat up straighter. "You're leaving?"

Don't leave, she imagined herself saying. *Not now.*

"I'll be gone only a week." Percy's back was to her as he gazed at the *Ariel*. The boat reared and tossed the rigging of her mane in the breeze, restless from where she remained tethered.

Just like Percy, whose very bones threatened to burst from his skin at any moment. He had given Mary so much, had even pulled her back from the brink of death through the sheer force of his will. "I need this, Mary." His voice was strung too tight. "To breathe the fresh air, to remember what it is to *live*."

Much as it pained her, Mary bit back her request that he stay with her at Casa Magni. She would be strong for him, just as he'd been for her. No matter how his absence would echo in her very soul.

"Just a week, then."

Percy seemed not to hear, already chattering about the nautical adventure at hand. It was one of the many reasons she loved him, that bottled spark of excitement that glowed like fireflies captured on a midsummer night. It was a shock of pure joy to witness that spark again.

He pressed a kiss to her hand before plucking up his papers like a boy about to head out on a holiday expedition with his mates, offering a vision of what their son might look like one day.

Later, she would remember he wore his favorite nankeen

trousers when he tramped away from her, a sheaf of Keats's poems poking from his pocket.

Tiny details of a seemingly inconsequential moment.

The sight of the *Ariel*'s colossal sails disappearing over the horizon seared itself onto the backs of Mary's eyelids, as impossible as the white-capped mountains of the Alps slipping from view. She already missed him.

Berating herself for her weakness, Mary reminded herself that Percy would return in a matter of days. Still, she breathed a sigh of relief when a letter arrived two days later, crowing that he had beaten Byron and would return in a week's time, on July 8.

The eighth came and went. An unexpected summer storm pounded the seas, and the *Ariel*'s mountains failed to appear over the horizon.

"He must have extended his stay." Mary's words over breakfast the following morning were directed to Claire as much as to herself. Percy Florence whimpered on her lap, his fingers shoved deep in his mouth while tears welled in his eyes. A tooth was coming in, making the poor mite miserable.

"I'll take him," Claire offered, and Mary let her. She understood the bittersweet pang of holding a child that was not your own, knew that Claire did it both to heal and to punish herself. While Claire sang softly to Mary's son, Mary penned a quick note to Percy at Lord Byron's, asking when to expect him.

A brief letter arrived from Byron a couple days later, apologizing for the delay and stating that he had decamped to Pisa. And that Shelley had left his villa at Livorno on time.

The paper trembled in the breeze from the open windows, then fell from her hand.

Three days late . . .

Byron's house was only seven hours away on smooth seas. For Percy not to have arrived . . .

An entire world could be created and destroyed in less time.

Where are you, Percy? Are you hurt? You'd never leave without my knowing, would you?

"I saw the post arrive," Claire said as she'd come downstairs, stopping in her tracks as she took in Mary's visage. "What's wrong? You're pale as a January moon."

Mary silently handed Claire the letter. Her sister had gasped as her fingers flew to the locket at her throat, which Mary knew contained a curl of Allegra's hair. Percy had urged Byron to send it to her when Allegra was still at the convent. "Oh, God," she whispered to Mary. "He's half a week late . . . Is it over?"

The question was the barrel of a musket that Mary was now forced to stare down.

"We go to Livorno." Mary was on her feet already, Percy Florence wailing at her hip while a desperate sort of courage infused her with a manic energy, tightly wound as if she could bend destiny to her will. "And learn our fate."

Leaving Percy Florence with his nurse, Mary and Claire were rowed by locals to the fishing village of Lerici, where they hired a carriage to drive the twenty miles to Byron's house in Pisa. All the while, Mary's mind tormented her with possible outcomes, each more terrible than the next.

Until they crossed the Magra River and Mary caught sight of the sea.

And she *knew*.

"My God, woman," Byron exclaimed when she finally poured from the carriage in Pisa, legs turned boneless and veins gone bloodless. She felt more ghost than woman. "You look like death."

"Where is he?" She allowed Byron to prop her up. "Where is Percy?"

A questioning glance from Byron to Claire had her sister shaking her head in answer. The two former adversaries seemed to declare a silent cease-fire in the face of this emergency. "He still hasn't arrived," Claire said quietly.

Byron tugged the lace of his embroidered sleeves and frowned at the overcast sky. "The weather was uncertain the day he left, but the sun was high when they departed in the afternoon."

"And his mood?" Mary loathed the question, but Percy's emotions had been so erratic of late. Mary recalled Fanny's and Harriet's deaths—and her own mother's attempt to drown herself—and understood what extremes she herself might have gone to after Everina's death. Even for a man who had seen only nine-and-twenty years, guilt and disillusionment could moth-hole a normally steady mind and make him ponder the very worth of his existence.

You are my everything, Percy. Without you . . .

"He was uproarious the entire trip, even laughed so hard at one of my jokes that tears ran down his cheeks." Byron touched Mary's elbow, as if to ground her. "He proposed founding a new magazine, *The Liberal*, so we might outrage Parliament and scandalize the remaining conservatives back home."

Mary smiled. That was hardly the mood of a man yearning for freedom from this life, or even one who sought to abandon his family as Gilbert Imlay had her mother. But the weather had been uncertain.

And Percy, God bless his merry soul, had never learned to swim.

"We'll find him, Mary," Byron said softly. "I swear it."

Inquiries as they retraced their path down the coast toward Casa Magni revealed that no accident had been reported. Despite the truth she'd seen in the sea, Mary decided that was a figment of her writer's imagination, penning a tragedy where one didn't exist. Percy had too much life still to live. This couldn't be how his story—*their* story—ended.

Until they reached Viareggio and Byron returned to the coach, his expression grim. Mary watched him tug at the golden hoop in his ear. The glass muffled his next words, but Mary's blood congealed as she understood the shapes of his lips. ". . . no tragedy on the stage so powerful . . ."

I will not despair. I will not break. I will not.

Byron scrubbed a hand over his face, suddenly haggard as he opened the coach door and lifted his eyes to hers. In that moment, the spell snapped, and Mary felt her world crest atop storm-tossed waves.

"A dinghy and a waterskin have been found washed ashore." Byron's face had gone as white as her knuckles. His voice was so quiet, so *small*. "The dinghy belonged to the *Ariel*."

Strange and harrowing must be his story, frightful the storm which embraced the gallant vessel on its course and wrecked it—thus!

The howling maelstrom of Byron's announcement and *Frankenstein*'s words broke over her. Mary looked down at her clasped hands, shocked that the hairline cracks she felt hadn't yet streaked down her skin. At any moment, her very being might fracture and she'd come apart.

"Find him," she commanded with a tightly leashed whisper. "Please."

Thrown about by hopes and fears, once they arrived back at Casa Magni, Claire held a terrible vigil, pacing the windblown portico while Mary stood by Percy's telescope. She'd envisioned him so often as a Greek god fallen to earth; now all that remained of her beloved likely lay at the bottom of the sea or scattered like jetsam across the stars.

When Byron returned, his face was a death mask. Claire fainted at the very sight and had to be carried inside before he could speak. Mary, however, listened to every word, needing to sear this moment onto the ephemera of her very soul.

"The bodies of Shelley, his friend Williams, and eighteen-year-old Charles Vivian—their extra hand—have been found washed ashore between Massa and Viareggio."

Somehow, Mary remained standing, buffeted by the death knell of this revelation yet unable to move. But she managed to speak, a single echoing sentence. "I need to see him."

Byron's normally swarthy coloring turned sickly. "No, Mary. Trust me—it's impossible." He hesitated, the great poet undone. "They could identify Williams only by his boots."

Mary swayed then. "And Percy?"

A long, terrible pause. Then: "Still wearing his nankeen trousers. And with this in his pocket."

Byron handed a thin sheaf of waterlogged papers to her—Mary could barely make out the blur of Keats's poetry, its cover doubled back as if put away in a hurry. An omen she now recognized too late, given that Keats had died only last year while here in Italy, and at the tender age of five-and-twenty. "A fisherman said he saw the *Ariel* out at sea," Byron continued, "trying to outrun the storm when the sky went black and the waves turned to mountains."

Mary's legs finally gave out, and Byron barely caught her as she plunged through all the flaming circles of hell.

"*Destiny was too potent*," she mumbled as he carried her inside, reciting one of Percy's favorite lines from *Frankenstein*, "*and her immutable laws had decreed my utter and terrible destruction.*"

In a moment of brutal clarity, Mary recalled their walk to Parliament Hill with Claire so many years ago, when Percy had lit his paper boat on fire and let it touch hers. How both boats had burned themselves out, their paper sails reduced to ash before the wrecks spiraled to the murky depths of the pond. It was clear now that the storm that would envelop them both was already hanging from the stars, just waiting for the *Ariel* to slip her moorings.

Now, with the gust of Byron's words, the sails of Mary's soul caught fire and turned to ash. She moaned and writhed in agony, unsure how she would ever speak or write or so much as *breathe* without Percy by her side.

Salty tears coursed down Byron's cheeks as he placed her upon a settee. "It's my fault. Percy made that damnable boat a death trap when he tried to make her faster than the *Bolivar*. With all that extra weight, she was doomed to sink if she took on water."

Mary pushed against Byron, but words still tumbled from his plush lips. "There was no greater poet, nor a more ethereal spirit," he babbled, but Mary blocked his words with her hands. *Too much, not enough.* He was *too late* in finally recognizing Percy's brilliance, couldn't he see that?

"A funeral," she whispered when she finally shook herself loose. "There must be a funeral. Percy should be buried with Everina."

Byron choked. Actually *choked*. "The authorities already poured lime on the bodies and covered them in sand. They can't be moved—due to current quarantine laws, the government says they must be cremated."

The thought of white-hot flames licking at Percy's battered body and devouring his mortal remains . . . Mary could only moan again.

"I'll make the arrangements, Mary," she heard Byron say. "All of them. It would be my honor—I've never met a man who wasn't a beast when compared to him. You were his heart. Let me do this for you. For *him*."

Mary couldn't speak. She'd always found such solace at her mother's grave, but there would be nothing left of Percy if he were cremated, no gravesite to visit, no tombstone to keep him tethered *here*, with her. He'd cease to exist, except in her memories and the words he'd written.

They weren't enough. They would never be enough.

> *But soon . . . I shall die, and what I now feel be no longer felt. Soon these burning miseries will be extinct. I shall ascend my funeral pile triumphantly, and exult in the agony of the torturing flames. The light of that conflagration will fade away; my ashes will be swept into the sea by the winds. My spirit will sleep in peace.*

Mary recalled Percy's pride at the closing scene of *Frankenstein*, how he'd crowed at her genius. Never had she imagined she'd been writing her husband's death scene.

Mary didn't attend the funeral.

It had taken Byron weeks of grappling with the local Italian authorities to allow Percy to be buried in Rome and to make the arrangements to build the two separate pyres—one for Percy and one for his friend Williams. It was too much to endure; the catacombs of Mary's heart simply refused to allow her to strap herself to that rack and turn the crank.

Better to remember Percy as he had been, not as a body left to decompose these past weeks, his limbs mere fuel for an unforgiving pyre.

Yet that did not stop her from imagining it. Or demanding the details from Byron when he returned, his clothes unkempt and his face unshaven, and found her sitting outside on the portico, facing the sea.

Percy's body exhumed, the flesh turned a dark and ghastly indigo from the lime used to preserve him.

Placing the body on the log pyre, the air shivering as the flames began their eager dance.

His mortal body slowly catching, the sky heavy with the scent of death and loss.

The waves lapping at the shore as the ashes—all that was left of the lips that had once laughed, the hands that had sketched sails and written stanzas, the mind that had dreamed of such beauty—were swept into a simple cedar box.

Listening, she'd wanted to turn away from the white-capped waters, but the cruel and unforgiving sea surrounded everything here in Italy. Better to face her fears. A letter she'd written to Maria Reveley Gisborne lay in her lap, ready to be sent.

> *All that might have been bright in my life is now despoiled—I shall live to improve myself, to take care of my child, and render myself worthy to join my love.*

Realizing she lacked even a portrait of Percy, Mary recalled that Maria had painted her mother's portrait and asked if she remembered Percy's visage enough that she might be willing to paint a miniature of him. Something, *anything* for Mary to hold on to.

Percy's absence cut off one half of her while the world expected her to go on living. She would—if only for their son—but while bearing an open wound for the rest of her life. Her mother's death had left her with a gaping, unexplored hole in her past; with Percy's death, now its twin yawned in her future.

She raised her eyes to Byron. So much effort, just to lift her head.

Lord Byron looked heavy, as if his grief were pulling on his very skin and bones. In his hand was an enameled box, which he held out to her.

"For you," he said, quickly amending as she moved to lift the lid, "don't open it."

"Why?"

Byron ran a hand through his hair. She'd never seen him look so disheveled. "I couldn't stand it as I stood there, the thought of you two being parted. So I took something before it was too late—I swear I heard Percy's voice urging me, instructing me . . ."

Mary simultaneously clutched the box and resisted the urge to drop it. "What is this, Byron?" she said. "What do I hold in my hands?"

Byron's eyes were a storm of warring emotions. "His heart," he finally answered.

Mary shrank back, repulsed, but Byron kept speaking. "There were others there who wished to claim it," he said, his eyes wide, nearly rolling in their sockets. "And his skull too. But I wouldn't let them. He was always yours, Mary."

She didn't speak, just remained in her chair on the portico while Byron finally broke down and howled his grief, as she held Percy's heart in her hands.

Cor cordium . . .

She and Percy had overcome so many trials together—her family's and society's censure, their lack of money, Fanny's and Harriet's deaths, the loss of their children . . . The one thing Mary had been certain they would always have—since the moment she'd decided to elope with him and in stark contrast to her own parents—was *time*.

Instead, Mary now faced the gaping maw of so many empty years without him.

Percy's spirit might be at peace, but from now on, her restless soul would always be seeking its other half. A snippet of poetry she'd once written for Percy came to mind, unbidden and unwelcome.

Oh, come to me in dreams, my love!
I will not ask a dearer bliss;
Come with the starry beams, my love,
And press mine eyelids with thy kiss.

Never again would Percy come to her and press gentle kisses to her eyelids. *My Elfin Knight . . .*

Now he lived only in her dreams.

CHAPTER 18

❦

September 1797

MARY WOLLSTONECRAFT

I lie here dying.

Today they took from me my daughter—Mary, whom William named after me, claiming she would always be a piece of me. When we parted . . . I knew.

I survived her birth, but this foul garden worm of a fever is slowly devouring me from the inside out. Alone in my room with the windows open, the summer jasmine has bloomed out. As have my days.

Sweating and shivering, I am determined to hold this pen, frantic to write even as death lurks patiently in the corner. I am angry over the years and the many future joys being stolen from me, but while death may claim my body—nothing I can do will halt that—it cannot steal my past.

My life . . . my dreams . . . my dearest loves . . .

William—you are a being of superior order caged in a mortal body. I fear we wasted the lamp of life, forgetful of the midnight hour that now draws near. My sapient Philosophership, I love you with my whole soul. How I wish we had more time . . .

Fanny—my sweet and gentle sparrow. You guided me to solid shores and for that I am forever grateful; may life's many darknesses never overcome you.

Mary—death will snatch me from you before you can weigh my advice, but I beg you to gain experiences and pursue your own happiness before the springtide of existence passes away. You are the heir to my immortality. I will watch over you always and revel in every moment of your living each day as I cannot.

The sleep of death creeps closer with each word I write. Turn away, I whisper, but mortality is persistent. You will all stay, my loves, and I will go.

A little patience and all will be over.

CHAPTER 19

❦

September 1822

MARY SHELLEY

In the months following Percy's death, curious Italian onlookers came to offer Mary their condolences. Everyone sought to comfort the poet's twenty-two-year-old widow. Save Claire, who had immediately decamped to Austria in search of solitude and a position as a governess. "I cannot bear more death and grief, Mary," she'd said hollowly. The carefree songbird of their youth had turned crow black, silenced by the bleakness that hovered always around her shoulders. "If I stay, I shall go mad."

Mary understood, and let her go. In truth, having Claire around was a constant and painful reminder of all the times they'd shared with Percy. Just this once, Mary wanted him—and her memories of him—to herself.

The tragedy of Percy's untimely death increased his fame overnight. However, the gawkers whispered behind their hands at Mary's aloofness, not realizing her soul was screaming in raw agony behind an impenetrable wall that was the only thing separating them from a woman driven insane with grief. Aside from Claire, there was only one person who might have understood what she was going through, but her father was still in London. It would take time for word of Percy's death to reach her father and for William Godwin's ensuing response. Thankfully, the deluge of visitors soon slowed to a trickle, leaving Mary to swim through the bottomless sea of her grief alone.

She was desperate for distraction, and the hailstorm of words she released in the following seasons—her daily journal, the first edition of *The Liberal*, which Percy had dreamed up in his final days, her short story "The Death of Despina"—were her only tool to keep the vortex of grief at bay. Lord Byron, upon visiting and sensing her manic need to work, paid her to copy his new poems and asked her advice about publishing his memoirs. Once she completed those tasks, she worked for months by candlelight to compile Percy's reams of unpublished poetry. Aside from his notebooks, there was also a motley assortment of scraps of paper with stray lines often scribbled next to sketches of sailboats that left Mary gasping through her tears.

When she craved peace, Mary took to rereading all her mother's works, especially *Letters Written During a Short Residence in Sweden, Norway, and Denmark.* There was fresh comfort to be found in those pages, as if Mary were reading an old friend's letters.

She found solace in the pages of her mother's past. And that of her son's future.

The childish giggles of Percy Florence while learning to walk in his leading strings reminded her of his father's laugh, and her toddling son loved gingerbread just as Percy had. "He'll never know his father," she said to a black-garbed Maria Reveley Gisborne when she came to visit, bearing her widower son, Henry, and a painted miniature that was a good likeness of Percy. Mary was grateful for the tiny portrait—it was comforting to keep by her bedside and would make it more difficult for time to erase her memory of Percy's laughing blue eyes and his always mussed hair. "It seems my family is cursed in this way,"

Mary added as she poured tea for the three of them. "Given that I never knew my mother."

"You may not have known her in the flesh," Maria responded as she sipped delicately from her porcelain cup, "but you know her through her words. And one day, when you return to England, you'll recover her memoir and meet her anew."

Mary was distracted for the remainder of the visit—the idea of some new project wriggling to life in the back of her mind—so she scarcely noticed when Henry Reveley hung back while his frowning mother climbed into their waiting coach. She vaguely remembered Maria's son Henry from her childhood, a rambunctious but kind boy who helped bind her knee once when she scraped it. Now he was a grown man who held the door open for his mother and offered Mary his polite condolences. "Mrs. Shelley," he began, "this may not be the most opportune time—indeed, my mother insists it is quite the opposite—but I understand all too well the loneliness that follows the death of a spouse. Allow me to propose that we unite our households, thereby increasing the happiness of both our families."

Mary blinked. "Are you proposing . . . marriage?"

"Indeed." A kindly smile. "My mother already counts you as a daughter. This would merely make it official."

Mary took in Henry's calm gray eyes and brown hair, nearly the same shade as Percy's but without his wildness. The idea of sharing her life with any man other than Percy was anathema; she would remain a widow until they were reunited.

Henry seemed to sense the direction of her pensive thoughts. "I know we've just reconnected under terrible circumstances, but I'm a man of some means. Our union would guarantee a life of comfort, for us both."

That was a subject that had kept Mary awake many long

nights—how she would support both herself and her son—until she realized she didn't require a husband to keep a roof over their head. Mary Wollstonecraft had made a living with her writing. So, too, would Mary Shelley.

"Thank you," Mary said. "But I'm afraid I must decline your kind offer."

Henry gave a sad smile as he tipped his black top hat. "I thought you might, but still, I had to try. It's my hope that time brings you comfort."

Mary didn't wish for comfort. She wanted her life with Percy, but since that was impossible, it was time to return home, to England.

Not her true home—that had been obliterated when Percy's lungs had filled with briny death—but the place where her mother's soul still lingered and her father still lived.

"Goodbye, Percy," she whispered as she locked the door to Casa Magni for the final time, that awful glittering blue bay behind her. To remain here would be to forever walk alongside grief and death. Still, even a year after Percy's death, it felt like she was excising some critical part of herself to leave behind the last place they had been together, the place where they had parted. "Until we meet again."

This time as Mary approached the sea-surrounded nook of England, it was to look upon a country transformed.

Not even ten years had passed since she'd returned from Scotland, but Mary might have had an easier time finding her way to the Coliseum in Rome than to Grosvenor Square. The freshly dug Regent's Canal ran a straight line of murky brown water through London, with newly built factories that belched black smoke into the air. Still, the sun was just setting in a burst of gold, and a city of gaslights bloomed to life, as if showing Mary the way.

Her father met her at London's wharf, just as he had all those years ago. This time, bent-backed William Godwin was alone, her stepmother, Jane, having remained behind.

Her father had a hired carriage waiting. Once Mary's trunks were attached to the back and she and Percy Florence were settled—her son curled next to her, his head of Percy's curls on her lap as he fell into an enviable sleep—her father thumped the roof of the carriage with his cane. "I'm glad you're home," he said quietly when they lurched forward. The darkened shop windows on the newly designed Regent's Street displayed mass productions from the nearby factories: ladies' fans and powdered cinnamon, cheap china dishes and ready-made cotton cloaks. "I've worried while you were away. Since Percy's passing, that is."

Mary felt the blow land and waited for the pain to pass. Not for the first time, she wondered when the mention of Percy would cease to make her heart ache, when his name or the remembrance of his laughing blue eyes might make her smile instead of further withering her heart. And yet, such a change would be bittersweet. While time would soothe her pain, so, too, was it already trying to steal away the sound of his voice and her memory of his laughter.

"How do I survive this, Father?" Mary's words caught on some rusty nail of emotion. Sitting here with her father—the one person who understood what she was going through—she realized she was terrified of the never-ending loneliness eating away at her just as it had done with Frankenstein's creature. Just as it had her father, despite his remarriage. "How do I withstand the death of my other half?"

Her father's pained smile reminded her of when she was younger, before Jane, when her father was her only family. When he had still seemed so broken, so fragile. She knew now that he'd been damaged her entire life, yet in this moment she sought the magical potion for how he'd pieced his bleeding heart back together. "I don't know," he answered slowly. "I didn't survive when your mother passed, not with my brightest hope beyond the grave. I merely made it through each day. And that, only because of you."

"Tell me," she commanded. She'd only ever *asked* about her mother, but this was different. Now she understood the importance of sharing those stories before they scattered to the winds. "Tell me how she died."

The raw pain that streaked through her father's eyes nearly made her rescind the demand, but she kept silent, especially as he removed the golden locket he kept either looped over Mary Wollstonecraft's portrait in his study or tucked into his waistcoat, the tiny treasure she knew contained a lock of her mother's hair. It was his talisman and he used it now, straightening his shoulders as if preparing to march into some doomed battle. She and her father were both warriors scarred—but not broken, at least not entirely—by the enemy of grief.

They were strong enough for this. They had to be.

"Your birth was difficult." He removed a handkerchief from his waistcoat—tomato red today—and blew his nose. Her stoic father, who never allowed the slightest bit of emotion to shine through the cracks of his heart. Was it her mother's death that had left him so wary of *feeling*? Had he been a different man before Mary Wollstonecraft's death? "But things improved after the doctor finished his surgery. Maria Reveley brought Fanny to meet you, but your mother was so weak that Maria offered to keep her a few more days. Your mother kissed her goodbye, not knowing it was the last time." He searched his pocket in vain for a handkerchief and finally scrubbed the back of his sleeve under his nose. "I even went to my office and did a little writing while Johnson came and visited your mother. We made plans for the future. We had three happy days together."

When he stopped, Mary reached for her father's hand with both of hers, willing strength into him. It seemed to help, for he continued. "On Sunday, your mother was resting in bed when there was a terrible banging. I ran upstairs—the fever had set in and she was shivering so acutely that our iron bed was bumping across the floorboards, shaking the entire house."

"Childbed fever," Mary whispered. She had always known this was the cause of her mother's death, but it was one thing to know it, another entirely to hear the details.

"There was nothing anyone could do but wait for the end." His lips twisted, his expression anguished. "We didn't tell your mother, but after a few days, she ascertained the truth. She always was too damnably smart." He sniffed—this time into the starched handkerchief he'd succeeded in digging from his pocket—and took a long moment before continuing. "The doctor instructed me to ply her with wine to ease her suffering, but I dared not play with the life that was dearest to me in the universe. It took a week for her to leave us."

"And in that week? Before she left?"

"Friends came to visit and pay their respects. She wrote a little and we named you Mary. In the last two days the shaking fits stopped and she slipped in and out of consciousness. During her final episode of alertness, she looked straight at me and told me I was the kindest, best man in the world." Mary could see what each word cost him. "I slept for a few hours that Sunday, but the doctor woke me at six. It was time. I sat with your mother for two more hours. Then she drew her final breath and she was gone. Utterly *gone*. We were formed to make each other happy, and I understood in that moment that I would never know happiness again."

William Godwin's stoic face crumpled before he pressed a fist to his lips and sucked in air as if to keep from drowning, all while tears leaked down his cheeks. Slipping her sleeping son into the corner of the coach, Mary moved to her father's bench and wrapped an arm around his quaking shoulders. She had never seen him cry—it was as if all his emotions from her entire life had been held back by a dam of silence that now broke.

"By all the gods," he was finally able to say after some time, "I wish I could shield you from the pain of Percy's death, of having to keep moving forward when all you want is to step back in time. I remember returning home to visit my parents after your mother had passed, dandling you on my lap while wondering how I was going to hold together in my bleeding hands the broken shards of our lives. I wasn't very successful, but I tried. For you, I tried. I know I failed every damnable day, and I'm so unbelievably sorry for it."

Mary pressed his hand to her damp cheek. "Never," she said. "You never failed me."

It was difficult to speak over the lump in her throat. She knew from Maria Reveley Gisborne that her father hadn't even attended Mary Wollstonecraft's funeral, that he'd been too broken by grief to endure watching his wife's burial at the same church where they'd married just five short months prior. It was a feeling she understood all too well. "I spoke to Maria Gisborne—Maria Reveley, as you knew her—while I was in Italy." Mary wondered whether she should continue, but she needed this, now more than ever. The coach was nearly home— only a few more minutes before her stepmother, Jane, and the rest of the world intruded on this conversation. "She said my mother wrote to me before she died—a journal of her life. I wrote to you about it, but you never answered."

William Godwin blotted his bleary eyes one final time before stuffing the handkerchief back into its pocket. "I didn't respond because I am so ashamed," Godwin said. "It was a memoir, you know. Your mother started it a few weeks before your birth—she thought I didn't know. Then at the end . . ." Out came the handkerchief again. "She wrote like a woman chased by the hounds of hell."

"Where is it?" Mary forced herself to breathe. In and out, over and over. "Maria told me she gave you the journal shortly before she moved to Italy."

Now Godwin's gaze was haunted when he lifted his gaze to hers. "It's gone." His voice was less than a whisper.

"What?" Mary's sharp question roused little Percy Florence, whose big eyes went wide and his lower lip quivered even as she scooped him onto her lap. She smoothed her son's hair back and calmed him with a kiss atop his head. "What do you mean, *gone*?"

"I read it the same day Maria Reveley—Gisborne, by then—gave it to me." He turned a ruined face to her. "And all the memories . . . I was so angry—furious at myself and angry that she had left me, left *us*—and I wasn't thinking . . ."

"Where is it, Father?" Mary dreaded asking, but she had to know. "The book?"

"I threw it on the fire."

Mary reared back. Her father must have read the betrayal on her face, for he grasped at her fingers, his words coming in a violent tumble. "Forgive me, Mary, please forgive me. I was so grief-stricken to read your mother's last words and to relive those days, and to know that I had ruined her legacy with that ghastly memoir, when all the while a more perfect account of her life existed, written by her own hand. When I realized what I'd done, I went back to save the book—your mother's final words—but it was too late. They'd already burned to ash."

Mary had been an infant when her mother passed, but somehow, this felt like losing her a second time. She wanted to blame her father, but he had obviously punished himself in the intervening years. And there was nothing to be done. If the journal was gone, there was nothing she could do to bring back her mother's lost words, no matter how she might wish the opposite.

However, this might be the only opportunity to ask the question she'd wanted to ask so long ago. "Why did you write that memoir about her? The way you did, I mean," she asked quietly. "I read it and . . . it was awful. To expose her in such a way."

"It was my duty, as the person who loved her the most. She had so many detractors, and I wanted to show you and your sister and the entire world everything she had overcome and protect her from malignant misrepresentation. Instead, I crucified her. Johnson didn't want to publish it, but I insisted. I should have kissed his feet when he refused to print more than a minuscule first run. It was terrible hubris on my part to think that my words—a man's words—could deify your mother more than her own writings, I know that now. How could I have loved her as I did and still have been so *wrong*?"

Her father's maniacal laugh degenerated into a fit of sobbing. Mary didn't know what to do as his shoulders heaved and he gasped for air while tears poured down his face. "I failed her," he continued. "I failed you, Mary. And I failed our daughters."

Mary's alarm over her father addressing her dead mother only grew as the coach halted outside the bookshop on Skinner Street, especially as Percy Florence started bawling as well.

She'd never been so relieved to see Jane standing outside in her gray day dress and sensible mobcap. Her stepmother took one look at the chaos inside and ushered William Godwin out of the coach with a single command before lifting Percy Florence into her arms. "Inside," she ordered. "All of you."

Still snuffling into his handkerchief, Godwin disappeared upstairs without a word. The latest generation of Jane's russet turnspit hounds silently watched him go, as if sensing his calamity. "I should go to him," Mary said, but Jane stopped her with the quiet command in her voice.

"No. Sometimes your father requires his solitude." Percy Florence quieted as Jane distracted him with a set of wooden blocks that Mary remembered from her childhood. Then Jane retrieved a plate of cookies from the counter and handed one to Percy Florence, who sucked on it with a toothy grin while petting the dogs until they, too, had cookie crumbs everywhere. When the spicy scent of gingerbread hit her, Mary herself nearly burst into tears as she remembered a letter she'd written to Jane, idly mentioning to her stepmother both Percy's and their son's love of the treat. "You'll stay down here," Jane instructed Mary. "With me."

Mary contemplated disobeying—she was a grown woman now—but knew Jane was right about her father needing his solitude.

"What was the cause of all that commotion?" Jane asked as Mary settled herself on the floor beside her son. Jane picked up the dusting rag she must have abandoned to greet the coach. Even though her hair was tinged with frost and ash, Jane Godwin still never seemed to stop moving. Mary suddenly recognized her stepmother's constant forward motion—she was a woman trying to keep ahead of an ever-rising tide. If a woman paused, the world might catch up and she might never extricate herself from the waters of its unceasing demands.

Mary pressed a hand to her heart, unsure whether she should answer Jane's question truthfully. She'd never had an amiable relationship with her stepmother, but she didn't wish to injure her with talk of Mary Wollstonecraft. Yet, Jane was proof that William Godwin had kept living—at least in some manner—despite what he'd said in the coach. "I asked my father about my mother. He told me he destroyed a memoir she'd written of her life. I'm sorry he did—I'd have liked to know her better. Especially now."

"Now that you're alone."

Mary winced at the stark truth.

"You really loved Percy Shelley." Jane didn't break from lifting books and efficiently destroying the dust beneath them. "I supposed it was just a youthful flight of fancy when you first ran off with him, but I understood it for what it was later. I'm sorry he's gone now and that you've been left alone at such a young age. I know how that feels."

Mary cocked her head, remembering belatedly that Jane, too, had experienced her own loss. "How did you do it?" At Jane's questioning expression she added, "Survive being a widow with a small child?"

Jane paused and glanced upstairs, where Mary knew her father had sequestered himself in his study, surrounded by the calming presence of his books and Mary Wollstonecraft's serene portrait over the mantel. He was likely holding one of his favorite volumes now, seeking solace from it and the locket of his dead wife's hair. "I'm afraid you've never known the real me, Mary. I was never widowed."

Mary's gaze ricocheted back to Jane. "What?"

Jane only shrugged. "My first husband was a fabrication created to lend me a sheen of respectability. Charles Gaulis Clairmont was indeed Claire's father, but he never married me."

Mary gaped. This was Gilbert Imlay and her own mother all over again, only with different names. "Does my father know this?"

Jane gave her a withering stare. "Of course. Contrary to what you may assume, I would never marry a man under false pretenses."

"You had a child out of wedlock, just like my mother." It wasn't an accusation; Mary had never looked for parallels between her mother and Jane, so it was startling to discover their existence.

"Two, actually. I was three months pregnant with your father's son when we were married. The baby boy died."

Mary recalled a sudden trip with Claire to visit her aunts in the countryside shortly after her father's remarriage. "I'm sorry," she said, and meant it. She felt an unexpected kinship with this woman who also understood the pain of losing a child. "I never knew."

"You didn't need to. Until now. I always wanted a son, but that boon was forever denied me. But I'm quite happy to have this little man underfoot."

Percy Florence fretted for a moment but calmed when Jane hid behind her hands and then surprised him into giggles. Sometimes it hurt to see Percy peeking out from his smile or shining through his blue eyes, but Mary was determined never to let her son see that particular pain. "Yet you raged when I ran off with Percy," she said to Jane. Despite the years that had passed, the scene in the French hotel lobby was still fresh in her mind. "And when Claire and I had our daughters."

"Of course I did. I didn't want you to suffer as your mother and I had. Society is cruel to women—a husband is one of the few shields we're allowed."

"Is that why you married my father?"

It was blunt; but then, so was Jane. She merely nodded and continued dusting the lacquered shelves of the étagère with its stacks of books. "I was willing to trade my freedom for that shield, for my daughter. Just as your mother had done." She set down the rag, folded it into a square with pristine corners. "Your father and I decided to be partners. William Godwin saved Claire and me from a life of ridicule and destitution. For that I shall always be grateful. Unfortunately, unlike his adoration of your mother, your father never loved me."

And then Mary realized: "But you loved him."

There was a long pause. Finally: "I did. I still do."

"And that's why you've taken care of him all these years." Mary glanced around the shop, seeing Jane's handiwork everywhere. There wasn't a book here that Jane hadn't personally curated, just as Mary knew that every item of William Godwin's clothing had been darned by Jane's meticulous hand. Even his boots by the door were freshly shined.

Mary rubbed her eyes—the rigors of the long journey and her father's confession finally threatened to overwhelm her. Percy Florence yawned and Mary thumbed a smear of gingerbread from his baby-smooth cheek. She hadn't noticed Jane slip away, but she appreciated the privacy. She'd put her sleepy son down for his nap and then rest herself.

Except Jane reappeared from the back room. She held tight to a battered leather hat case cradled in her hands, each step toward Mary purposeful yet hesitant.

She stopped only when she stood before Mary. "It's my turn to ask your forgiveness."

Mary picked up Percy Florence, thinking back to the sharp words Jane had so often used to cut her, all the times she'd reprimanded her and sent her to bed without supper. Now that she was older and a mother herself, she saw in Jane a stepmother who had done the best she could to raise another woman's child. All the while knowing she would always be the outsider. "There's nothing to forgive," she said.

"There is." Jane frowned and ran a quavering hand over the top of the leather case—the only time Mary had seen her stepmother look less than self-assured. "The journal your father mentioned? I knew about it."

"What?"

"There was an incident early in our marriage, mere days after our wedding, actually. The door to his study was locked, but I could hear him within. It took me a moment to realize the sound—he was *weeping*. I was still upset over an earlier disagreement. You see, I'd finally demanded he move the portrait of your mother out of our bedroom."

"The one Maria Reveley painted." Mary winced to realize the pain that would have caused both Jane and her father.

Jane nodded. "When I knocked at his study, he yelled at me to go away. I'd never heard William Godwin raise his voice—I worried something had happened to you, but you were snug in your bed. When I came back downstairs, the study door was open and I went in, thinking to apologize to your father."

"And?"

"The study was empty and there was nothing untoward inside, just that painting of your mother serenely staring down at me. He'd made a shrine of it, hanging it over the fireplace, with a locket looped over the frame."

"The one with her lock of hair?"

Another nod. "The one he doesn't want me to know he often

carries in his pocket. I wanted to hate her then, truly I did, but how could I hate a woman who died and lost everything I now possessed? I nearly turned around and locked it all behind me, but then I saw it . . . a book smoking in the corner of the grate. It hadn't caught fire yet—as if your father didn't truly want to destroy it. I was young and curious and couldn't leave alone the mystery of why my knowledge-loving husband would burn a *book*, of all things."

Mary's heart thudded and her eyes stretched wide as Jane set the leather crate on the counter and undid its tiny metal lock. She riffled inside. "We women are allowed to have our secrets. And sometimes it's our job to protect other women's mysteries. Your mother's secrets joined mine that day."

Mary's heart skittered to a stop when Jane retrieved a weary journal, its green leather cover faded and singed around the edges. Mary scarcely dared to breathe. "Is that . . . ?"

"Your mother's journal." Jane pursed her lips as if remembering something bitter. "I read it the night of your father's outburst. I'd known that Mr. Godwin viewed our marriage as a business transaction, but I'd harbored secret fantasies that we might still fall in love." She gave a wry chuckle. "Probably the effect of reading too many novels. Reading *this* disabused me of that notion—your mother and father shared one soul in two bodies, and I could never compare to the illustrious Mary Wollstonecraft. I was and always have been jealous of what they had. And for that, I ask your forgiveness."

Mary would have forgiven Jane just about anything as her stepmother set Mary Wollstonecraft's final journal onto the counter and took Percy Florence into her arms. He laid his head on his grandmother's shoulder, his eyelids with their thick fringe of lashes already fluttering toward sleep. "Why didn't you just finish what my father had begun?" Mary whispered, her vision blurring as she touched the smooth leather cover. Her mother had *touched* this same journal, had poured her most precious memories into it. "Why didn't you let it burn?"

Jane pressed her temple to Percy Florence's. "My own mother died when I was young. There were many times over the years that I'd have traded my soul to talk to her one last time. I couldn't deprive you of that, no matter how jealous I might have been of the woman who wrote this."

Mary hugged the journal to her chest. "Thank you," she whispered. "For returning her to me."

Jane only shifted Percy Florence to her other hip. "They called your mother the first of a new genus," she said begrudgingly. "But that *Frankenstein* of yours is something new too. I'm sure you heard that they made it into a play, you know, over at the Lyceum Theatre—*Presumption; or, The Fate of Frankenstein*. The masses don't read, but put a story on the stage and lo and behold, I find my stepdaughter as famous as all the other writers I ever stocked in this bookshop."

Mary couldn't recall the last time Jane had complimented her, even if it was reluctantly. However, she'd already had plenty of experience with scandal sheets and public scrutiny, and didn't care for either. "The idea of fame is discomfiting."

"Perhaps, but fame can also be useful. Will you keep writing?" Jane nearly smiled when Percy Florence yawned and snuggled closer. "Make a living by your pen as your mother did? After all, you have to maintain a roof over this little boy's head."

Now, *there* was the pragmatic stepmother that Mary recognized from her childhood. "I'm editing Percy's final works and just finished a new story, 'The Death of Despina.' Beyond that, I have no idea what I'd write."

Jane pressed a kiss to Percy Florence's temple. The child may not have shared her blood, but it was obvious Jane was already smitten with Mary's son. "Write whatever you fancy—travelogues, poetry, novels. You're only five-and-twenty, Mary. You have your whole life ahead of you."

Mary looked down at her dour widow's weeds. The color matched her soul; perhaps it always would. "It feels as if the best years of my life are already behind me."

"Your mother once wrote that it was better to have experienced love and lost it than to never have loved at all." Jane headed toward the staircase, so she couldn't see Mary's surprise that she had read *A Vindication of the Rights of Woman*. "There's a box of beeswax candles in your room, enough for several hours of reading." Jane ascended the stairs. "I'll keep an eye on this little man while you become reacquainted with your mother. Your sister Fanny is in there, too, young and carefree as you never knew her."

Mary paused, taking in the image of her son in Jane's arms, so trusting and pure, before following them up the stairs and reentering the girlhood room she'd once shared with Fanny. So much had changed since the last night she'd slept here, that moonlit eve when she and Claire had slipped out to meet Percy and set into motion their own vibrant lives.

With the door tightly closed, she lit several candles and gingerly fingered open the journal. Two aged papers slipped from between its pages, an eerie echo from when she'd opened her father's memoir about her mother. The first was dated December 11, 1800, and written in Maria Gisborne's hand, beginning with *My Dear Reader* and serving as a reminder of all the trials and tribulations women throughout history had overcome. Mary smiled at her friend's words, recognizing her mother—

and perhaps even herself—among the lines. On the second letter, her father's handwriting flickered in the candlelight.

> *We love as it were to multiply our consciousness, even at the hazard of opening new avenues of pain and misery to attack us.*
>
> *—W*

Feeling the palpitations of her every artery, Mary knew this piece of paper her mother had saved was a message for her, and so, too, was it a gift from her quiet, staid father. Tucking the letter in the back and opening the journal to its first page, Mary was awestruck as she stared down at the thoughts and memories her mother had set there in midnight ink.

> *I yearned to disappear.*
> *It had been two days since I'd last eaten and still longer since I'd bathed, but those were inconsequential trifles at this moment . . .*

Mary had lived for her mother for so long without ever truly knowing her.

Sapere aude. Dare to know.

And so . . .

Mary dared.

EPILOGUE

❦

1831

MARY SHELLEY

Mary, you are your mother's daughter. Your veins probably run with ink; you just haven't discovered it yet.

Percy had been right that long ago night at Villa Diodati that began their writing competition: *Frankenstein* was the cut that opened Mary's veins. And finally reading her mother's memoir all those years ago had unleashed her.

Mary Wollstonecraft's brilliance was undeniable. Mary's mother *was* the first in a new genus, and Mary had done her best in the years since reading her memoir to follow in her footsteps. With *Frankenstein*, Mary was recognized as the creator of the first in a new species of literature: science fiction.

Can you imagine, Percy had once asked her in the shadow of Frankenstein Castle, *being able to cure death?*

She *could* imagine such a thing now, for words were an alchemist's stone that protected one's ideas from death's scythe.

A deluge of works had poured from her pen since she had read her mother's memoir—*Falkner*, *The Last Man*, and finally, *Lodore*. Books by female novelists were supposed to celebrate beauty, but Mary wasn't made to write soft and tender themes, not after the life she'd lived. Darkness shadowed the world, and her words exposed that.

She believed her mother would be proud.

"The critics poleaxed *The Last Man*," she announced to Jane after reading the latest reviews of her most recent novel. It was morning, and Percy Florence—now twelve and growing into the awkward lengths of his limbs—had left for his lessons, so Mary had decided to visit her father and stepmother at their new accommodations in Westminster Palace. Her son would be boarding at the prestigious Harrow School next year, and while Mary had hoped that Percy Florence would one day follow in the literary footsteps of his parents and grandparents, her son preferred time spent climbing hills or rowing the Thames. He was cutting his own path, more young country squire than poet or philosopher. And that was enough. "One reviewer calls my imagination *diseased*," Mary added as she turned back to the paper, "and another says my writing is *perverted and morbid*. They simply cannot fathom what sort of woman would create such a nightmare."

"They are little people with small minds, *corculum*." Her father had just come down the stairs, leaning heavily on his cane. Today's waistcoat was saffron with apricot embroidery, more colorful than a Turkish souk. Her father had been awarded a sinecure position as Office Keeper and Yeoman Usher of the Receipt of the Exchequer—no more hawking books and dusting shelves for the humble Godwins now that they lived a life of leisure. Mary was thankful for the roaring fire in the grate and the overflowing tray of breakfast on the table—her father's new allowance meant she no longer worried about his finances. Fortunately, Percy's financial settlement upon his death would pay for Harrow, and Mary was currently enjoying the signal honor—and very lucrative position—of being the only female contributor in compiling the 1,757-page volume *The Cabinet Cyclopedia*. Chosen among many literary luminaries for her varied writing and lingual abilities, Mary had signed on to write essays about the literary men of Europe but then taken it upon herself to expand her scope to include historical female figures. When her editor rejected the idea, Mary did what her mother would have done—she sneaked the women into the official version, oftentimes allowing them to overshadow the men who crowded the pages.

Her writing provided a comfortable living for her and Percy Florence, plus the terrier she'd just given him for his most recent birthday. "A literary protest against war and violence was never going to win admirers," her father added as he assumed his place at the head of the table. "Not in this day and age."

"It almost makes me wish I had published this anonymously," Mary muttered half-heartedly as she rubbed at the ink that perpetually stained her fingernails. "The reviews of *Frankenstein* were tame in comparison to this."

"None of that nonsense." Jane bustled to pour her husband's tea. One sugar and a twist of lemon, just how he liked it. "You keep writing and publish everything under your own name, just as your mother did."

Mary smiled at that. Since her stepmother had handed over Mary Wollstonecraft's journal, a sense of equilibrium had settled over Jane and their entire family. Mary's father and Jane even seemed to have started a new and more amicable chapter of their story together. "I suppose. Although I've been thinking about that. In regards to *Frankenstein*."

Her father held his cup in his hands, inhaled the fragrant steam. "Go on."

"What if I were to republish the book?" Of all her works, it was imperfect *Frankenstein* that refused to fade from her mind.

"With a revision—taking into account some of the early reviews—and put my name on it?"

She held her breath, expecting her father and Jane to endorse the idea immediately. Instead, her father merely looked at her over the rim of his cup. "Why would you do that?"

Mary faltered, but only momentarily. "Because I've been raked over the coals for my writing" —with a shake of the latest reviews—"and still lived to tell the tale. And because I revised Percy's final poems and released *Posthumous Poems* to rapturous reviews, but only because no one knew that I edited them and wrote the preface."

That project had been a labor of love.

Percy had left behind many published works, but there had also existed a trove of unrefined poems that only she had ever seen. Thus, Mary had preserved for posterity every memory, every poem, and every word that her husband had ever been part of. Mary's mother had preserved her thoughts for her daughters, and Mary was determined to give her son that same gift. Percy Florence would know his father—Mary had guaranteed it.

Percy had once claimed they shared a soul, and somehow she knew that he'd have smiled upon her polishing the uncut gemstones of his words until they gleamed with wildfire.

Except Percy had also left behind the tainted legacy of his radical political views and society's gossip about his supposed harem. That wasn't the *real* Percy, but Mary had understood from the cautionary tale of her mother's memory what might happen to the story of Percy's life if left in the wrong hands. Although Percy was reviled and mocked while he was alive, Mary's pen had doggedly recast him from a radical atheist into a revered and visionary Romantic poet who sought to shield those he loved from every sort of heartache.

Mary had enshrined her husband's final legacy. Now she wished to ensure her own.

"I take pride in all my works," Mary continued, "but I'm proudest of *Frankenstein* and I want people to know *I* wrote it. And I want it to have a *real* publisher and to finally be taken seriously."

Her father sipped his coffee. "Then it seems you know what to do next."

Mary released a breath and melted back into her chair. Leave it to her father to force her to put her feelings and motivations into words. Infused with a sudden energy, she leapt to her feet, already gathering her hat and cloak. "Then I should get to it, shouldn't I?"

Her father turned his face so she could kiss his cheek, still full of stubble, as he'd declared a man of five-and-seventy need not impress society by shaving every day. "I'll expect a full report this Sunday over supper."

"Tell Percy Florence I'm baking gingerbread for dessert," Jane called as Mary bustled back outside, into the fresh air. Already, the introduction to *Frankenstein* was unspooling in Mary's mind, changes that she'd mulled over the past thirteen years now begging to be written.

When the muse spoke, one must hurry to listen.

It was time to finally own her creation.

This new edition of *Frankenstein* must be a flawless tale that she would be proud to stamp her name on, come what may.

Seated before the oak and brass slope desk that had witnessed the creation of so many of her recent works, Mary pressed a kiss to the polished box that still contained the fragments of Percy's heart before tracing a finger over her first edition of *Frankenstein*, its cheap binding already breaking and the pages gone yellow before their time. In its margins were notes from her younger self—to rewrite the first two chapters where the incidents were tame and ill arranged, to modify the language where it was childish and unworthy of the rest of the narration. She smiled at her well-loved copy of *A Vindication of the Rights of Woman*—the same she had read on her way home from Scotland—as she dipped a quill into her mother's old inkpot, the one with *Sapere aude* etched onto its side. "Wish me luck."

But she didn't need luck. Now her writer's intuition nudged her when her prose became too florid or when she needed to delve deeper into one of her characters. This time it whispered praise as she relegated the women of *Frankenstein* even further into the story's background, a bit of social commentary on the role of modern women. That moment felt as if Mary Wollstonecraft herself were nudging Mary's pen, all the while smiling over her daughter's shoulder.

When she finished her work for the day—this session saw her lengthen Walton's letters to his sister and Frankenstein redouble his fruitless warnings against ambition—she looked it back over. "I wish you were here to read the changes I've wrought," she murmured to Percy's portrait. Sometimes she even found herself wishing the indomitable Lord Byron might cast his critical eye over her writings. Except that was impossible now.

No one could have predicted that the mercurial poet would follow Percy to the grave less than two years after the *Ariel* sank. He'd tired of his life in Italy and decided that a man ought to do something more for mankind than pen verses, leading him to become the victim of a violent fever while helping Greek patriots fight their imperial Ottoman rulers. Mary had watched Byron's London funeral procession—almost as obscene as the processions he arranged during his life—from her window while penning the initial draft of *The Last Man*. Much as she'd swung between liking and loathing Lord Byron, even she had to admit as his funeral sledge passed by that one of the literary greats had abandoned the earth forever. And while he could hardly be called a friend, his appearance and verses were a form of beauty that in life she had often delighted to behold.

Claire was still in Russia then, working as a governess. Mary didn't begrudge her sister her travels. It was what Claire had always craved—to be an independent woman, seeing the world. Mary and her sister had trod more similar paths than she'd ever imagined, had been forged into stronger women for it.

In order to *dare to know*, they had to dare to *live*.

As a girl, Mary had never planned on living past eight-and-thirty, her mother's age when she died, but Mary Wollstonecraft's journal had taught her that pain and joy and suffering were part of the complicated matrix of life. Percy and Byron were gone, and while Mary missed their literary conversations, the truth was that she no longer needed them as she had in those fledgling days when she'd first unfurled her writing wings. Having lived alone these past nine years, she was more independent and had lived a more complex life than her nineteen-year-old self. Thus, this version of *Frankenstein* would be more layered.

Unlike that first draft, this time when she finished, Mary signed her name to it.

For she was eager for everyone to know what impossibilities women—like she and her mother—had been capable of.

What *all* women were capable of, when they *dared* . . .

I do not know how briefly to give you an idea of the whole tale—a Mother & Daughter are the heroines—The Mother who after sacrificing all to the world at first—afterwards makes sacrifices not less entire, for her child—finding all to be Vanity, except the genuine affections of the heart.

—Mary Shelley, letter to her publisher,
dated January 31, 1833

Author's Note

❧

Her Lost Words is my love letter to two brilliant women who lit the way for not just women writers but *all* women. Mary Wollstonecraft is regarded as one of the world's founding feminist philosophers, and her daughter Mary Shelley is renowned for being the mother of modern science fiction. However, as with so many women in history, both Wollstonecraft's and Shelley's personal triumphs and tragedies have generally been forgotten. The fact that these two talented female writers achieved so much and are not better known made me determined to share their unique stories.

While Mary Wollstonecraft didn't write a memoir recounting the entirety of her life, she did produce an imposing body of work including a conduct book, a history of the French Revolution, travel narratives, novels, and her two *Vindication*s. (The most famous of these is, of course, *A Vindication of the Rights of Woman*, which has become increasingly important in the twentieth and twenty-first centuries as we continue to strive for gender equality.) All of these projects allow us to follow the movements and motivations of Wollstonecraft's storied life. It is unfortunate that William Godwin—in trying to preserve his wife's legacy—wrote a grief-stricken biography in the weeks after her death that scandalized society with its depiction of an overly emotional woman who attempted suicide and engaged in not one but two premarital affairs that resulted in illegitimate children. Thus, Mary Wollstonecraft was reviled for over a century and nearly forgotten before feminists like Virginia Woolf began to rehabilitate her legacy.

Mary Shelley, on the other hand, is better known, although mainly for her revolutionary creation of *Frankenstein*. However, even this work by a woman has been called into question, as some claimed that Percy Bysshe Shelley's edits of her masterpiece meant that he should be considered a coauthor. (This is no longer the case, as the differences between the 1818, 1823, and 1831 versions show that Percy's edits were no more than any editor's contributions to novels, be they new or old.) Most people forget how young Mary Shelley was when she finished writing *Frankenstein* (only nineteen!), along with her tragic personal life and her many literary contributions in the years following Percy's death. Like her mother, Mary wrote many other novels, short stories, and travel narratives, along with her copious personal correspondence.

I hope readers will forgive the liberties I've taken with both Mary Wollstonecraft's and Mary Shelley's lives in order to tell the tales of these two trailblazing women, given the need to fit both their stories into one novel.

First and foremost, in a history full of Marys and Janes and Claires (and nearly every variation of all three), I shifted some names for ease of reading. Mary Shelley's stepmother was in fact Mary Jane Clairmont, and her daughter was Jane Clairmont until she changed her name from Jane to Clara to Claire around the time that *Frankenstein* was published. Mary Shelley's daughter was also named Clara, but I settled on her middle name—Everina—to avoid making readers' eyes cross. Also, while Mary Shelley was born Mary Wollstonecraft Godwin and was often referred to as Mary Wollstonecraft Shelley following her marriage, I omitted *Wollstonecraft* for clarity's sake.

Regarding compressing time and combining characters, Mary Wollstonecraft's father moved their family from village to village during her early years, but I focused only on Hoxton while pulling in some of her experiences from Epping and Barking. Mary's childhood was indeed a house of horrors—I didn't have to make up her family's poverty, her father's drunken rages, or even his hanging of the beloved family dog. I did, however, omit mention of Mary Wollstonecraft's two sisters, whom she paid to set up as teachers, and her brothers, one of whom she helped to attend Woolwich to earn a naval commission and another whom she assisted financially in emigrating to America. Mary Wollstonecraft actually made a prior journey to revolutionary France before the one detailed in this story, but I condensed that visit to better focus on the Revolution rather than have her travel back and forth. Maria Reveley's character has also been merged with that of Mary Hays, one of Mary Wollstonecraft's acquaintances. (And yet another Mary!) Mary Wollstonecraft actually attempted suicide the morning after her fight with Imlay and his mistress and left instructions that Fanny be raised by Mary's German friends. I moved this up for pacing and left out the German friends, as it seemed likely that Gilbert would raise Fanny and give her legitimacy in the event of Mary's death.

Aficionados of Mary Shelley will note that I've included only two of her living children here, which is probably the largest departure I've made from the historical record in these pages. (In the same vein, I also left out Mary Jane Clairmont Godwin's two sons, Charles and William Godwin the Younger.) In reality, Mary Shelley had five pregnancies but only one surviving child. Mary's first pregnancy resulted in a two-months-premature daughter who lived only eight days, and William "Willmouse" and Clara "Ca" Everina both died very young before Mary gave birth to Percy Florence. His birth was followed by a miscarriage. In depicting a life fraught with tragedies, I chose to combine events from Willmouse's and Everina's lives and include Mary Shelley's miscarriage, in which Percy saved her life with the ice bath. In the historical timeline, eighteen-year-old Mary Shelley gave birth to Willmouse in December before meeting Lord Byron. Mary Shelley was pregnant again when she wed Percy, and Clara Everina was born after Claire's daughter Allegra. *Frankenstein* was published in January 1818, and then the entire crew decamped for their fateful trip to Italy in March. Willmouse died only nine months after his younger sister, and as Mary witnessed her son's final hours, she wrote, "The misery of these hours is beyond calculation. The hopes of my life are bound up in him." Percy Shelley also suffered greatly over the loss of his children, as evidenced by his poem: "My lost William, thou in whom / Some bright spirit lived . . . / . . . If a thing divine / Like thee can die, / thy funeral shrine / Is thy mother's grief and mine."

In regards to Percy and Claire's terribly complicated relationship, some biographers believe it likely that the two had an affair and perhaps even had an illegitimate child together, but in a letter to Isabella Hoppner on August 10, 1821, Mary Shelley stated emphatically that "Claire had no child," save for Allegra. Mary also insisted:

I am perfectly convinced in my own mind that Shelley never had an improper connexion with Claire . . . we lived in lodgings where I had momentary entrance into every room and such a thing could not have passed unknown to me . . .

Given that *Her Lost Words* is told from Mary's point of view and she was obviously dedicated to Percy, I leaned into her perspective regarding the relationship between her sister and husband. If Mary Shelley wrote that the rumors were wrong, then in this story, the rumors were just that: *wrong*.

As for other characters, I combined Claire Clairmont with the historical Jane Williams near the end of the story when Percy goes sailing, and also merged Byron with Edward Trelawny, who actually accompanied Mary and Jane Williams back to Casa Magni while waiting for news of Percy. (It's also Trelawny who retrieved what was believed to be Percy's heart—some believe it was his liver—during his cremation and reluctantly gave the organ to Mary Shelley. It was found in her desk after her death, along with a copy of Percy's "Adonais," which he had written upon the death of Keats. The heart was eventually encased in silver and buried in the family vault with Mary and Percy Florence Shelley.)

As for Mary Wollstonecraft's female friends, Maria Reveley didn't paint the portrait of Mary Wollstonecraft in the final stages of her last pregnancy that hung in Godwin's study; her friend John Opie did. However, given Maria's worldly education, it seemed likely that she was well versed in painting like so many gently raised women of that age, and I wanted her to give her friend one final gift, aside from keeping her journal safe. Maria also didn't paint Percy Shelley's miniature, but Mary did discover that she had no portrait of Percy in the days following his death, so she wrote to Irish painter Amelia Curran to ask for the portrait of Percy that she had painted while the couple visited Rome in 1819. Unfortunately, the end of larger-than-life Théroigne de Méricourt is accurately depicted in this story, although she wasn't admitted to the Salpêtrière Hospital until 1807, by which time Mary Wollstonecraft had long since passed away. However, Méricourt was certified insane in 1794 following her attack and injuries at the Tuileries Garden. Jean-Paul Marat did intercede to stop the mob on her behalf, but it was too little, too late.

To end this confessional on a happier note, Mary Wollstonecraft and William Godwin's unusual and entirely adorable partnership is based on their letters and journals, including some of the notes they sent to each other when Godwin was working down the street following their marriage. Their slow-burning relationship was certainly founded in friendship. Godwin waited three weeks after returning from Bristol to first kiss Mary, but after they experienced an already delayed courtship, I decided to speed things up!

Readers will note the inclusion of many snippets of Mary Wollstonecraft's, Mary Shelley's, Percy Shelley's, and Lord Byron's written works. As best as possible I have included excerpts from *A Vindication of the Rights of Woman*, *Frankenstein*, Percy Shelley's and Lord Byron's poems, and even the love letters written between William Godwin and Mary Wollstonecraft. These words are entirely their own and I cannot take credit for their eloquent wordsmithery.

Writing a book is never a solitary pursuit, and I have so many people to thank for helping guide this story to publication . . .

As for research, I stumbled upon a true treasure trove as I explored the Keats-Shelley House in Rome, where I gaped at Mary Shelley's original travel desk and squealed over signed copies of *Frankenstein*. The quote at the end of the novel is preserved in a letter Mary Shelley wrote to Charles Ollier, the publisher of her final novel, *Lodore*, on January 31, 1833. I gasped out loud when I read it, recognizing immediately that her words were the perfect close to this novel about one of history's most dynamic mother-daughter pairs. I am indebted to the Keats-

Shelley museum staff and the Keats-Shelley Memorial Association for preserving these treasures about Mary Shelley, Percy Shelley, and Lord Byron.

During my research trip to Geneva, Margit Schwiegelhofer was a font of knowledge about how the city would have looked to Mary Shelley and where she drew inspiration as she began to write *Frankenstein* during that fateful night at Villa Diodati.

I couldn't have written this story without the clear-eyed support of my brilliant literary agent, Kevan Lyon, who enthusiastically cheered me on from the idea's very inception. I owe a debt of gratitude to her pride of talented female historical authors, the Lyonesses, for chiming in with all manner of brainstorming, most especially Renée Rosen, Christine Wells, and Stephanie Dray, who generously took their red pencils to early drafts of this book, and Georgie Blalock, who rescued me from the ninth circle of Title Hell. Thank you to my editor, Kate Seaver, and the entire team at Berkley—Claire Zion, Craig Burke, Fareeda Bullert, Jessica Mangicaro, Jeanne-Marie Hudson, Chelsea Pascoe, and Amanda Maurer—for taking on a novel about these two pioneering women writers.

A huge thank-you to all the readers who have read my novels over the years. It's an absolute honor to share these women's stories with you.

Finally, I'd never be able to do any of this without the support of my family. To my dad, Tim Crowley, who never lets a phone conversation go by without asking about my books, and to Daine Crowley and Hollie Dunn and Heather Harris. Most especially to Stephen and Isabella, who keep our three bossy cats off my laptop keyboard while I'm trying to write.

Recommended Reading

Godwin, William. *Memoirs of the Author of A Vindication of the Rights of Woman*. London: J. Johnson, 1798.

Gordon, Charlotte. *Romantic Outlaws: The Extraordinary Lives of Mary Wollstonecraft & Mary Shelley*. New York: Random House, 2016.

Marshall, Florence. *The Life & Letters of Mary Wollstonecraft Shelley*. London: Richard Bentley & Son, 1889.

Shelley, Mary. *Frankenstein; or, The Modern Prometheus: The 1818 Text*. Oxford: Oxford University Press, 1998.

Shelley, Mary. *History of a Six Weeks' Tour Through a Part of France, Germany, Switzerland, and Holland*. London: T. Hookham, 1817.

Shelley, Mary. *The Last Man*. London: Henry Colburn, 1826.

Shelley, Percy Bysshe. (Shelley, Mary, ed.) *The Poetical Works of Percy Bysshe Shelley*. London: Edward Moxon, 1839.

Wollstonecraft, Mary. *Letters to Imlay*. London: C. Kegan Paul, 1879.

Wollstonecraft, Mary. *Letters Written During a Short Residence in Sweden, Norway, and Denmark*. London: C. Kegan Paul & Co. Paternoster Square, 1879.

Wollstonecraft, Mary. *A Vindication of the Rights of Woman*. New York: Penguin Books, 2004.

HER LOST WORDS

Stephanie Marie Thornton

Questions for Discussion

❧

1. Mary Wollstonecraft styles herself as a revolutionary, even traveling to Paris to witness the French Revolution firsthand while others are fleeing. How did her early life experiences shape her character and bring her to that point?

2. Mary Shelley—then Godwin—is so young when she decides to elope with Percy Shelley. Why do you think she made this fateful decision? Was it the right choice for her to make?

3. Mary Wollstonecraft and William Godwin experienced the opposite of love at first sight—*loathing* at first sight—when they met at Johnson's dinner party before Mary's departure to Paris. What experiences most changed them in the intervening years so they could become friends and then lovers after Mary's return to London?

4. Claire Clairmont and Percy Shelley reputedly had a very close relationship, which often caused friction between Claire and Mary. What did you think of their unique living arrangement, both before and after Claire met Lord Byron?

5. Mary Wollstonecraft railed against women losing themselves to love in *A Vindication of the Rights of Woman*, but then finds herself in the same situation with Gilbert Imlay. What lessons did she learn from that relationship, and how did they guide her relationship with William Godwin?

6. William Godwin—a liberal philosopher in his own right—plays a huge role in Mary Wollstonecraft's later life. How did her death shape his relationship with Mary Shelley?

7. Lord Byron is an example of the type of man Mary Wollstonecraft warned about in *A Vindication of the Rights of Woman*—the domineering sort who saw women only as trinkets and who was protected by the law when it came to property rights, divorce, and custody of children. How did Percy and Mary Shelley try to circumvent him? Was there anything they should have done differently?

8. While Mary Wollstonecraft and Mary Shelley take center stage in this novel, other women from history had important roles as well. How would the story—and both Mary Wollstonecraft's and Mary Shelley's lives—have been different without Théroigne de Méricourt, Maria Reveley, and Jane and Claire Clairmont?

9. The title of the novel is *Her Lost Words*. Whom do you think this applies to more: Mary Wollstonecraft or Mary Shelley?

About the Author

Photo by Katherine Schmeling Photography

Stephanie Marie Thornton is a high school history teacher, a librarian, and the *USA Today* bestselling author of *A Most Clever Girl*, *And They Called It Camelot*, and *American Princess*. She is also the author of four novels and one collaborative novel about women in the ancient world. She lives in Alaska with her husband and daughter, where she enjoys hiking, beekeeping, and being entertained by her three rescue cats.

CONNECT ONLINE

StephanieThorntonAuthor.com
f AuthorStephanieThornton
⊡ StephanieMarieThornton
𝕏 StephMThornton